A VIOLENT MAN

He was running, arms pumping, chest heaving, sweat streaming from his forehead down his face, blurring his vision, burning the corners of his eyes.

His right arm dangled, useless, broken in two places, and each step jarred it, sending a fresh wave of pain into his shoulder.

Thrummmm!

The stunner bolt hummed past him, close enough to spur his already flagging steps.

He could feel the pair of Imperial Special Operatives closing in as he tried to reach the tube train station from the Grand Park.

Thrummmm!

His right leg buckled with the stunner paralysis, and he pitched forward, headfirst down the ramp toward the platform, trying to tuck himself into the approved combat roll, but hampered by the broken arm and unresponsive leg.

Thrummmmmmmmmmmm!

MAJOR JIMJOY EARLE WRIGHT IS IN TROUBLE. TO SURVIVE, IT'S EITHER HIM OR THE EMPIRE!

Tor Books by L. E. Modesitt, Jr.

L.E. MODESITT, JR.

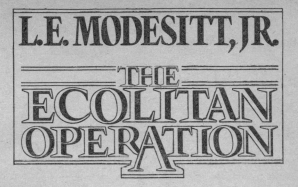

THE ECOLITAN OPERATION

A TOM DOHERTY ASSOCIATES BOOK
NEW YORK

THE ECOLITAN OPERATION

Copyright © 1989 by L. E. Modesitt, Jr.

A TOR Book
Published by Tom Doherty Associates, Inc.
49 West 24 Street
New York, NY 10010

Cover art by Wayne Barlowe

ISBN: 0-812-54582-6   Can. ISBN: 0-812-54583-4

Library of Congress Catalog Card Number: 88-51637

First Tor edition: June 1989

Printed in the United States of America

0 9 8 7 6 5 4 3 2 1

To Elizabeth Leanore,
  For her love
    of words,
      of the books that contain them,
        and of her father who writes them.

... I ...

The man in the power technician's white jumpsuit scanned the control board with the same bored ease and critical eye that the real technician would have used.

His forearms rested lightly on the angled and flat gray padding at the base of the control board as his eyes continued their scan.

Technically, the failsafe systems were supposed to catch any imbalances long before they showed on the main board, but the destruction of the Newton quarter on Einstein had not been forgotten over the three centuries since it had occurred. There, the failsafes had not functioned, and the duty technician had gone with the plant when the magfield had contracted a magnitude more than the plant had ever been designed to handle.

The man who had replaced the duty technician smiled a bored smile as he waited for the failure he knew would come. His eyes flicked to the time readout in the center of the board.

2146—two standard minutes until the magfield began a series of pulses so minute that they would not be perceived for another twenty minutes outside of central control. More important, it was 2146 on Landing Eve, forty-six minutes after the Grand Commandant had arrived at the Military Pavilion to begin the celebration. Nearly the entire Halstani government would be present.

The Military Pavilion was twenty-five kays from the power station—well beyond the maximum damage capabilities of a malfunctioning fusion bottle—but not beyond range of the EMP factors that had been designed into the fluctuations, nor of the power pulses that the fusion system would begin to feed into the power net.

2147—the man in the technician's suit surveyed the board again, following the pattern he had rehearsed so carefully, leaning forward slightly, his elbow brushing the square plate in the middle of the right side of the board.

He lifted his head perhaps three centimeters as he eased back and began the scan pattern again.

2148—his eyes crossed the feedback constriction loop indicator as the fluid bar flickered minutely. He did not nod, but continued his scan pattern.

At the end of another scan circuit, he turned as if to wipe a speck of dirt, an eyelash, from the inside corner of his right eye with the forefinger of his right hand. He leaned forward as he did so, and his elbow tapped another control plate, this time in the second row.

The replacement technician leaned back, as if satisfied with the readings displayed across the board, all of which continued to appear normal. The duplicate readings in the backup control center, in power control central, and at Military Central also would continue to appear normal.

2150—a second pulse registered on the feedback constriction loop, larger only to an eye looking for the minute difference. The man in the operator's control seat could feel the beginning of dampness on his palms, but his face was as impassive as it had been when he had assumed the duty nearly two standard hours earlier. His heartbeat remained unchanged, as was absolutely necessary. The chair in which he sat monitored the vital signs of the operator, and his departure from that chair, until relieved, would trigger alarms in five separate locales.

The operator repressed a smile, taking a deep breath of the carefully filtered air, as he thought about the special circuitry woven into the suit which he wore and the special modules in the heels of his boots. The air, despite the filtration, carried a tang of ozone and metal.

He stretched, carefully, to ensure his weight remained in the chair, then returned to scanning the board, his professional look glued firmly in place, waiting for the hidden, but routine, 2200 military scan.

2152—a third pulse on the feedback loop, this time larger, almost above the noise level.

Click.

The light pen slipped from the narrow front ledge of the control console and dropped onto the floor. Bending forward and carefully leaving his body weight on the seat, the operator reached for the instrument.

He paused to touch the back of his right boot heel, detaching the bottom section in a single motion and slipping it into the prepared pocket on the inside of the jumpsuit's right trouser hem. The special conducting male and female couplers slipped together soundlessly. The operator sat up, stylus in hand, and scanned the board quickly, to assure himself that he had missed nothing.

2154—a fourth pulse on the feedback loop, this time edging barely above the normal noise range.

The operator rested his left hand on his knee, letting his breath out slowly as he invoked his internal-system function control disciplines.

2156—a fifth pulse, clearly into the high noise range.

The operator looked toward the sealed portal, as if checking to see that no one had entered. His left elbow touched another control plate, this time in the third row on the left side.

2158—a sixth pulse, high, but now masked by a higher energy noise level since the automatic signal dampers had been disengaged.

2200—a seventh pulse, fractionally above the highest of

the damped noise levels. The operator continued to breathe normally, now concentrating more upon maintaining normal bodily function signals than upon the board before him, as he waited for the double pulse on the output monitor line that signified a full data pull by the HALDEFNET monitors.

2202—the feedback loop pulse was clearly reaching above the noise level. The operator spent exactly the same amount of time checking the readout as he had for each previous scan.

2203—on the fourth panel from the left in the second row down, twin pulses wavered for an instant and were gone.

The operator took a deep breath, then shook his head as if disoriented, and dropped it between his knees, out of sight of the direct visual monitors. His hands detached the left boot heel, guiding it into the pocket on the left trouser leg of the single-piece coverall. Once again the couplings in the pocket and those on the heel slipped together without a sound.

He had less than half a standard minute to complete the next phase of his mission.

Squinting his eyelids shut tightly, and still keeping his head down, he tossed two small squarish cubes over the top of the control console.

Flrrrrt.

A flare of intense light flooded the room, a brilliance that seared the monitors into uselessness. Even as the glare continued, the operator, eyes closed, taped down the seat cushion on four edges. While the pressure would not be as great as if he remained sitting there, it would be adequate to convince outsiders that the operator was slumped halfway out of the seat. Next he jerked open the front closures on the singlesuit and wriggled out, carefully leaving the suit itself in the operator's chair, where the electrical circuits he had connected would now continue to mimic the bodily patterns of an unconscious man. The chair would dutifully report that an injured operator remained within the control room.

Eyes still closed, he walked twenty measures steps through the glare to the portal, slipping the counterfeit of the special military key into place, and easing out into the lock. Once the portal closed on the searing light, he opened his eyes and placed the beret of the Halstani Marines on his head to complete the uniform he had worn under the technician's suit. The only substantial difference between his replicated uniform and the standard Halstani Marine Major's uniform was that all the insignia and accoutrements were comprised of plastics transparent to the metal sensors used by the Halstani security systems.

Outside the lock, as he had calculated, the immediate area was vacant. He turned and slapped a thin line of instant-weld taping across the portal. Breaking it would require a laser cutter. He turned and began to walk down the corridor. His steps were precise, clicking as he marched down the tech access corridor and turned right at the first intersection, then left at the second.

The power station's main security checkpoint, the only one in operation on holidays, was less than fifty meters before him. Less than fifty meters and two guards, neither of whom was likely to let him go unchallenged. One was on the inside of the security portal, waiting for him. The other, unseen for now, was on the outside.

He did not shrug, but he could have, as he maintained his stiff posture all the way to the first security checkpoint.

"Who . . . pardon, Major? What are you doing—?"

The false Major launched himself over the low console.

Thud.

Clank.

The uniform had obtained for him momentary respect, the extra instants he had needed to disable the guard.

He frowned, not liking the next step, as he retrieved the standard-issue stunner, the one the guard had dropped.

Thrummm!

The unconscious soldier twitched before his breathing lightened. Then the man in the Major's uniform began to reprogram the security console, setting it to seal the lock behind him. As he stepped forward to enter the lock to the outer security station, he touched the "execute" key.

Thrumm!

Thrummm!

Clank.

Again the Major had been faster than the guard. He rubbed his sore knee as he lurched to his feet from the dive he had taken out of the lock.

The second guard lay sprawled across his console, stunner scattered a good meter away where it had skidded across the hard plastone flooring. The Major eased the guard off the console and laid him down out of sight. Once more the Major's fingers flew across the console, adding a series of codes. Next he retrieved the stunner and pocketed it before straightening up and marching toward the exit, less than five meters away.

As he approached, the automatic door swung open. Though he carried one stunner ready to use, the ramp and the groundcar lot it led to both appeared virtually empty under the searing blue glare of the arc lights. The summer evening air was warm on his face as he headed down the ramp.

With a wrinkle of his nose at the dank smell of the nearby Feloose Swamp, he glanced back over his shoulder, realizing that he should not have done so. Trying to make the glance casual, he returned his gaze to the lot ahead.

The technician's car was where he had left it, and he eased himself inside, taking off the beret as he closed the door. As the electric whined into operation, he slipped out of the uniform tunic and into the travel tunic that he had left folded on the other front seat.

By now he was well out of the lot and onto the highway away from the city and toward the shuttleport. After stuffing the uniform tunic under the seat, he began to peel the plastic striping off the pseudo-military trousers.

One-handed, he continued to drive as he took a small towel from the dashboard storage box and began to wipe his hair. The mahogany-red hair color broke down under the enzyme, and a muddy brown color, not his own, replaced it. The rest of the changes were complete by the time he parked the electrocar at the tube station that served the shuttleport. He locked the car and walked briskly into the station and onto the downward ramp leading to the tube platform below for the five-minute ride to the port.

Ignoring the flashing full-color hologram that asked whether he was "man enough to give your best for Halston? Can you meet the test of the best Marines this side of the Arm?" he slipped the system pass into the gate.

Hmmmmmmm.

The bars turned to allow him onto the platform. At the same time, the identity of the pass holder was automatically flashed into the movement control section of the planetary police monitoring network. Since the pass holder was clearly not on duty or supposed to be at work, the automatic alerts did not flag one of the duty officers.

The man who was not the pass holder smiled faintly as he waited on the empty platform. A faint vibration and an even fainter high-pitched humming notified him of the approaching maglev tube train.

Still alone on the platform when the doors on the two-car train hissed open, he stepped inside and took a seat near the doors, letting his eyes skip over the single other passenger, a rumpled-looking technician in a gray suit, to the train security officer in his shielded booth. The doors hissed closed.

The power fluctuations would not be noticeable for another twenty minutes, nor would the explosion occur until he was well clear of Halston—assuming that things went as planned.

The maglev arrived at the port two stops and four minutes later. He and the other technician both departed, heading for two different concourses.

The man who had been Major, technician, and several other roles along the course of his efforts took the last seat on the 2300 shuttle.

The two explosions occurred nearly simultaneously.

The main power station went at 2257.

Military Central, and eighty-five percent of the Halstani High Command, went at 2258, when the EMP set off three tacheads stored nearby, tacheads whose fusing systems had been modified for electrical pulse detonation.

The beta shuttle for Halston orbit control had lifted at 2259, carrying a man with muddy brown hair.

At 2330, Planetary Police Movement Control, under orders from the acting senior Military Commandant, declared a state of emergency and suspended all off-planet travel.

... II ...

After placing the plastic square into the public comm console, the man with the muddy brown hair and incipient paunch began to code his message, slowly, almost laboriously, his tongue protruding from his lips as he punched in each word. He seemed to grunt slightly, from time to time, with the effort.

The clerk behind the transmission counter shook her head slowly, wondering how the man had ever gathered enough funds for the message, let alone for the trip he was obviously about to take, or had just taken.

At last he finished and pressed the display button to check his handiwork.

Malendr Fristil
Drop 23A
High City
Alphane
Sector Blue, Empire

Aunt Malendr,

Finished the replacement of the trim. The cabinet was completely rotten near the top. The job required removing the entire top. I had to use power tools, and they probably left scars on the inside.

I am taking my vacation now, and I will see you when
I get back.

                                                    Thorin

He nodded at his work with a pleased smile and punched
the eject stud, taking the plastic square in his hand to the
dispatch clerk.

"Alphane, Sector Blue," he mumbled apologetically to the
woman.

She inserted the card in the reader, scanned the number of
characters, weight, and routings.

"Twenty-three credits."

The workman fumbled through his battered pouch, finally
coming up with a stained twenty and three chips, all of which
he plopped on the counter.

"Thank you." Her voice was simultaneously warm and
bored.

The man bobbed his head. "How long, miss?"

"Let's see. The Alphane run goes through Scandia. No
more than two days at the outside."

"Much obliged."

The cabinetmaker smiled a toothy grin, almost a leer,
before he picked up his traveling satchel and headed back into
the orbit control concourse.

The clerk routinely bypassed the privacy safeguards, as she
had been taught by Halstani Security, and was reading his
message to Aunt Malendr even before he had disappeared
into the sparse crowd swirling through the station's curved
corridors.

She had forgotten the cabinetmaker within a few minutes,
her fading memory of yet another nondescript traveler blotted
out by the news of the disaster on Halston below when the
carefully scripted presentations of the explosions began to
flash across the station's main screens.

... III ...

While the glamour of the *Empress Katerina* had not entirely departed the ship, most of the old moneyed passengers who had once sworn by the *Empress* on the run between Halston and New Avalon had. Instead, they took the newer *General Tsao*, even while deploring the stark lines and functional decor of the newer ship.

The man who currently bore the name of Thorin Woden, sitting in the dark-paneled, but cramped, lounge of the *Empress*, enjoyed the faded ambience of the about-to-be-retired dowager ship.

In his hand was a well-thumbed manual on woodworking, although both hand and book lay along the arm of the heavy-appearing armchair. The chair was bolted to the deck, the mountings concealed beneath the thin but rich-looking carpet that was beginning to fray. Neither old nor heavy, the chair was a lightweight imitation comprised of well-connected struts, stiffened fabric, and first-class plastwood veneer. Thorin Woden appreciated both the appearance and the illusion, for reasons beyond the ambience.

"For those passengers with a destination of New Avalon, we will be entering orbit in fifteen standard minutes. On behalf of the *Empress*, we wish you a pleasant stay in New Avalon.

11

"Passengers continuing to Tinhorn should remain on board. Because of delays in returning to Halston, the New Avalon orbit station requests that only those passengers actually bound for New Avalon leave the *Empress.*"

Thorin Woden shook his head slowly, surveying the near empty lounge. Through passengers preferred the observation deck, where remote screens relayed the approach to orbit control, while most departing passengers were gathering their belongings, luggage, and spouses or offspring.

The man called Woden had little enough to gather, and while his vacation on New Avalon would be brief, he intended to enjoy it. He was too well aware that each vacation could be his last.

Finally, a faint *clink* ran through the hull, and he stood, holding a satchel and a nondescript carrying bag generally filled with clothes.

"We regret to announce that there will be a short delay before departing passengers can disembark. This delay is caused by the lack of available lock capacity. The *Empress* regrets the delay, but we are informed that it will be minimal."

Woden frowned.

Lack of an available lock or docking capacity normally meant waiting off-station, not locking in and waiting. Lock capacity wasn't the real problem.

New Avalon enjoyed chilly relations with Halston. So the delay could not be at the request of Halstani officials. New Avalon was too proud of its quiet efficiency to deliberately allow anything to halt smooth passenger services.

Woden's hands moved to the heavy workman's belt, his fingertips skimming over the hidden openings. Then he lifted his luggage and stepped toward the lounge exit.

Abruptly, he stepped back into the lounge just in time to avoid two figures moving quickly toward the minimal amenities passenger cabins, more accurately termed closets, he reflected.

The first was a flushed and angry junior officer of the

Empress Katerina, a third pilot by the stripes on her sleeves, flanked by an Imperial Marine Commander, who also looked out of sorts.

Woden frowned again, then forced his face to relax and headed toward the disembarkation lock.

If there were to be a confrontation, he needed witnesses.

Smiling thinly as he heard the heavy pounding on the cabin he had left hours earlier, he continued in the opposite direction, toward the main lock, where he was certain he would find another Imperial functionary of sorts.

"Wrong," he muttered to himself as he reached the central section of the hull where all the corridors connected.

A crowd of passengers stood lined up before the lock, which was flanked by a pair of Imperial Marine guards in combat suits, their stunners unholstered.

Each passenger faced a credentials check, followed by a full-body scan, designed to compare the passenger against a preselected body profile. That was not the public explanation for the scanner, which was touted universally as a routine method for discovering internal body smuggling and for concealed weapons. Other methods, less conspicuous and just as effective, if unpublicized, already detected smuggling and unathorized weapons.

The man called Woden let out his breath slowly, shaking his head, and letting his bags droop in his hands.

"You there. Either wait until you're cleared or get in line," snapped the Marine on the right.

The cabinetmaker grinned.

"I said to get in line." The guard raised her stunner, as if to emphasize the command.

"That won't be necessary," suggested the cabinetmaker. "You can either take my word that I'm the one you're looking for, or you can put me through the scanner first."

"You wait your turn."

"Fine, and you'll spend your next turn on Adark, both for ignoring a reasonable suggestion and for unnecessarily delaying debarkation from a innocent commercial—"

"What's this?"

The cabinetmaker turned toward the red-faced Commander, the one who had already been pounding on cabin doors.

"Major Wright, Commander. Jimjoy Wright. Presume you're looking for me?"

The Commander's mouth dropped momentarily, and his nose wrinkled as if the air smelled of rancid fish.

"How . . . yes, Major. The Service does happen to be looking for you."

"Too good to believe I might get leave after all. The mess on Halston?"

The Commander swallowed, as if to say something, then choked it back, finally answering, "If you wouldn't mind the scanner, Major?"

"Not at all. Only have my word I'm me."

With that, the Major picked his two bags and handed them to the officious Marine. "Take care of these, please. Thank you."

Next he stepped in front of a bewildered young woman, black-haired and thin-faced, wearing a purple shipsuit that made her look even more washed out than her apparently natural pallor.

"Excuse me, miss, but this will speed up everyone's departure." He half bowed, smiled, and stepped through the scanner, then glanced at the technician operating the equipment.

She avoided looking at him and tried to catch the eye of the Commander, who was now engaged in conversation with the ship's third officer. The Commander did not look up, and the technician tried to keep from looking at the strange Major.

The ship's officer's voice was low, but intense.

". . . dangerous, you said . . . need to block the ship . . . quarantine the station . . . and he announces himself . . . Regency Lines . . . protest . . . consider the matter of compensation . . ."

The third officer was leaning toward the Commander, who took one step backward, then another.

The Major let a faint smile cross his face as he watched the

Commander endure the civilian pilot's complaints. He had no doubt that he would hear from the Commander in turn.

"Commander?" asked the Major, loud enough to break into pilot's monologue. "Believe your technician has something to say."

"Yes, Aldora?" asked the Commander, half turning from the pilot, who glared at both the Commander and the Major, switching her glance from one to the other.

"The Major . . . I mean . . . the comparison . . . he's Major Wright," stammered the technician.

"Thank you." The cabinetmaker and Major inclined his head to the technician.

"I can believe it," announced the Marine Commander. Turning back to the pilot, he inclined his head. "Thank you, Officer Shipstaad. A pleasure to work with you."

The third pilot inclined her head stiffly. "My pleasure, Commander." The words came out harshly.

The Major noted that the Marine guards appeared more tense, rather than less, now that he had been positively identified.

"Major?" The Commander gestured toward the ship's lock, where yet another pair of Marine guards waited.

The Major nodded and marched toward the lock and the second set of guards. He had no doubt that he could have escaped, but there was no reason to, not now.

He'd only done his duty, if not exactly in the way in which he had been ordered. But he had completed the job, and about that, High Command couldn't quibble.

On the other side of the *Empress*'s lock, inside orbit control station, waited a third pair of guards.

The Major shook his head. All this to deny him his hard-earned leave. He grinned at the pair, who had leveled their stunners at him and motioned for him to stop.

"If I'd decided to take your toys away, technicians, you'd be long gone." His smile was friendly, and so was his tone, but the man on his right paled slightly. The woman aimed directly at his midsection, in approved Service fashion.

"Major, I would greatly appreciate it if you would refrain from threatening my personnel. They might believe you, and I would have a hard time explaining why I was shipping your body, rather than you."

"Commander, appreciate your suggestion and solicitude, but I do need some relaxation now that High Command has decided unilaterally to cancel my hard-earned leave."

The Commander coughed.

"Where to?" the Major asked.

"Lock six. To your left. There's a courier waiting."

The Major who had briefly been a technician, a Halstani officer, a cabinetmaker, and assorted other occupations smiled again, briefly, and turned to his left.

A trailing guard raised an eyebrow at the other guard, the one who had arrived carrying the Major's bags. The baggage-carrying guard glared at the other, who looked away.

A third guard whispered, "The Major's supposedly a Special Operative. You wouldn't argue either."

A handful of civilian passengers, cordoned off behind a rope, viewed the military procession with open eyes and closed faces, waiting for the Imperials to leave so they could get on board the *Empress* and on with their trip to Tinhorn.

. . . IV . . .

A man who believes in nothing will support the status quo, not oppose it

A man who believes in himself first can be trained to support his society.

The true believer will place his ideals above action, because no action can attain the perfection of his ideals.

These are the people who compose most of society.

The others? The criminals, idiots, writers, politicians, and fanatics?

The politicians pose some danger because they are interesting and employ popular vanity and the illusion of ideals to make small changes in society. Small does not necessarily mean insignificant, and for this reason the politicians must be watched.

Of the remainder, the greatest danger comes from the altruistic fanatic, who believes simultaneously in himself, his ideals, and the need for action. Such individuals should be killed at birth, if they could but be identified that early.

Failing that, they should be made military heroes and given the first possible chance at a glorious death. That is the Empire's current policy.

Unfortunately, someday one of those heroes will survive . . .

> *Private Observations*
> Sanches D. P. Kwixot
> New Augusta, 2456 A.E.F.F.

... V ...

Cling.

At the sound of the console chime, the officer in dress grays stiffened, though he did not leave the straight-backed chair.

"Yes, Commander. Yes, sir."

The orderly's voice, soft as it was, carried through the outer office, a room empty except for the orderly and a Major in a gray uniform and recently cut black hair.

"Major Wright?"

"Yes." The Major stood, flexing his broad shoulders, shoulders that did not seem as broad as they were in view of his equally broad torso and muscular lower body. He looked through the orderly, who avoided looking in the direction of his eyes.

"You may go in, sir. Commander Hersnik is ready to see you . . . sir."

"Thank you." The Major's voice was expressionless.

The orderly continued avoiding any eye-to-eye contact with the Major until the Special Operative had passed him and was stepping through the security portal to the Commander's office.

The security portal flashed green, signifying that the Major carried neither weapons nor energy concentrations on his body, not that he would have required either to deal with the single senior Commander who awaited him.

Major Wright stepped from the portal ramp onto the deep gray carpet and halted, coming to attention before the Commander. The Commander sat behind a wide wooden console with an inset screen.

To the Major's right was a wide-screen reproduction of New Augusta, as seen from the air, distant as it was from the Intelligence Service station, showing the broad boulevards and clear golden sunlight of the Imperial City on a cloudless summer day.

The Major repressed a cynical smile. The view had been carefully chosen to avoid showing the blighted areas that remained on Old Earth, whose ecology still remained fragile.

"Major Jimjoy Earle Wright, Special Operations, reporting as ordered."

"Commander Hersnik, Major Wright. Have a seat." The Commander, black-haired, black-eyed, olive-skinned, neat, and proper, did not leave his swivel, and presumably the energy-defense screens mounted in the console, but gestured toward a straight-backed armchair across the console from him.

"Thank you, sir." Once again, the Major's tone was politely expressionless as he took the proffered seat.

"You are wondering, no doubt, Major, why you were diverted from your scheduled leave to report to Intelligence Headquarters." Commander Hersnik, elbows on the arms of his swivel, steepled his fingers together, then rested his chin on them as he waited for the Special Operative's answer.

"Figured it had to be important, to risk my cover. Did wonder about it . . . sir . . . Especially when your . . . security forces . . . delayed an entire civilian ship and insisted on my immediate return. Seemed . . . unusual."

"Unusual. Yes, that would be one way of putting it." The Commander paused. "Tell me, Major, your own evaluation of your last mission, the Halston mission."

Jimjoy Wright shrugged. "Instructions were clear-cut.

Halstani Military was ready to annex the Gilbi systems. Need to immobilize them to give us time to deal with the situation appropriately." He smiled self-deprecatingly. "My efforts along the immobilization line never got far. Once they had those accidents outside the capital, it didn't seem there was much else I could do."

"Uhhh . . . accidents?"

"They had to be accidents, didn't they, Commander? Who would possibly conceive of deliberately turning a fusion power system into a nuclear mishap on purpose? And coincidental detonation of tactical nuclear weapons followed the power failure, according to the fax reports. Attempting to create that kind of EMP-induced accident would have been awfully chancy, even if it had been deliberate."

"I see . . ." The Commander frowned. "Assuming these accidents . . . they were rather unfortunate accidents from the viewpoint of the Halstani *Military*, wouldn't you say?"

The Major ignored the emphasized word, shifted his weight in the straight-backed chair, and looked straight into the Commander's eyes. His own eyes were flat and expressionless. "Most large-scale accidents with fatalities are unfortunate, sir. Some have minor consequences, except for the casualties themselves. Others have major impacts."

"If such an accident had not occurred, then, Major, I take it that you had a plan that would have been more targeted?"

The Major smiled widely, seemingly enjoying the falsity of his expression. "Can't say that I did, Commander. That's the problem with trying to stop a government's war machine. You remove the top admiral, the marshal, whoever . . . and someone else takes up the gauntlet. And they have a martyr to make it even easier. Even if I could have destroyed a goodly section of their fleets, why . . . they'd rebuild.

"So the accidents were rather fortunate, at least from Intelligence's point of view. And from mine, I'd guess. Looked like an impossible job for any conventional approach."

The Commander's lips pursed, and he drew into himself, as if he were repressing a shiver.

"Are you disclaiming the credit for accomplishing your assignment, Major?"

"Not disclaiming, Commander. Wouldn't be true, either. Just suggesting that it continue to be classified as a regrettable accident, and one for which the Emperor sends his heartfelt condolences."

"Then you take the responsibility for fifty thousand casualties, many of them civilians?"

"You know, Commander, you have a rather unusual approach to a poor Special Operative who managed to carry off an assignment that at least four others had failed to accomplish."

"How did you—never mind. I asked you a question, Major. Do you take the responsibility for fifty thousand casualties?" Hersnik's chin was now off his hands, and he leaned intently toward the Major.

"My orders specifically required that I not consider casualties, Commander. Obviously, every Special Operative will be held accountable and responsible for his actions. War creates casualties. When a system supports a warlike government, the distinction between civilians and military personnel becomes semantic. Under the circumstances, we do what we can, sir."

"Were I the strictest of military traditionalists, Major, I would find your attitude less than perfectly acceptable."

Major Jimjoy Earle Wright said nothing, but retained the open and falsely expansive smile as he waited for the Commander to get to the main point.

Commander Hersnik coughed, steepled his fingers together again before looking at the captured panorama of New Augusta to his left. He kept his glance well above the broad shoulders of the not-quite-stocky Special Operative.

"The Fuardians have begun to annex Gilbi, Major. And there's nothing we can do about it. Not now."

The Major's smile vanished. He shrugged, but did not comment.

"Would you like to say something now, Major, about the fortuitousness of your 'accidents'? Would you?" Commander Hersnik's voice was soft, cultured.

"Not much to say, is there, Commander? Except that Special Operatives aren't theorists. We're operatives, and we solve the problems we're handed. Wasn't told I had to worry about being successful."

"Major Wright," continued the Commander even more softly, "it's worse than that. The Woman's Party has taken control of the Halstani government. Military Central was the only group strong enough to hold them off. Now there's no military presence to speak of, not with political expertise."

Wright shrugged again. What could he say?

"The Woman's Party has made known in the past their extreme displeasure with the Empire. They are far more likely to take a hard line than Military Central did."

"Why?"

"Because the Halstani military relied on hardware and did not have complete heavy-weapons design and manufacturing capability. The Woman's Party is more inclined, shall we say, toward more economic attacks."

"So why didn't someone suggest to the former Halstani military leaders that they leave Gilbi alone?"

"It was suggested, I am told. On more than one occasion. The Halstani military refused to believe that the Empire was cold-blooded enough to act. Now the Woman's Party is claiming that we had a hand in the 'accident' and that any further Imperial interference in the Gilbi area will be proof enough of that."

"But you want me to single-handedly stop the Fuard annexation anyway?"

The Commander smiled a smile even more false than the early smiles of the Special Operative. "That is not a bad idea, and one which I enthusiastically supported, Major, since you and the Fuards seem tailor-made for each other. But High Command would like the real estate in the Gilbi sector to remain undamaged.

"That leaves us with the question of your next mission, Major Wright, and one which, given the circumstances of your . . . diversion . . . should be nonactive and relatively distant from your last episode. High Command has such a mission. Strictly reconnaissance." The Commander paused again. "Does the name Accord mean anything to you?"

"The eco-freaks out on the Arm?"

"The very same. It has come to our attention that they are beginning to develop a rather nasty biotech system that could prove, shall we say, rather difficult. You are to determine whether that is in fact the case. You are to report back with your findings without taking *any* action. Any action at all. Do you understand?"

"I understand, Commander." The Major's flat blue eyes were flatter than ever, as was his voice.

"Fine, Major. Fine. My orderly has your new orders and briefing package. You may go."

The Special Operative slid from the chair to attention, waiting.

"You may go, Major. And let us hope that you are tougher than the eco-freaks, for our sake, if not for yours . . ."

Jimjoy Wright could follow the train of unspoken thoughts beyond the words, but did not comment, even in his expression, as he turned to leave the Intelligence Service officer.

"Thank you, sir."

"My pleasure, Major. My pleasure."

. . . VI . . .

"What are you going to do about him?"

"Nothing."

"Nothing?" The one Commander shrugged to the other. "At least, not until he's on Accord. Then . . ."

"Perhaps, but will he make it that far?"

"With the new Matriarchy, the Fuards, and a few others all looking for him? I doubt it."

"He's good."

"At destruction, but not necessarily at the undercover business. You told me that yourself."

"You're probably right, but I think we'll prepare. Just in case he turns out to be better than you think."

"I think? That was your assessment."

"That was then. After seeing the report on the New Avalon encounter, I wonder."

"He turned himself in, didn't he?"

"Exactly . . . when he didn't have to. That bothers me, because he used the situation to dominate it."

"You handle it, then."

"I always do. I always do."

. . . VII . . .

"Space Available Passenger White . . . Space Available Passenger White . . . please report to control lock three. Please report to control lock three."

A muscular man, no longer quite young yet not middle-aged, stood. He wore the too tight clothes affected mainly by graduate students aping the Slavonian muscle elite. Unlike most graduate students, he and his obviously exercised upper-body muscles would have passed on Slavonia as well.

Unfortunately, his cheap clothes would have marked him as nonelite, as did the muddy brown hair and the tightness around his eyes. The Slavonian elite wore only the finest in natural fabrics and leathers. Their oiled golden, or black, hair glistened above carefully relaxed expressions.

The man, easy on his feet, and the subject of not a few not-so-covert gazes by a handful of female passengers and by at least one interested male passenger, hefted a pair of crew bags and turned toward the counter waiting under a larger number three on the corridor wall.

As he turned, his eyes traversed the rows of seated passengers, all waiting to embark upon the *Morgan*, without stopping to study any single individual until he locked gazes with a woman who had shoulder-length black hair. He smiled faintly but, without waiting for a response, turned his concentration back toward the lock control counter he had almost reached.

The counter held only a screen, a speaker, and a scanner.

"White," he said softly to the screen.

A face appeared on the formerly blank screen, the face of a pleasant young woman.

"May I help you, citizen?"

"You called me. Space Available Passenger White."

"May I help you, citizen?" the screen repeated mindlessly, the carefully constructed female face showing the proper degree of abstracted concern, dark eyebrows rising with the words' inflection.

"Yes. My name is Hale White." The man looked down at the keyboard, finally touching one of the studs.

"Yes, citizen White," the computer persona answered. "There has been a late cancellation. If you will accept a minimal amenities cabin, Republic Interstellar can fulfill your request for transportation to Haversol on the *J. P. Morgan*. If you accept, please depress the lighted panel on the console and insert your credtab."

The man called White tapped the "inquiry" stud instead.

"You have a further question?"

"Price. My funds are limited." At the same time, he touched the "Cr" button, followed by another tap on the "inquiry" stud.

"The total price, including Imperial tax, Haversolian entry fees, pilotage surcharges, and minimal sustenance charges, will be Cr 1,087. If you accept, please insert your credtab."

He reluctantly pulled the thin strip from his belt and inserted it into the slot.

"Your funds are sufficient, and your place on the *J. P. Morgan* is confirmed. Place your hand on the scanner."

A flash followed, creating a combined record of handprint and picture, against which any passenger claiming to be Hale White could be compared at the actual lock entry control port.

"Thank you for choosing Republic Interstellar. The *J. P.*

Morgan is currently disembarking passengers through lock three. We anticipate beginning boarding passengers within one standard hour. Your boarding time will be in approximately one and one half standard hours. Please be at lock port three by 1430 Imperial Standard time.''

The muscled man, who could have been a Solarian tough, an out-of-work steel-bending spacer, or someone even less reputable, turned away from the now blank screen and picked up the set of heavy bags, almost with contempt. Crossing the corridor back to the waiting area for lock port three, he ignored the scrutiny of women too young and too old, and another admirer of roughly the right age but the wrong sex.

From the handful of empty chairs, he picked one away from the single large wall screen displaying the planet below, and nearer the lock port itself, where shortly the departing passengers would be entering the station for either shuttle service planetside or transfer to another ship.

"Down on luck, spacer?" asked the white-haired and thin man in the flimsy chair next to him. His eyes were shielded behind heavy old-fashioned, black-lensed glasses.

"Not yet," the younger muscular man grunted. "Actinic burns?"

"Laser."

The younger man shifted in his seat carefully, as if he were worried that the thin tubes and stretched fabric would collapse under him. He noted the thin wires running from the mirrored glasses to the bioplugs behind the older man's ears.

"Scanner glasses? How do they work?"

"All right. Can't do color, and they blur clothes. Some places shut me down. Don't like broadcast energy, even low power. Hell on shapes, though. You look like ex-commando pilot type. Sort of like Dubnik."

"Dubnik? Friend of yours?"

"Dubnik? That spineless musclehead? Hardly. When I was chief on the *Alvarado*, he gave me these scanners. Used to paint—old-fashioned watercolors. You know what these are . . . can I paint now? Sculpture, but it's not the same.

"No, that bastard had to use lasers, had to. The Serianese threw high-speed torps. Dubnik put the screens back up. Didn't tell the laser battery chief. That was me."

In spite of himself, the younger man winced. "You still here?"

"You see me, spacer. But you don't. Half flesh, half synth. Better than not being here. Dubnik . . . he didn't make it. Still spineless musclehead. Torps never even brushed the screens. Serianese couldn't shoot then. Can't now. That's why they belong to the Fuards."

The spacer did not look away, but had nothing to say.

The lock door had opened, and the first passenger out was a young woman in a Republic Interstellar glide chair guided by a man in the uniform of a steward, light gray, with green stripes down the sleeves and trouser seams.

"She's a grav-field para," announced the ex-technician.

"Anything you don't see, chief?"

"Not much. Don't call me chief. Call me anything; call me Arto. Hell-fired pun, but it's my name."

"What about that woman sitting on the end over there, with the case by her feet? She really that muscular?"

"Legs are. Shoulders, too, but she's got something wrapped around her middle. Not much density. Sort of like rope, I'd guess."

"Cernadine rope. Ship scan will pick that up."

"Won't do anything. Cernadine's legal on Haversol. Empire doesn't care much about it anyway."

"Does seem that way." A hint of bitterness tinged the spacer's words.

"For now, spacer."

"Stow the spacer. Name's White. Flitter driver—till I told a Special Op suicide wasn't my department. His maybe."

"And you're still here?" asked the older man ironically.

"He was easy on me. Lots of bruises, concussion, and a month in rehab. He didn't like suicide either. Went off and did it, though."

"Him or you?"

"I was out cold. He went. Didn't come back. None of them did. Teryla two episode."

"Heard about it. Two men cashiered. Rest dead; one casualty before the drop."

"Me. Casualty. Career and respect."

"Sounds like Haversol is just a transfer point."

"Does, doesn't it?"

The last of the departing passengers left the *Morgan*. The door to the lock closed.

"Embarkation on the *J. P. Morgan* will begin in fifteen standard minutes. In fifteen minutes, those passengers holding gold status accommodations will be embarked."

"Wonder how many of this group rates gold?" asked the younger spacer.

"To Haversol? Not many."

"What about the blonde? Sorry . . . the thinnish woman in the middle of the second row, the one sitting taller than the others?"

"Built like a Special Operative herself, under all that fluff. Muscles like yours, just not quite as obvious. Has a plate in her shoulder, and some sort of metal behind her left eye."

"Probably is a Special Op with all that."

"Not Imperial," answered Arto. "Empire makes sure their boys got no metal anywhere. All plastics, if anything. Second, never saw a female Special Op. Fuards, Halstanis, Serianese—everyone else uses women. Best we do is commando corps. Should be the other way around. Bulk counts for commandos, doesn't count near as much for undercover sneak and thief."

"Wonder who?"

"With all those muscles and height, probably Halstani. One of their flamed sisters."

"Could be. Won't the lock scanners catch her?"

"Sure. But the Empire's not at war. So the crew just forgets she's there. Just like the Fuardian and the Halstani flag lines forget about our ops, unless there's trouble."

"Makes sense, I guess. But why's she here?"

"Not here, White. Haversol. Haversol's a happy hunting ground for everyone—us, them, the outies, even see some of the Ursans once in a while. Good reason to be careful there."

"Why are you headed there?"

"Not headed there. Headed to Accord. Understand they *might* be able to fix my eyes. Good biologics there."

"Like the genetic wars under the Directorate?"

Arto shook his head. "No. Not quite the same, the way I understand it. The Directorate tried to create superkillers. Accord works with what already exists."

"Not what I heard." The younger man shrugged, and let his eyes check the still-closed lock port. "But I guess you hear what they want you to hear."

"Isn't that the truth," snorted Arto. "Never changes."

In the lull in the conversation that followed, both men looked around the waiting area.

"Attention, please. Your attention, please. In just a few standard minutes, we will be embarking full status passengers on the *J. P. Morgan* through lock port three. Those passengers with gold status should be prepared to embark. Those passengers with gold status should be prepared to embark."

Arto glanced from the far seats back at the man beside him. "Wouldn't mind that kind of status."

"No. Beats the stand-up closet I got."

"Bet you spend most of your time in the common lounges."

"No bet."

"Be careful, White. You look just enough like an Imperial agent to get in trouble, and you haven't got any metal plates in you. Every two-bit operator, like that sister, or like the fellow over on the end with the heavy boots—bet he's a Fuard with the steel tubes built into his forearms—will be angling to find you out. Doesn't matter that you're what you say you are. Because only an Impie agent could have cover that good."

"Hades! That why everyone keeps looking at me? Thought it might be my good looks."

"Just a guess, friend." The scanner glasses, their mirrored

surface impenetrable, looked away from the spacer and toward the lock.

"So who do you work for? Knowing all the agents and what makes them tick?"

"Me? I work for me, no one else. Couldn't afford it otherwise. One stun beam my way and I'm blind. Direct hit and I'm out for a week, with a headache for a month afterward."

The spacer nodded, ignoring the evasion. "So what should I do? Act my normal dumb self? Hope someone doesn't decide I'm am Impie agent? Pretend I am? Pray?"

"Prayer won't help. Neither will playing the agent unless you can carry it off. Acting innocent might, particularly if you are. At least until you land on Haversol. Then all bets are off."

"Wonderful." The brown-haired man shook his head, lifted both shoulders as if trying to relax them.

"And that shielded personal kit in your bag would make anyone suspicious, at least anyone with a scanner."

The other shook his head again. "That why I've opened the damned thing every time I've turned around?"

"Your attention, please," interrupted the message system. "Your attention, please. Republic Interstellar is now embarking gold status passengers on the *J. P. Morgan*. Gold status passengers only. Through lock port three. Would those passengers with silver status please prepare to embark? Passengers with silver status prepare to embark."

Arto reached down and pulled a single kit back toward his feet. "Time for us to separate, White."

"Have a good trip. Good luck with the eyes."

"Hope to, and thank you." The older man stood, then leaned toward the younger spacer. "Someone's out for you, but it won't be me. Good luck."

With that, Arto was up and in the waiting line of passengers, his bag in one hand.

The man called White did not shake his head, but studied the remaining passengers waiting to board the *Morgan*.

So someone was already looking for him? That was scarcely the most auspicious beginning he could have hoped for. Not at all.

He shrugged and brushed back his hair with his left hand, not that his hair was long enough or messed enough to require attention.

"Standard amenities passengers, please stand by for boarding. Standard amenities passengers, please stand by for boarding on the *Morgan*. Destination Haversol."

The level of deference in the carefully controlled voice announcing the passenger boarding schedule was definitely declining.

The apparent Halstani Intelligence Operative glanced in his direction before standing. Her eyes passed over him, but he had no doubt that the woman already knew who he was. Her look was confirmation, not search.

He would have liked to sigh, but that wouldn't have been in character.

His supposedly uneventful trip to Haversol was looking less and less uneventful.

... VIII ...

Jimjoy stretched as he studied the small room.

One double bed, scratched plastic drawers built into the wall next to a narrow closet with dual doors—bent—which looked as if they squeaked every time they were opened. A lopsided and cracked plastic table squatted in front of two armchairs that would have been out of style three centuries earlier in most of the Empire. The drapes, spread, upholstery, and floor padding were all either brown or orange or both, and two colors, faded as they were, clashed.

The Imperiale was anything but imperial, though in character for the itinerant pilot/electrical worker outlined in Jimjoy's cover papers.

He shook his head. Hale Vale White—whoever had saddled him with such an absurd cover name should be on the mission, rather than the overtired and overworked Major who was.

Lifting the single hanging bag from the floor, he opened the closet doors.

Skkreeett.

Wincing, he hung up the bag, but did not close the door. Instead, he glanced over at the other bag, squat and lumpy. With a sigh, he dragged it over and used his right foot to give it a final shove inside the shallow closet, where it barely fit.

Then he sat on the edge of the bed, which sank alarmingly under his weight, and pulled off his dusty boots, letting them clump to the floor.

He half turned, half eased himself back into the central valley in the bed, the depression created by his own weight. Even sleeping one night at the Imperiale was likely to give him a backache, and there was no guarantee that he would escape with a single night. But he wasn't up to trying the floor, or to fighting with what might appear on it once the lights were out.

With the first Accord ship not available for two days, and with the supposedly few credits, the poor pilot named White could be expected to catch a few hours' sleep, especially in the warm midday of Haversol. Besides, if Arto were right, the longer he stayed around Haversol, the more he would have to be on his guard. The sleep he got now might be his best.

At least the Imperiale had climate control, reflected Jimjoy as he adjusted the pillow under his head. He hoped that no one would bother him, not yet. The last thing he needed was his combat reflexes jolting him into full awareness because some cheap hotel's valet wasn't certain who belonged where.

In a more affluent system, he wouldn't have had to even leave the orbit station, but Haversol had no quarters in orbit, except for the extraordinarily wealthy, which raised the costs of travel beyond Haversol considerably. And the Empire certainly wouldn't help Haversol out, not to improve transit toward the Arm. Neither was it in Haversol's interest.

Jimjoy shook his head and let the economics lapse.

The dim light of late afternoon angling into his eyes woke him from the latest in a series of nightmares.

He recalled only the last, in which he had commandeered a slow freighter and was being chased toward some system jump point by a full Imperial flotilla, all because he had failed to give Commander Hersnik the proper salute.

"Must be a moral in that," he muttered as he struggled up into a sitting position to wipe his dripping forehead with the back of his sleeve. He eased his feet over the side of the bed, his back to the narrow single window, cradling his aching head in his hands.

Finally, he stood and made his way into the antique bathroom, where he began to splash the lukewarm water that was ostensibly cold over his face. Slowly, he wiped his face dry.

Then, taking a deep breath, he stepped back into the empty floor space next to the bed and began the muscular relaxation exercises designed to relieve tight muscles and the symptoms of tension.

The sagging bed had left his back stiff, but not actually sore—not yet.

The exercises relieved that stiffness, as well as the remnants of the nightmare-induced headache.

Once he had completed the exercise pattern, he returned to the bathroom and cleaned up. Then he extracted a clean, but slightly faded, tunic from the hanging bag, leaving the squeakprone closet door still open. He pulled on the tunic.

He bent down and touched the squat kit bag, as if to adjust the clasp, and then straightened, stepping away from the shallow closet again and toward the door that represented the single exit from the room. With a glance around the not-quite-shabbiness, he touched his hand to the door, then listened before actually opening it.

No one seemed to be outside in the hallway.

Feeling more rested and slightly more relaxed than when he had entered the dingy room hours earlier, Jimjoy started down the empty hallway toward the center stairs, avoiding the ancient elevator.

Four flights down and he stood in the dusty lobby, inhabited by one bored clerk hunched behind a faded plastone-facaded counter, and a white-haired man who stared at the main doors.

Jimjoy touched his chin, wondering whether to try the equally aged saloon or to chance finding something nearby which might be even more dismal and expensive.

The Special Operative walked over to the open portals, the

first actual portals he had seen so far on Haversol, and peered in. Despite the early hour, nearly half the tables were taken, and the majority of the patrons were actually eating.

He shrugged. The posted prices were reasonable, and he was no more likely to find trouble in his hotel than outside it.

Scarcely inside the portal, he found a tough-faced woman in a gray tunic before him.

"Dinner or drinks? Or both?"

"Dinner . . . maybe drinks later."

"Unhh-hunnnn," mumbled the hostess as she turned.

Jimjoy shrugged again and followed her, letting himself amble along in the style of his current persona. The walk was that of an outwardly careless man who had actually never let down his guard. For all that the style reflected Jimjoy's current feelings, the motion was more obvious than he would have normally used. But he had the strong feeling that he was being tracked closely.

"Here," grunted the green-haired tough who had led the way. The small table was in a corner, jammed under a planter from which a tattered nightfern spilled over the sides and brushed Jimjoy's shoulder as he ducked under it in moving behind the smeared and nonreflecting black table.

The would-be out-of-luck spacer eased himself into the straight-backed wooden chair on the back side, glancing at the two dark-bearded and burly men and their companion at the nearest table. The first looked up from his mug of ale. The second continued to stare at the tabletop. Their companion, a younger male with collar-length blond hair, was clean-shaven and held a heavy wineglass.

The four tables on the other side, to his right, each designed for four, were filled, and all were lined up with minimal space between the tables and the rear wall.

Even as he positioned himself in the battered chair to survey the saloon, he could feel the chair back grate against the already scraped and dented paneling behind him. Although the planter stand projected nearly half a meter from the wall, he still had a good view of the threesome to his left.

He edged the chair farther away from the planter to give himself a bit more room, hoping he wouldn't need it.

Another woman, tired-looking, wiry, with white-streaked black hair, dropped a bill slate on the adjoining table and turned, in two swift jerks, to face him.

"Eats? Or drinks?"

"Eats. What do you have?"

"Here." She slapped a cube on the table, which projected the menu right into the air before Jimjoy. "Be back in a minute."

She jerked back toward the three men who hunched around the table to Jimjoy's left. The younger man was still drinking from the wineglass, but the two bearded men had drained their heavy and transparent mugs.

Jimjoy glanced at the blond man and decided that he was a she . . . despite the masculine appearance and garb.

Jimjoy frowned as he watched the hard-looking blond woman proffer a handful of credit discs to the waitress before standing with a sudden movement.

"Let's go . . ." The low and gravelly voice grated on Jimjoy's nerves, and he wished the woman and her two bearded friends would depart quickly. He also hoped that the adjoining table would remain empty, but with the saloon filling up so early in the evening, he doubted that.

"Come on," said the blond woman. Standing, she was taller than Jimjoy.

One man, the one closest to the Special Operative, rose quickly. The other did not.

Jimjoy's mouth opened. He closed it quickly.

"Now!" snapped the blond, as her right hand reached down and lifted the man who had remained seated from his chair and onto his feet.

The waitress scuttled backward, nearly upsetting Jimjoy's small table, at the sight of the tall woman yanking a nearly hundred-kilo man from his chair as if he had been a disobedient infant.

"We're going . . ." said the tall woman, quietly this time.

The laggard male did not look at her, but nodded . . . after mumbling "Sorry" under his breath.

The waitress slid sideways past Jimjoy's table in an effort to avoid the argument and brushed into the shoulder of another woman, violet-haired and hard-eyed, who immediately looked up with a glare. The violet-haired woman's look softened as she realized it was the waitress, even as both watched the blond woman escorting her male friends toward the doorway.

". . . used to be a Hand of the Mother . . ." That whispered scrap of information came drifting down from the line of tables to his right.

The woman was not massively built. Solid, but certainly not heavy, and if that episode had been the casual effort of a retired or resigned Hand, Jimjoy would just as soon avoid one on any terms, but especially on professional terms.

Quite suddenly, Commander Hersnik's concerns about the Matriarchal takeover of Halston seemed much more believable.

"You decided?" asked the waitress. Her tired voice sounded as though nothing in the world had happened minutes before, even though the Halstani trio were not quite out of the saloon.

"Samburg steak, whatever else goes with it."

"Salad or local veggies."

"What do you recommend?"

"Local veggies."

"I'll take them."

"Drink?"

"El Parma, with dinner."

He hoped the local beer was palatable, but the out-of-luck pilot of his cover would not have wasted credits on anything more elaborate. Hale Vale White indeed.

He snorted.

By now almost all the tables were taken. As he watched, the green-haired hostess escorted two couples to the table next to him, barely before the glasses had been removed and the table surface further smeared by the quick hand of a scarred youth wearing a faded brown singlesuit.

As the four sat down and were quickly abandoned by the hostess once she had gestured at the table, Jimjoy glanced from one face to the next. He wrinkled his nose, afraid he might sneeze, so heavy was the scent of rose perfume emanating from the false blonde. She and the spurious redhead were obvious joygirls bent on separating the younger men from their paychecks and whatever else could be separated.

Jimjoy sighed at the lustful innocence in the face of both men, wondering how long before they lost more than innocence, wondering if lust was ever innocent for all its singlemindedness.

Rather than dwell further on the neighboring set of mismatched couples whose companionships were doubtless financially based, he began to study people at other tables.

Across the nonreflecting tabletop toward his right and past the three closer tables was a corner table, pulled out fractionally. At it sat three people: a silver-haired woman, apparently in her late twenties or early thirties, as measured in standard Terran years; a dark-haired and slender man whose age seemed indeterminate in the dim light; and another woman, clearly older and heavier. Although he could not have said why, Jimjoy felt that the younger woman's silver hair color was natural. He knew of no world where such color was widespread, but it looked natural—and not the natural color that came with age or premature aging.

The woman looked in his direction momentarily, although he could not tell whether she had actually looked at him.

Jimjoy dismissed the urge to smile and continued to survey the room. The table closest to him on his right held four men, all bearded, silently chewing on their main course, occasionally swallowing gulps of beer. One, his red beard shot with silver, thumped his heavy mug on the table, empty, wiped his mouth and beard with the back of his faded gray sleeve, and waved wildly toward the tired-looking waitress.

She looked at the bearded man, who held up the empty mug. With a nod toward the bar, she accepted his order.

For all the diversity in the saloon, Jimjoy became aware of

one thing. The two couples next to him did not fit. Nowhere else could he see such an obviously commercial relationship.

Slowly he edged his chair back until it rested firmly against the wall behind him. Then he quietly shifted his weight until his legs were coiled under him.

"What you doing, bud?" demanded the nearest of the young men.

Jimjoy recognized the accent and coldly looked at him, bringing his hands up under the edge of the table.

"Nothing."

The other man began to move.

With that, Jimjoy yanked the table up to interpose as a momentary shield between him and the other two, or four, agents.

Crash.

Pssss.

Water splattered from somewhere, as if sprayed.

SSSSSZZZZzzzzzzttttttt.

"AAAcceiiii!"

Jimjoy cleared the table area, spraying the remaining chairs aside and landing in the open dance area. He glanced back at the two couples, ignoring the pain in his right bicep, which felt like a low-grade burn.

A smell of smoldering electronics permeated the area.

The agent who had received the table struggled to his feet, half cradling his arms against him. Either wrists or forearms, or some combination of both, were broken or unusable.

The others?

The second man and his female companion were sprawled facedown against the table, while a set of cubes sputtered and sparked on the floor under the table. The second woman edged away from the table, as if the cubes were about to explode.

Jimjoy wanted to touch his injured arm, but just looked down at the narrow slit in his sleeve as he slipped away from his table. He tried to implement the relaxation techniques he had learned years earlier as he moved. His concentration was unequal to the task, and besides, he needed to finish getting out of the way before someone focused on him rather than on the devastation he had inadvertently created.

"Screamers!"

WWHHHEEEEeeeeeee!

Belatedly, the saloon alarm had gone off, and two blocky men carrying riot sticks and tangleweb guns burst through the tables to level their equipment at the table where the four agents had been.

Jimjoy eased himself into a vacant stool at the long bar.

The woman with the fake red hair had disappeared, but the riot police grabbed the man with the injured arms from a corner table after gestures from several patrons and a nod from the bartender.

"See that?" asked the man on the adjoining stool. "Weren't you sitting there?"

"Next table. Place exploded when I got up." Jimjoy shook his head. "Needed to use the facilities. Just lost my samburg steak."

"Didn't miss much. Should have ordered the grilled colpork. What happened anyway? They say anything?"

Jimjoy ignored half the questions.

"Thanks for the tip on the steak. She doesn't find me, and I'll have the colpork instead."

The Imperial Special Operative shook his head again, doing his best to look confused, which wasn't difficult, since he was anyway. He still couldn't understand how the Fuards had found him so quickly. Or been able to arrange the table next to him on such short notice.

"Buster . . . you ordered samburg?"

Jimjoy repressed a rueful smile at the efficiency of the tired-looking waitress, who didn't wait for his reply to start setting his order on the bar.

"That's fine. No way I'm going back there."

"Can't say I blame you . . . Say, you're bleeding . . . What happened?"

"Flame!" Jimjoy looked at his arm. He could see some

blood, and the tunic sleeve was darker above the cut on his upper arm. The wound still burned. "Must have been cut by all the flying glass." He eased the fabric away from the skin. From what he could see, the wound looked like a combination between a razor knife cut and a tangler burn, but was little more than skin deep. It would probably leave a bruise covering most of his upper arm within a few days.

"Just a cut. Got some spray?"

"Cost you . . ."

"If it's just a few creds, fine. Otherwise, I'll just bleed until I finish eating."

"Five credits."

"Spray it."

"Cryl, spray here." The waitress's voice was low, but carried to the bartender.

Jimjoy realized that the saloon had quieted as the two men with the riot gear had been joined by three other men in dark black uniforms.

The waitress took the thin can from the bartender and sprayed the heal/seal solution through the slit sleeve and right over the threads of blood running down his arm. Jimjoy bit his tongue to repress a shudder at the pain. Definitely a nerve scrambler of some sort.

"So what happened?" asked the waitress in the same low voice.

Jimjoy did not look back over his shoulder at the methodical cleanup he knew had to be going on, but anticipated a tap on the shoulder at any second. He took a bite of the samburg steak, managing to choke it down. Colpork couldn't have been any worse. He looked for the El Parma and swallowed more than he should have. Between a steak that made sawdust taste good and the bruise and burning in his arm, not to mention his being a target for who knew how many agents, things were definitely headed downhill, if not farther.

He managed to clear his throat and recall the woman's question.

"Oh . . . hadesfire if I know. Got up . . . to use the

facilities, and the big guy grabbed at my table. Then there was water everywhere. Somebody screamed, and the guy let go of me . . . ducked away . . ."

"All right . . . cart them off . . ." The voice of one of the men in the dark uniforms stilled the room.

Jimjoy realized that the local authorities had not attempted more than a perfunctory questioning of the people at the few adjoining tables, and were basically just cleaning up the mess.

The two blocky men tossed the two bodies on a stretcher which was quickly covered with a stained gray cloth. One of the dark-uniformed men escorted out the man with the injured arms. And no one even looked for the missing redhead.

". . . swear there were four there . . ." he muttered, trying to see if the waitress would comment.

"One of the women's gone. Havvies don't care . . . so long as types like that don't cause more trouble . . ."

"Don't care?"

"How could they? You want to be a target of every system's sneaks?" With that, the waitress was gone, heading for the table where the four agents had been sitting. She picked up a battered pitcher from beside the table and handed it contemptuously to the youth in the singlesuit who was cleaning up the rest of the mess around the table, waiting for the two Havvies to finish.

". . . water . . . who threw it . . ."

Jimjoy had seen the pitcher, had felt the water. But who had thrown it? And why?

His forehead furrowed as he glanced over his shoulder, scanning the area. The table where the silver-haired woman and her two companions had been sitting was vacant, without a water pitcher. More interesting was the service station next to the table, without any water pitchers either.

The remaining two uniformed men were gingerly collecting the two fused cubes of metal. They ignored a second battered water pitcher on the floor.

He returned his glance to the plate in front of him.

". . . be even worse if you don't eat it warm," offered the talkative man.

"Thanks," mumbled Jimjoy as he took a mouthful, though he failed to see how the samburg could be any worse cold.

The threesome had been the only ones close enough to have reached the water pitchers, but why had they bothered? Were they somehow tracking the Fuards?

He shook his head again as he methodically chewed the so-called steak. The advice had been correct. The cooler the samburg got, the more it tasted like oily sawdust, as opposed to hot sawdust.

The two Haversol officials completed their cleanup, scooped up their equipment, and left. The waitress and the busboy finished resetting the table, and the green-haired hostess showed a threesome to the smeared tabletop.

The conversations around the room returned to normal chaotic volume, as if the scene had happened before and would again.

Jimjoy was becoming more aware, minute by minute, of his aching right arm. Within another hour, it would be virtually useless for at least a day. And that meant he would have to be even more careful when returning to his room. At the same time he doubted that more than two pairs of agents would be tracking him in such an out-of-the-way place as Haversol.

The silver-haired woman's group had wanted either him alive or the Fuards out of the picture, for which he was grateful, if puzzled. The remaining Fuard was in no shape to want anything, and by the time he could summon much aid, Jimjoy would be on Accord. That left the Havvies themselves, and from what he could tell they didn't take sides.

He pushed aside the inedible remnants of samburg and took a series of swallows from the bottle of El Parma. Then he tried the vegetables, which were far better than the samburg. He finished them all, then swigged the last of the local brew.

He forced himself to use his right hand in signaling the waitress, who never seemed to look his way.

"Here." Still without more than a sidelong glance, she slapped the bill on the counter.

Jimjoy could feel her apprehension, but he ignored it and turned to the bartender.

"You or her."

"Either. Leave her hers."

Jimjoy handed the rail-thin man the Imperial twenty-credit note, waited for the change, and left two small notes on the counter. He did not look back as he headed for the still-open portals.

He found the effort to keep from wincing increasingly difficult as he climbed the stairs to his room. The arm was like a series of knives ripping at his shoulder, although the heal/seal had stopped the blood from the thin parallel cuts.

Slamming the door open, Jimjoy staggered in, ready to use his left hand, and the palm weapon it held, if necessary.

His room was empty, dust showing it as untouched as when he had left. Either that or the lightest footed or fingered of intruders had come and gone. He was scarcely up to analyzing the situation as he bolted the door and swallowed one of the emergency painkillers from his kit . . . before sinking into the valley in the center of the too soft bed.

. . . IX . . .

He was running, arms pumping, chest heaving, sweat streaming from his forehead down his face, blurring his vision, burning the corners of his eyes.

His right arm dangled, useless broken in two places, and each step jarred it, sending a fresh wave of pain into his shoulder.

Thrummmm!

The stunner bolt hummed past him, close enough to spur his already flagging steps.

He could feel the pair of Imperial Special Operatives closing in as he tried to reach the tube train station from the Grand Park.

Thrummmm!

His right leg buckled with the stunner paralysis, and he pitched forward, headfirst down the ramp toward the platform, trying to tuck himself into the approved combat roll, but hampered by the broken arm and unresponsive leg.

Thrummmmmmmmmmmmmmmm!

Another stunner bolt chased him, the sound rolling like thunder after him as he tumbled helplessly toward the stone wall where the ramp made a half circle down and around toward the tube train platform.

Crack!

A projectile ricocheted off the stone.

Crackkkk . . .

The sweat was still running off his face, and the throbbing in his arm continued to send waves of pain into and up through his shoulder, but Jimjoy realized he was lying on his back.

On his back? Where? Had Hersnik caught him?

Crack. Tap.

"Room cleaning."

Room cleaning?

He shook his head to clear his thoughts. The Imperiale . . . was he still there?

Glancing around the darkened room, he noted the still-open metal closet doors, his pack on the floor.

"You want your room cleaned?" repeated the voice through the closed door.

"No," he croaked. "Not now."

"No later. Maybe tomorrow."

"Maybe tomorrow," he responded through his all-too-dry throat.

Thrummmmmmmmmmmmmmmm. The muted roar of the cleaning machine continued down the corridor away from his room.

Slowly, he eased himself into a sitting position, using his good arm. Then he eased off the tunic, blinking back the involuntary tears when the fabric ripped away from the cuts and the heal/seal.

Surprisingly, his upper right arm appeared only slightly swollen. Although the throbbing intensified when he moved his arm or fingers, he could move it, a good sign so soon after the injury.

He shifted his weight and let his legs dangle over the side of the bed, taking one deep breath, then another.

The nightmare memory of the chase was clear, terribly clear, although he had never been on either end of such a pursuit in real life.

He started to shrug, then aborted the motion as he felt the pain from his arm increase. Instead, he gingerly slid from the bed to a standing position, then took a step toward the dingy bathroom. He needed to feel clean.

. . . X . . .

The narrow screen beside the lock port flickered, then changed from a blank gray to a fuzzy image of the Accordan ship as it edged in toward the lock.

With its bulbous shape and plasteen plates, the Accordan vessel had certainly not been designed for anything besides full space work, or much beyond service as a transport. Jimjoy doubted that the structure could have taken much more than a full gee under any circumstances.

As his eyes surveyed the screen image beside the inner lock portal, he could not help but note the symmetry and the smooth plate joints that proclaimed a level of workmanship higher than technically or practically necessary.

"Stand by for locking." The metallic voice rasped through the compartment where he stood with two dozen others, including the silver-haired woman with the enigmatic smile. He had noticed that she also had green eyes, eyes which seemed to bore into his back when he wasn't able to check whether she was looking at him or not. Then again, it could have been his imagination.

He turned suddenly as a flutter of white in the corner of his eye caught his attention . . . and wished he hadn't made the motion quite so abruptly as a sharp ache in his right arm reminded him again of his first night on Haversol.

The second night had been far less eventful, if more painful. But he had not seen any of the characters from his first dinner, including the silver lady, since then. Not until he had gotten off the shuttle and caught a glimpse of her hair in the corridor of the small orbit station. But while the pain of whatever stunner or nervetangler that had raked his arm had subsided, it was far from gone, particularly when he used his right arm or moved suddenly.

Whunnnkkk.

The dull thudding sound echoed through the closed space, and the floor vibrated, but not enough to cause any of the travelers even to have to shift their footing.

"Locks linked," the unseen speaker announced unnecessarily. "Have your passcards ready for boarding."

Jimjoy took a deep breath and fumbled with the thin folder he carried, turning to his left just enough to catch sight of the silver-haired woman—the young silver haired woman, he corrected himself. This time he caught her eyes momentarily before she looked past him without a glint of recognition. She had her passcard ready as well.

"Please enter the portal in single file. Your passcard will be taken once you are in the lock." The voice from the overhead speaker was a new one, a voice with an accent, as if the speaker used Panglais as a second language.

After all the polite jostling, Jimjoy Wright discovered that the silver-haired woman, as well as a number of others, had ended up in front of him. His bemused smile faded as he began to wonder.

He was assuming that she was the woman from the Imperiale. What was the likelihood of her being in both places, en route to Accord, merely by chance? If not by circumstance, then for whom did she work? Hersnik? The Matriarchy? Was she a contract agent for Hersnik?

He nearly shook his head, but repressed the gesture. After all, he was merely an itinerant pilot and technician—that was all he was.

The short line moved quickly. The dozen-odd people before him had disappeared through the inner lock portal so swiftly that he had to take three long steps to close the gap before stepping inside.

He held up his card.

"White?"

"Yes?"

The ship's officer ignored his response, instead waiting for an answer from a second official, who stood behind and to the right of the card checker.

"Have him stand aside."

"Would you please stand here, Ser White?" asked the checker with a polite smile on her lips. "We need to discuss several matters with you before you embark."

"What matters?" responded Jimjoy, equally as formally.

"Nothing wrong. We just would prefer you understand your options on Accord before the fact." With that she gestured for Jimjoy to move to the side, even as she took the next pass.

"Fliereo?"

"Clear."

"Simones?"

"Clear."

When the remaining ten men and women and the sole child, a boy of perhaps ten standard years, had been passed on by the officials, Jimjoy found himself standing with the two Accordan ship personnel and a thin and red-haired woman.

"Ser White. You first. Your credentials sheet indicates background and experience in various piloting duties, including flitters, skitters, and even space scout craft. You also claim experience as a journeyman electronics technician. We'll pass on the obvious Imperial connection and take you at face value." The checker pursed her thin lips and nodded her head at the man who had first suggested that he step aside.

"Afraid I don't understand," interrupted Jimjoy.

"It's not a question of understanding. Accord is a new planet with colonization started less than two centuries ago. The current and potential food supply system, and the entire economy, are geared to that development level. The native hydrocarbons and metals are on the light side. That means that there isn't much industry, except in the satellite community off Four. So there isn't much demand for pilots or electronics types, and that job market is rather tight right now. That makes you category three—useful but not in high demand.''

"So how does that affect me?''

"There's a bond requirement . . .''

"Bond?'' Jimjoy frowned. This didn't sound like the happy-go-lucky, back-to-the-trees bunch that rumors had portrayed or that all the Havvies had been talking about. They sounded much more like the hardened and practical would-be rebels that Headquarters feared—and that he had discounted. "Still don't understand.''

"Because you may not be able to support yourself as an unofficial immigrant, you must post a bond equivalent to the passage cost to the nearest system which will employ you. In your case, that is relatively low, since Haversol needs both pilots and electronics types.''

Jimjoy sighed.

"How much? With whom?''

"Five thousand Imperial credits.''

"That's . .'' This time he did shake his head.

"Can you post it or not? Do you choose to?''

"You don't take immigrants?''

"Unless or until you take the immigrant aptitude tests, Accord takes no responsibility for your employability. Anyone who does not have verified long-term current employment must either post bond or take the tests.''

"You can't win, Major,'' added the woman checker.

After a moment of shock, barely managing to keep his jaw in place, Jimjoy laughed. She was right.

"I'll post the bond.''

"Since you're being reasonable, Ser . . . White . . . by being relatively direct, in turn, we'll spare you any delusions about our lack of vigilance.''

The thin red-haired woman's eyes went back and forth in puzzlement as she watched the byplay between Jimjoy and the ship's officers.

"Assuming I am what you think I am, I'd be interested in the basis for your statement."

The checker grinned before answering.

"We test all immigrants for skills and aptitudes. The profile would tell us what your passcard shows, and a great deal more. That would go on the record, of course, which is periodically inspected by the various Imperial services, since Accord is a dutiful colony, fully aware of its indebtedness to the Empire."

Jimjoy refrained from grinning in return and shrugged. "What next?"

The man responded this time, nodding at the woman. "Cerla is the third officer. Doubles as purser, customs, immigration, and tourism. Technically, once you post bond, you're a tourist, although we don't stop anyone who wants to from working. But you're a tourist even if you stay your whole life, with no local citizenship rights unless you officially change your mind and go through testing." He added, "Cerla will guide you through the formalities in her office."

Cerla, her short brown hair bouncing slightly, turned and headed through the inner ship lock into the Accord vessel, assuming he would follow.

He did, but not before overhearing the beginning of the conversation between the man and the red-haired woman.

"Sher Masdra, you have no skills beyond the commerce . . . shall we say . . . of your own person . . ."

When it came right down to it, reflected Jimjoy absently as he followed the purser, neither did he or anyone else. Especially, it appeared, on Accord. He hurried in pursuit of Cerla.

By the time he had caught up with the quick-moving purser, she had stopped by a portal that was beginning to open.

"My office, quarters, and general place of business." The woman gestured for him to enter.

Jimjoy slipped inside, ready for anything—except for the four-by-four-meter room, tastefully accented in shades of blue and cream, with a console and four small screens on one wall, a recessed double bunk on the opposite wall, a small table and two chairs. His eyes lighted on the built-in beverage dispenser, then flicked to the overhead lighting strips.

"Everything from business to pleasure," he noted dryly.

"Have a seat." Her tone ignored his sarcasm.

The Special Operative looked over the choice. Either the luxurious and padded sink chair or the utilitarian swivel before the console.

He settled into the sink chair, since he knew she would not sit down if he took the swivel. As he eased himself into the chair, he inadvertently put his weight on his right arm, and was rewarded with a renewed throb from the muscle all the way into his shoulder.

"You looked like you were sitting for an execution, Major."

"What's the Major bit? The name's White."

Cerla raised an eyebrow. "I thought we'd gone through that already. No charades, as I recall."

Jimjoy smiled expansively from the depths of the padded sink chair, designed clearly to keep upstart passengers from leaping at the purser/government agent. "Only admitted I wasn't an immigrant. Didn't deny I had Imperial ties. You said that I was a Major . . . or whatever."

Cerla shook her head, and her bobbed brown hair bounced away from her round face and suddenly flat brown eyes.

"All right. You are Major Jimjoy Earle Wright the Third, Imperial Space Service, Special Operative, Intelligence Service, on special detail for reconnaissance of Accord. Your cover name is Hale Vale White. You have orders limiting you to strict observation, without any specific time limits.

"You graduated from Malestra College with an I.S.S. scholarship, completed pilot training at Saskan during the '43 emergency, served one tour as junior second pilot on the courier *Rimbaud* before being transferred to Headquarters staff for independent assignments. You are qualified to pilot virtually every class of atmospheric and space vehicle. You are persona non grata to the Fuards, the Halstanis, the Orknarlians. You are the tempter incarnate on *IFoundIt!* And your profile has been circulated to every non-Imperial world by the Comsis Co-Op.

"Besides, even if you aren't exactly *who* we think you are, there's absolutely no doubt about *what* you are."

Jimjoy frowned. "Care to explain that?"

Cerla smiled faintly. "I probably shouldn't, but you've obviously been set up. That means that the Empire either wants you dead or to create an incident. It also means that the Empire won't listen to anything beyond an in-depth factual report, if that. Something as ossified as the Empire cannot afford to change, not beyond the cosmetic."

"Hope you're going to explain," Jimjoy pursued. He was annoyed by the woman's patronizing attitude—even as attractive and friendly as she projected herself. Even if what she said made a certain disturbing kind of sense. He took a breath slightly deeper than normal and tried to relax.

"Yes . . . although I am tempted not to."

"Appreciate it if you would. I'm too Imperial not to be put off by your rather patronizing attitude toward the Empire. Even if you turn out to be right."

This time the purser smiled more than faintly, pursed her lips, and cleared her throat. "It's really very simple, so simple that anyone could use the technique, not that we had to in your case. First is the question of identity." She paused. "I'm getting there, Major. Believe me, I am. But there are a lot of pieces of information you need, and it's not exactly easy to blurt out these things, even though it's necessary now." Her smile was broad, but somehow forced.

While he appreciated the effort, and the smile, Jimjoy was leaning forward, wondering what came next, a cold chill settling inside him, reinforced by the hot throbbing of his still-unhealed arm.

"Every Imperial Special Operative falls within certain clearly defined parameters—male, with an optimum muscle, fat, and bone ratio that never varies by more than five percent; never less than one hundred eighty-one centimeters nor more than one hundred ninety-five centimeters; primarily Caucasian genetic background; strong technical education and mechanical skills; generally between twenty-eight and forty-five standard years; and always with a surface carriage index of between seven and eight."

Jimjoy looked at the purser blankly.

She said nothing more.

Finally, he spoke. "I understood everything until you got to the last item."

"I thought everyone knew about surface carriage indices." He could see the steel in her eyes and repressed a shudder, not quite sure how he had thought she might be friendly. Or was she just being mischievous?

"Afraid I'm rather uninformed."

"Surface carriage index is a measure of underlying muscular tension and emotional stability. It was originally developed by Alregord's psychiatrists as an attempt to provide a long-range visual indication of intentions. For that, it was a failure, because the only thing the index is really good for is showing the unconscious attitude of the individual toward humanity in general. The higher the number, the less socially oriented the individual. This gets complicated because the index varies with some individuals depending on their surroundings. For our purposes it doesn't make much difference, because the variations are generally less toward either end of the scale. Above ten, and a person is sociopathic or psychopathic. Below two, and there's almost no individual identity. The seven-to-eight range indicates a loner with little or no interest in permanent attachments to people."

"Sounds like psychosocial mumbo jumbo."

"Think about it, Major. Compare my description to any Special Operatives you may know before you condemn the analysis."

Jimjoy felt cold. If Accord had discovered such a readily apparent pattern, who else knew? His thoughts returned to the meeting with the retired spacer. Arto, had that been his name? Had he been an Accord operative? Or had he seen part of the pattern?

Jimjoy was brought back to the present by Cerla's next question.

"Now . . . do we continue the charade, or do you want to give me some idea of what you happen to be looking for?"

Jimjoy nodded. He'd been set up, at least to some degree, because his actions were a problem to the Empire . . . or the Service. It almost seemed as though no one wanted him to be successful. Every time he'd pulled off the difficult, they'd given him something tougher. The apparent ease of the Accord assignment should have been a signal, especially now, after the incident on Haversol.

The quiet of the cabin was punctuated only by the hissing of the ventilators, and by a dull *thunk* that echoed through the ship, indicating that the ship had unlocked from the Haversol orbit control station.

"While you're still deciding, would you like a drink?"

"I'll pass on the drink for now. How about a piece of information? I know your name. Period. You seem to know everything about me. Seems you'd have to be a part of colonial intelligence or armed forces . . . or that Institute . . . but why does anyone care?"

Cerla poured herself a goblet of a lime-green fluid and set the other glass back in the rack by the dispenser.

"Anything the Empire does affects us. How could anyone concerned not care?"

"Suppose you're right—"

"And you still haven't decided whether you're going to play it straight. What other options do you have? We know who and what you are. And . . ."

"And . . . ?"

". . . you're intelligent enough to see that."

Jimjoy was positive she had been about to say something else, but there was no way to determine what.

"Reluctant to affirm or deny," he said with a half smile.

"If I deny I'm this Wright character, I have to spend forever proving I am who I am. And you won't believe me. If I lie outright, that's trouble. If I agree, that's a confession, and people have been known to disappear for less. This Wright character sounds like he's on everyone's hit list. Very popular man."

"You make a good point. Good . . . but irrelevant."

As she spoke, Jimjoy eased himself forward in the depths of the chair, trying to shift his weight in a way not to seem too obvious, yet ready for action if necessary. He doubted that he could escape untouched, but he had to try.

Cerla ignored his tension and sat in the anchored swivel less than a meter away. After speaking, she sipped from the goblet, swallowed, and cleared her throat.

"I will make one further observation which might help you decide. While Accord is not unknown for its ability to obtain intelligence, the background on you was there for the taking, laid out. This leads to certain disturbing conclusions, which is why you were warned on Haversol."

"Warned?"

Cerla said nothing, but waited.

"I see," temporized Jimjoy.

"Not totally, but we can always hope that you will." She stood, swiftly, though so gracefully that Jimjoy did not move. "Are you sure you wouldn't like something?"

"How about some juice?"

The purser/agent filled the second goblet and tendered it to him before reseating herself on the swivel, one leg tucked under her.

Her posture reassured the Special Operative . . . slightly. The sink chair felt somehow sticky under him and he shifted his position again.

"So where does that leave us?" he asked.

"You refuse to admit anything, and we're forced to take you on faith, at least in part. Assuming you are who we think you are, Accord would like to see that your visit is successful and that you return safely from our poor colonial outpost to your headquarters.''

''And how much will you hide?'' He didn't bother with questioning their assumption of his being an Imperial agent. That was probably all that was keeping him alive, even if he were being stubborn and not wanting to admit it outright.

''Nothing. We obviously will not volunteer anything, but should you find something or wish to observe something, we will certainly not hinder you in any way.''

''That bad?''

''Yes.''

''And who are 'we'? You talk about some group, but you've never identified who you are.''

Jimjoy took a sip from the goblet. The green juice reminded him of a combination of orange and lime with a hint of cinnamon, except the combined taste was somehow whole and clean.

''We?'' he prompted.

''Let us just say that most of Accord has a vested interest in your safe return, including the colonial forces, the local government, and the Institute.''

Jimjoy wanted to shake his head. The situation sounded far worse than Hersnik or the briefing tapes had portrayed, and he wasn't even on Accord yet. Instead of commenting, he chose the inane.

''Very good drink. What is it?''

''Lerrit. Native.''

She waited.

He waited.

''The *Carson* is approaching jump point. Approaching jump point.''

The announcement from the hidden speaker was the first indication Jimjoy had of actual operation since the delocking maneuver. The crew was smooth . . . very smooth. And that brought up the question of why a ship's officer was spending so very much time with an apparent down-and-almost-out spacer—even one thought to be an Imperial operative.

Jimjoy had a momentary feeling of being into something over his head, very far over his head. He ignored it.

"So you fear the Empire—and my safe return, with whatever information I pick up, allows the Empire no pretexts, whereas my demise would allow them to blast two orbs with one bolt?"

"That's half of what the—what we had determined."

"And the other half?"

"If you're such a headache to your own Service, we're certainly not out to do them any favors." This time the smile was nearly malicious.

Jimjoy took a deep swallow of the lerrit, and waited again.

"What about all that noise about the bond requirement?"

"Forget it. That was for public consumption. Besides, the Empire might not clear any credit line or voucher you wrote, and that would be just another problem for us."

Jimjoy looked over at Cerla dubiously.

"We will, of course," Cerla continued, as she shifted her weight in the swivel and placed her nearly empty goblet on the console, "claim that you did post bond, and customs records will show that it was posted and returned to you when you left."

Jimjoy could see Hersnik causing problems over that transaction, but since it would be a while before he had to break that particular orbit, he said nothing about it. Instead he took another gulp of the lerrit, nearly finishing it.

"Would you like some more?"

"Not now." He looked for some place to put the goblet down, but finding nowhere within arm's reach, retained it. "Aren't you afraid I'll find something?"

"We're certain you will. We just don't think it will do the Empire much good."

"You obviously know it won't," concluded Jimjoy. "That means you either intend—" He broke off his statement, not sure where his words might carry him.

"We think it won't. We don't know. What were you going to say?"

Her last question had been idly asked, but Jimjoy did not miss the sharpening of attention.

"Not sure. Except that when something is this clear, there's more than meets the eye."

Cling!

"Standing by for jump."

The announcement was delivered in a bored tone from the same unseen speaker.

Cling! Cling!

The ship's interior was flooded with the pitch blackness that accompanied every jump, a blackness that seemed instantaneous and eternal all at once.

Normal lighting returned just as instantaneously.

"The next jump shift will occur in approximately one half standard hour."

Cerla picked up her goblet to drain the last half sip. Then she set it back on the console.

Thud.

The sound echoed through the quietness of the cabin.

Jimjoy avoided looking at the woman and tilted the goblet back to drain the last drops out.

"Are you sure you wouldn't like some more?"

"No, thanks." He extended the empty goblet with his left hand. His right arm was beginning to throb once more.

She took it and set it next to hers.

Thud.

"So where do all of these orbits within orbits leave me?"

"You're cleared into Accord. Your papers are here." She gestured vaguely at her console. "Once we arrive, the shuttle from orbit control will deposit you at the port outside Harmony. You're free to pursue your observations and inquiries. If you need special assistance or transportation to places not served by normal commercial channels, we suggest that you request such transportation through the Institute, rather than flying yourself in equipment of potentially dubious performance. If you prefer to be the pilot, the Institute will provide a flitter and a backup pilot.

"In return for this openness, Accord will know what you see, or at least have a good idea."

"Being unduly generous?"

"Practical. Short of assassinating you, Major, which would be easy enough to do, no one could stop you. We'd rather you didn't expire on our watch." She fixed his eyes with hers.

Jimjoy found their opacity disturbing in their intensity.

"We may also request that you actually observe other activities, from time to time, if we feel you may be missing information for your report."

"Indoctrination now?"

"Hardly. We hope for a limited balance in your findings, and more information shouldn't exactly hurt you. Your report will need to be more than brilliant, in any case."

Jimjoy smiled wryly. In that respect, Cerla was right. Dead right.

"That it?" He stood, ignoring the burning in his right arm.

"Almost." She stood and turned back toward the console, where she picked up the folder from the flat top. She took two steps back toward Jimjoy and extended the documents. "Those are your clearances, as well as a list of fax numbers you may find helpful. At the end are the particulars circulated on you, which you may find of some interest."

Cerla inclined her head toward the portal. "That's it, Major. Turn to the left as you leave. Your cabin is the last on the left. You won't need it that long, though. This is a short hop. Less than twenty-four hours before we swing orbit." She paused again. "And, Major, you might consider that being a loner is not the same as being independent."

"I'll think about it. Sleep on it, in fact, since that's what I need most right now."

Cerla raised her eyebrows, but said nothing. She continued to extend the documents.

Jimjoy took them, meeting her eyes. He nodded and stepped away, turning.

The portal opened before he approached and stepped through,

heading to the left. He could feel the purser's eyes on his back as he departed, knew she was watching since he had not heard her close the portal. She was interested in him, but not in any romantic or sensual way.

Her parting comment bothered him, even more than the implications about Accord's use of the so-called surface carriage index. While Accord could have invented the concept just to fluster him, that didn't make sense either.

He found himself shaking his head again. Accord wasn't going to be any picnic, not if they were all as sharp as he'd seen so far. And that was scary for another reason. Accord wasn't even independent. Just a colony with a few scattered colonial forces, a colonial council, and a ragtag Institute pretending to be a university.

. . . XI . . .

Any power which merely opposes its own destruction or the loss of its territory almost never wins the ensuing conflict unless it defines its objectives beyond survival or the perpetuation of the status quo.

In warfare, status never remains quo. All things change, and success for the defender rests on the ability to shift the fight from defense to offense, to place its attacker or attackers on the defensive.

Without such a de facto switch in positions, the most that can be gained is a stalemate, and the result of such a stalemate is inevitably a change in the actual governments of both attacker and defender, even if the outward forms remain apparently unaltered.

Thus, the eventual outcome of any war is a change in the government of at least one of the parties. For this reason, no war should be undertaken by any government interested in its survival without change, not unless the alternative is wide-scale death and destruction.

Patterns of Politics
Exton Land
Halston, 3123 N.E.

... XII ...

Jimjoy stepped through the shuttle portal and onto the open ramp that led down to the white tarmac below.

No impenetrable plastarmac, no lines of shuttles, and no throngs, either of officials or of welcomers. Just a handful of men and women. And, also unlike the central systems of the Empire, there was no baggage handling. Jimjoy carried both his hanging bag and the heavier and bulkier bag which contained equipment, folded clothes, and personal items.

"Excuse me . . ."

He looked back as he realized that his hesitation was blocking the other passengers.

The woman who had spoken was the silver-haired one, the one he suspected of lofting the water pitcher onto the Fuards to help him.

"You did a very nice job," he said, trying not to let the sarcasm creep into his voice. "Thank you."

"Just my job, Major. Now . . . if you will excuse me . . ."

"Sorry." He stepped aside, gestured broadly for her to proceed, following quickly. By now the upper right arm only ached, although it would be days before the bruise disappeared.

". . . about time . . ." Jimjoy ignored the whispered complaint from the heavyset man who had been standing behind the Accord agent. Except, he wondered, how could she be an agent? As an Imperial colony, Accord could not operate an intelligence service, nor any armed forces other than the domestic police forces.

Jimjoy had been operating outside the Empire too long and had totally missed that simple fact. Yet the woman, as well as the ship's purser and the other ship's officers, had acted as though she were representing *something*. Did the Ecologic Institute, or whatever it was called, actually run the colony? Was that what worried Hersnik?

He filed the thought and hurried to keep close to the silver-haired woman.

From the scattered group of people waiting a woman stepped forward, her tanned face and short-cropped blond hair giving her the appearance of an outdoor professional of some sort. "Thelina!"

"Meryl!"

The two women exchanged hugs, and Jimjoy fixed both faces in his mind as he skirted them and headed for the transportation terminal ahead. He could hear them talking as they followed in the same general direction, but he could not make out anything beyond pleasantries.

Thelina—that had been what the blond woman had called the Accord/Institute agent. He mentally noted the name. Then he took a deep breath and lengthened his stride, trying to ignore the tired feeling in his right arm.

The air was crisp, with a tang, not salty like the sea, but like a mountaintop above a fir forest. The shuttleport was west of Harmony, on a plateau of sorts, but certainly not one high enough to qualify as a mountain. Jimjoy looked up in front of him toward the west, where he could see a hint of clouds above the peaks on the horizon.

The gravity was a shade stronger than Terra-norm, but not enough to bother him, certainly not the way it would have on Mara or on the Fuard heavy planets.

He entered the transport terminal, glanced up at the high ceilings supported by arched wooden beams, and realized that the open area was both dimmer and cooler than he would have expected without climate control.

"Ser Wright?"

Jimjoy looked at the young man, scarcely more than a schoolboy, who wore a forest-green tunic and matching trousers.

"Yes." His voice was noncommittal.

"I am apprentice Dorfman, from the Institute. Your flitter is waiting to take you either to your hotel or to quarters at the Institute, if you prefer."

"The Ecologic or Ecolitan Institute?"

"Yes, ser."

"I plan to visit the Institute later, but I think I will take commercial transport to my hotel."

"Very good, ser. I hope we will see you later. The commercial transport sector is to your left."

With that, the apprentice turned and left.

Had there been a certain relief in the young man's expression? Had the Institute hoped he would refuse its offer? He shook his head and continued toward the ground-transport gates before him.

Once through the four-meter-wide polished wood gates that looked as though they were never closed, he put down both bags with relief, shrugging his shoulders, particularly the right one. Although he wanted to rub the still-tender muscles, he did not, instead leaning down as if to check the heavy squat bag.

Although he had been the first passenger from the shuttle through the gates, he waited until several others, in groups of twos and threes, began to appear and line up for transportation. He inserted himself third in line, watching to see whether any prearranged groundcar pulled into line to pick him up. None did.

He got the third car in the lineup. As the driver, a slender, white-haired man, opened the door, Jimjoy swung the bags into the rear seat with him.

"Your destination, ser?"

"Colonial Grande."

"Colonial Grande it is."

The electrocar hummed as it slowly built up speed leaving

the shuttleport, turning right on the first boulevard, which contained a center parkway lined on each side with ten-meter-high trees. Each tree was the same, with a thick black trunk that rose five meters before branching out into stubby black branches. Along each branch, particularly at the end, sprouted long and thin fronds of yellow and green, enormous narrow leaves that swayed in the gentle breeze.

"The trees?" asked the Imperial Operative.

"Corran. They almost look T-type until you study them up close. They shimmer in the sun after a good rain, like they had a light of their own."

From the first boulevard the driver made another right turn onto a second, less expansive boulevard with a narrower center parkway that held but a single line of the corran trees.

Gray stone slabs, finely cut, composed the walks on the edge of the boulevard, and the grass was emerald green and neatly trimmed. For all the careful design of the streets, the dwellings abutting them were modest, muted in color, and generally of one story.

Almost as if it were a scene from the past, reflected the Special Operative, without metals, synthetics, and plastarmac, when people built with wood and stone and brick.

He asked no more questions as the car hummed through the morning quiet of Harmony, instead concentrating on gathering impressions of Accord. He could see the people, could even see an occasional small child, too young to be in school. Although he saw one or two individuals in a hurry, the general impression he received was of a peaceful town. Too peaceful?

There was none of the haste and self-importance of Tinhorn, or Madeira, or New Washton, or even of New Avalon. Certainly none of the lurking impression of power conveyed by New Augusta, or even the hidden fantaticism of smaller capitals—such as *IFoundIt!*

"Colonial Grande coming up on the left, ser."

Jimjoy recalled himself from his dreaming mood and took a deep breath.

As the groundcar hummed up to the Colonial Grande, which, with its plank-and-stone facing and heavy walls, resembled a lodge more than a hotel, Jimjoy surveyed the circular entry driveway, more from habit than from any feeling of need.

His eyes swept past the thin man working on the wide flower bed beside the main entry, then halted and looked back. No reason for a gardener not to be working on a nice morning, but something about the man bothered Jimjoy.

Instinctively, he checked the concealed belt knife, whose plastics would trigger no detectors, and the small stunner the Accord officials had pointedly ignored and probably should not have let him keep.

The electrocar purred to a stop.

Jimjoy watched the gardener, who had arranged his weeding chores so that he faced the entry canopy.

"The Colonial Grande, ser."

"Oh . . . yes. Thank you. How much?"

"Nineteen credits, ser."

Jimjoy fumbled a twenty note and a five-credit piece from his belt while still watching the gardener. Finally, he opened the door with his right hand, his left poised to use whatever might be necessary.

As the morning sun struck his face, Jimjoy caught the look of recognition on the gardener's face.

Zing!

Thrummm!

Even while flying toward the turf on the right-hand side of the entry pillar, Jimjoy fired one charge from the stunner.

A quick look around the base of the pillar reassured him that, while the other agent's needler had missed, he had not. Scrambling to his feet, ignoring the scrapes that his knees had taken even through his trousers, he scanned the area, checking the roofline.

"Hades . . . and . . ."

He launched himself back behind the next pillar.

Zing! Zing! Zing!

Chips from several needle darts sprayed around the pillar and into the area where he had first flung himself. They had come at an angle from behind the gardener.

Thrumm! Thrumm! Thrumm!

Several stunners responded to the needler, even before Jimjoy looked around the pillar to catch sight of a figure disappearing over the roofline. He pulled himself up, then lurched forward toward the inert form in the garden.

A small squad of men and women dressed in forest-green tunics and trousers, without insignia, had deployed across the entry area, appearing as if by magic. Their stunners had clearly been those responding to the rooftop sniper.

As Jimjoy finally reached the man, who was not breathing, so did a familiar figure, one with silver hair, but still wearing her traveling clothes.

"No warning from you this time."

"You didn't seem to need it," observed Thelina.

Jimjoy noted with amusement that Thelina had apparently made a dive similar to his and was now brushing the dirt and dust from her tunic.

Jimjoy took in the needle dart in the gardener's back, recognizing the dead man's facial structure through the disguise and changed hair color. He glanced back up at the roofline.

"Did you tell anyone where you were going?"

"Hardly." He looked around. The groundcar was gone, his two bags lying in a heap. "Except the driver."

"That wouldn't have counted," responded the woman flatly. "That leaves exactly one possibility, Major. I suggest you think about it."

Jimjoy didn't like that possibility at all, not at all. He looked away from the woman to see an armored groundcar purr into the circular entrance drive.

"Institute?"

"Yes."

"All right if I change my mind about lodgings?" He wondered if he were making a mistake, but so far, his opposition was treating him much better than the Empire had.

"Took you long enough, Major." His title was delivered almost in a tone of contempt.

"So I'm a slow learner."

Thelina flipped her shoulder-length hair away from her thin face, mumbling under her breath.

". . . damned hair . . . nuisance . . ."

"I rather like it, Thelina."

"Ecolitan Andruz to you, Major Wright."

"I rather like it, Ecolitan Andruz." He stooped to check what he already knew. Commander Allen had disposed of another disposable partner. Some other lieutenant, since anyone with seniority avoided the Commander whenever possible. That meant either that the Service didn't want to reveal to the colonials the need to dispose of one Major Wright or that two Special Operatives were acting independently. The second possibility was laughable.

Jimjoy shivered, feeling lucky that he had never had to work with the Commander. Allen and Hersnik both after him—just what he needed.

"You know him?"

"No," answered Jimjoy, "but I'd seen him before. That was enough."

"Nice partner. That last needle wasn't exactly an accident."

"Doesn't look like it, but you or I will take the blame. Do you think your people will find him?"

"No. Too professional, unless we did a total search, and that would leak out. Besides, that would lead to another embarrassment."

"Embarrassment? Is that all you people think about?"

"Considering that you are relying on that same protection, Major, I wouldn't push too hard. You're here . . ."

Jimjoy shrugged. "Defer to your wisdom, Ecolitan Andruz." He tried to keep his voice level. Clearly, the Institute had little love for any Imperials, or at least Thelina Andruz had little affection for either him or Commander Allen.

Jimjoy glanced back at the roof from which the Commander had disappeared, wondering when Allen would make another attempt. Probably not until Jimjoy left Accord, or until Allen had another expendable partner.

That left Jimjoy—and the Institute—some time.

He just hoped he was reading the situation right. It would be rather embarrassing, to say the least, if the Institute had set all the circumstances to encourage him to visit the Institute right off. On the other hand, maybe the good Commander did not want Jimjoy at the Institute.

He shook his head. No matter what, he was probably wrong.

"Head shaking won't help, Major. Here's your transport." She gestured at a second groundcar purring into the drive.

With a last look at the dead man, Jimjoy straightened up and walked slowly back to where the commercial driver had dumped his bags. He picked up both to carry them to the second groundcar, now waiting behind the armored one.

"Are you coming, Ecolitan Andruz?"

"No. Someone has to clean up the Imperial messes, Major, even coming off leave."

"Appreciate your efforts, Ecolitan Andruz, and I do like your hair, even if it's not fashionable to take compliments."

"I do take compliments, Major. From friends . . . or good enemies." She began to turn to face a younger man in the dark green uniform of the Institute. "Perhaps we can get around to clarifying your status as an enemy of sorts, at least by the next time we meet."

Jimjoy wondered whether he had caught the hint of a smile, or if he were just imagining things.

. . . XIII . . .

Jimjoy opened the rear door of the groundcar and glanced inside, then stood back.

The driver was female, dark-haired, and tanned, wearing the same sort of uniform as the apprentice who had offered him a ride from the shuttleport.

The Imperial Major looked aside, then back at Thelina Andruz. She was already turning away, as if her duty were complete. She still wore the informal green shipsuit in which she had left the *Carson*, and she wore it with the authority of an Imperial Commodore.

Seeing that the Ecolitan had already dismissed him, Jimjoy returned his attention to the groundcar, realizing that his right arm was beginning to stiffen up from holding the heavy kit bag while he stood there.

Thelina continued her conversation with a young trooper, her voice low enough that Jimjoy could not pick up more than fragments of words. The uniform worn by the man was unfamiliar, as was the single insignia on the collar, a dark green triangle within a silver circle. Because planetary police and local Imperial reserves normally adopted Imperial-style uniforms, Jimjoy decided that the man, with the tunic's similarity to that of the driver's, had to be some sort of member of the Institute.

The idea of an Institute with a range of uniforms indicated more than tailoring, as did the lack of insignia.

"Are you coming, Major Wright? Ser?" The driver's voice was low, polite, and mildly insistent.

"In a moment." Jimjoy decided that Thelina was not about to halt her conversation for good-byes or other pleasantries, and swung the heavy kit bag through the open door of the groundcar. He then slung the hanging bag into the car, leaning inside to drape it over the kit bag. After another look at the oblivious Ecolitan Andruz, he swung himself into the groundcar, closing the door behind him.

Thudd!!

He repressed a wince at the force with which he had shut the door and decided against rubbing his still-sore arm.

The Ecolitan behind the wheel did not blink as she let the vehicle hum smoothly away from the circular drive of the Colonial Grande.

Jimjoy refrained from looking back, but settled himself as comfortably as possible on the rather firm and drab green rear seat.

"Standard transport?" he asked.

"Hardly, Major," answered the young driver. Her response seemed to be in Old American.

Jimjoy frowned. Had he addressed the question in Panglais or Old American?

While the Panglais of the Empire was the official language of Accord, since it was part of the Empire, most of the settlers had been refugees from the ecollapse of the western hemisphere of Old Earth, assisted and joined by the remnants of the marginally successful colony on Columbia. Yet until the driver had spoken, all he had heard, he was certain, had been Panglais.

"Old American the normal language at the Institute?" He phrased his question in Old American.

"We still call it Anglish, Major. But . . . yes."

"How did you know I understood it?"

The driver did not take her eyes off the road, but Jimjoy thought he saw a faint flush at the back of her neck, under the dark skin he had thought was tanned but now suspected was a naturally dark complexion.

She swallowed once, then answered. "I didn't. I thought you must if you were coming to visit the Institute."

Jimjoy nodded. A full background on one Major Jimjoy Earle Wright had been circulated. What hadn't been broadcast to the winds?

"How far is it?"

"By groundcar? Another two standard hours."

"Are we going all the way by groundcar?"

"I was told you were adverse to Institute flitters, and that you wanted to see as much of Accord as possible. The car was available."

Jimjoy sighed silently, letting himself enjoy a rueful smile. The transportation arrangements had to have been the idea of one certain Ecolitan Andruz.

Why, he couldn't say. Not yet, at least. But he would have bet that her sense of humor was warped, or warped enough for her to enjoy the thought of his sitting on a hard groundcar bench for two hours rather than spending a few minutes in a flitter. The object lesson was clear, intended or not.

He turned his eyes outside. Already the car was leaving Harmony, with only a few scattered homes along the still-broad boulevard that stretched ahead. Two hours! He owed the striking lady something.

Thelina—yes, the lady was certainly striking. Natural silver hair that reminded him of Accord's sunlight, green eyes, and a complexion that seemed like silvered bronze.

Striking indeed.

His mouth dropped open. Of course she was striking. She had been put there for him to notice. To distract him from noticing others. Once he had been allowed to discover she was an Institute member or agent, he would find it difficult, if not impossible, to recall who else might have been observing him, who else might be tracking him.

He shivered. Such an obvious ploy, and he had swallowed it whole. The undercover business was clearly not his. Clearly. So why was he in it?

He shook his head. A bit late for him to be understanding the difference between espionage and Special Operations.

"You do want to see as much of Accord as possible, Major, don't you?" asked the driver, interrupting his belated understanding of Thelina's role.

He forced a grin. "That's the way it's been presented. Would you like to provide some commentary on the sights we are passing? Their economic, historical, and military significance?"

"I'll do my best, Major," replied the driver without looking back at him.

Jimjoy straightened himself in the seat.

"We are now turning onto the Grand Highway. The highway climbs gradually west from Harmony and is the most direct route between the east and west coasts of Atlantal, at least in the mid-latitudes."

The Imperial Special Operative concentrated, trying to bring back into clear mental focus the screens upon screens of map projections he had studied.

Atlantal, the main and first settled continent, ran from nearly the north polar ocean to past the planetary equator, the only continent with such a great north-south range. Harmony was roughly forty degrees above the equator, with a temperate climate moderated further by its seaside position on Muir Bay and by the prevailing winds.

Jimjoy did not immediately recall the Grand Highway, but then the Imperial maps had been climate- and relief-based, rather than showing highways or local political jurisdictions.

"Grand . . ." he muttered, struggling to recall whether there had been an east-west range of hills or mountains near the latitude of the Accord planetary capital.

"Officially, the highway is called the Ridge Continental Transit Corridor. Basically, it follows the mid-continent ridge from coast to coast," the driver elaborated as she completed a sweeping turn onto an empty highway even wider than the boulevard they had just left.

Jimjoy nodded, visualizing the geography and remembering the odd intersection of continental plates that had left Atlantal with both east-west and north-south lines of mountains.

South of Harmony, the mountains ran generally in east-west bands. North of the capital, the even older hills swept north-south, climbing into the Saradocks, which peaked near the northernmost point of Atlantal.

He pursed his lips briefly as he returned his full attention to the driver and the scenery.

Outside, the well-tended but forest-bordered fields displayed a range of green and dark green plants. The space between the individual plants indicated to Jimjoy that the growing season had a while to go before harvest—certainly consistent with the local calendar of early summer. He saw few dwellings. Given the small total population of Accord, that wasn't surprising, although he personally would have suspected a larger population center than Harmony. Yet the capital was by far the largest urban area.

Most surprising was the highway. Far too wide and smooth and with far too little traffic for such an impressive engineering work.

Ahead, the road arrowed straight into the haze that cloaked the horizon and muted the dark green of the more distant hills and peaks.

"Rather an imposing highway . . for so little traffic."

"It wasn't our idea, Major. A legacy of the Empire. Look at it closely." The driver was smiling.

He shrugged and flexed his shoulders, trying to unstiffen the sore arm and to get more comfortable on the hard seat.

Item: The pavement itself was smooth, without visible joints.

Item: The highway was straight, even when the geography would have dictated some curves.

Item: The cuts through the hills were glassy smooth, so smooth that no vegetation had taken hold.

Item: Tall local trees towered over the edges of the highway shoulder, where the pavement ended, as if cut by a knife.

Jimjoy almost slapped his forehead. He was getting flamed tired of missing everything.

"Imperial Engineers? Another Road to Nowhere?"

The driver nodded.

"Suppose it dates back a good two–three centuries."

"Almost two. The Institute figures it will last another 2,000 years before the underlying stresses reach the total structure break point."

"Wouldn't want to be around then." Jimjoy laughed harshly.

"Not much chance of that, Major."

"Suppose you're right there."

Impervious to virtually all natural forces except the basic stresses of geology, used or unused, the road would outlast them both. And the resources used to build it probably represented close to as much as the total colonization effort. Needless to say, there had only been two Roads to Nowhere built, according to the footnotes in Engineer history. One was on Tinhorn, and the other had not been mentioned. Obviously, it was on Accord.

Just as obviously, there was more to Accord, far more, than he was seeing, or likely to see. And someone in the Imperial forces didn't want him to see it.

. . . XIV . . .

After nearly two hours in the groundcar, Jimjoy was more than willing to admit that his inadvertent refusal of an Institute flitter had been a terrible choice, not even considering the near assassination. Unhappily, he had not thought that turning down the flitter had meant making a choice between ground and air transport.

For the last sixty minutes the highway had not only continued straight but remained absolutely level, roughly five hundred meters below the highest points on the ridge lines of the mountains to the south. Neither had the vegetation visible from the car changed much, nor the tenor of his desultory conversation with the Ecolitan driver.

He was only relieved that his trip had encompassed less than ten percent of the highway's length, and hoped that it would not encompass much more. The dull silver of the pavement was boring, engineering masterpiece or not.

"Mera, how much farther? What's on the other side of the hills to our right?"

"Major, we're less than ten minutes from the Institute. On the other side of the hills are the grounds belonging to the Institute. Training areas, research farm plots, some specialty forests, all sorts of things like that."

"Airstrips?" he asked innocently.

"A few, but just for transport and medical emergencies. We're still pretty thinly populated up here."

Jimjoy smiled wryly. The cadet, or Ecolitan, or whatever they called senior student types, hadn't liked the idea of driving him all the way on the ground either and had used the incredible smoothness of the highway to best advantage, moving close to the speed of a slow—very slow—flitter, and well above the recommended speed for a groundcar.

During the trip, they had seen only three or four other vehicles, all slow and bulky cargo carriers with wide tires.

"Steamers," according to Mera, running on actual old-fashioned external combustion engines.

"Why not?" she had answered his question. "They're cheap, efficient, nonpolluting, and suited to the road. They represent maximum efficient use of resources."

The last comment had puzzled the Imperial Major. Accord would not have to worry about resource shortages for centuries, if even then, especially with some of the metal-rich moons circling the fourth and fifth planets in the system. So why were the Accordans so preoccupied with resource efficiency, rather than in building up their manufacturing and technical infrastructure as quickly as possible?

That also scarcely sounded like a colony planning revolt, especially when Mera had pointed out that Accord was attempting to develop the fewest number of mines and mineral extraction sites and was investigating "other" extraction processes.

The young Ecolitan could have been lying, but Jimjoy didn't think so.

"Other?"

"Biological. You'll have to get that from the research fellows. They can lead you through the details, Major."

Jimjoy paid more attention to the outside surroundings again as the groundcar began to slow. He could see a break in the hillside ahead and to the right, as well as a green triangle perched upon a wooden pole beside the road, and set perhaps two meters above the level of the smooth road surface.

"We here?"

"Another few minutes once we leave the Grand Highway."

"Grand Highway? Thought it was the Ridge Corridor."

"We're not quite so prone to take Imperial terminology literally. Besides, what else would you call it?"

Although he shrugged at the young woman's cavalier references to a great engineering feat, he was a little surprised at her flippant tone with him. Her feelings he could understand. The highway might be a great engineering wonder, but it didn't exactly appear to be necessary. He decided to push further.

"The Grand Fiasco?"

"Not totally. It does make coast-to-coast surface cargo traffic both practical and economic, so long as you don't have to factor in the amortization of the construction costs, which we don't."

Jimjoy kept his jaw in place. The driver, young as she appeared, had been educated in more than mere ecology, that was certain.

"Economics, yet?"

"If you can't make something economical, its ecology or engineering doesn't matter. Except for something like the Grand Highway."

Jimjoy agreed silently—with reservations—and braced himself when the groundcar slowed as it took the banked curve through the narrow cut in the hill. The steeply sloped sides of the exit road were covered with vegetation, a sure sign that the exit road postdated the highway.

The much narrower road they now traveled did not follow the imperious straight-line example of the Engineers' masterpiece, but arced around the more imposing hills in wide, sweeping curves, gradually descending.

"How far?"

"Another five kays. Just around that last curve and downhill from there."

Although he saw one short and low stone wall, Jimjoy noted the general absence of fences, as well as a mixture of familiar and unfamiliar flora. He saw no animals.

"Animals?"

"The Institute research farm is farther west. Most native animals are nocturnal, those that the Engineers left." While her voice was carefully neutral, that neutrality provided a clear contrast to her previous tone.

"I take it the Institute has questioned the Engineers' policy of limiting local fauna?"

"That was before our time, and there's not too much we can do about it, except to modify things to fill in the gaps."

"Gaps?"

"Ecological gaps. If you need a predator, one will evolve. In the meantime, you discover something else overpopulates its range, usually with negative consequences.

"Here we have the additional problem of fitting in Terran flora and fauna necessary for our own food chain. We don't need as much as the Imperial Engineers calculated. But they always thought bigger was better."

Jimjoy listened, but concentrated more on his surroundings as they presumably neared the Institute.

No power lines, often common on developing planets, marred the landscape. Nor did he detect any overt air pollution, not even any smoke plumes. No glints of metal or rusted hunks of discarded machines.

The bluish-tinged trees with the angular leaves had a well-tended look. Interspersed with the native trees he could see Terran-style evergreens, but nothing which looked like T-type deciduous stock.

The Accord-built road, although narrower than the Grand Highway and curving, appeared equally smooth, without a sign of patching or buckling.

"How active is Accord? Geologically?"

"Slightly less than Terra, but the geologists claim that the current era is the most stable in several eons. And a geologic disaster is waiting in a decaying orbit."

"When does the disaster begin?"

"I understand we have somewhere between twenty thousand and fifty thousand years local."

Jimjoy caught just a glimmer of a smile as she answered his last question.

Mera had slowed the groundcar evenly as they neared the next curve. Jimjoy tensed, wondering if he were about to be ambushed or whether they were merely nearing their destination.

As the car decelerated to slightly faster than a quick walk, it came around a wide curve and through two cylindrical pillars, one on each side of the road. Each rose five meters and was topped with a bronze triangle set inside a dark metal circle. The dark gray stones were set so tightly that the joints were hairline cracks. No mortar was visible.

Below, in a circular valley, stood the Institute. The placement of the low buildings, the muted greens and browns, and the symmetry of the landscaping all stated that the valley housed an institute. Beyond the buildings, the ground rose to a lake, then to a series of small hills that flanked the lake before climbing into a series of foothills, then into low mountains nearly as high as those whose flanks had been scored by the Grand Highway of the Imperial Engineers.

"Impressive."

"You think so?"

"Yes. Very powerful."

"Powerful?"

Jimjoy nodded before speaking. "Tremendous sense of power, of knowledge, of purpose. Especially purpose."

"So that's why you're here."

"I'm not sure I know why I'm here myself, young lady. Would you care to explain?"

"I shouldn't have spoken out."

"No reason to stop now, and besides, your thoughts won't doom either one of us."

The driver laughed lightly, uneasily. "No." Her voice turned more serious. "Not this time. I suppose I do owe you some explanation." She did not look back at him as she let the groundcar roll down the curving drive toward a circular building at the front of the Institute. "Most visitors make some comment about how rustic the Institute is, or how isolated, or how beautiful. All that's true, but it's not why we're here. You're the first I know of who instinctively saw—really saw—it as it is."

Jimjoy wondered if she had shivered or merely shifted position as she completed her admission.

"Are you as dangerous as they say, Major Wright?"

Jimjoy repressed a smile. After more than two hours, Mera had finally used her own admitted weakness as a lever to ask a question to which she had wanted an answer.

"Don't know who *they* are. Or what they say. Done some dangerous things, and a lot of stupid things. Probably more dangerous to me than to anybody else. Don't know how else to answer your question."

Mera nodded. She pursed her lips, then licked them and looked at the building she was guiding the car toward.

Jimjoy followed her glance, realized that he had seen but a handful of vehicles. He was betting that some of the gentle hills were artificial and housed both aircraft and groundcars.

"Major . . ."

Jimjoy waited.

"If you're dangerous to yourself . . . what you learn here can only make that worse . . ."

He frowned and opened his mouth to question her observation.

"Here we are, Major. It looks like the Prime himself is here to greet you. That's quite an honor, you know."

Jimjoy focused on the silver-haired and slender man in an unmarked forest-green tunic and trousers who was walking from the circular building down the walkway lined with a flowering hedge. The tiny flowers were a brilliant yellow.

Both car and Ecolitan would arrive nearly together.

Jimjoy smiled wryly, briefly.

Mera's pause on the hilltop overlooking the Institute had been for more than just letting him get a good look at the facilities. He just wondered what other signals he would discover after the fact while he was at the Institute.

... XV ...

"He's addressed as 'Prime,' " noted Mera, as Jimjoy reached for the groundcar's door latch.

"Prime what?"

"Just 'Prime.' He's the Prime Ecolitan."

The Imperial Major shrugged, then opened the door.

"Don't worry about your bags. We'll get them to your quarters. Besides, you don't need to drag them out."

Jimjoy released his grip. "All right . . . Thank you."

"No problem, Major. No problem."

He looked at the approaching Ecolitan, then back at the driver. "And thank you for the scenic tour."

"Anytime, Major." She was already looking at the driveway before her.

Jimjoy closed the door and straightened, absently deciding that, even had he been in uniform, a salute would have somehow been improper.

"Honored to meet you," he stated, with what might have passed for a slight bow to the slender man who stood waiting.

The Ecolitan seemed several centimeters taller than Jimjoy, but whether the differential was created by an effortlessly perfect carriage or by actual physical dimensions, Jimjoy wasn't immediately certain.

"The honor is mine, Major Wright. It is not often we

receive Imperial officers here at our isolated and rather provincial outpost of erudition."

The statement was delivered by the lightly tanned man without even the hint of a smile, although Jimjoy thought he caught the hint of a twinkle in the dark green eyes as the Prime extended his hand. "Welcome to the Institute."

"Pleased to be here. Not certain I had all that much choice, under the circumstances, but look forward to learning all about the Institute."

"We would be more than pleased to offer what we have, although what you find may not be what you seek."

"Mysteries within mysteries," noted Jimjoy with a shrug.

The Prime smiled. "No mysteries. My name is Samuel. Samuel Lastborne Hall. I am called Ecolitan Hall, Prime, Supreme Obfuscator, and other terms less endearing. Also Sam, mostly by dear friends and enemies."

"Pleased to meet you, Sam." Jimjoy nodded again. "I've also been called by a number of names."

"Currently . . . Jimjoy Earle Wright, Major, Imperial Service, or Hale Vale White, unemployed pilot?"

"Whichever you prefer. I'd prefer not to acknowledge anything."

"I trust you will not object if we use your real name, Major Wright."

Jimjoy felt as though he were fencing on the edge of a cliff, rather than standing on a gray stone walkway lined with a flowered hedge, and bathed in a weak sunshine that struggled through the high, thin clouds.

"Can't control what you acknowledge," he finally admitted with a smile.

Jimjoy realized that the groundcar had not left, even though he had shut the door.

"We need to continue our talk, Major, but it's rather impolite to keep you standing here. My office is not far."

The Prime Ecolitan turned.

Jimjoy followed.

As the two men headed back toward the low two-storied,

stone-walled building, the electrocar began to whine as it rolled away toward its storage spot or next assignment. Jimjoy wondered when he would run across Mera again, or if he would.

The main doors to the Institute building, simply carved, were the old-fashioned manual type. No automatic portals for the Ecolitans.

Holding one open for Jimjoy, the Prime used just his fingertips, indicating the apparently well-designed counterbalancing of the heavy wood.

Jimjoy stepped through, then slowed to wait for his escort. "My spaces are at the head of those stairs."

The air was as fresh as that outdoors, if slightly cooler, and the stone underfoot was identical to that of the outdoor walkway, except for the wax or plastic film that protected the interior stone and imparted a faint sheen.

Heavy, open wooden slabs, smoothed to a satin finish and protected with a transparent coating that neither was slick nor showed any signs of wear, composed the stairs.

Despite his intentionally heavy tread, Jimjoy could feel absolutely no give in the three-meter-wide staircase. He did not nod to himself at the craftsmanship, but added that assessment to those of the doors and the stonework.

Double doors to the Prime's office stood open, and the Prime made no move to close them after he and Jimjoy entered the simply furnished room.

Jimjoy had seen no one else except Samuel Lastborne Hall since leaving the groundcar.

Besides the wide one-drawered table that served as a desk, the all-wooden armchair behind it, and the three wooden straight-backed armchairs for visitors, the only other furniture in the modest room consisted of built-in bookcases, which lined all the wall space, except for three wide windows reaching floor to ceiling. The half-open tinted glass windows were flanked by simple-working inside wooden shutters. Although the woods in the room's furnishings showed differing grains, all were light, nearly blond.

The Prime gestured to the chairs before the table.

"You'll pardon me if I take the most comfortable, but these days I am not quite as limber as I once was."

Jimjoy sat in the chair on the far right, closest to the middle window.

Smiling as he seated himself in his own chair, the Prime slowly let the smile fade.

In turn, saying nothing, Jimjoy deliberately scanned the rows and rows of bookshelves, picking up the eclectic flavor of the titles arrayed there. Most he did not recognize, but the titles showed an impressive range. At last he returned his glance to the head Ecolitan, waiting.

"Did you wonder why I met you myself? Why there were no subordinates? Or have you thought about those implications?"

"Didn't think about it one way or another."

Ecolitan Hall smiled faintly again. "The behavior of those in power is reflected in their actions. So . . . perhaps I have no power.

"In any case, I would like you to consider several points while you remain here at the Institute. First, while we do believe you should stay for at least a few days, we hope you will remain longer. How long you stay is entirely up to you."

"Not entirely," interjected Jimjoy wryly, his attention directed at the Prime even though he could hear a flitter approaching and wanted to turn to check it out.

"True. You do owe some allegiance to a higher authority, such as it is, but you do have some leeway. It is in your interest, and in ours, for you to understand the Institute as fully as possible.

"Second, we would like you to talk to as many people as possible, as often and as deeply as you feel comfortable.

"Third, any and all classes here at the Institute are open to you, and the entire staff has been instructed to answer all your questions. Completely, I might add."

Jimjoy continued looking past the Prime toward the bookshelves behind the man, wishing he had chosen the chair farthest from the window to be able to see the incoming flitter while still looking at the Prime.

"Completely? Doubt that. Should be at least a few secrets around here."

The whine of the incoming flitter sounded military, with the fuller sound and overtones of maximum-performance turbines.

"There are quite a number of secrets here, Major. If you can find them, you are welcome to inform the Imperial Service of them all, should you choose to do so."

"Assuming I were an Imperial officer . . . not seriously suggesting I would be able to hide anything from any superiors I might have?"

"I am not suggesting anything, Major. Your report is your report. We are providing some incentive for you to stay, and I personally feel that any additional information you obtain will be of benefit both to you and to the Institute. We should both end up profiting from the experience."

Jimjoy returned his full attention to the Ecolitan as the flitter landed, and its turbines whispered away into silence.

"Why would such a peaceful organization as the Institute require military-style flitters? Would you care to answer questions like that?"

"Might I first inquire if that is theoretical or based upon your own observations? Or upon rumor?"

"Observation."

"You have actually seen a military-style flitter? Here? I don't see how." The Prime shook his head rather dubiously.

"If we're splitting neutrons, honored Prime Ecolitan, I should state that my observations have not noted an actual military flitter, but only one flitter with full military engine and lift capabilities."

The Prime nodded. "You are well above average in your observations, as well as basically honest. It may be too bad for you that you were not born on Accord. Then again, it may be better for all of us that you were not."

"Do I get an answer? For all the supposed openness?"

The older man shifted in the wooden armchair, smiled easily, and nodded.

"We do not operate any armed flitters at the Institute, but all our flitters are built with full armor-composite fuselages and are powered with the highest-powered turbines possible for each class. We manufacture our own fuel through a modified biological process which, although time-consuming, is based on renewable feedstocks and is relatively less expensive than synthetic fuel engineering. That process is also much cleaner in environmental terms."

"Armor implies defense, and defense implies attacks. There are no reports of attacks."

"Defense . . . true. But defense against what? Against more severe weather, against a wilder ecology in some ways, and against early breakdown. Also, there has been some sabotage, and you yourself were the subject of an armed attack."

Jimjoy pulled at his chin. "That wasn't exactly a complete answer."

"Your follow-up question was not based on either fact or observation."

"So I have to know at least part of the question before anyone will answer?"

"For me, that is true, but I am sure that the students and most of the instructors will answer most of your questions, whether or not you know what you are asking about, to the best of their knowledge."

Jimjoy grinned. "Sounds like you really want me to learn what you're doing. Either that or you don't intend for me to ever leave."

"Major, we cannot afford for you not to return. You, Major Jimjoy Earle Wright, will return able to report and discuss anything and everything about the Institute."

The assurance sounded absolute.

Jimjoy tried not to frown.

The Prime stood, then walked around the desk table.

In return, Jimjoy stood. "Appreciate your hospitality. And the transport."

"Let me know personally should you find any trace of inhospitality. And I do mean that." The Prime's handshake was firm. "Now I will be taking you to meet Ecolitan Thorson, who will take care of your quarters and any other logistical and scheduling requirements you may have while you are here."

Jimjoy followed the Prime back down the wide wooden stairs that should have been slippery and were not, trying to keep from shaking his head.

. . . XVI . . .

"Gavin Thorson," offered the painfully thin man in greens. His freckled face and smooth complexion gave the impression of a man younger than he had to be.

"Hale White or Jimjoy Wright, depending on whose word you take," answered Jimjoy, extending his hand.

"Major Wright, a pleasure to see you. I must admit that you look less fearsome in person than on paper." He took Jimjoy's hand and gave it a healthy squeeze, then stepped back. His smile, like that of the Prime Ecolitan, Samuel Lastborne Hall, was open and friendly.

"Careful, Gavin," interjected the Prime from near the doorway. "That's part of his effectiveness. All the while he looks at you guilelessly, he listens, and more important, he understands. Then he analyzes what he hears."

"Too much credit," said Jimjoy with a laugh.

"There he goes again. Watch out for your secrets."

"Thought you said there weren't any, or none that I couldn't ask about."

"Gavin will tell you anything you want to know, provided you can ask the question to show you know what you're talking about."

Jimjoy glanced back at Thorson, who had remained next to his comparatively cluttered desk.

"The Major should have one of the standard staff rooms in the short-term quarters."

"That's no problem. Anything else, Sam?"

The familiarity caught Jimjoy off guard.

"We don't stand on ceremony around here. I do put up with the students and junior staff calling me Prime, and I reluctantly have to insist that all the staff be accorded some deference by the students, although that's never been a problem after the first two weeks anyway." The Prime Ecolitan nodded as he returned his gaze to the thinner Ecolitan. "The Major is a visiting lecturer and staff member. He may observe, or he may choose to share some knowledge with us. That is entirely his decision."

The older man glanced back at Jimjoy. "Now, if you will excuse me, there are a few things still pressing on me."

Jimjoy inclined his head and waited until the Prime had left.

"Amazing man, Sam is. Hard to believe he's nearly ninety."

"Ninety! He looks scarcely fifty." Jimjoy paused, then added, "Is that a benefit of Accord biotechnology?"

"Probably, but not in the way you would suppose. Diet, physical condition, genetics, and mental outlook are still the best retardants of age. Sam just comes from good stock, and he's taken care of himself."

The Imperial Major could not restrain a skeptical glance at the gangly Ecolitan.

"Ah, yes, the Empire is concerned about our great biotechnology secrets. I only wish we had them."

"What I've read indicates you've already done plenty."

Thorson brushed the remark aside with a gesture as he suddenly stepped away from the puddle of sunlight where he had been standing.

"We have. We certainly have. But not with humans. We've accomplished a great deal in integrated ecologic studies, experimental plant genetic manipulation, and the development of Accord-specific plant crossbreeds. We've even managed some limited tissue clones and some success in suppressing the genetic reaction syndrome. But conquer the aging process? Hardly. Do you have any idea how complex that is?'' The fussy-looking Thorson nodded his head. ''Now, I need to get you to your quarters, and we need to get you some greens. Street clothes just won't do, and while we could probably find Imperial uniforms, I doubt that you really want to wear them, not after that nasty incident in Harmony.''

''Greens would be fine.''

''Come along, then. After that, I need to have you assigned an I.D. number and plugged into the information net for schedules, library access, and all the little details that you need to know about. Then there's an account to use your funds . . .''

''Details . . . ?'' But Jimjoy was talking to the Ecolitan's back. He turned to follow the thin man.

Thorson bounded down the wide stairs two at a time, his feet scarcely seeming to touch the wood.

Jimjoy felt like his steps shook the building.

''Where—''

''First, your quarters, where Mera should have put your bags.''

Jimjoy had wondered about that, but had let the young woman take his bags, particularly since there was nothing absolutely vital in them. While some material was convenient, it all could be replaced, with a little effort. What would be interesting was whether it was all there, and how deeply the Ecolitans had snooped.

He shook his head. It would all be there, with the seals intact.

Two doorways, two covered walkways, and what seemed a half a kay later, Thorson flapped down a corridor and flung open a doorway.

''Here you are.''

The sandy-haired man was not even breathing hard, despite the breakneck pace he had set. If an older administrator were in such good shape, what conditioning would he find in Ecolitans who could take the field? And would he find Ecolitans who were trained to take the field?

Jimjoy looked around the room, which had a single wide window and four-meter-square floor space.

"Not exactly a palace, but it should be sufficient for your stay. I am pleased to see Mera has delivered your two bags."

Jimjoy looked down, convinced that they had not been touched. The two bags had been laid next to the narrow bed. The bed was unmade, but a set of linens and a heavy dark green quilt were folded at one end.

Beneath the window, which was closed off by blond wooden shutters, were a study table and chair. On the desk was a bronze lamp with a parchment shade. The chair was carved and straight-backed. Both table and chair were of matched bronze woods, slightly darker than the shutters.

White plaster walls lightened the room. From what Jimjoy could see, the exterior walls were solid stone, but whether the plaster had been applied directly to the stone or whether there was an extensive internal wooden support structure was another question. He wasn't immediately ready to start thumping or probing the room's walls to make that determination.

A rectangular gold rug, edged with a dark green border, covered most of the gray stone flooring. A second bronze lamp was attached to the wall beyond the foot of the bed. The bed itself was against the right, or north, wall, while a built-in closet and drawers were on the left-hand side.

Crossing the soft rug, Jimjoy walked toward the window, glancing down at the triangular design in the center of the gold central section.

"That's the Institute's emblem," answered Thorson to the unspoken question.

Jimjoy stopped in front of the window and unhooked the shutter latch, folding the hinged shutters back against the casement. The sunlight outside had begun to fade as the clouds from the west crept along the mountains.

The base of the window, more than a meter wide, stood about one and a half meters above the neatly clipped grass. The lawn sloped gently downhill toward a garden. On the far side of the garden, the ground again rose toward another single-story building, one which had the look of classrooms, or laboratories, with close-spaced and near continuous windows.

Turning back to Thorson, Jimjoy nodded. "Very pleasant. These are short-term quarters?"

"Short-term staff quarters. Provided for Ecolitans who are here for a few weeks, or at most a few months. The longer-term quarters range in size from two or three rooms with kitchen and bath facilities to separate houses in the family quarters section."

Jimjoy nodded again.

Thorson smiled his awkward smile. "This is more central to all that's going on here, and Sam was most specific that he wanted you to be able to see everything.

"Now . . . I need to show you the dining area, and we need to get you over to the tailor to pick up your greens, and then to Data Central to provide you with an I.D. to use the datanet system."

Jimjoy grinned as the tall, thin Ecolitan flew down the corridor like a giant stork. Then he shrugged, closed the door—which had no lock, he noted in passing—and followed the older man.

... XVII ...

The stocky man who was in fact a muscular thin man puffed up the ramp into the shuttle.

The embarking officer glanced at the checker, who batted her eyelashes and turned to address the boarding passenger.

"Ser Blanko . . . so glad you enjoyed your stay on Accord."

"Who said I enjoyed it? Business is business is business. That's my motto." He swung his case around.

"If you wouldn't mind, Ser Blanko . . ."

"Mind what?" grumbled the stocky man with a touch of a whine to his response.

"Just being careful with the case until you get home. That's all. After your partner, we wouldn't want you to have any problems . . ."

Barely an instant's stiffness froze the man. "You got the wrong person, officer. Never had a partner, never will. Business is business, like I say. No time to educate someone else. Just enough time to get the sale made."

"So sorry, Ser Blanko. We hope you have a pleasant trip back to Alphane."

The man did not correct the embarking officer.

Although his destination was Alphane, his card indicated Frostbreak.

. . . XVIII . . .

"Thelina . . ." He rolled the sound of her name out into the whispers of the night, his voice scarcely more than a murmur.

As he walked toward the experimental orchard, he wondered why he had spoken the woman's name. After all, she had scarcely said more than a handful of words to him, and he was certainly no more attractive than a score of senior Ecolitans, all intelligent, well muscled, and tanned. Most important, in her brief words to him, Thelina Andruz had made it perfectly clear that she was less than thrilled with his success at wholesale and individual murder and civil disruption.

He frowned in the darkness, not that darkness had concealed anything in the centuries since the development of night vision scanners and snooperscopes. He concentrated on stretching his legs, trying to make each stride perfectly even, perfectly balanced, trying to feel his way across the uneven ground without looking.

Training his body to operate as independently of conscious perceptions as possible, he had practiced the technique for years. While he still had to scan the terrain, he did not have to spend time consciously plotting his route or progress.

Jimjoy paused to listen, catching again the sound of someone trying to match his stops. The unseen watcher continued to miss the irregular pauses on a continuing basis.

The Imperial Major grinned. Obviously, some poor apprentice or student had been assigned the task, probably either as penalty or to improve clearly deficient skills.

Jimjoy suddenly broke into a full sprint toward the orchard, still at least a half kilometer away.

A faint gasp whispered across the high grasses from his left, and he grinned as he concentrated on breaking away—at least momentarily.

Within three steps he was close to full speed. Tempted as he was to come to a full stop and listen to the chaos that might result from his tracker's lack of ability, he did not. Jimjoy was a sprinter by build and should have been doing more distance running, far more distance running, than he had been doing recently.

Training was boring, inanely boring. This time, with someone trailing him, he could make it into a game. If the tracker were a good distance runner with a lighter build, by the time that Jimjoy reached the orchard, the odds would be that his pursuer would be catching up, no matter how hard Jimjoy pressed.

He tried to keep his breathing deep and even, matching breath to strides, once the early exhilaration passed and his legs began to feel heavier.

Listening as he ran, he tried to pick up the sounds of his shadow but could hear nothing beyond the sounds of his own footsteps, his own breath rasping in his throat and chest.

As the low stone wall separating the meadow from the road drew closer, he darted a glance back over his shoulder down the gentle incline up which he had run. No sign of the other person.

Looking across the wall and to the left and right, he hurdled the waist-high barrier, landing relatively lightly, for him, on the pavement. Two more steps, and another hurdle, and he was running between the rows of the orange/trilia trees. With the level ground underfoot, the effort was not quite as great, although he was becoming more aware of the fractionally higher Accord gravity with each step.

The trees were past the blossom stage, and in the daylight only green buds would show where the full fruits would be by autumn. In the starlight, Jimjoy could not see those buds, only know that they were there, only smell in passing the faintest hint of the bittersweet odor of trilia.

The more he thought about it, step after hard step, the more he wondered about the sound of the gasp he had heard as he had sprinted away.

With a shake of his head, he slowed and made a circuit around a tree and headed back toward the walled road and the meadow beyond.

As he passed the trees closest to the road, he checked for traffic on the road, even though he saw no lights, before hurdling the first wall. He landed heavily, his feet thudding down one after the other. The pavement felt hard, much harder than on the way uphill. He forced the second hurdle, which became half jump/half hurdle, and stumbled as he landed on the softer meadow ground.

His breathing was close to gasping. His steps were shortening, and his feet were hitting the ground with almost no spring. The knee-to-waist-high meadow grass seemed more of a drag than on even the uphill sprint, but he forced the pace and adjusted his direction toward the spot where he thought he would find his would-be pursuer.

Short of the area, he slowed his stride into little more than a jog and began to look, listening for any sign.

He stopped, then began to inch forward, drinking in the sounds around him, trying to pinpoint any area of silence where the night insects did not chitter or whisper, where only the sighing of the grass occurred.

A faint crackle from the left caught his attention.

Wondering how much he should play the role, he decided, with a grin, to overplay it to the hilt.

With that, he eased down into the grass and began to edge silently toward his unseen target.

Something promptly bit him on the neck, not once but

three times. He tightened his lips and continued his inching along. The silence ahead was perceptible.

Several sharp stones jabbed into his legs, but Jimjoy ignored them, still easing himself forward.

A warbling call echoed across the night.

In spite of himself, Jimjoy nodded. Almost perfect, but not quite.

So the person in the grass before him had a partner.

A froglike sound chirruped perhaps five meters ahead, to his left.

The warbling call repeated.

So did the chirrup.

Neither changed position, and Jimjoy edged forward, listening as he moved.

In time, he could sense a figure stretched out in the grass, could hear the lightly ragged breathing of someone trying to use breath exercises to control pain. Less than two meters from the youngster now, he suspected the youth was male.

"Twisted your ankle . . . or do you think it's broken?" he asked conversationally.

A sharp intake of breath was the only response.

"Look, young man. This isn't war . . . it's training. Besides, if I'd been after you, you'd have been out of the way long before I started running."

Jimjoy stood and, with two quick steps, knocked the truncheon/short staff from the young man's hands with a quick blow.

Even in the darkness, Jimjoy could see that his would-be tracker was in a great deal of pain from trying to sit up.

"Damned fool . . ." mumbled Jimjoy. "Never attack when you're wounded, especially in training. Not unless you're dead anyway. Now lie back and let me look at that leg.

"And signal your partner that you need help," he added. "I assume that bird call was from her."

The student's body posture answered both questions, but he still refused to answer.

"Idiot . . ." Jimjoy cupped his hand to his mouth and rendered a credible imitation of the imitation bird call.

"Major . . . I wish you hadn't done that. That will only get us both in trouble."

"Not in any more trouble than you're in already." He gently edged the youth's leg from its doubled position. "Hades if I can figure out how you did it, but looks like you've got at least one broken bone there. Not to mention some severely torn muscles."

"Can't. Need the credit."

"So I was an extra-credit assignment. Wish I'd known. What course? Field training?"

"Stet."

"Ecolitan Andruz?"

"No. Sabatini."

"I'll have to talk to him."

"Her. I really prefer that you didn't, Major."

Jimjoy ignored the comment.

"Is there anything . . . hovercraft . . . that can track out over this soft ground?"

"Never seen anything here. Maybe nearer Harmony." Even in the dimness, he was ghost-white.

The Major studied the meadow, concentrating on the section from which he had originally come, where it sloped upward toward the trees that separated the meadow proper from the low quarters buildings.

He warbled again, more urgently.

"That about right?"

"Nightcaller is a little higher-pitched. Two short and a trail-off."

Jimjoy tried again.

"Pretty good, Major."

Jimjoy could see a figure at the edge of the trees.

"Come on down. Your partner's broken his leg!"

The figure disappeared into the trees.

"Hades! Now she's convinced that I destroy students. Hang on."

Jimjoy picked up the youngster, who was bigger than he looked, perhaps as much as eighty percent of Jimjoy's own mass.

"Major, you can't carry me."

"Don't sell me short."

Jimjoy took one step, then another, concentrating on maintaining his footing as he made his way up the hillside toward the footpath that wound through the trees.

The young man wore blacks, he observed absently, which were really too dark for night work.

"How's the leg?".

"It hurts."

"Any more than before I lifted you?"

"A little less, except when you sway."

By now they were approaching the trees. Jimjoy heard several sets of footsteps.

Three people emerged from the shadows as he neared the path—one in blacks and two in greens.

All dark-haired. That disappointed him.

"Suspect your student will be laid up for a while, Ecolitan Sabatini."

"Practicing your night combat skills, Major?" The woman's voice was low. The sarcasm was undisguised.

"No. Did try some night running. Didn't think any real Ecolitan would put so much pressure on a student that he'd lie silently in the grass with a broken and twisted leg."

"Excuses, now?"

"Sabatini, you want a fight . . . I'll give it to you. You want an apology . . . we'll talk about it. After you point me to the infirmary. Or the hospital or whatever."

Jimjoy could see the pallor on the older woman's face, even in the dimness of the starlight. The two standing beside her were students, one female and one male. The female wore black coveralls.

"And by the way, black doesn't work that well in a night wilderness setting. Not natural out here."

Sabatini said nothing, but he could see the tenseness in her body posture.

"You two . . . it's been a long night already. Where's the infirmary?"

The woman student nodded to the right, where the path meandered back toward the instructional buildings.

Jimjoy shrugged his shoulders gently. The one arm, where he had taken the hit on Haversol, was beginning to tighten up. He walked around the three without a word and marched forward, using his anger as fuel for his quick strides.

A single set of steps followed his along the smooth stones.

"What's your partner's name?"

"Mariabeth."

"Mariabeth? Come on up here and lead the way."

She said nothing, but darted around him and his burden and briskly set the pace. At the first fork, she followed the left-hand branch.

So did Jimjoy, hoping that the health care facilities were not too much farther, since both arms were beginning to ache. But Hades would freeze over before he would let any of the stiff-necked Ecolitans know that.

Ahead, one of the doors in a long and low building showed a faint glow.

Mariabeth took the stone walk that led there.

Jimjoy followed, breathing deeply, wondering if he'd been a damned fool or merely an idiot for dressing down Sabatini before students.

Mariabeth held the door. In the glow of the shaded lamp, she turned out to be a muscular girl with black hair and black eyes, a mouth that could probably scowl, pout, or smile with equal facility and expressiveness, and shoulders that could bear the weight of the Institute's regime without too much trouble.

Jimjoy squinted hard as he stepped inside. Even though the interior light was still dim, his night vision was scarcely ready for the abrupt change.

The waiting area was empty, but a wheeled stretcher stood vacant on the far side of the room.

After taking the last three steps with his burden, Jimjoy

laid the young man on the white cover of the stretcher trying not to express too much relief as he eased the youngster down.

Taking a deep breath instead of sighing, he glanced around.

Mariabeth pushed the ''Emergency Call'' plate as he watched, and Jimjoy squinted even more as the light level in the room rose again. He could feel the involuntary tears as his eyes adjusted once more.

''Thank you, Major.''

''No problem. Some ways, I caused your injury. Not that I meant to.''

''I understand.''

Mariabeth stood waiting by the interior door.

''What's the problem?''

Jimjoy's eyes turned toward the newcomer, another Ecolitan, male, and about his own age.

''I'd guess that the young man has at least one broken bone in the right leg, if not a compound fracture. Probably some ripped muscle tissue when he tried to stand on it and hadn't realized how badly he was hurt.''

The newcomer took in Jimjoy, then moved to the stretcher.

''How did it happen?''

''Running in the dark,'' answered Jimjoy.

''How did it happen?'' repeated the medical man.

''The Major happens to be right . . . oooohhhh . . .''

''Sorry. Looks like the Major was right about several things . . . First, who are you, just for the record?''

''Oh . .. Elting, Elias Winden, Student Third, Fifth Wing.''

''Been here recently . . . any other injuries . . . any drug allergies . . .''

Jimjoy waited to see if the medical type needed anything else from him.

''. . . well . . . the Major was apparently right about several things . . . but why did you try to run on this leg?''

''Sabatini—''

''That was my fault, Doctor. He was trying to keep up, and I didn't realize he was hurt that badly when he fell.''

"He came back for me as soon as he knew . . ."

"He carried Elias all the way from the meadow." Mariabeth's soft voice cut off both Jimjoy and Elias.

"That's nearly a kilo . . ."

"That's right. And that was after he'd sprinted more than a kilo already," added Elias.

Jimjoy managed to keep from frowning, not certain where the two students were going.

"Well, young man, you certainly aren't going to be doing too much with that leg for a while." The doctor looked back at Jimjoy and Mariabeth. "Either of you coming?"

"I am. Elias is my partner."

"Major?"

"He's in good hands with you two. Not much I can add now. Just wanted to get him here. Stay with him, Mariabeth." Jimjoy didn't know why he had added the last words, but he did not retract them.

"I will, Major. I will."

"Thanks, Major. For . . . just thanks."

Jimjoy did not turn until the three disappeared into the corridor down to the treatment center. Then he took three deep breaths.

He slowly turned, walked to the door, and opened it, listening before stepping outside. The path was quiet, deathly silent, and he took another deep breath, another step, flexing his shoulders, trying to loosen the muscles. His steps kept him in the center of the three-meter-wide pavement as he directed himself back toward his own small room.

Three minutes—that was the minimum he needed for night vision adaptation, even forcing it, and he wondered if he would get that much.

Stopping for a moment, he rubbed his chin, then shrugged his shoulders once again. The slightest hiss behind him indicated a foot set down gently, but not quite silently, in the grass to the side of the walkway.

He continued walking, slowly, breathing evenly.

After a time, he looked up briefly, scanning the midnight

skies. The afternoon clouds never lasted into late night. By now the stars of the Arm were low in the western sky. Above the Arm was the Rift, a jagged half-heaven width of starless black running overhead north to south. In the east shimmered a few double handfuls of stars.

He lowered his eyes. Someone was waiting, ready to follow. The muted sounds of the local insects told him that much.

Jimjoy shrugged again, glancing down the empty path ahead to his room. Whether he liked it or not, if the Institute itself wanted him dead, he was dead. Which meant that his big worry was the amateurs, assuming he could tell the difference.

He picked up his pace abruptly, straining for the sound of steps, but he heard no sounds at all.

He stopped nearly in mid-stride, but still heard nothing.

With a wry smile, he resumed his strategic withdrawal toward his room, and perhaps sleep.

Just before he stepped inside the quarters building, he looked back at the night sky overhead, at the wide sleeve of sooty darkness that comprised the Rift, and then at the Arm. Rift and Arm. Arm and Rift.

He shook his head and opened the door. The inside corridor was as empty as the stone walk behind him, as empty as the Rift overhead.

As empty as the future before him.

. . . XIX . . .

For a moment Jimjoy did not move. Finally he squinted, yawned, and dragged himself upright, at last swinging his feet from the narrow bed and onto the dark green of the rug.

"Hades . . ."

He did not shake his head, but glanced at the partly open window. The small room held a hint of chill. Flexing his shoulders to relieve some soreness, he sat for a moment longer, then stood swiftly.

A glance at the white square of paper half underneath his door told him that his suggested daily schedule had been silently delivered, as usual. Some poor student or junior faculty member delivered it sometime after midnight, but well before the time he woke, even on the few mornings he had risen before the summer sun.

Jimjoy, bare-chested, hairy, wore only briefs. His unshaven black beard imparted a faintly sinister look. His forced smile as he reached for the heavy shower robe did nothing to dispel the sinister impression. He bent down and retrieved the schedule.

"Microcellular biologics—permanent genetic alterations . . . theory of unified ecological balances . . . practical analysis of the Imperial political structure . . . linguistics as a predicate for cultural analysis . . . field training briefing . . ."

He paused at the last item.

"Field training briefing . . . instructor . . . Regulis . . . too bad it isn't Andruz . . ."

After laying the schedule on the desk, he pulled his shaving kit off the shelf and draped the heavy towel over his shoulder. With a tuneless whistle, he opened the door onto the empty corridor and trudged, barefoot, down toward the washroom and showers.

How much of the biology he would understand was uncertain, but try he would, if only to see what the Ecolitans seemed to be able to do.

He shrugged his shoulders again.

... XX ...

As the chimes rang the second time, Jimjoy put down the orientation manual he had coerced from the librarian and stood, watching the student Ecolitans flow quietly from the library carrels and the frozen data screens toward the open double doors of the main corridor.

The silence amazed him. Although he had not been an Academy graduate, he had visited the Alphane Academy, with its iron discipline, and the Imperial cadets resembled rowdy toughs compared with the student Ecolitans. Yet the Accord students appeared to be in at least as good a physical condition, and they certainly did not hesitate in questioning their instructors. Politely phrased as those questions were, many constituted direct challenges to the instructors' beliefs or conclusions.

He glanced at the orientation manual, one of the few hard documents on the Institute itself, then at the dwindling stream of young men and women in greens.

Shrugging, he tucked the manual under his arm and headed for the doors himself.

"Major," called the librarian, a stocky man with silver hair, "please feel free to keep that as long as you need it." There was no sarcasm in his voice.

"Thank you." Jimjoy nodded and marched out the door

after a pair of students, both male, as they silently marched toward the main servarium.

After slightly more than a week at the Institute, the Imperial Major still felt confused. The daily printout offered a choice of classes and activities to observe. Without its guidance, he would merely have been shooting blind. There were no class schedules printed anywhere. Everyone seemed to know where to go. Only notices for special activities appeared on the computer bulletin boards or the scattered public notice boards around the Institute.

Jimjoy had used the library terminals to access the main schedules, and all the abbreviations and schedules there matched those in the master course file. But like all university catalogs, the brief course descriptions told him little enough, particularly since he didn't share the same cultural background.

So he had attended the majority of recommended classes, ranging from hand-to-hand combat, where he had observed but not participated, to an advanced seminar on techniques of cellular manipulation, where he understood only enough to come away fascinated and awed.

The Ecolitans were adequate in the martial arts, better than any other colonies or any of the independent systems, with the exception of the Fuard Commandos and the Halstani Hands of the Mother. While Jimjoy would have hated to deal with the Commandos or the Hands, he would have given the edge to most of the Imperial Marine Commandos and virtually all Special Operatives. Nonetheless, the Institute looked to have a large number of well-trained personnel, especially considering it wasn't even supported, at least officially, by a planetary government.

Even more impressive were the apparent skills of the Ecolitans in ecology, biology, and all the related sciences. Though not a scientist himself, he would have bet that their understanding of the ecologically related fields would shame virtually all the top Imperials in the field.

He shook his head as the two junior students slipped into

the servarium and into the quickly moving line of students on the right.

Jimjoy paused, as he always seemed to do, then walked to the left, toward the shorter line reserved for Institute staff.

No menu was ever posted.

"Yes, Major Wright?"

Jimjoy grinned. Every last member of the Institute had to have been briefed on his appearance and presence, down to the lowest cook.

"Whatever's good."

"Both the parfish and the baked scampig are good."

"Scampig."

The cook handed him the heavy earthenware plate, pale green, and Jimjoy placed a salad and a glass of the iced liftea on the tray with the plate.

Surprisingly, every staff table had at least one occupant.

He studied the tables.

"Major Wright?"

The voice seemed familiar, and he turned to the right.

"Here, Major."

Temmilan, one of the younger history instructors, motioned to him, pointed to a vacant seat.

He nearly shrugged, but moved easily through the widely spaced tables toward her. Smiling wryly, he reflected on the spaciousness of everything on Accord, from the city of Harmony to the table spacing at the Institute. Even his room was far more spacious than anything the Academy would have granted a visitor.

The spaciousness—and the grant of personal space without the chill of the Empire—still amazed him. The Accordans granted each other personal space without crowding or ignoring one another.

"You look bemused," observed Temmilan, as Jimjoy pulled out the wooden chair.

"More like amazed."

"Amazed . . . what an interesting choice of words."

Jimjoy did not immediately answer, but set his dishes and

glass on the polished wood and placed the tray, also wooden, in the rack in the middle of the table, which immediately sank slightly under the impact.

"Surprised, whatever," he finally answered. "The business of friendly quiet."

"Quiet isn't exactly business."

Jimjoy grinned. He wondered who the others were at the table, particularly the older redheaded man with the analytical appearance. Instead of asking, he took a sip of the liftea.

"And friendship certainly should have elements of quiet . . ." pursued the thin-faced instructor. Her straight black hair was cut short, and her eyes seemed to slant more than their natural inclination when she smiled.

Jimjoy frowned, then readjusted his chair.

Temmilan waited, then added in a low voice, "If you do not mind, I would like to introduce you to some other philosophy staff members."

"Thought you were history . . ." mumbled Jimjoy, caught with a mouthful of bitterroot salad.

"You cannot separate history and philosophy. We try not to make such an artificial distinction. History inevitably reflects the philosophy of the historian." She paused, with a sheepish look on her face. "But that makes us sound so pedantic."

"But we are pedagogues," added the older man.

"Next to you is Sergel Firion. He's the head philosopher, so to speak."

"Or the head historian," chuckled the department head, "if you believe in the impartiality of historians." His blue eyes twinkled under a short-cut thatch of red hair shot with silver.

"Across the table is Marlen Smyther, and you know who I am," concluded Temmilan.

Jimjoy swallowed another mouthful of bitterroot salad. "Temmilan, also teaching history or philosophy or whatever."

"We'll make it complete, then, Major Wright." The smile

disappeared. "I am Temmilan Danaan, instructor in history and moral philosophy and practicing Ecolitan."

At the words "practicing Ecolitan," Jimjoy caught a trace of a frown on the face of the woman whom Temmilan had introduced as Marlen.

"I thought all Ecolitans practiced what you preach, or is there organized hypocrisy as well?" Jimjoy regretted the sarcasm as he spoke, but he still wanted to see any reaction.

"Practicing Ecolitans," answered Sergel Firion, still with a hint of laughter in his voice, "take themselves much more seriously than the rest of the Institute. They like to extol the virtues of our little school to outsiders and to anyone else who will listen."

"If you're teaching here, how?"

"Through example," responded Temmilan. "We take sabbaticals on a regular basis and go where we are needed." She smiled. "That's not always where we would like to go, I assure you."

Jimjoy speared another mouthful of salad. He could see that the majority of student Ecolitans were already finishing up, although he had barely started his meal.

"No need to hurry," observed Temmilan. "None of us have a class right after lunch."

The Special Operative managed not to shiver. He disliked espionage because he was so transparent in personal interactions. The history instructor's comment reminded him all too clearly how out of his depth he was. Demolition, piloting, problem-solving—those he could handle. But not people problems, and he was sitting among the individuals comprising perhaps the biggest people problem facing the Empire with an assignment to *do* nothing. Just report. He did have to return first, and that might prove a problem.

KKCHHhhewww!!

Jimjoy started at the sneeze from Sergel.

"Excuse me. That shouldn't have happened. I'll have to check my antiallergen levels."

"Some of us are still not fully adapted to a few of the local histamines," added Temmilan.

Jimjoy nodded, although something about the comment bothered him, and took a bite of the scampig, which remained warm under a coating of tangy cheese. The meat was far tastier than the salad. He had tasted better weeds on some survival-level assignments.

Another odd fact tickled his brain with the third bite of scampig. He had not seen a single dessert in his stay at the Institute. Fruits, yes. Cheeses, yes. But no cakes or sugared pastries or the equivalent.

Perhaps because he avoided desserts, as a result of their all-too-positive impact on his waistline, he had not noted their absence earlier. The observation brought him up short. What else was he missing?

"Why the frown?" asked Temmilan.

"Not sure." He shrugged as if to pass it off, then sipped the iced liftea. The taste was somewhat bitter, but remained as palate clearing and refreshing as usual.

"Are you really a member of the Imperial Intelligence Service?" blurted Temmilan.

Jimjoy debated whether he should even reply, then smiled. "I could deny it, but there's probably not much point in that, since virtually everyone at the Institute seems to be convinced that I am."

"You didn't exactly answer the question."

"The answer is sufficient, but I'll amplify a bit. As the entire galaxy from Haversol to Accord apparently knows, I am a Major in something connected with the Empire. I did not graduate from the Academy on Alphane. I have seen service on a number of worlds, the latest of which is Accord."

Jimjoy coughed to clear his throat, then inclined his head to Temmilan. "And what is the real reason why the Institute combines philosophy and history?"

He hoped she would answer at enough length so that he could finish more of his meal.

He waited, taking another mouthful of the scampig. She

did not answer. So he took another bite, then another. The meat remained tasty, for all that it was now cool.

A nod, which Jimjoy ignored, passed from Sergel to Temmilan.

She finally spoke. "It may be as much tradition as it is anything, but Jimbank, the first Ecolitan on Old Earth before his corruption, is reputed to have said that without history, philosophy is meaningless, and without philosophy, history is irrelevant.

"Certainly, history is determined in large part by the philosophy of those who wrote it, and how it is recorded is determined in even larger measure by those who record it."

"Victors write history," mumbled Jimjoy through another and final mouthful of scampig. "Nothing new about that."

"Not all history is written by the victors, Major. And much history is rewritten once the losers later triumphed. And that rewrite may have been rewritten even later."

Jimjoy held up a hand, swallowing quickly, to speak before the conversation moved further.

"All true," he admitted. "But what's the point? Does understanding the philosophy of the historian change what happened? What happened happened. Your historian can write all he wants about two hundred deaths in a battle, but if three thousand soldiers died, three thousand died. All the words and tapes around won't change the real number of deaths. Or what power controls the territory in the end."

"You're absolutely right, Major," interjected Sergel, "so far as your argument goes."

For some reason, Jimjoy felt feverish, yet strangely clearheaded. He blinked several times.

Marlen nodded to Temmilan.

"A moment yet," said Sergel to no one in particular. "We may be able to integrate the entire proceeding." He focused on the Special Operative.

"Major, is it not true that all successful governments, directly or indirectly, control the curriculum of public education? In fact, is it not true that one time-honored purpose of education is indoctrination in the system in which one lives?"

Jimjoy frowned, trying to grapple with the words.

"Yes . . . in some cases." He felt he should say more, but he could only respond to questions.

"Don't you feel, deep inside, that the Empire has changed the way it presents history to show itself in a more favorable light?"

Jimjoy nodded. It was easier than talking.

"Is not the Academy designed as much to instill loyalty as to educate? And is that not the reason why few Imperial officers who are not educated at the Academy ever make the most senior ranks?"

"Yes . . . probably . . . makes sense . . ."

"Do you think that your not being an Academy graduate made it easier for your superiors to send you to Accord?"

"Yes . . . maybe . . . not—not sure . . ." he stammered, wondering why he was answering the question at all.

"Then why were you sent here? And why was every outsystem intelligence service allowed to discover your posting?"

"Thought it was because I was too direct. Hersnik implied I was being punished for undermining the Halstani Militarists and allowing the Matriarchy to take control."

Jimjoy noted Marlen's mouth drop open, but it seemed unimportant. It was crystal clear to him, and the Ecolitans ought to be bright enough to figure that one out.

"How did you undermine the Militarists? Did you do that because you believed that the historical picture you received showed them as undesirable?" pressed Sergel.

"How?" fumbled Jimjoy. "Not hard. Redid the controls on the main fusactor system. Set a delay constriction for the mag bottle. Created a critical mass. Then used the EMP to trigger some loose tacheads they weren't supposed to have. They couldn't complain because they were already breaking the Concordat."

"But why did you do it? Just because you were ordered to?"

"Mostly. You either believe in a system or you don't. You believe, and you obey. You don't . . . you run like hades."

Jimjoy could feel the sweat breaking out on his forehead, but the clearheaded feeling seemed to come and go.

"Do you still believe in the Empire?"

"No." Jimjoy wanted to shiver at the matter-of-fact way his damning admission had slipped out.

"Do you really think anyone here believes in the Empire?"

"No. Not unless someone's a spy."

Sergel nodded at Temmilan, who asked the next question.

"But aren't you a spy?"

"Yes. You know that."

"Are you here to destroy something like you did on Halston?"

"No. Forbidden to destroy. Just observe."

"You no longer believe," interjected Sergel, "and now you doubt. Doesn't that show how what you are taught affects your own philosophy?"

"Not sure about that."

"We are," continued Sergel. "That is why we feel that philosophy and history should not be separated. Do you see why?"

Jimjoy could feel the clearheaded feeling leaving him. He wiped his forehead, took a deep breath, then shivered. But he found himself answering. "I think so. You argue . . . philosophy controls . . . both what is taught and how it is taught."

"Exactly," added Temmilan brightly. "If you understand philosophy, you can understand why history is written the way it is or was. More important, you can analyze today's events and see why they become the type of history that they do."

"But people are still people. Deaths still happen, and the dead are just as dead," responded Jimjoy, wondering why he bothered. With all the admissions he had just made, he was probably as dead as the history they were discussing.

"We are not certain all those deaths have to happen, Major. Philosophical analysis of history can be a projective tool as well. One can project the impacts of a culture's interpretation of history into the future. A culture that blames the rest of the world or the rest of the galaxy for its ills is likely to stoop to anything. One which is obsessed with explaining legalities will have to justify itself before acting, which could provide some restraint.

"Those, of course, are gross examples . . ."

"Does that apply to individual behavior?" asked Jimjoy. He was getting a headache and afraid he knew exactly why.

"Not really," answered Marlen, an edge to her voice. "An individual can be a contradiction—honorable and a trained killer. Or dishonest, but compelled to act honorably."

"And individuals change," added Temmilan, "which seldom happens with established cultures—except through force."

"I'm not sure that individuals are any different," reflected the Imperial Major. "They do react more quickly to the threat of force." He wiped his forehead with the napkin. This time his skin stayed dry.

Jimjoy looked around the dining area. No one remained except those at his table and a man and a woman at a corner table. He glanced away from the pair as he recognized their function.

"Do the practitioners of moral philosophy and history have any overriding ethical obligations?" he asked almost casually, not wanting to acknowledge overtly the effectiveness of whatever they had slipped into his liftea, but wanting to twist some of their supposed ethic back at them.

"I would suppose so," responded Sergel. "They should live in accord with their moral code, if at all possible. But in any culture, survival transcends morality, or there is no culture. The danger there, of course, is that if one stoops to anything for survival, one may become one's own greatest danger."

Jimjoy laughed, once, harshly. "As if man is not always his own worst enemy?"

Sergel nodded slowly.

"Some merely have to worry about their place in the Empire . . ." murmured Marlen.

"That's true," offered Jimjoy evenly, fixing her eyes with his. "Especially those of us who have to return."

He stood abruptly. "I appreciate the education, both practical and theoretical. I do not doubt that you all have given me a great deal to consider." He scooped up the orientation manual and tucked it back under his arm. Then, half bowing, he smiled quickly and falsely at the three before turning and walking quickly toward the doors that opened onto the main garden.

As he passed by the pair in the corner, he half waved, half saluted, then continued onward.

"What else can you do?" he asked himself. "What else could you do?"

He hoped that the three were not a problem, but the rule of three probably held.

Where there are three rebels, one is a spy for the government.

The question was which one. He would have picked Marlen, but he knew his judgment of character in women was suspect. Why else would he keep hoping to attract Thelina Andruz?

"Check . . . and mate." He shook his head as he stepped into the garden.

He glanced around and had to smile. The Institute and its gardeners had a way with plants. That he could not deny.

. . . XXI . . .

Through the predawn mists of the upland valley slipped Jimjoy, his long and even strides silent as he moved through the parklike forests west of the Institute.

His quick steps took him toward the taller hill he had noted earlier, and as he progressed, he glanced overhead. The mist, swirling and green-gray, was already thinning as if anticipating the sun.

Before him, the ground changed from spongy green turf into a sparser grass barely covering the rocky and dark red clay that slanted upward in a progressively steeper incline.

Terwhit . .. terwhitttt . . .

The gentle call whispered from the woods behind him. He halted for a moment to pinpoint the direction, but the call was not repeated.

Sccrrrttt . . .

The scraping sound was distant, but clear in the muted time before sunrise. Jimjoy shook his head and continued the climb. Let whoever it was follow as they wished. He hoped that his followers would be more careful, and this time he would not run.

He stepped up his pace again, to a walk that bordered upon the speed of a trot. His breathing quickened, yet remained regular at an effort that would have prostrated most others.

Crunnch . . .

This time the sound paralleled his course.

He nodded without breaking stride. As he had suspected, there was a trail up to the hilltop. He hoped that the view from the overlook shown on the contours map was as good as the map indicted. Still . . . the hike was good exercise, if nothing more.

He grinned and broke into a trot. That shouldn't push anyone into a careless mistake. Trail or no trail, he intended to be there before his shadow. Either of his shadows, the one that presently trailed him or the one that would arrive with the sunrise.

The faint sounds dropped back, although he knew his own progress was certainly no longer silent. But that was usually the case. Difficult as hades to be both quick and quiet, whether on foot or in a courier or a scout.

Jimjoy could feel the hillside steepen further, then after fifty meters flatten out as he neared the clump of trees that seemed to begin just short of the hill crest.

He was now panting slightly as he entered the copse of trees with the blue-black trunks, irregular and heavy branches, and needle-pointed green leaves. Then, all the trees on Accord had blue-green or yellow-green leaves—never just plain green—except for the obvious Terran imports, which didn't seem to be that widespread.

His shoulder itched, and he absentmindedly rubbed it. The trees.

The hard clay of the lower slope had become a softer humus under the trees, easier on his booted feet. A stickiness seemed to ooze from the branches, like a fine mist parted by his passage.

Ahead, he could see where the trees ended, and between the gaps at the edges of the grove before him, the swirling mist. Through the mist he could see the outlines of the lower hills on the eastern side of the Institute. The gap of the Grand Highway was partly visible to the right.

Terwhit . . .

He looked for the source of the soft call, nearer than the earlier one, but saw nothing, not that he expected to.

As he stepped out from under the last trees, he nodded. In front of him, the turf inclined gently to the drop-off. In spite of himself, he frowned and bent down to check the grass. Another piece of the puzzle.

With slow steps he ambled toward the drop-off, toward the rustic but sturdy black-wood rails and posts planted securely short of the rocky cliff edge. The trail he had surmised was indeed present, but approached the overlook from his right, as if it wound around the crest of the hill, avoiding the trees.

His shoulder itched, and he absentmindedly rubbed it. The fabric parted under his touch. He checked the skin under the disintegrating greens and saw no redness or irritation, then laughed softly.

Live and learn. He checked the rest of his tunic and trousers. Whatever the trees exuded hadn't seemed to hurt his skin, but the greens he wore wouldn't be good for much besides rags.

The sky brightened as he looked eastward, watching yellow streaks fan from the horizon above the mist, then fade into green. Directly above the horizon the purple-misted sky lightened toward its normal green-blue. But the mists in the valleys swirled like golden flames above the tree-cloaked hills as the sun reached them.

He looked down at the low and spread-out buildings of the Institute, still shrouded and shadowed, then back at the flame-dance on the horizon.

Light footsteps crinkled toward him from the trail, but he did not turn. Before long the sunrise glory would fade into day, and he wanted to remember it without interruption, without conversation.

The flames faded from the mists, which, ghostlike, dropped back into the distant trees like druids seeking refuge from the light. Slowly, the rising sun bleached the gold from the horizon, and the skies lightened into full dawn.

Finally, the first shafts of sunlight began to fall across the

Institute below, striking the lake, casting long shadows from even the single-story buildings.

With a deep breath, he turned.

"Good morning, Ecolitan Andruz."

Thelina studied his face without saying a word, then looked toward the white-gold orb that hung just above the eastern hills. She glanced back at him, but said nothing.

In turn, he only nodded, then turned and began to walk down the trail and back toward the Institute and the day ahead.

Thelina walked beside him. Both were silent, even as the querles began their soft morning calls from the meadow grass.

Again his long strides were noiseless, despite the heavy boots on his feet.

. . . XXII . . .

Jimjoy stepped out of the flitter wearing an unmarked green tunic and trousers whose cut and quality were those of a dress uniform. Even before he had taken a dozen steps, the flitter lifted off.

Ahead of him was a set of wide stone steps leading down from the elevated flitter pad into the hotel garden. On the far side of the garden was the entrance to the Regency.

After he had taken the last step, he stopped, as if he had not even realized the garden was there until he came upon it. Bending over, he studied the single pink flower, from the dewdrops still not lifted by the early morning sun to the thorns on the stalk beneath flower and leaves.

"We're both far from home."

Then he straightened and began to walk through the garden toward the hotel, not quite so quickly as he had descended the steps from the flitter pad. His steps crunched on the fine white gravel.

He followed the winding path through the waist-high evergreen hedges, glancing first at a circular flower bed, watching as a silver night-bloomer entered its daily hibernation. Like all too many of the "flowers" on Accord, it was not technically a flower at all, but a form of green fungus that filled the flower niche.

126

He let his steps slow further to study a pair of thin, silver-trunked trees he did not recall seeing anywhere before.

The first polished wooden bench he passed, looking golden in the sunlight, was empty, and the drops left from the evening rain glittered like cheap jewels. The second bench was equally empty, but had obviously been used. No raindrops remained, and a silver lizard the size of his thumb scuttled into the bushes, abandoning the crumbs remaining from a breakfast roll.

He smiled, briefly, then continued onward from the garden's white gravel path out of the last of the hedge borders and back onto a stone veranda. On the veranda stood several tables set for breakfast. Set, but without occupants.

After passing the tables, he turned under the colonnade and in through the open portal to a wide carpeted corridor leading through the lobby of the Regency.

"May I help you, ser?"

"No. Just passing through."

The doorman stepped back with a puzzled look on his face, although the man had spoken in Anglish.

Without another word, Jimjoy, taller than the average Accordan, though not noticeably so, proceeded through the lobby and out onto the front walkway leading to the Avenue of Anselad. His steps picked up as he left the hotel. And upon reaching the avenue, he abruptly turned left, heading downhill toward the mastercraft shops.

From the near silence surrounding the hotel he walked into a gradually increasing number of Accordans, apparently on their way either to work or to transact some sort of business.

The first shop he passed bore a simple sign—"Waltar's Implements."

He half smiled as he looked in the wide window at the range of hand tools displayed, and at the limited power tools. But he did not stop, passing in succession an electronics emporium, a small cafe, and a decorator's shop with paint, fabric, and paper wall coverings displayed in coordinated settings.

The next doorway opened into a bookstore, which was still closed, although he could see a man apparently getting ready to open for business.

Rather than wait on the street, he continued forward, studying the surroundings. Most of the buildings were built from a native stone, a grayish granite, and finished and framed with wood or timbers. The roofs uniformly bore pale green slate shingles. All the walks were finished stone, with central panels of the dark stone surrounded by a narrower border of a white-green similar in color to that of the shingles, all carefully fitted together with a minimum of mortar.

Flower boxes, as much greenery as flowers, were everywhere, and even the Avenue of Anselad itself, the central business-and-shopping area, was split by a central mall of trees, hedges, and grass—nearly twenty meters wide. All told, the avenue was nearly seventy meters wide.

Farther north, the central parkway widened into a square flanked by three imposing stone buildings. Jimjoy could see only their tops from where he stood, but it was clear that all three were considerably taller than anything else in Harmony.

The clean smell of baked goods wafted his way, reminding him that he had eaten little before catching the flitter from the Institute.

"Christina's" was all the sign stated, but there were several cases heaped with breads, muffins, turnovers, ellars, and ghoshtis. He stepped inside, noting that although a number of people were waiting at the display cases, several small tables were vacant.

"Try the ellars, especially the greaseberry ones . . ."

". . . have two loaves of the spicebread . . ."

". . . told me that she would quit . . . Ansart will be furious . . . all he wants is for her to support him anyway . . ."

". . . and one more turnover . . ."

"Can I eat it now, daddy? . . ."

"Yes, ser, may I help you?" The woman was light-haired, youngish, but with slight circles under her eyes and a pleasant smile. Like the two men helping her at the counter, she wore khaki trousers, a pale yellow shirt, and a wide black belt.

"Just wanted something warm and filling. Any possibility of getting some liftea with it?"

"The tea's on the end of the counter there. Just help yourself. The nutbread muffins are the best, if you like nuts. If not, the berry ellars are good." She pointed to a tray of lightly browned pastries. Each appeared to be tied in a knot, but the slight differences in each indicated their handmade origin.

"Two ellars and the tea."

"Two creds fifty, ser." She handed him an earthenware plate with the ellars on it. "Hope you like them."

"Sure I will," he answered, again in Anglish, handing her a five-credit piece.

"Don't see many of these," she observed, making change.

"The coins?"

"They only mint small coins here. Here's your change."

He nodded and made his way to one of the small empty tables, where he set down the plate before moving back to the counter to pour some liftea from the heavy crockery teapot into an equally heavy and large earthenware mug. The mug itself was bright yellow with a green sprout as decoration. He did not recognize the type of vegetation depicted.

". . . must be from the Institute . . . but no stripe . . ."

". . . don't recognize him . . ."

"Mommy . . . want a turnie . . . now!"

". . . and a loaf of the rye . . ."

He sat at the table and took a sip of the steaming tea, then another, savoring both the warmth and the taste, even though he had not been cold to begin with.

"Is that order ready . . . for the Colonial Grande . . . ?"

". . . shipped him off to Four for a research assignment of some sort . . . talks, but I never understand—yes, the mixed rye and the spicebread, please—so what can you do . . ."

". . . is that one over there? In the corner . . ."

"The same uniform, I think . . ."

"Here you are, ser. Will there be anything else?"

The ellars were a mixture of two kinds of pastry, a light and flaky crust twisted together with a heavier and richer one, wrapped around the filling. He finished both and almost licked the crumbs off his fingers.

"Pardon me, ser . . . if you're through with the plate, I'll take it."

"Are you Christina?"

"No . . . I'm Laura. Christina's my aunt." She lifted the plate, then turned back to him. "You are from the Institute, aren't you?"

He thought for a moment before answering. "For now, at least. I'm classified as a visiting instructor."

"I didn't know they had any outsider professors . . ."

"May be the first . . . but that's probably up to Sam . . ."

"Sam?"

"The Prime."

The sandy-blonde paused. "How long will you be here?"

"In town? Just for the day. Hadn't seen much of Harmony."

"You from Parundia?"

"A bit farther than that, I'm afraid."

"Off-planet?"

He nodded.

"But you speak Anglish, not Panglais. That why I figured you were from one of the out-continents."

Her last statement seemed forced.

He shrugged. "The Institute invited, and it seemed . . . so I accepted."

"Do you intend to stay at the Institute?"

He laughed, gently. "Now, that is not my choice, one way or the other."

"I suppose not." She paused again. "How did you like the ellars?"

"Good. Quite good."

She nodded and headed back into the kitchen area, through a swinging door, still carrying the earthenware plate.

The crowd at the display cases had diminished, and only a single man stood there.

"Order for Waltar's."

"The usual?"

"Same as always."

"Here you go."

Aware as he was of the Ecolitan-style uniform, Jimjoy forced himself to sip the last of the liftea before slipping a fifty-unit piece next to the mug when he finally finished the liftea and stood. One youngster, also in khaki and yellow, waited behind the counter.

"Quite good."

"Thank you, ser. Come again."

"I hope to."

Outside on the avenue, there were fewer people. The temperature was at least another five degrees warmer, and steamier than at the Institute. He shrugged and headed back to the bookstore.

"Readables." That was the name of the establishment, and despite the modest title, the shop was even bigger than the implement store, with shelf after shelf of bound hard-copy books. The disc-and-cube section comprised less than one-fifth of the floor space.

Jimjoy began at one end of the hard copy section, scanning the titles one after another, listening as he did to the half-dozen people scattered throughout the shop.

"Do you have . . . *Politics and the Age of Power*?"

"Section three on the right, about the fourth shelf down."

". . . can you believe he said that . . . to her, of all people . . . and right after she finished hand-to-hand . . ."

". . . mangle him? . . ."

". . . didn't bother, but when he realized . . . should have seen his face . . ."

". . . all of them out there like that? . . ."

". . . guess so —oh, look over there . . ."

"So how is the weather in Parundia?"

He smiled as he continued with his survey of the bookshelves, noting a wide array of volumes openly displayed which were unavailable even in the restricted section of Alphane Academy library.

He reached for a small volume. *The Integrated Planetary Ecology*, Samuel L. Hall, The Institute Press, Harmony, Accord. He scanned the title page. Eighth Printing.

"Hmm." He slipped the book under his arm as he continued his study.

"Are you looking for something in particular?" The young woman addressed him in Panglais.

He repressed a smile and looked at her blankly.

She repeated the question in Anglish.

"No. Just looking."

"That's fine. Let me know if you need help." She returned to her position behind the counter by the door.

A few moments later, an older man joined her. The two whispered.

Jimjoy listened as he browsed.

". . . doesn't acknowledge Panglais . . . Parundian accent in Anglish . . . but official dress tunic . . ."

"One of their specialists? . . . Growing so big you don't know them all anymore . . ."

". . . said that there's even an Impie there now . . ."

"Him? . . "

". . . speaks Anglish . . ."

Cling!

"Readables, this is Tracel. May I help you? . . .

"No, we don't have that right now. If we get the cubes on the next downship, we can have it bound and on the shelves by next week. If you have disc or cube, we'll have that the day after . . .

"That's no problem. Let me take down your name . . ."

Jimjoy moved across to the compact cube-and-disc section, checking off the titles. While the technical and professional titles seemed about the same, the hard-copy fictional and poetry sections, not to mention crafts and hobbies, were more extensive.

He nodded to himself and stepped up to the counter, laying Sam Hall's book on the counter, along with a twenty-credit note.

Tracel finished entering something on the small terminal and looked up.

"That's an old one . . . seventeen-fifty, please."

"But still popular, I see."

"Is it still required reading at the Institute?"

He shrugged. "Couldn't say. Just a visiting lecturer. But it was recommended."

"My sister said it was pretty interesting. I never read it, though." Tracel made change and handed him three coins. "Do you need a bag?"

"No, thank you." He nodded politely and left.

Outside, the temperature was even warmer, with correspondingly fewer people on the streets. With several hours before he was to meet the Institute flitter, he crossed the avenue between the infrequent groundcars and began to wander northward again, listening and taking in the shops.

Sometimes, sometimes, just walking and listening taught as much as anything, if not more.

... XXIII ...

". . . two, three, four . . . two, three, four . . . two, three, four . . ."

Jimjoy whispered the cadences to himself as he wound up the exercise routine. Sweat poured down over his forehead, as much a consequence of the humidity and stillness of the air in the room as of any real heat.

Outside, the rain poured down, more like a tropical storm on most T-type planets. On Accord, the storm qualified as the normal evening shower. The summer pattern was relatively constant—cool, crisp mornings, increasing warmth and humidity as the day unfolded until late afternoon or early evening, when the clouds piled up and poured over the low mountains to the west and saturated the Institute. Once in a while, there were days that remained clear into the night, and when that happened the temperature dropped another ten degrees.

Not that the rains seemed to stop Institute activities. The only concession was the number of covered walkways between the major buildings. That and the solid construction, although Jimjoy wondered why all the buildings consisted solely of natural materials, either woods or stone. No synthetics, no metals, and no buildings of more than two stories.

That had been true in Harmony as well. Only the buildings

housing the Council, the Court, and the Governor had exceeded that height.

He pushed away the delaying thoughts and squared himself for the next series of exercises, designed to exercise his combat training reflexes. They did little more than keep his skills from deteriorating too rapidly. Jimjoy needed practice with others, and used the Service facilities on Alphane or elsewhere to the maximum whenever possible. By himself, he found it hard to push hard enough to keep the edge he needed. Solitary exercises were neither fun, interesting, nor competitive. Only necessary.

Outside the window, the even sound of the heavy rain lessened as the evening storm began to lift. Jimjoy noted the decreasing precipitation, but doggedly continued his regime, pausing briefly every so often to wipe the sweat from his eyes with the short sleeves of his exercise shirt.

As the rainfall drizzled to a halt, so did the Special Operative, panting from a routine that should not have left him quite so exhausted, although his endurance had improved slightly since he had first arrived at the Institute. He hoped the better condition would balance somewhat his lack of combat practice.

He swallowed, still finding it hard to accept that the marginally higher gravity of Accord should have made such a difference. It did not seem that much greater than T-norm, not enough to affect short bursts of exercise, but it still took a toll during prolonged exertion.

"Wonder if it would make a difference in combat troops . . ."

Shaking his head at the unconscious verbalization, he pulled off the soaked exercise gear and laid it on the rack in the closet. Then he pulled on the standard heavy cloth robe supplied by the Institute and draped a towel over his shoulder.

He trudged out the door that had no lock and down the hall toward the showers, wondering once again why there were no showers attached to individual rooms.

"No locks, no theft, no showers . . ."

There was no theft at the Institute, or so he had been told.

And he had lost nothing. As far as he could determine, no one had even entered his room while he was gone, not even for cleaning. Each resident was responsible for that.

Jimjoy smiled. No Imperial officer ever had to clean his own base quarters. With his limited cleaning experience, Jimjoy doubted that his room matched the sparkling state of the student rooms, but neither was it obviously cluttered or grubby.

The showers were empty, and Jimjoy sighed as he immersed himself in the stream of hot water. At least the ecological purists had not done away with the basic pleasures of a hot shower and soap.

Unfortunately, each shower was vented with liberal quantities of cool fresh air coming from outside through angled louvers. The Special Operative decided he did not want to be showering there in winter.

He shivered anyway as he cut off the water and began to towel himself dry—quickly. He wrapped the heavy robe around himself, grateful for the warmth of the thick cloth.

Thlap, thlap, thlap.

The shower clogs, also Institute supplied, were big and heavy, announcing his presence with every step back toward his room. Half the time, especially in the morning, he just went barefoot.

Back inside his room, he stuffed his exercise clothes into the bag he used for laundry, estimating that he had another day before he had to take care of the mundane business of wash.

Given his lack of previous experience, he was glad he was using the Institute-supplied uniforms rather than his own.

He smiled faintly as he sat down on the narrow but comfortable bed, still wearing nothing but robe and clogs, and reflected on how sharp most of the senior Ecolitans looked in the same tunics he wore. He had watched some of them wash them right alongside Jimjoy, but somehow they didn't look like the end of the day first thing in the morning.

With a sigh, he stood up and walked back to the closet,

where he stripped off the robe and pulled on a pair of briefs. Even though he had been informed that most Ecolitans slept in the nude, with nothing but a sheet and a standard quilt, that was one accommodation Jimjoy found himself unable to make.

By now, with the window completely open, both the temperature and the humidity in the room had dropped, and there was already a hint of night chill. The Imperial Major turned off the lights, wondering again at their concession to modernity, and settled into his bed, drawing the heavy comforter around him.

Aside from a few murmurs, occasional light footsteps, and the calls of night insects, the Institute was still. So still that virtually every night the quiet left him thinking. Was it the architecture, with the solid walls and natural materials? Or were the Ecolitans all ghostlike and silent people?

He turned over as the faint sound of footsteps came down the hallway from the shower rooms.

He sat up as the footsteps stopped outside his door, swung his bare feet onto the rug as the door opened noiselessly. In the backlight from the hall he could see a figure in a robe sliding inside the doorway and the door closing as noiselessly as it had opened.

Just as noiselessly, he hoped, Jimjoy slid to the foot of the bed, hoping to catch the intruder unaware.

The robed figure moved toward the bed.

Jimjoy jumped—to find himself holding all too closely the warm figure of a woman who was clearly wearing nothing beneath the robe.

"Do you always attack so directly, Major?" The voice was low, almost breathless, with the hint of a laugh . . . somehow familiar to the Special Operative.

Not Thelina. No . . . Jimjoy released his hold and stepped back, to find the woman close against his chest again, her arms going around his neck.

"Are you always . . . this . . . direct?"

"My secret . . ." Her voice was low in his left ear.

"Temmilan—" he blurted.

"It took you long enough." Her lips brushed his earlobe.

Jimjoy's hands slid down to her waist and lifted her away and onto the bed. Sitting, not lying, he told himself. He sat down next to her, conscious now of her warmth and his chill. He stifled a shiver.

Her arm went around him, her fingers digging into his right shoulder, drawing him closer.

He disengaged himself and stood up, crossing the room to get his robe, knowing that if he had not immediately separated himself he never would, knowing how vulnerable he was to her softness and warmth. This time, as he reached for the robe, he did shiver.

After momentarily debating whether to turn on the lights, he decided against it, but belted his robe firmly and sat down at the foot of the bed, keeping some distance between them.

"You don't accept gifts, Major? Even willing ones?"

"I enjoy the packaging, Temmilan," he answered, knowing that what he said was stupid, but trying to say something that would neither entice nor antagonize the Ecolitan. She could make his mission even more impossible if she chose.

"Someone else, or someone left at home, then?"

"Something like that." He paused. "Not that I don't appreciate the thought . . . and the interest."

"Not enough, apparently."

He winced at the bitter edge to her voice, glad she could not see more than his profile, he hoped.

"Too single-minded, I guess . . ."

"*Most* men are."

Jimjoy had to repress a laugh at her attempt to insinuate that his rejection was tied to his lack of masculinity. He wondered what attack would be next.

"I can only share the weaknesses of my sex," he added.

"You do have them, I'm sure."

"You know them already, or you wouldn't be here."

"Perhaps you have more than I guessed."

Jimjoy stood, then walked over to the study table, where he turned on the small lamp.

"Should I shed some light on the subject in question?" He turned back to the Ecolitan historian. "Assuming you would like to have some illumination."

"Puns, and erudition yet, and from a clandestine ki— source."

Jimjoy picked up the straight-backed wooden chair and twisted it. He sat down with his forearms resting on the back, facing Temmilan, who had let her robe fall open. He avoided the view, instead looking her in the eyes.

"Too many assumptions, Temmilan."

"Oh?"

"Assume that because I'm clandestine, I'm inherently a killer. That because I'm alone, I'm vulnerable to the advances of an extraordinarily attractive woman. That because I don't respond unthinkingly, I can't." He paused. "Shall I go on?"

"You do reason well." She pushed a stray lock of her jet-black hair back over her right ear. "You have obviously had to learn to rationalize on a grand scale. Not that it's surprising."

"So . . . what do you really want?"

"Haven't I made that clear?" She lifted her weight and let the robe gape further.

Jimjoy kept his expression bemused, struggling to keep his eyes well above her shoulders, and trying to figure out the strange contradiction between seduction and hostility.

"I suppose so . . . though why is still a bit unclear . . ."

"Perhaps I think you need conversation of a less violent nature, Major."

"That's true. We Imperials eat children for breakfast. Raw, preferably, and then ravage the women."

"Major . . ."

"And we go in for whips and chains as well, even while we remember the last books we read, perhaps a decade earlier . . ."

"Major Wright . . ."

"But I don't understand . . . do I? One look from a lovely lady is supposed to turn me around. One promise of rapture . . . and this Imperial officer will be defenseless."

This time, Jimjoy waited for a response.

"You want me to say you're impossible. You know, that would be the standard feminine line—"

"And if there's something you can't stand, it's being predictably feminine." His voice was soft. "Even if you've just set up a predictably feminine situation."

He was rewarded with a laugh, slightly ragged, but a laugh nonetheless.

"Sometimes, Major, just sometimes, you show flashes of inspiration."

Temmilan's right hand drew the robe close enough to cut off the most provocative angle of the too revealing view, as she straightened up and shifted her weight on the bed.

Jimjoy tensed fractionally, wondering why Temmilan was dragging out the situation, rather than either throwing herself at him or withdrawing gracefully.

Was there a sound in the corridor?

"Only sometimes?" he countered, easing himself off the chair gradually and standing, then shrugging his shoulders, inching backward.

"Fishing for compliments?"

"Hardly. Just fishing." As he spoke, he reached the door, opened it quickly, and grabbed the fully dressed Ecolitan leaning toward it.

Crunch!

Clannk!

The green-clad man stared at the stunner on the tiles and shook his wrist.

"Sorry about that, friend," said Jimjoy conversationally. "Now, Temmilan," he began, as if to finish his talk with her.

Sccr—

"Oooofffff," The Ecolitan collapsed in mid-leap from the force of the Major's kick.

"This is getting all too predictable. Temmilan, why don't you take this poor fellow back to whichever garbage heap he came from . . . and jump in with him."

Jimjoy yanked the white-faced young Ecolitan from the rug and set him on his feet.

"Very clever, Major. Is dragging in poor bystanders and abusing them your idea of impressing me?"

Jimjoy sighed. Loudly.

"Spare me the posturing, and get the hades out of here."

Temmilan slowly got up, again letting the robe gape open, nearly baring her breasts and swaying slightly as she did so.

Jimjoy ignored the brazen motion, stepping back and kicking the stunner into the corridor and shoving the still-gasping Ecolitan after the weapon.

"Keep your hands to yourself, killer." Her voice was so low that only Jimjoy could have heard the words.

"I always intended to."

Jimjoy waited in the doorway, watching, until the pair disappeared around the corridor corner ten meters away. He almost laughed when he saw Temmilan begin to console the younger man.

Then he closed the door, shaking his head.

The setup was brazen, so brazen, so unlike the underlying sophistication and simplicity he associated with the Accord and the Institute.

He shivered as he understood the full implications.

Then he chuckled, realizing that neither he nor Temmilan could say anything, for exactly the same reasons.

Shaking his head again, he propped the straight-backed chair under the door lever, not that he expected more visitors. But he decided he did need a bit of warning the way things were going.

He took off his robe once more, turned off the light, and climbed back into bed. Intrigue within intrigue or not, he needed some sleep.

... XXIV ...

Jimjoy angled along the corridor, following the young man he had seen the night before—and who seemed vaguely familiar. From what he could tell, the man was an apprentice Ecolitan—one who had finished all his course work and was now assisting various instructors for roughly a year before being sent on a field assignment.

Not all apprentices remained at the Institute, but exactly where the others went, Jimjoy had yet to discover. As for field assignments, that could mean just about anything.

The program of studies only noted that "apprenticeships may occur at the Institute or at other Ecolitan facilities." The library held no actual listing of such facilities under the apprenticeship notation, but did list separately two dozen small ecological field stations, two weather satellites, and a half-dozen satellite and on-system but off-planet research centers.

The apprentice strode out through the double doors and under the covered walkway that led to the physical training facilities.

The walkway was virtually without traffic. Jimjoy raised his eyebrows and stepped through the doors, following the brown-haired man.

About fifty meters away from the covered training arena, the Ecolitan apprentice glanced back over his shoulder.

Jimjoy smiled broadly, then watched the other stiffen as he looked away and continued toward the training complex. Jimjoy wiped the smile from his face and increased his steps to narrow the gap. He noted a number of students approaching on the intersecting walkway from the southern classroom complex.

Apparently, the apprentice was assigned to help with a physical training class.

The apprentice disappeared through the staff doorway.

Jimjoy grinned. His own locker lay through the very same doorway.

Before entering, he paused, listening, then flung the door open and marched through, watching two instructors look up in surprise from their conversation at the small table in the center of the room.

"Can we help you, Major?" asked the one on the right, a muscular blond woman with the triangle of senior staff on her short-sleeved and three-quarter-length, padded martial arts clothing.

The apprentice was quietly dressing in the far left corner of the room, sandwiched between two rows of lockers.

"Just like to observe, perhaps work out a little."

The blonde smiled. "I'm Kerin Sommerlee. You're certainly welcome. We're probably not up to your caliber."

Jimjoy and the instructor both ignored the snort from the apprentice.

"Have to see. Not in the shape I should be. You don't mind?"

"Not at all." She pointed toward a rack on her right. "You might want to change, though. Take whatever fits."

"Appreciate it." He nodded. "When do you start?"

"As soon as the students finish straggling in. Take any locker that doesn't have a silver triangle."

"Thanks. I have one at the end." He moved toward the rack and studied the choice of available jackets and trousers, finally selecting one of each. As he carried them toward his own locker in the corner opposite the apprentice, Jimjoy noted a locker with both name and silver triangle—Andruz. He also noted, once again, that while the showers were individual, the locker areas were common, at least for the staff, without separate dressing areas by sex.

He shrugged as he pulled off tunic, trousers, and boots, and slipped on the padded short jacket and trousers. He went barefoot, although his feet were no longer as tough as he would have liked.

He did not miss the once-over by Kerin Sommerlee, or by the other instructor, a blocky man with the muscles of a powerlifter. At one hundred and ninety centimeters, Jimjoy was neither outstandingly tall nor replete with bulging muscles. But technique was another question, and why he worried about losing touch without continual practice. For him, timing was especially important.

"Warm-up mats?" he asked the blocky man, since Kerin had already left.

"I'm Geoff Aspan, Major," answered the Ecolitan. "The warm-up area is through that door. That's where the class is meeting."

"Appreciate it."

"Our honor."

Jimjoy found the nameless apprentice and Kerin talking quietly as the two watched students arrive and begin their warm-ups. Again he felt he had seen the young man before, but could not remember where. He had seen so many faces wearing the forest-green tunics lately, and his thoughts had not been primarily on the student or apprentice Ecolitans.

He pushed away the questions of where he had seen the apprentice and what he might be discussing with the blond instructor and decided to warm up. Taking a vacant mat, he began his own routine, concentrating especially on stretching out his all-too-tight back and leg muscles. The backs of his thighs were always tight, too tight, and even in tip-top condition and limberness, he had trouble touching his toes easily.

Jimjoy repressed a grin as the nameless apprentice watched in disbelief while Jimjoy struggled to put his hands flat on the floor with straight knees and legs. The young man did not quite shake his head at the obviously poor shape of the Imperial Major.

Continuing through his routine, Jimjoy concentrated on stomach-centered exercise as the students completed filtering in. Finally he stood up and shrugged his shoulders, moving toward the wall as Kerin Sommerlee walked toward the center of the mat. The powerlifter stood behind her, and the apprentice next to him.

"Today is basically a review class. We'll break you into groups and evaluate your progress individually . . ."

Jimjoy looked over the students—obviously one of the youngest classes at the Institute. Several of the girls were repressing giggles at something, and the casualness of the boys was too artificial to be real.

He watched as Sommerlee split the class apart, carefully separating the gigglers into different groups. All the groups had varying sex mixes, but none was of a single sex.

"Now . . . responses . . . one at a time."

Sommerlee stood before one group, the muscular man before another, and the apprentice before another, as each student reacted to an attack by the instructor.

The near mechanical student responses almost brought a smile to the Major's lips as he recalled his own sessions years earlier. Perhaps five of the twenty students in the class showed some flair, either from a natural ability or from earlier training. One was a petite redheaded girl, who used the muscular instructor's own weight and momentum to considerable advantage.

Thud.

Even Jimjoy winced, but the muscular Ecolitan smiled.

"Nice, Jerrite, nice. Don't forget to keep your position. You won't usually be facing just one single attacker."

Nodding at that, Jimjoy looked over the progress of the other groups, easing along the back of the mats, studying the moves used and the instructions given.

He frowned. Something about the course nagged at him,

but he couldn't immediately say why. Looking at the open-worked beams overhead, their smooth workmanship, did not help his concentration. So he looked at Kerin Sommerlee, who was busy "attacking" one of the larger male students.

Then Jimjoy slowly nodded, understanding what about the course, about most courses, had bothered him.

He frowned, debating whether he should share the insight, or how he could convey the message.

Ambling toward Sommerlee, he waited for a break in the class pattern.

"Major . . . care to play attacker?"

"No . . . thank you." He paused. "Not for a moment, anyway. But if you'd care for a match . . . no one defined as attacker or defender . . ."

"The class isn't ready for free form yet."

"Understand. But . . . like to claim the right to share something. And I can't share it without a demonstration. Also, without a demonstration first, I doubt if my unsupported word would have much credibility. It might be better if . . ." Jimjoy gestured toward the heavily muscled instructor.

"No . . . you don't get off that easily. Geoff has yet to take me, even with a handicap."

"All right. Rules?"

"What do you suggest?"

"No gouging. No broken bones, and no action once someone's on the mat."

Sommerlee frowned in return. "Of course. We wouldn't do that normally."

"Thought so, but I haven't worked out here."

"All right." She raised her voice. "Gather round, everyone."

Jimjoy waited.

The students were silent as they ringed the mat.

"Major Wright has requested a free-form demonstration. Some of what you see will be beyond your current ability. *Do not try it.* Trying something without the fundamentals is a quick way to break your neck, if not worse.

"We are fortunate to have Major Wright here, and since he will not be able to stay until you are ready to try some of what he may show you, try to remember the basis of what you see for *future* reference."

Sommerlee backed away and faced Jimjoy.

He took a deep breath, then moved, aiming at her right, then cutting left.

Keeping a balanced stance, which he had calculated, she countered—and Jimjoy struck.

Thud.

Sommerlee shook her head groggily.

"Whoa . . ."

"You all right?" he asked evenly.

"In a moment."

Jimjoy ignored the whispers.

". . . so fast . . ."

". . . and she's the best . . ."

". . . used his weight . . ."

He offered her his hand, knowing she might attempt to throw him with it.

She did, and he went into a dive carrying her along. At the last instant, he twisted and released her hand.

Thud.

Jimjoy came out of the roll and looked back at Sommerlee. She did not move, but she was breathing evenly. After a moment, she sat up very slowly.

"I think you have made your point, Major, whatever it was."

"I don't, Ecolitan Sommerlee."

Jimjoy did not bother to hold back his smile at the apprentice's comments.

"Would you like a chance at the Major, apprentice Dorfman?"

"Yes, please, Ecolitan Sommerlee."

"Try to take it easy on him, Major." Kerin Sommerlee got up gingerly and walked to the side of the mat.

Jimjoy faced Dorfman, realizing where he had seen the apprentice before last night—on his arrival at the Institute. Maybe it had been better that he had taken the cab.

The younger man did not move for a moment, then tried to flank Jimjoy.

The Major moved, as if to avoid the pass, then lashed out with a foot.

Dorfman twisted, but could not undo his momentum, finally turning it into a twisting roll. Coming out of the roll, he launched himself back at the Major, in an imitation of the attack Jimjoy had used earlier.

Thud.

"Had enough, Dorfman?" he asked in a deliberately annoying tone.

Sommerlee frowned. So did the other instructor.

Dorfman shook his head, looked down at the mat, and slowly stood, as if unsteady.

This time, Jimjoy waited.

Crack.

Thud.

The openhanded slap had caught Dorfman on the cheek, lifted him, and dropped him into a heap.

"He'll be all right in a moment."

"Are you sure?"

Dorfman twitched, then pulled himself into a sitting position.

"Enough is enough, apprentice Dorfman." Jimjoy's voice was cold enough to penetrate. Dorfman slumped, almost as if in relief.

"Now . . . if no one minds, I'd like to share a few observations. About this class. About hand-to-hand combat. Based on my own training, not that different from yours, but mostly from my experience, which is a great deal different."

"Be our guest, Major."

Jimjoy tried to overlook the edge of bitterness in her tone. He could scarcely have expected charity.

"First . . . watched you train. Something bothered me. Took a minute to see." He glanced out over the students, finally fixing his eyes on Sommerlee.

"Most courses like yours, like my original training, assume the strength of a defensive position, only conceding to overwhelming brute force. That's not necessarily so. The stronger position is the stronger position." He could see the puzzled looks.

"Let me show you. A volunteer?"

The petite redhead stepped forward.

"Take a defensive position, as if I were going to attack. I won't," he added as she looked up at him warily. "But I need to illustrate." He moved to her side. "You're balanced against an attack from roughly here to here. From here—" He touched her shoulder, and she wavered. "So what? Any good martial arts student constantly changes position to present what you could call a 'defense for attack.' That's still a defense.

"You can sit down," he added in a lower voice.

"What I did to both Ecolitan Sommerlee and apprentice Dorfman, in the simplest terms, was force them into a defense that was vulnerable to attack at the time I actually attacked." He paused. "That sounds simple. And it is—*if you think in those terms*. But if you begin by assuming that defense is the best position, you won't think that way."

Jimjoy looked at Dorfman, whose expression was still blank.

"Look. Why do you learn combat? Not to toss someone aside. You learn it to kill or disable someone. Period. No other reason, except exercise, and there are a lot better ways to exercise. If you have to really use your skills, they shouldn't be defensive. The point is disability or death. Period. Not defense. If you don't want someone disabled or dead, don't learn the skills . . . because you'll end up dead instead." He lowered his voice. "Doesn't apply to practice, but your practice should always keep that in mind."

Jimjoy paused again, studying the students, whose faces, if not blank, mirrored subdued shock at his bluntness.

"Put it more bluntly. Most times you use hand-to-hand combat when you've screwed up once already. If you have to kill or disable someone, the worst possible way is to do it hand-to-hand.

"Second point. You will screw up. We all will. I'm human, and you're human. We make mistakes. But the universe doesn't give you three chances in a row, and damned few enemies will give you even two. So you can't risk losing *even once* with hand-to-hand. Fighting has no honor. Except in learning or improving your skills, you fight to win."

He scanned the faces, repressing a sigh at the ignorance, the naïveté.

"That doesn't mean you attack all-out like Dorfman did. See where it got him? It does mean any defense should only be temporary . . . just until you can destroy your opponent. End of sermon."

He half bowed to Sommerlee. "Your class, Ecolitan Sommerlee."

"The Major has just delivered a rather convincing lecture. While we may not share all his political views, what he says about hand-to-hand combat has a great deal of . . . validity."

Jimjoy walked toward the locker area, not certain whether he had hurt or helped himself, but hoping that some of them had listened. Behind him, the exercise area was silent, almost dead silent. The whispers would begin, he suspected, only after he had disappeared into the staff dressing area.

He took a few deep breaths as he stepped through the doorway.

"Another great success, killer?"

Sabatini stood next to the table, her black eyes glinting.

"Another great success, Sabatini. If that's the way you look at it. If any of them listen, it might save their lives. Not into propaganda. Just survival."

"How touching."

He walked past her to his locker, where he pulled off the jacket, then the trousers. He draped a towel over his shoulder and headed for the shower.

Sabatini surveyed him from head to toe as he passed.

"Try the meat market, Sabatini. Steers don't fight back."

"You have a way with words, killer."

"I know. The wrong way."

He turned the shower on as hot as he could stand it, letting the steamy spray bathe him from all sides.

By the time he had toweled off and opened the door, Sabatini was gone. Instead, Kerin Sommerlee was standing by the table, clad only in underwear and examining bruises on leg and thigh.

She shook her head as she saw him. "Hate to face you when you really were out to kill."

"Too enthusiastic out there." Jimjoy mumbled, making sure the towel was clinched firmly around his waist, and avoiding looking directly at the woman's body, far less stocky and more shapely than he had realized. She reminded him of Thelina, though the two looked only vaguely alike.

"Major . . . you pulled the last throw . . . or whatever it was?"

He shifted his weight uneasily, conscious of the dampness of his bare feet on the slightly roughened stone underfoot. "Yes . . . could have killed you otherwise."

"I know. I could feel it. Geoff knows, too. He was white when I looked at him."

"Dorfman doesn't. Most of the students didn't."

"Dorfman's a fool."

He shrugged, not quite looking at her, but toward her face. "And the students?"

"Some were beginning to realize, especially after Geoff's comment."

"Geoff's comment?"

"You didn't hear? He said that the Institute had never had any two people who could have taken you, let alone one. You shook him up a lot. I don't think he ever realized just how good the Special Operatives are."

Jimjoy automatically opened his mouth to protest.

"Please save the objections, Major." Her voice was tired. "After about thirty seconds with you on that mat, I know who and what you are. There aren't half a dozen people on this planet or three others where I've been who could do to me what you did. None that quickly and effortlessly.'' She winced as she examined her leg. "That's what upset Geoff. Suddenly, you're real. All too real. The kids—that's all they are—can't see that . . . except maybe Jerrite.''

"Sorry.''

"Don't be. You provided a lesson we couldn't have learned so painlessly—relatively, at least.'' She pulled her padded robe and trousers back on in quick but smooth motions.

"I have one more class this morning. Then I can soak out what I know is going to be even more sore.'' She looked up. "You're one of the best. Right?''

Jimjoy said nothing.

"Aren't you?''

"Probably. Not the top, but close.''

"Attitude?''

He nodded.

"I thought so.'' She flexed her shoulders, trying to relax her muscles. "Like to do any instruction here? Say . . . for the advanced classes?''

"Not sure it would be a good idea. I'll think about it.''

"Do. And don't worry about Sabatini. She's on her way out. She was under review even before you arrived. She'll blame you, of course, but there's not much the Institute can do about that.''

"Whatever's convenient.'' Jimjoy hitched up his towel and headed for his locker.

"And whoever she is, Major, she's lucky.''

Jimjoy shook his head at the nonsequitur, but decided against asking for an explanation. He had too many problems already without asking for another.

. . . XXV . . .

Finding Thelina Andruz's quarters had been neither difficult nor helpful. While the silver-haired Ecolitan lived in a separate house with another Ecolitan in the senior staff section of the Institute, and while there were no guards or restrictions, every nonstudent Ecolitan seemed to live on his or her own personal clock. The pathways and corridors of the Institute were never quite completely deserted. Just as frustrating, for his projected schemes, was the lack of centralized personal communications. Without going to her quarters, he could not discover if she were actually there.

After his encounter with the historians, and then his night visit from Temmilan, the last thing he wanted was to broadcast any intentions of anything. Yet it was clear that he was close to transparent to at least some, if not all, of the Ecolitans. Part of that was their training in physical character reading—he'd been fascinated by the classes on surface carriage and physical intent. So interested that he'd actually read through most of the student assignments, hoping that they would prove helpful in the future.

The Major stopped his pacing and sat on the edge of his narrow bed. Then he stood back up again. He frowned. Who else could help him? Could she? Or was he just rationalizing because she intrigued him? How could he possibly learn what he needed to know quietly, when everyone seemed to follow him, to pay attention automatically when he appeared?

Someone seemed to be there to watch his every action, from the books he borrowed to the material he accessed from the datanet, from the classes he attended to the limited instruction he had undertaken. Almost as if they were compiling a dossier on him, or on every Imperial agent. Probably both, he concluded gloomily, and from that would follow a profile of the Imperial Intelligence Service, at least a profile of the Special Operative section.

But that left his problem unsolved. He didn't dare chase Thelina.

"So . . . if you can't go to the mountain, get the mountain to come to you . . ."

Easier said than done. He looked out at the darkness before dawn. Thelina was not about to chase down one Jimjoy Wright. Not from any indication he had seen so far. Not when she had refused to say a single word after sharing a clearly breathtaking sunrise.

What about illusions? Or coincidences? Could he arrange a circumstance where she had to talk to him . . . alone? And would she listen?

Could his maneuvering get her beyond the obvious contempt of him and of the Empire he was bound to represent? Most important, would she help, however inadvertently, to get him on the right path? Before the Empire put him back on the clearly marked path to Hades already reserved for him by Commander Hersnik?

Special Operatives did not just resign. Jimjoy had never heard of a resignation. Some graduated from field work to Intelligence. One or two were medically retired, after a year or two of quarantine duty and extensive psychological "readjustment." But he didn't want the Empire's idea of medical retirement, and movement to Intelligence from the Special Operative section meant a promotion to Commander. And there was no way he would get a promotion, not after the Halstani incident, not after being tagged, he was certain, with complicity in the killing of Commander Allen's partner. Even though Allen had clearly killed his partner to keep the facts behind the assignment from coming out.

If he stayed on Accord, he'd be the target of every spare agent around, from the Empire to the Hands of the Mother. Not to mention the fact that his delay on Accord would give the Empire another excuse to move against Accord. Even his "disappearance" on Accord could trigger that, which was probably why he was still alive and being protected by the Institute. And why Temmilan could do nothing fatal to him, since such an action would blow her cover.

Jimjoy snorted. The Ecolitans had to know about her, or he was missing something. And Temmilan was far from stupid, which meant she had to know they knew. He shook his head, trying to refocus on his own problem.

If he did return on schedule . . . At that, he shuddered. His return would never be noted, and the records would show his disappearance in action, with the finger still firmly pointed at Accord.

He continued to pace, knowing that his time was growing shorter. He stopped, stared at the rough white ceiling, still grayed in the foggy predawn light that misted through the casement. Outside, the whispered shrilling of a dawn lizard punctuated the fog with its intermittent calls.

Muted voices from down the corridor indicated that the junior Ecolitans were rising and beginning their morning routine, a routine he thought not nearly as intense as it should be . . . as if he cared.

In the meantime, his time on Accord continued to dwindle, especially with the good Commander Allen running loose, reporting back and pinning everything on Jimjoy. If he could just saddle Allen and Hersnik with all the problems . . . if . . . if . . .

He looked back out the window, not really focusing, then at the triangle in the middle of the rug.

Jimjoy smiled, tentatively at first, then with nearly unconcealed joy. The whole idea was so preposterous, so silly, that it might work. The longest of long shots, but better than anything else, assuming he could get some limited cooperation from the good Ecolitan Andruz. Assuming he could move quickly enough when the time came . . .

He sat back on the edge of the bed, then swung his feet up and stretched out, since there was nothing he could do.

Not yet.

. . . XXVI . . .

Although Jimjoy wore the unmarked greens of the Institute and could have been taken for an Ecolitan at first glance, even with the black hair and blue eyes, his lightly tanned complexion had not seen the outdoors to the extent required of Institute faculty and students alike. And the raw and unconcealed intensity in his eyes was not that of the Institute.

The Ecolitan greens had represented a compromise for Jimjoy. He had not brought a uniform, nor did he intend to wear one, or admit publicly that he was an Imperial officer. At the same time, civilian clothes would have been even more out of place.

While the greens had scarcely been a major consideration, they were now critical to his plan. If his calculations were right, the one Ecolitan named Andruz would finally be coming along the walkway before long. If she didn't eat at home or skip lunch like she had for two out of the last four days. Or bring her friend Meryl along again. Or lunch with the entire field training staff . . .

He continued his glances down the ramp until he caught sight of the distinctive silver hair.

At that, he turned away from the old-fashioned bulletin board and started toward the dining area. According to the literature, few people ever considered someone in front of them to be following them, although that was exactly what Jimjoy had in mind. He let the gap between them narrow.

As he entered the dining area, he took the left line, the one always used by the Institute staff, and slowly moved through, listening to see if Thelina, who was alone today, unlike the last time, had any comments. She said nothing.

"What will it be, Major?"

He could have cared less today, but he grinned in spite of himself. The staff behind the counters still seemed to delight in announcing him and his rank.

"What do you have?"

"No meat. Just fish—grubber, parfish, or lingholm."

"Parfish." He'd seen it before, and the Ecolitans seemed to enjoy it.

"The lingholm's better."

"Then I'll take the lingholm."

The student serving as cook's helper grinned broadly back at him.

That was another thing he didn't understand. Virtually the entire Institute took his presence with an amused seriousness, yet denied to outsiders that he even existed. He had heard two beginning students tell, with tears of laughter running down their cheeks, how they had played dense colonials to a Fuardian faxer tracking down a rumor that Imperial officers were being trained by the Institute.

Chalk up another angle for the ubiquitous Commander Allen, getting yet another stooge to do the work. But he was glad the Institute ignored the potential danger and could still laugh.

Jimjoy did not look back. If his scheme were to have a chance, Thelina had to be convinced that he had not seen her.

At the end of the food line, he paused by the salads, as if trying to decide upon fruit or greenery. Finally, after the man behind him had slipped by, he picked a small fruit plate and straightened, blocking Thelina without seeing her.

He turned and carried his tray toward the dining area, slowly scanning the tables as if searching for someone, but carefully avoiding anyone's glance while straddling the aisle. He could feel Thelina moving closer. He stopped momentarily, then leaned forward, as if to head for a table, then stopped again, leaning back.

Her tray jabbed him in the back, and something hot sloshed onto him.

He turned, hoping his calculations had been correct.

"Oh . . ." he said, letting his mouth drop open as he looked at the silver-haired Ecolitan. Then he grinned ruefully. "Still throwing things at us poor Imperials? Were you trying to alert me this time?" His voice was gentle and good-humored.

Thelina Andruz sighed. "It would be you, wouldn't it? I should have guessed."

"Guessed?"

"Who else but you or a visiting dignitary would be ambling around?" She glanced over her shoulder. "We're crowding the aisle. Take that table over there. Your company won't hurt, as long as I can eat quickly."

Jimjoy said nothing, but eased over to the two-person table toward which she had inclined her head.

He took an extra napkin from another table as he passed, and, after setting his tray down, awkwardly tried to mop up the liquid that had splattered across his lower back.

"Scampig broth," explained Thelina as she slid into her chair. "It shouldn't stain anything, and . . ."

Jimjoy nodded. "And I probably deserved it for stalling around, right?"

"Probably," observed Thelina, before taking her first bite out of a thin sandwich.

"Since it's taken me more than a week to engineer this," Jimjoy commented softly as he seated himself, "I hope you'll stay long enough to listen."

"Engineer what?"

"Your running into me."

"You . . . unwhoooo . . ." For a moment, Jimjoy wondered if she were choking or laughing or swallowing, or all three.

The Ecolitan coughed again and cleared her throat, before swallowing and taking a sip of her iced liftea. "For what reason? You certainly could have just walked over to see me. I'm hardly inaccessible."

"That's assuming I wanted the entire world to know I was looking for you."

"That, in turn, means you are up to no good whatsoever, Major Wright." Her voice had turned distinctly cooler.

"Half right," answered Jimjoy, before taking a bite of his salad. He said nothing else and bit into a bright green fruit, trying not to let the large piece pucker his mouth too much.

"First time I've ever seen anyone try to eat an entire sourpear at once."

"Could be the last," mumbled Jimjoy as he reached for his own iced liftea.

"Your half-right proposal, Major?"

He refrained from glancing around the crowded dining area, hoping that the overall noise level and the apparently spontaneous meeting were enough to allow him a quick comment. "I would like your help in leaving Accord and getting to somewhere like Sligo or even Alphane without the Empire being alerted to my departure."

"Why?"

"Because I'm not likely to arrive, otherwise."

"You believe that of the glorious and saintly Empire which you serve?"

"Flamed right." His voice was low.

Thelina did not respond, but cocked her head slightly and took a spoonful of the scampig broth, that which remained. Then she pursed her lips, but still said nothing.

Jimjoy watched the green eyes, noted that the silver hair was twisted up short behind her head in some sort of bun.

"That's right, Major. Worn up or short now that I'm back here in a physically active billet." She took another spoonful of the broth.

Jimjoy repressed a sigh and tried another fruit, a reddish one with a pink interior. Unlike the sourpear, the red fruit was sweet, with only a hint of tartness. He wondered if the tartness were part of the Accord character and fostered by its foods. He continued to eat methodically, occasionally studying the silver-haired woman, but refusing to bring up the subject again until she acknowledged interest or rejected the idea.

"Greetings, Major."

Jimjoy kept from jumping, barely. Instead, he glanced up at the thin-faced professor with mild interest. "Greetings, Temmilan. How is the philosophical history business?"

"About as practical as ever . . . or, as you suggested, as impractical as ever." The historian transferred her study to the Ecolitan across from Jimjoy. "You're in the field unit, and we met last year, but I'm not good with names. Temmilan Danaan."

Thelina nodded. "Thelina Andruz. Field Two."

"Pleased to see you again. You know the Major well?"

"Not terribly well, Temmilan," answered Jimjoy. "This is the second time we've met. She was considering making amends for running into me with a full tray of scampig broth."

"Major Wright is always accurate, Temmilan. It is one of his worse faults."

"You may be right, Thelina. Make what amends you can . . . if he will accept them." Temmilan nodded to them with a pleasant, if distant, smile and eased past the table.

"And what did you do to her?" asked Thelina dryly.

Jimjoy found himself flushing, and shrugged.

"That bad?"

"No. You might say it was what I didn't do."

"That's worse." By now the silver-haired Ecolitan was smiling an indecently broad smile.

Jimjoy looked down at the last few bites of the lingholm and speared a small morsel, gulping it down.

"Well, you have some ethics, if no taste."

"Won't claim either."

"Let's take a walk. Whether you intended to or not,

you've just told the whole world you're looking for me. After that confrontation, half the Institute will be told that we're lovers.''

"Uhhnn . . ." choked Jimjoy.

"Temmilan's the biggest gossip around, except for old Firion.''

The Imperial Special Operative managed to choke down the last of the fish. He followed that with a deep swallow of liftea to clear his throat.

"Am I that unattractive, Major?''

"I believe you mentioned a walk.'' He stood.

"I did. The main garden would be nice, if you don't mind, the one by the biology quad.''

"Lead on, Ecolitan Andruz.''

Neither said anything until they had entered the garden and taken the second path to the left, which led toward a bench surrounded by a low hedge on three sides and shaded by a large evergreen.

Jimjoy glanced upward.

"Silft . . . native. This bench is proofed for conversation. Have a seat, Major.''

Jimjoy raised his eyebrows, but followed her directions. Thelina seated herself next to him, as closely as he could have wished under other circumstances.

"Look toward that building. See the lack of focus?''

Jimjoy nodded. Obviously the raised hillock on which rested tree, hedge, and bench contained more than mere earth.

"Why don't you trust the Empire? And why should we help you, assuming we could? Specifics, please, Major.''

He took a deep breath before starting. "Simple. My cover was broadcast to every outsystem agent possible. Commander . . . the agent at the hotel . . . were clearly after me. If I leave on any recognized transport, there's no way I can count on recognizing my own assassin. You and your people are clearly able to track me anywhere and keep me from getting off-planet without your consent.''

Jimjoy shrugged. "And if I tried to stay here, the Empire would put pressure on you. Insist that you send me back on a planned schedule, during which I would meet some sort of unfortunate accident. If you stood up to them directly . . . that gives them an excuse to come down hard, say with three or four fleets.

"Doesn't leave you many options. Odds are that if anything happens to me, and that's exactly what the Service wants, they'll tag you with it. I'd like to stay in one piece. You'd like that, too—professionally, at least. That means I have to get off-planet and to a location where I can show up so visibly that the Empire has a problem with me, not with you."

Thelina looked straight ahead, not meeting his eyes. "This one time, Major, I agree with your logic and all your conclusions. You did forget one option."

"My death here by doing something wrong? No . . . that would still get me out of the Empire's hair and allow them to use me as a martyr and a cause to move against you."

"That was not what I had in mind. What if you stayed here, at least for a few weeks longer, then suddenly appeared back at your original duty station?"

"Some risk for the 'local' Major Wright, isn't there?"

"Not if he stays at the Institute."

Jimjoy grinned at the thought of confounding Commander Hersnik.

"What do we get from it, Major?" The Ecolitan's voice was soft but cool.

"What do you want? Editing rights to my report? Future information? My gratitude? Mutual survival? Those are the options, but my chances for future information and long-term survival are slim."

"They're probably nonexistent." Her voice was flat.

"Where there's life . . ."

"I suppose so. You don't offer much."

"Editing my report . . ."

"Major, we would only edit your report to point out

factual errors. Frankly, we want it to be as complete and accurate as possible. That is one reason why we would prefer to keep you in good standing, officially, until someone in authority actually reads it.'' She paused, then added, ''That's because the rumors about us are far more deadly than the facts.''

And more true, probably, thought the Major, not vocalizing the thought.

''That should do it,'' concluded Thelina. ''Now, put your arm around me for a moment, as if we're about to say good-bye. A bit more affectionately, Major. There will be some speculation as to why we're seen together, and we need to give the gossips the right flavor. You were right about that also.''

Jimjoy put his arm around her, as requested, and leaned toward her, although he could feel his eyebrows raised in question.

''How else can I see you? Especially after hours. Everyone will think you've made another conquest, Major.''

He could feel himself blushing, and resenting it. She leaned into his arm, briefly resting her head against his. Just as he was beginning to enjoy the feeling, she sat up and looked at her wrist.

''I'll be late, again.'' Her lips brushed his cheek, and she was gone, leaving him standing by the bench.

He did not shake his head, but he wondered if he had actually had his arm around her.

... XXVII ...

"How long do we wait?"

"You just arrived back. His orders give him up to six standard months. The idea was to let him hang himself. Besides, we still don't have a report from our contact at the Institute."

"That could be a problem. You may not."

"Definitely a possibility, since they clearly know at least one of our contacts. But better one we're allowed than none."

"And you stand for that?"

"You have a better idea? Besides our current operation to force them into the open?"

"You should have sent Wright after them the way he did the Halstanis. Either way, we would have gained something."

"You are rather impatient. Remember, the Emperor and the Senate both frown on blowing up our own colonies. Or have you forgotten that small fact? Besides, Wright was never trained in espionage. Subtle as an old-style cruiser, and he's certainly bound to make mistakes. They don't forgive easily."

"Do we really know that?"

"No." He paused. "But do you have any other explanations for the disappearances? And our inability to plant anyone they don't want planted?"

"Perhaps you picked the wrong people?"

"Wrong people . . . perhaps. Speaking of which, how did you lose the other half of your team? Again, I might add?"

"Wright shot him."

"No. Better to claim *they* shot him. Wright was probably looking for you."

"You know me too well."

"All too well, my friend. All too well. And how will you report the incident?"

"As you suggested. Reconnaissance disrupted by unknown agents, presumably attached to the underground rebel force associated with the Institute. You'll have to explain the need for reconnaissance."

"Unfortunately . . . unfortunately. Is there any way our contact could be persuaded to goad Wright into action? His actions are always so drastic we could probably recoup everything."

"I've suggested that, but no response. And what happens if Wright goes over to the rebels?"

"Then we can move. Claim he was either killed or reconditioned, and that he was destroyed uncovering the rebellion. Get rid of him and them."

"Why bother?"

"You're asking that?"

"Outside of the personal thing, I meant. It would be years before the Institute would be a threat, if ever."

"I wish that were true."

"Then the rumors *are* true."

"It's time for you to file your report. And make sure it's filed correctly, especially this time."

"Don't I always?"

. . . XXVIII . . .

Jimjoy stood up from the table where he had eaten alone. The unmarked Ecolitan greens offered no real protective coloration, although he continued to ignore the low comments from the young man with brown hair seated beside a darker-haired history and moral-philosophy instructor and an older professor.

After glancing absently around the room, Jimjoy flexed his shoulders and walked toward the trio, looking beyond them toward the garden. As he neared the table, he glanced down, casually letting his eyes take in the two Ecolitans and the apprentice.

"Oh, good day, Temmilan, apprentice Dorfman. And you, too, Professor Firion." His voice was pleasantly false, as he had meant it to be.

"Good day, Major," responded Temmilan.

Dorfman did not meet Jimjoy's eyes, instead looked away.

"A very pleasant day, indeed," observed the graying Sergel Firion.

"Yes, it is. A day for cheerful quiet." Jimjoy paused briefly, then added, "Once you said something about friendship being able to rest in quiet, and I questioned that. Now I find, rather surprisingly, that I agree with Temmilan's original assessment."

"My, you're such a quick convert." Temmilan's voice was only slightly warmer than glacial ice.

"We Imperials have no moral philosophy and can be converted quickly." He laughed softly and concluded, "And sometimes we even stay converted." He paused again, then added, "Have a pleasant day." But before he could turn to leave, he found his right arm engaged by a silver-haired woman.

"Major Wright." Despite the formality of the salutation, the words sounded warmer. Much warmer.

Thelina squeezed his upper arm gently before releasing her grip.

"Thel—Ecolitan Andruz." He inclined his head to her.

"He's still rather formal, don't you think, Temmilan?" Thelina Andruz smiled brightly at the two historians and the apprentice.

"Rather."

Thelina turned her bright smile on the Imperial Major. "I'm sorry I couldn't make it in time for lunch, but I do have a few moments. Shall we go?"

"Nice to see you all," Jimjoy said warmly as he nodded to the historians and left with the silver-haired Ecolitan, who had reasserted her grip on his arm.

"You have such a way with words, Major."

"Thank you so much."

The two walked out of the staff area arm in arm. Jimjoy could not resist a grin, even though he knew the scene was a charade.

"The main garden, or somewhere else?"

"Have you seen the small formal garden?"

"No. Don't even know which one it is."

"Then you should, Major. You certainly should. How else could you bring back an accurate picture of the Institute and what it stands for?"

"Guess I couldn't."

"You are absolutely correct *this time*. You couldn't."

He winced at the emphasis in her statement.

Thelina disengaged her arm from his and reached for the door before he could.

"Don't you let a poor Imperial do anything by himself?" Even as he walked through the open door and the words tumbled out, he shook his head.

Thelina was silent. Jimjoy glanced back at her as she let go of the doorway.

In turn, she was shaking her head.

"I know. I know. It's a good thing I don't have to operate just on words."

She nodded in agreement with a solemn smile and stepped back beside him. She did not take his arm. "Take the left walkway."

"Left it is." He decided against offering any more statements. With Thelina, every time he opened his mouth, he seemed to swallow either his tongue or his boots.

Less than ten meters from the doorway, they stepped out from under the covered walkway onto a path with rectangular gray stones which curved in a gentle arc beyond the edge of the nearest academic building, the one that housed the library where Jimjoy had spent more than a few hours wrestling with the Institute's datanet and finding out more than he suspected the Ecolitans would have liked, for all their professions of openness.

Thelina's steps were unhurried, forcing Jimjoy to slow his pace.

"We are not on a field march, Major. You should enjoy the scenery, especially the garden. It's close to a replica of the more famous English formal gardens."

"An Anglish garden? Generally a replica?"

"*English* was the way it was most properly pronounced. And generally a replica because there have been no gardens there for some time." She paused before continuing. "There. The bushes—they should properly be boxwoods, at least chest-high. But boxwoods do not grow well here, if at all. So we have used a dwarf delft on the outer hedges and even lower smallwood on the inside."

"Which path?" he asked as they entered the green chest-high maze. Jimjoy could see that the inner part of the maze consisted of bushes less than waist-high.

"Whichever you wish. There are benches on either side, and this is a symmetrical pattern."

In time they reached a bench, partly concealed, resting on four of the gray paving stones, with the delft on three sides, and a narrow single-stone-width path from the main path to the bench.

Jimjoy started to step across the grass.

"You could take the path, just for the sake of form."

He glanced across to see her smiling gently and brushing a stray wisp of silver over her left ear. Her hair was again twisted up on the back of her head.

"Still long?" His eyes took in the wound silver, which seemed to glint, almost haloing her face, despite the afternoon overcast and the absence of direct sunlight.

"So far, Major. I probably will get around to cutting it one of these days, assuming that I remain here for more than home leave."

He raised his eyebrows. A training slot counted as *leave.*

"The Empire seems to feel that short-haired women are automatically from Halston or Accord. Who needs that kind of attention on field duty?"

That made an unfortunate kind of sense, Jimjoy reflected. He followed her suggestion and walked the curving spiral of stones behind her, putting each foot in the middle of a slate-gray stone and taking a good dozen extra steps to get to the smooth wooden bench.

The bench itself was typical of Accord, smoothly and finely finished, with a high back and with each slat grooved into place.

Jimjoy saw neither bolts nor nails, but only the smoothed traces of well-fitted pegs.

Did the Accordans carry everything to the extreme craft he saw at the Institute? Harmony had certainly looked much the same. Was anything done quickly or without precision and care?

"Why the frown?"

"Just . . . thinking," he murmured.

Thelina gestured toward the space beside her as she sat down. "Might as well sit down and tell me, Major."

Jimjoy sat.

"Closer. You'd think we were strangers, and we certainly aren't that, Major. Are we?"

Jimjoy sat dow, puzzled because there was no edge to her statement. Neither was her tone inviting. She had merely stated a fact.

"What were you thinking about?"

"About the degree of craft that goes into everything, even wooden benches."

"You find craftsmanship unusual?"

Jimjoy laid his arm across the back of the bench, above her shoulders but not actually touching her, and leaned slightly closer, as if the conversation were more intimate than it was certain to be.

"Not craftsmanship. Seen nothing here without it. Not sure all things are worth doing well."

"There's a difference between actions and objects, Major. You seem to value the reverse, faulting yourself when your actions are not perfect. Yet you say not all actions need to be done well. If you spend the time to create something, shouldn't it be made honestly and well? Not elaborately, but honestly and well?"

"You may be right. Hadn't considered that distinction."

"You're remarkably open-minded when you're not on the defensive."

"Could be. Seems a few people here want me on the defensive."

Thelina turned in toward him, touched his right shoulder with her left hand, and brushed his cheek with her lips. The semi-kiss, without emotion, was followed by an announcement lower than a whisper. "This is not shielded, but we're making arrangements. We'll be eloping some night in the next week when I visit you."

He leaned closer to her. "Then why here?"

"Why not?" her voice was louder, soft but carrying. "Everyone knows about us."

Jimjoy brought his other arm up, holding her loosely. He felt awkward.

"You're blushing, Major."

He was, he knew, and tried to refocus the conversation before he really got in over his head. More over his head, he corrected himself.

"What can I say?"

"Nothing, Major. Your intentions are completely and totally transparent."

Jimjoy wrenched his thoughts back to what had been bothering him earlier.

"Historian . . . has to be working for Allen . . . has to be . . ."

Jimjoy kept his voice as low as he could, and his arms around Thelina, who felt as responsive as a mannikin, though warmer.

She turned as if to nibble his ear, whispering back, "I can hear you. So can anyone with a directional cone. Who's Allen?"

He tried to keep his voice even softer. "Man who got away . . . first day here . . . Commander . . . Special Op . . ."

"Cold," she said, half aloud.

"I agree," he answered, not agreeing with anything.

"Why don't you like her?" Thelina moved away from Jimjoy and her question was asked in a normal tone of voice.

He let his arm drop away and shifted his weight. "Too forward. Too obvious."

"Remind me to avoid that pitfall, Major."

"Now we're back to being formal?"

"I'm only allowed so much off-duty time, Major."

Jimjoy shifted his weight totally away from her, stretched his shoulders with a shrugging gesture, and stood up beside the bench. He looked around the garden.

"Well, shouldn't keep you for too long." He kept the

puzzled look off his face, though he wondered why Thelina had taken his comments about Temmilan with so little reaction.

She turned on the wooden bench to follow his movement without standing up. Her green eyes focused on him and seemed to sharpen. "You're right, Major. It's time for me to get back to work, and time for you to get back to view any of those classes you missed. You have a lot left to cover, I'm sure."

He nodded. "Always learning something new. Hard to tell what you people don't already know, though. Some things don't surprise you at all. Almost as if you already knew it all and hadn't bothered to let anyone know."

She shook her head as she in turn stretched and stood up. "No. You know military skills and tactics far better than we do. Kerin told me about your little exhibition. You weren't just impressive, she said. You awed a woman who's never impressed, especially by men."

Jimjoy flushed, again, and glanced at the low hedge around the bench. He saw no sign of the blurring that would have signified a distortion screen.

"Then, too, Major, we also watch for reactions, or overreactions. The fact that your judgment was so accurate in heated circumstances was interesting, especially given the 'stress' you were under. We had a bit longer to make our conclusions."

Jimjoy forced a smile. He knew now all too well to what incident she was referring.

"As I suspected, Thelina, you have been ahead of me all the time. Cool and calculating." His voice was almost as cool as hers had been at times.

Thelina was standing facing him, grinning widely. "It makes no difference. Your reactions are unique enough to throw all our calculations off."

He shrugged again, still coolly angry, still aware that he could say nothing that surprised her. He wondered why so many of the Ecolitans, Thelina in particular, left him feeling verbally inadequate.

"Anyway," she added lightly, "I do have a field lesson for the newbies."

"Newbies?" He glanced at her, his eyes picking up on the small monogrammed Ecolitan emblem on her tunic.

Her eyes followed his and, surprisingly, she blushed. "New—new—"

"Brats?" he offered.

"Not exactly, but accurate enough, thank you." Her voice was again moderated and cool, and the momentary color in her face was gone as quickly as it had appeared.

"Field session?" he probed.

"Survival indoctrination . . . edible plants and animals. The usual. Basic principles."

"How many planets' worth?"

"That, Major, depends on how receptive the students are. First, they have to learn this planet. Enough . . . in any case."

Jimjoy could not tell from her tone whether she was putting him down or leading him astray, or both. He did not shrug, though he felt like it.

A brief gust of wind ruffled his hair and pulled several strands of hers loose.

"See you later." He stepped around her, brushing into the hedge, feeling several sharp points digging into his hip. She did not move, though an amused smile played across her lips. He ignored it as he put his feet on the narrow stones and headed back toward the main walkway that would eventually lead him to the physical training facility.

Now that everyone was awed, he obviously couldn't hide anything and might as well get a decent workout. A workout he clearly needed to untangle his thoughts. He hadn't planned on that, but he clearly needed it, for more than one reason.

"Have a good workout, Major."

Jimjoy tightened his jaw, but did not look back or acknowledge the pleasantry as he kept his steps even.

... XXIX ...

"Name?"

"Laslo Boorck."

"Imperial I.D. or passport?"

The hefty man handed across the Imperial I.D., looking down on the purser from near two hundred centimeters. In turn, the purser placed the flat card in the reader.

"Palmprint."

"Yas . . ." The hand went on the scanner.

The scanner remained silent for a moment, then flickered once, then turned green.

Bleep.

"Welcome aboard, citizen Boorck."

Citizen Boorck ambled a few steps, then waited.

"Next. Name?"

"Lestina Nazdru." The woman, with her red-and-silver-streaked hair, was clearly a different type from the sedate and overweight agricultural specialist whom she accompanied. Her nails glittered, and her eyelids drooped under their own weight.

The purser did his best not to stare at the translucent blouse.

"I.D., please."

"Of course, officer."

She placed her hand on the screen with a practiced motion. The long nails glittered alternating red and silver.

Again the scanner hesitated, but finally flickered green.

Bleep.

"Welcome aboard . . ."

"Thank you." Her voice was low, a shade too hard but pleasant, if vaguely professional.

The purser smiled faintly as the woman rejoined her husband, if their reservations could be believed. He'd seen all types, and a lot of the October-May marriages looked like the pair he had just passed on board the *M. Monroe*. Older and heavier man, wealthy, but with minimal taste, and an attractive wife not that much younger, but of even more questionable taste and background.

Remembering the hesitation of the scanner, he glanced at the short list on his screen to compare profiles, but neither the heavy man nor his companion matched the handful of names and profiles. The automatics were supposed to match names against prints. The list contained individuals for whom various law enforcement or military authorities had placed a detention order. He scanned the list again, then looked up.

"Next."

Behind him, the October-May couple walked toward their silver status stateroom, holding hands casually.

"You like the ship?" asked the man.

"A touch beneath you, Laslo, but it will do." She looked along the narrow corridor. "Shouldn't we turn here somewhere, dear?"

"I believe so, honeydrop. I do believe so."

The man stopped and fumbled with the silver-colored card.

"All passengers. All passengers. The *Monroe* will be leaving orbit station in five standard minutes, bound for Certis three. We will be leaving Accord orbit station in five minutes, bound for Certis three, with a final destination of Alphane four. If you are not bound for Certis three or Alphane four, please contact ship personnel immediately."

The stateroom door opened, and the man withdrew the silver card, gesturing to the woman.

"After you, dear."

"You can be so courtly when you have to, Laslo."

He followed her inside. Two built-in and plush chairs flanked a table. Over the table was a screen. The view on the screen showed the mixed blue-green of planetary continents and water covered with swirls of clouds, as seen from orbit.

The woman closed the door and flopped into one of the chairs.

"Take a load off, Las."

"In a minute . . ."

"They got any entertainment on the screen? Who wants to see a dumb planet every time you travel? Seen one, you've seen them all."

"You're so right, dear. But Accord has such marvelous agricultural techniques. I thought it might look different from orbit."

"Laslo, you dragged me here on business, left me in that tiny hotel while you went running through the countryside. You still smell like manure. Once we get to Alphane . . . We're going to Alphane for some civilized times and some real fun. And some comfort. Freshers with perfume, not old-fashioned showers. Real Tarlian caviar. You promised!"

"So I did. So I did. And where are we? We are on an Imperial ship bound for Alphane."

The silver-and-red-haired woman kicked off one shoe, then the other.

"Are our bags here yet?"

"They should have arrived before us. Let me check." He opened the artificially veneered closet door. Two expensive and expansive black leather bags, matching, were set on the racks, side by side.

"They're here."

"Tell me, Laslo, why was that ship's man looking at his screen every time he checked someone in?"

"Looking for some criminal, I suppose." The heavy man eased himself into the other chair.

"Do they ever look for women?"

"I would suppose that they might. Women break the law as much as men . . . although, dear, I suspect that they do not get caught as often."

He took her left hand, the one on the table.

She disengaged it deftly.

"Laslo, I feel rather tired, and it's likely I will continue to feel tired until after I return to civilization."

The man sighed. "I understand, dear. I do understand."

"You're always so understanding, Laslo. It's one of your great strengths, you know."

"Thank you." The man looked up at the screen. A slight shiver passed underfoot.

"The *Monroe* is now leaving orbit. The *Monroe* is now leaving orbit. The dining room will be open in fifteen standard minutes. The dining room will be open in fifteen standard minutes. Please confirm your reservations in advance. Please confirm your reservations in advance."

The woman smoothed her long hair back over her right ear, then over her left ear, tapped her fingernails on the table.

"You might damage the grain of the wood, dear."

"What grain? Can't you recognize cheap veneer?"

"I suppose it's the principle of the thing." He looked straight into her muddy brown eyes. "Will you be ready for dinner soon?"

"I will be ready for dinner when I am ready. That shouldn't be long."

"In that case, I will meet you in the lounge, dear." The man levered himself out of the chair, straightened his short jacket, and moved to the stateroom door.

"That's a dear."

The doorway opened, then closed with a firm *click*.

... XXX ...

"Welcome to Alphane station, ser Boorck, lady Nazdru. We hope you enjoy your stay. Will you be taking the shuttle planetside or transshipping?"

"The shuttle . . . for now . . . for . . . some culture . . ." answered the man.

"That we have. That we have. The shuttle concourse is to your left."

"Laslo, you are so masterful," commented the woman with the sparkling red-and-silver hair and the matching nails, blissfully unaware of the stares she was receiving from the conservative Alphane residents returning planetside.

"Thank you, dear. You know how I value your judgment."

"You should, dear. You should."

"But you know I do. Why else would I be here?"

"Now, Laslo, don't get sentimental. We have a shuttle to catch."

The big man sighed, loudly, and motioned for a porter to follow with the two heavy black leather bags.

The three stepped onto the moving strip in the center of the corridor and were carried toward the shuttle concourse. Lady Nazdru continued to draw stares. Few noticed Ser Boorck at all, except as an overweight man obviously dominated by a younger, if experienced, woman.

"You'd think that they'd never seen someone with colored hair, dear."

"Not like you, dear."

"You're so kind, Laslo."

The porter coughed. "Ser . . . lady . . ."

"Oh, yes, thank you." The man stepped off the moving strip and toward one of the staffed counters.

"May I help you, citizen?"

"I unfortunately neglected to arrange for shuttle passage . . ."

"That shouldn't be a problem. Do you have an Imperial I.D. or an outsystem passport?"

He handed over the flat I.D. card.

"Your print, citizen?"

The man complied.

"Does she need mine, too, Laslo?"

The woman behind the counter scanned the red-and-silver-haired woman. "I don't think that will be necessary. Your . . . husband's I.D. is clearly adequate." She shifted her glance back to the man. "How do you wish to pay for passage?"

"How much is it?"

"Three hundred each, plus tax."

"This should do." He handed over a credit voucher.

"Just a moment, citizen." She laid the voucher on the screen.

Bleep.

"That will clearly suffice, ser." Her voice showed much greater respect. "It will take another moment to print out a revised voucher."

"When does the shuttle leave?"

"You should not have to wait long, ser. The next one is for Alphane City. That is in thirty-five standard minutes. The next shuttle after that is the one for Bylero. That is in fifty minutes. If you want the southern continent, take the shuttle for Dyland . . ."

Burp.

"Here is your credit voucher, ser. And your passes. They are good on any shuttle. Just check in at the lock, or make arrangements at any service desk."

"Laslo, have you reconfirmed our accommodations at the Grosvenor Hill?"

"I will, dear, I will, just as soon as I arrange for our shuttle."

The shuttle clerk suppressed a smile as the man motioned to the porter and waddled toward the service counter. With her eyes on the woman, she did not notice that the man made no attempt to reconfirm the accommodations.

The heavy man and the woman leaned toward each other, out of apparent earshot of the shuttle clerk.

"But, Laslo, dear, I did so want to see Dyland *first*."

"I understand, honeydrop . . . I understand."

The shuttle clerk smiled amusedly and returned her attention to the screen.

"You didn't tell me you had *business* in Alphane City." The woman shook her red-and-silver hair.

"Put the bags here." The man nodded at the porter, then extended his hand with a five-credit token.

"Thank you, ser. Will that be all?"

"You promised, Laslo. You promised . . ."

"That will be all."

The porter left with his cart.

"You promised . . ." Her voice trailed off.

"I can only do my best." The man shrugged. "What if I meet you in Dyland . . . the day after tomorrow?"

"Laslo . . ."

"Tomorrow?"

"And you'll take me to the Crimson Palaccio?"

"Yes . . . the Crimson Palaccio."

"You're a dear, Laslo." She threw her arms around him and gave him a theatrical hug, whispering in his ear, "Look behind me." As she broke away, she added more loudly, "And be careful. Don't forget your diet, dear."

"I'll see you then, honeydrop. Don't buy too much . . ."

"I won't, Laslo. You know I won't. And we'll talk about *that* at home." She beckoned to a porter.

He watched as she waltzed away, shaking his head slowly.

. . . XXXI . . .

Jimjoy squinted as he studied the set of carefully crafted orders. Captain Dunstan Freres, it was. He set the orders on the battered dresser.

Then he sighed. According to his rough calculations of the probabilities, there was literally no chance of another name matching Dunstan Guillaume Freres in the entire Service, but the syllabic and semantic contents were unusual enough to convince the skeptical that no one would create such a name as a cover.

The authorization codes were genuine, taken from the Service's reserve list, which meant that he had roughly three standard weeks before they triggered any alarms. Jimjoy intended to surface before that.

Sighing again, he ran his left hand through his short hair, dark brown to match his temporarily swarthy complexion. Then he looked down at the closed and nearly depleted emergency make-over kit, then back at the uniform on the sagging bed. Next to the uniform lay a baggy and ancient raincoat and a shapeless cap.

One complication led to another. He couldn't exactly walk out of his less-than-modest room in a crisp uniform, but neither did he want to attempt donning the uniform in a public fresher, knowing what he knew about the ways of Special Operatives and the Imperial surveillance network.

"Curses of knowing the work," he muttered under his breath.

Although the gray-green walls, with the scuffs that even the heavy plastic wall coating had been unable to resist, seemed to press in on him, Jimjoy let himself slump onto the edge of the palletlike mattress, avoiding the uniform laid out on the other side.

If he left before the rest of the conapt tenants began to stream out, there was always the chance that someone would notice. More important, the base duty officer was bound to take notice of an early morning arrival.

No Service Captain with any understanding would check in before 0800 or after 1200. Before 0800, and there was the chance that you'd be required to report to your assignment immediately. After 1200, and you were docked the extra day of leave.

As Dunstan G. Freres, Captain, I.S.S. (Logistics), Jimjoy intended to be as forgettable as possible.

Forgettable or not, he was bored. While he could wait, and did, the room was boring, just short of being dingy, and all too typical of the short-term quarters that had surrounded military bases since they first moved from tents to fixed emplacements with roofs and floors.

The bed was nearly the worst he had slept on, except for the one on Haversol. Not that he had gotten much sleep that night, not after the incident in the saloon, when Thelina had indirectly saved him from the hordes of assassins snooping around after the fresh meat he had represented.

The Special Operative smiled a long, slow smile. In time . . . in a comparatively short time, Commanders Allen and Hersnik would get a taste of being on the other end—one way or another.

He stretched and stood up, checking the time, walking back and forth at the foot of the bed.

Checking the time again, he looked at the uniform on top of the bed and perched on the edge once more.

Lack of patience, if anything, had been his undoing before, and now he couldn't afford any undoing. So he looked away from the Service-issue timestrap and began counting the scuffs in the wall plastic, since they were the only finite details within the room.

This time, he lost track around number 277.

"Roughly one quarter of one wall . . . makes a thousand plus twenty-seven times four or a hundred eight . . . eleven hundred eight times three walls is thirty-three twenty-four. Say the short wall's half the others . . . half of eleven hundred eight is five fifty-four . . . added to thirty-three twenty-four . . . thirty-eight seventy-eight. Three thousand, eight hundred and seventy-eight blemishes and scuffs on the walls . . ."

What else could he count? Or should he reflect back on Aurore to see what else he had missed?

Either way, it would be a long, slow early morning.

... XXXII ...

Jimjoy eased into the vacant console, tabbing the proper entry and access codes. His bored appearance and gray-flecked hair matched the rating stripes on his tunic sleeve. Another not-too-bright, but technically skilled, file follower, with the intelligence to ensure that the records of all the officers under his care were complete, that they had current physical examinations and training schedules that matched their promotion profiles, and that they met all the other bureaucratic requirements.

He, as the most recently arrived technician, accessed a series of files, profiling physical examinations. The senior duty tech noted the screen coming on line, nodded, and returned his attention to the problem before him, the question of how to schedule the senior Commander performance review-board interviews within the operational and deployment requirements.

The senior technician did not notice the subfile called up by the technician, nor the immediate split screen, since he was supervising from three cubicles away. Not that he really knew any of the horde of personnel technicians other than by their files and his reviews of their data-handling capabilities.

The graying rating with the youngish face accessed another file, this time adding an item on various positions, subtracting

186

others. He checked the cycle times, the times at which current masters would be updated with present file information. At that point, the changes would be relatively permanent.

He returned the second file to storage, then called up five files consecutively, nodding minutely as he did, and as the supporting information was added to each.

In time he returned to the tedious business of transferring and editing, satisfied that Commander Allen's records now showed all his physical examinations as having been performed by the same physician in the same Intelligence clinic.

That had been the hard part, reflected Jimjoy, finding a good Service physician at Headquarters who had recently died of sudden causes. But he had had three options—debriefing officers, dental officers, or medical officers. Finally he had located a medical officer, and, not surprisingly, the late Major Kelb had actually examined Commander Allen after one mission.

Getting to the actual medical records had been the easy part, for him.

The major difficulty had been finding the people to impersonate.

He shrugged, touched the console again, and forced a frown.

"System four beta inoperative."

He tapped another access code, and was rewarded with another set of files. He glanced around to see if the senior technician were nearby. But the senior tech remained locked in his own cubicle, still wrestling with the promotion board schedules.

Jimjoy stood, eased back the swivel, and headed down the corridor toward the fresher facilities, leaving his dress beret beside the screen. Once around the first corner, he took the left-hand corridor back to the security desk, pulling another beret from beneath his belt.

"Leaving a bit early, aren't you?"

"Not leaving," he mumbled. "Beta four's down. Need to get a debugger from Tech-Ops."

"Personally?"

"Syndar says I have to explain *personally*. The authorization is on the screen."

The thin-faced Marine at the shielded console nodded sympathetically at the thought of one personnel technician's having to explain how he had scrambled an entire system.

"Wouldn't want to be in your shoes. Let's see your card."

Jimjoy handed over the plastic oblong.

The guard checked the screen codes and inserted the card into the verifier.

"Handprint."

The verifier, after a moment, flashed green. The Imperial Marine did not remark on the slight hesitation, which could not have been avoided, but handed back the card and touched the portal release, opening the barrier that separated the closed personnel section from the rest of the facility.

"See you later. Good luck."

"Thanks."

"You'll need it."

Jimjoy nodded as he stepped through the portal, then continued his even pace until he was around the next corner, where he entered the public men's fresher.

Shortly, a heavyset Major of Supply waddled forth, proceeding toward the main security gate.

The pair of Marines at the main gate, male and female, passed the Major with bored looks, logging the screen pass into the console and dismissing his average muddy looks and brown hair as soon as his waddling gait had carried him out of sight.

. . . XXXIII . . .

The white-haired Commodore bustled down the corridor, the tightness of the tunic and trousers indicating either vanity or a recent weight gain. The gold sleeve slashes glittered, indicating a recent promotion, in contrast to the row of faded ribbons across a heavy chest.

He passed a junior officer in exercise shorts and shirt, sweat streaming from his forehead, who stared at the sight of a Commodore in full-dress uniform hurrying through the Intelligence sector's physical training and demonstration facilities.

The Commodore felt the look and withered the unfortunate with a single steely glance, continuing his short quick steps until he arrived at the locked portal. His fingers proffered the entry card, danced over the console to enter a code, and presented a full handprint to the screen.

Bleep.

The portal irised open, and the senior officer hurried through, immediately turning left toward the combat simulation sector.

The multiple-target simulator was behind the third portal on the right side.

Taking a small plate from his belt, the Commodore deftly made two adjustments to the entry log console, then stepped through the portal. The small anteroom was empty, two chairs vacant for users who might have to wait their turn. Two additional closed portals confronted the older-looking officer.

Without hesitation, he took the one on the left, and bounded up the two steps into the simulator control room.

"What . . . Commodore? This—"

Thrummm!

Even before the young technician had collapsed over the console, the Commodore had reached her and pulled her and the swivel in which she had slumped away from the board.

His fingers tapped three studs, and light flooded the simulator below and back up through the armaglass window. He tapped another stud and spoke into the directional cone. "Maintenance problem. The system seems to have dropped the lighting parameters. We should be able to bring the backup on line. Do you want to begin the sequence again, or to continue from where it broke?"

"Hades! Can't you techs ever run anything right?"

The Commodore smiled a wintry smile through the one-way glass as he saw the man in the camouflage suit stand up in the far corner. Another man moved on the far side of the now large and empty room that had been filled with holographic projections not moments before.

"We do our best, sir." The Commodore paused, then continued. "While we're getting back on line, there's a Commodore Thrukma here. He says he needs a moment with Commander Allen, if one of you is Commander Allen."

"Thrukma? Never heard of him. What does he want?" The leaner and older man holstered the needler and turned toward the portal that would lead him back to the anteroom.

"He says that you already know."

Commander Allen frowned, but said nothing as he palmed the portal release. "Be back in a minute, Forstmann. Try the sequence yourself."

The Commodore obliged by rekeying the holotrack and tapping the "resume" stud. Then he turned to the portal through which he had entered, his own needler in hand.

Thring.

Thud.

The man who wore the name Thrukma on his tunic shook his head slowly as he looked at the body sprawled halfway through the portal.

Commander Allen wore the same frown with which he had left the simulator. Not even the neat hole through his forehead had erased all the lines on his face.

The Commodore checked the body, to ensure that the good Commander was as deceased as he looked, to slip several items into the Commander's equipment belt, and to make the changes and adjustments to the two needlers.

Then, moving quickly, he ran his fingers over the console. Next he dragged the body all the way into the control room before locking the control room portal behind him.

Finally, he locked the portal into the simulator, making it difficult, if not impossible, for Lieutenant Forstmann to leave the simulator without outside assistance. That would ensure Forstmann raised no alarm until either someone finally broke into the simulator or the technician recovered.

With a last look around, the Commodore palmed the portal to the main corridor, stepping outside. Without seeming to, he scanned the corridor and, seeing no one, made a final entry on the console portal controls, an entry that effectively locked them to all comers. While the tampering would be recorded under Commodore Thrukma's name, the Commodore would long since have vanished by the time it mattered.

The white-haired man turned from the portal and picked up his short steps toward the less secured section of the Intelligence physical training facility.

With the same deft manipulations, he logged himself out of the secure section and into the regular training area.

He began to bustle toward the main exit.

"Commodore?"

The voice came from a senior Commander, wearing, unfortunately, the Intelligence Service insignia on his collar.

"Yes, Commander." The Commodore's voice was neutral, yet condescending at the same time.

"I do not believe we have met, and your name is not posted to Headquarters . . ."

"Thrukma, Commander. If you check the most recent listing, I believe you will find it. It's spelled T-H-R-U-K-M-A. From Tierna, Fifth Fleet. Had the *Alaric*."

"*Alaric*? That the one—"

"Exactly. The same one, for better or worse." The Commodore's dark gray eyes focused on the Commander. "And you, Commander Persnal, if I recall correctly, were the watch officer on the *Challenger* at Landrik."

A slow flush crept over the collar of the dark-haired Commander, and his jaw tightened.

"Your pass, please, Commodore."

"Of course, Persnal. Of course. You always were a stickler for the rules, and I see you haven't changed at all." The Commodore flashed a purple oblong and nodded toward the main exit. "I believe the nearest verification console is there."

Persnal swallowed, but said nothing, standing well aside from the senior officer. The flush had subsided, and his sallow complexion had become even paler as he trailed the quick-stepping Commodore.

Two Imperial Marines and a duty technician waited behind the shielded consoles, bored looks on all three faces.

"Problems, Commander?"

"Problems, Commodore?"

The Marines had addressed the Commodore. The duty technician had addressed the Commander.

"No," answered the Commodore. "Just posted here, and the Commander does not know me personally. He has suggested, as ranking Intelligence officer, that I verify my clearance and identity." The Commodore stepped up to the console and inserted the purple card, tapped in his codes, and presented his hand to the scanner.

Bleep. The console flashed green, after an almost undetectable pause, and displayed an authorization code. All three ratings scanned it and nodded, virtually simultaneously.

The Commander frowned, studied the screen, studied the Commodore, then checked the screen again.

"Now," suggested the Commodore, "how about verifying who you are?"

"But . . . I'm the duty officer . . ."

"I don't know that . . . and I don't think you look like the Major, I mean Commander Persnal who was . . . on the *Challenger*. So be a good officer and oblige me, Persnal."

The Commander looked at the suddenly blank-faced technician and the impassive Marines, then back at the Commodore. The flush returned to his face, but he extracted a purple card seemingly identical to the one that Commodore had proffered and placed it on the console, adding his own keycode and placing his hand on the scanner.

Bleep.

"Good," noted the Commodore. "Good day, Commander. A pleasure to meet you again and to know you still regard the rules as paramount. I'm sure we'll be seeing more of each other." He palmed the portal release and stepped through, out into the afternoon sunshine.

With a glance at the senior officer quarters, he stepped toward the transportation center, where the dispatch records would indicate that Commodore Thrukma had requisitioned a flitter for Central City.

. . . XXXIV . . .

The nondescript brownish groundcar rolled into the parking area behind the visiting officers' quarters, swinging carefully into an unnumbered and unreserved spot.

After a delay of several minutes, Jimjoy stepped out, wearing the rumpled working ship blues of a Service Captain and carrying a ship bag. He locked the car and stepped away, scanning the area, but saw nothing out of the ordinary.

The cubelike building before him, three stories tall, with its greenish-white permacrete finish, looked like a smaller-scale transplant from Alphane City. The few straggly trees between the parking area and the quarters had managed to hang on to a few handfuls of yellow-green leaves, and the yellowish dust collected around the permacrete walk from the groundcar parking area to the side entrance to the quarters.

Nearer the building were the reserved spaces, only one of which was filled, with an official-looking black car with tinted windows.

Jimjoy smiled. That one had to belong to the Security duty officer. He walked across the spaces, stepping aside as a small blue electric runabout darted toward him. He waved, then waited, as the runabout screeched to a halt.

Another officer, female, also in ship blues, popped out of the runabout.

"Off early, Freres?"

"Off late. Been on since 2400."

"Ooooo. That sounds like you've had a few problems."
The solid and pale-skinned Lieutenant shook her head. Her
lacquered hair scarcely moved.

Jimjoy grimaced. He didn't have to act. The jungle-flower
perfume was overpowering. "Who hasn't, these days?"

"I know what you mean. It seems as though everything is
happening. All at once. And the Intelligence types . . . something really has them unglued."

"Can't believe that. Nothing upsets that bunch. Deep-
space ice in their hearts."

"Not today. Why, Captain . . . well, I shouldn't say, but
they are really turning the base upside down . . . and they
won't say a word."

"Still don't think it sounds like them." He turned and
matched her shorter strides as they headed for the quarters.

"I suppose they're human. Something must upset them, at
least sometimes." She tossed her head again, but the lacquered blond hair under her uniform cap still remained immo-
bile. "And what about you? You up for something later?"

He grinned widely.

"That's not what I meant."

"It isn't?"

"You know it's not."

Jimjoy grinned even more widely.

"You're impossible!"

"That's entirely possible." He swung the bag over his
shoulder. "Unfortunately, I have been on my feet—"

"For once."

"—since 2400 this morning. And to be up for anything,
possible or impossible . . ."

"You need some sleep. I know. All you do is sleep off
duty."

"Not all." He grinned again.

"Let's avoid that. If you actually manage to rouse yourself
after obtaining whatever rest is necessary, and are interested

in something besides the impossible, you might think about calling me later.'' She entered the quarters before him.

''Kkkkchewwww . . .'' He sneezed from the combination of the perfume in the enclosed area and from the drifting yellow dust that swirled around them as the portal swished behind them.

''Maybe you do need some rest.''

''Just dust.''

''Think about it, Freres.'' She smiled warmly as she took the right-hand corridor away from him.

''I will . . . after I get some rest.''

Jimjoy admired her spunk, though not necessarily the solidity of either her figure or her makeup. Without the over-abundance of artificial fragrance, it would have been even nicer to chat with her.

He took the left-hand corridor, heading around the corner toward his own small, but adequate, room.

Although he had hoped for a bit more time before the Intelligence community began turning over stones, in some ways he was surprised to have gotten as far as he had before the reaction had become obvious. The fact that it was obvious indicated that they had no real leads—yet.

Still, he let his steps slow as he neared the room where he had spent the last several weeks, on and off.

Quiet. Far too quiet.

''Shoooo . . .''

He turned and moved back around the corner, wearing the disappointed expression of a man who has suddenly remembered that he forgot something. He maintained that disappointed look as he marched back up the hall and out to the small groundcar.

Knowing that his current official identity as the good Captain Dunstan Freres could come under scrutiny at any time, he had left only a few uniforms in the officers' quarters, and a few real and a few spurious papers and documents supporting the identity of one Dunstan Freres.

The additional funds supplied by the Institute had come in

very useful in procuring the range of uniforms and accessories necessary to his plans. He'd been more than a little surprised at Thelina's insistence on his accepting the funds.

But he certainly trusted her judgment, at times perhaps more than his own.

His steps clicked lightly on the pavement as he headed back toward the groundcar, hoping that Prullen had not seen him, although she probably wouldn't have thought of his mere return to the car as anything more than a personal rejection—he hoped.

It was almost time for him to surface at Intelligence Headquarters, assuming that his information packages had reached their intended destinations—the key media, the Admiral, and Commander Hersnik.

The media would probably attempt to verify the noncritical sections first, and that would blast a few more orbits, and another Intelligence crew would likely end up nosing around trying to discover who had leaked certain classified material.

Hersnik he trusted not at all, but he needed Hersnik to make the decisions, preferably without too much chance to think things over. So his reemergence and entrance would have to be abrupt enough and public enough to avoid the kind of unpleasant details that the late Commander Allen had specialized in.

He shrugged as he climbed into the groundcar. He had done what he could. Now he would see what kind of fool he had been.

. . . XXXV . . .

Commander Hersnik had been in his office roughly five standard minutes, according to Jimjoy's calculations, when the Special Operative stepped through the Security portal and into the Commander's outer office. In a single fluid motion, his fingers traced a series of patterns over the interior controls of the portal.

"What . . . why did . . .?"

Jimjoy smiled at the orderly. "Security. Very tight security, Lieutenant."

"I suggest that you unseal that portal, Major—quickly, before the Commander has to summon the necessary assistance." The Lieutenant's hands were moving toward the small red keyboard.

Thrumm.

Clunk.

Jimjoy shook his head as the junior officer slumped over the security console, unconscious. The Special Operative slid around the end of the bank of screens and entered several codes and messages into the system, all indicating that the office was temporarily vacant as a result of a strategy conference and that the Commander would be available at 1500 for his normal appointments.

While there was a risk that Hersnik might be scheduled to

meet with a superior, conceivably a Commodore or an Admiral, such immediate postluncheon meetings were rare, or nonexistent.

He smiled as he tapped the access panel.

"Yes?" Hersnik had left the screen blank, but his voice was as annoyingly clear as the last time Jimjoy had visited him.

"Major Wright to see you."

"Wright . . . Major Wright . . . here?"

Jimjoy nodded, then realized that he had left the orderly's screen blank—obviously.

"That is correct. He claims he has some unique information for you, Commander."

"You're not Jillson!"

"No, I'm Wright? Do you want the information, or do you want to face a court-martial?"

"Court-martial? Who are you kidding, Major?"

Jimjoy sighed, loudly, since Hersnik wasn't the type to appreciate subtleties. "Since when have I ever overstated my case, Hersnik?"

"Commander to you, Wright!"

"Hardly, and not much longer, unless you're willing to listen. And don't bother to try your out-lines. They've all been shunted into a delay loop."

Jimjoy waited for Hersnik to realize that he was effectively isolated.

"All right, Wright. Come on in."

Jimjoy smiled at the false levity in Hersnik's tone. The voice patterns told him what he needed to know. As he stepped up to the second portal, the one into the even more secure inner office, he picked up the long-barreled stunner again, touched the access plate, and stepped inside.

Thrumm.

Thriiiimmm.

Clank.

Hersnik was grabbing for the fallen stunner with his left

hand as Jimjoy pounced from the portal and swept the weapon away from the Commander's grasp.

"Sit down."

Hersnik looked at Jimjoy, then at the weapon, then slowly eased back into his seat.

"Keep your hands visible, and listen."

Hersnik said nothing, but pursed his lips.

"You know, Commander, you really didn't need the stunner," Jimjoy observed, as he moved to the side where he could see both the consoles and Hersnik's hands. "I really am a loyal Imperial officer, difficult as you seem to be making it for me. And I meant what I said. Check the information on your console under 'Allen, double eff, star-cross.'"

Hersnik's usually neat black hair was slightly mussed, and there were circles under his eyes.

"That's nonsense . . . and how did you get here?"

"Not nonsense, and I got here on schedule, as set forth in my orders. Was there some reason why I should not have been able to return on schedule, Commander?"

Hersnik looked blankly at Jimjoy.

"Let's lay those questions aside for a moment, Commander, and get to the reason why I came back so quietly. That happens to be because Commander Harwood Allen is a Fuardian agent, and because he knows I know that." Jimjoy paused, then shrugged, still watching the Commander's hands and eyes. "And because I really didn't want him to have another shot at assassinating me."

This time, the Intelligence officer behind the wooden-framed consoles swallowed hard. "Allen . . . a Fuardian agent? Ridiculous!"

"That's what I thought, even after the first time he tried to kill me, then killed his partner when the Accord locals had him surrounded. That didn't make sense, you know. They would have had to turn the Lieutenant over to the local Imperial representative. So why didn't he want another arm of Imperial authority to know that he was out to kill off an

Imperial Special Operative? Unless there was something strange about their mission? Besides, the Accord types already knew that we kill each other off all the time. So it just couldn't have been that he had hush-hush orders to do me in, could it?''

Hersnik said nothing for a long moment, then, rubbing his numb right hand, cleared his throat. "Go on, Major. That is all pure speculation.''

Jimjoy shrugged again.

"When he tried the second time, it seemed rather strange, especially since he usually doesn't work solo. That's probably why his report won't show the second attempt.''

Hersnik raised his eyebrows.

"By then, I'd managed to find out a few things on my own, like his connection to Major Kelb, and his hidden credit accounts, and the gaps in his time accounts and early personal history.''

"Interesting— if true. But what do those things have to do with you? Or with your ridiculous assertion that he is a Fuardian agent?''

"Commander, isn't it obvious? Commander Allen knows that I know about him. He's tried to kill me twice. If I tried a direct return to base, he would have had me either fried in obscurity or locked away in some dark cell forever.'' Jimjoy smiled humorlessly. "The options aren't exactly wonderful. I can't desert because Allen leaked who and what I was to every agent within sectors of Accord, and I couldn't come home because some of my own team was laying for me. My only chance was to sneak back here and present the evidence.''

"What evidence, Major? I have yet to see a shred of anything remotely resembling factual evidence.''

"Oh . . . that. Once I realized what was really going on, that was easy enough to dig up. Bank records, holo shots of Allen with Fuardian muckety-mucks, alterations to service records, even his original birth records, not to mention his off-duty training with the Fuards during his official Imperial leave.''

"You have documentation?"

"Brought you some copies. You can tell how good they are. The originals are safely tucked away. The Fuards have some. But everything will stay safely buried unless, of course, I don't show up back on duty pretty quickly.

"But let's get back to Commander Allen and that code. 'Allen, double eff, star-cross.' Remember?"

"What nonsense . . ."

"Commander, no nonsense. Doesn't hurt to look, unless you're in with Allen on this, in which case I'd start running. So don't bother protesting. Key it in. 'Allen, double eff, star-cross.' "

Jimjoy watched as the Commander laboriously tapped out the codes with his left hand. He refrained from shaking his head at desk-bound officers who were nearly helpless if their right hands were incapacitated.

The Commander's eyes widened as he read the material appearing on the screen. Finally, Hersnik swallowed. "Am I supposed to believe this?"

"You can or you can't. That's your choice. The Admiral will receive his transmission in less than two standard hours, and he'll read it because it will come in under the Imperial star coding. His staff also has the same information, and they will ensure, I suspect, he receives that information in his afternoon briefing. That's in less than an hour.

"There's a timedrop to Galactafax and Stellarview first thing in the morning. I came to alert you, and to request immediate reassignment to field duty."

"You what?" blurted the Commander. "You think that will change your . . . destiny?"

Jimjoy grinned once more, widely. "Have to be a gambling man, Commander. My bet is that it will be a lot easier for you to give me an impossible assignment that will probably kill me than to murder me on Service territory and risk a stink, particularly if you think about it."

"Why don't you just let us make the decisions?"

"I am. Just want to give you the complete picture before

you do." Jimjoy bent toward the Commander. "Look. I'm good at what I do. Hades good. You can use me or not, but there have to be tough problems where you can. I'm not after diamonds and braid. If I disappear now, you risk a stink, and you can see from the information in the packets that it could involve you personally."

"Me?"

"It's on record that I entered your office, and that you are in charge of both assignments for me and for Commander Allen." Jimjoy paused, surveying the room and the telltales on the consoles.

"Assuming that the Service were out to . . . shall we say . . . make your life difficult . . . what future insurance would you have that the same preposterous set of circumstances might not occur again, purely through chance?"

"None, except for my own abilities and wits." Jimjoy smiled tightly, before adding, "And, of course, some insurance that if I disappear, except on assignment, such information as you see there will appear in various media outlets. There would be enough confirming data to make it sticky."

"Are you through threatening the Service, Major?" Hersnik asked coolly.

"Don't think you understand, Commander. I'm not threatening anyone. I've been threatened. Simply want to do my job, and try to ensure that I have some chance to keep doing it—since it doesn't look like I can do anything else."

"If you felt so threatened, why didn't you just disappear? You certainly have some talent for it."

Jimjoy kept his expression impassive. "For how long? How long could I stay hidden with every Imperial agent, and everyone who owes Intelligence something, on my track?"

Hersnik nodded. "So you accept the extent of Imperial Intelligence?"

"Be a fool if I didn't."

"Then why did you come back? With that power, couldn't Commander Allen have you disappear tomorrow and not ever reappear?"

Jimjoy hid his puzzlement over Hersnik's continued reference to Allen as if the late Commander were still alive. While it was certainly in Jimjoy's favor to act as if Allen were hanging on the other side of the portal, was Hersnik trying to test him? Or could it be that Hersnik didn't know?

"I don't question the Service's power, Commander. My only hope is to set up a situation where it is easier and more profitable to use me than to dispose of me."

Hersnik nodded once more, as if some obscure fact had become clearer. His fingers tapped the console, but he left them in clear view. "You seem to find the Service untrustworthy on one hand and extraordinarily trustworthy on the other. That's either naive or exploitive on your part, isn't it?"

Jimjoy shrugged. "The Service is trustworthy, at least as an institution, Commander. I have found some individuals less than trustworthy, and I have brought back some evidence of their failures. They seem to be out to stop me from bringing back that evidence, but I seriously doubt that most of the Intelligence Service has ever even heard of one Major Wright, much less concerned itself with his fate."

The Commander chuckled mirthlessly. "So what do you want? Really want?"

Jimjoy took a deep breath. "Immediate orders to the toughest assignment possible. Preferably as far from Headquarters as practical."

"How immediate is immediate?"

"Next shuttle off-planet."

Hersnik nodded again.

Jimjoy found the gesture annoying, but did not react.

"I take it you are worried about Commander Allen?"

"Put it this way, Commander. Either you believe me or you don't. If you do, you're going to detain Allen, and the Fuards will be after me. Or you won't, but you'll tell Allen, and he'll be after me."

"Commander Allen is an Imperial officer."

"Commander Allen damned near killed me twice," responded Jimjoy evenly. "Was he under Imperial orders to do so?"

"Hardly," answered Hersnik, with a twist to his lips.

Jimjoy could tell that Hersnik was relieved to be able to answer the question truthfully, since Allen had been ordered to kill Jimjoy once, and only once.

"In that case, Commander, you shouldn't find it that difficult to provide me with orders to do my job somewhere."

"That assumes the Service finds, after an appropriate investigation and inquiry, that your assertions are correct."

"My life is somewhat more important than your inquiries. Do you intend to give me orders or place me under detention—and face an inquiry yourself, along with me?"

"You leave me little choice, Major Wright. Not exactly for the reasons you thought, however. I cannot afford to turn down your generous offer. We've already lost three operatives on New Kansaw." He nodded at the keyboard. "May I?"

"In a moment, when I release some of the blocks."

"You might also be interested to know that we have already discovered the late Commander Allen's double game."

"Late. Late? You mean he's dead? You already tried and executed him?"

"Not exactly. It appears as though someone else found out first. He was shot through the head with a needler in the combat simulator. It seems as if it might have been done by another inside agent. We have some idea who might have killed him, but it would be impossible to prove, especially now, since the needler used was the Commander's own. It was fully charged, and not for simulator work, either."

"Then why did you string me along here?"

Hersnik smiled coldly. "Why not? Your entrance was not exactly designed for friendliness, although, in retrospect, I can understand your concerns. At least you appear willing to handle another assignment, and we have a much better lead on the late Commander's demise.

"As for the New Kansaw assignment, Major, you seem to

be the perfect choice, because, frankly, I really don't care how many rebels you butcher. I'd rather not ruin another officer doing it.''

Jimjoy forced a frown. "I don't have to like it . . ."

"Neither do I . . ."

"But you get the credit for uncovering Commander Allen's espionage, while I get a black mark, another one, for unconventional behavior, if I'm lucky."

"Don't press your luck, Major. Standard procedures . . ."

"Didn't seem to hamper you when you assigned me to the Accord mess. By the way, that report is completed and filed under 'Accord, biotech one,' with my order code."

"What did you find out?"

"It's all in the report. Basically, they have taken the science of genetics further than anyone in the Empire. I suspect they may even be beyond the accomplishments of Old Earth in the pre-Directorate days. How far only a skilled scientist could tell you. I tried to put all the technical jargon in the report. There probably are future military applications, but the Accord types seem to be concentrating mainly on plant genetics and removal of lethal human genes. They've done a great deal with plants.

"Accord really has no way to disseminate the information beyond its own people. No one outside of the top Imperial scientists seems to understand what they're doing. I suspect that's what led to the Fuardian actions and Commander Allen's presence there, perhaps as a way to get the Empire to crack down on the Institute, rather than learn from it."

"I'm not sure that follows."

"Look at it this way. Only Accord and the Empire have the scientific background to benefit from the Institute's research. Halston's still in an uproar, and the fundamentalist leanings of the Fuards have always prohibited genetic research. If Commander Allen could have persuaded the Service to destroy the Institute *before* gaining the knowledge the Institute has developed, then the Empire could not use that information against the Fuards. And since genetic research is against the Fuard creed, they'd want to destroy the Institute anyway. But since Accord is still an Imperial colony, they can't move directly. Of course, I'm sure you've already figured that out."

"True . . . uh . . . ummm," offered Hersnik, glancing at the small security screen wistfully, and rubbing the numbed fingers of his right hand with his left.

Jimjoy took a step toward Hersnik, who looked up nervously. "Seems to me you have two choices—get me out of here and clean up the mess, or be unavailable when the Admiral is looking for you and wants to know why his staff knows and why you haven't let him know."

"That sounds like blackmail . . ."

"No. Letting the Admiral and the media know is merely insurance." Jimjoy sighed. "If I'm alive and this drags out, you'll always have the chance to blame me for forcing the issue—once you've shunted me off to somewhere like Gilbi or New Kansaw."

Hersnik steepled his fingers, awkwardly, since his right hand seemed not totally controlled. His black eyebrows furrowed. "You forget I could still place you under a security lock."

"You could." Jimjoy laughed, harshly, "But then you'd have to explain that in addition to everything else, and it would look like you were trying to cover up something worse. Do you really want that, Hersnik?"

At the use of his name without its accompanying rank, the Intelligence Commander glared at the Major.

"Explain what?"

Jimjoy leaned forward, with an intensity that forced the Commander to lean back in his swivel. "Do you think that the Admiral is going to explain to the media how a Fuard agent infiltrated the Service's most inner circles? Do you think the Admiral will go before all those fax crews? When the news is bad? When that's your job? When my reports show that the Fuards are manipulating the Intelligence Service?"

"What?"

"A portion of my report was leaked to the media . . . the part that shows Commander Allen was trying to kill me to prevent his identity from being revealed."

"And . . ." said Hersnik slowly.

"If anything happens to me right now, it would seem that you were covering up everything to save our own neck. I doubt it matters to the Admiral one way or another whether you explain your way, or face an inquiry and a possible court-martial. Not to mention explaining my disappearance. Of course, you could just say that everything is well in hand, and that I have been reassigned at my own request . . ."

Jimjoy could finally see the trace of sweat on Hersnik's forehead. He waited.

"You really don't think this will protect you for long, do you?"

"No. As soon as the furor dies down, I imagine someone will try again. But I'm a good enough operative to have a chance. And it will probably cost anyone who tries at least a few good men, which would also have to be explained. And I really don't think you want to make those explanations for a little while."

"That's not enough, Wright. Good try, but it won't wash."

Jimjoy smiled. "All right. I'd hoped you'd be reasonable. Unless I cancel the drop personally, and I won't until and unless I have a courier to my assignment and I'm the copilot, 'Halston Fuse One' will hit the fax circuit."

"Halston Fuse One?"

"Call it up on your Security two base. You can call up from your data banks. You just can't get outside."

Hersnik frowned, but the Commander's hands touched the console. His mouth dropped open.

"Not even the Admiral knows about this, Commander, and if I get safely off-planet in my courier, he won't have to."

Hersnik glared.

"No threats, please." Jimjoy sighed. "I've already had to do more than enough just to carry out my mission."

"Your mission . . . your mission . . ."

"The one you sent me on. The one you didn't want me to return from, Commander. You and I both know who Commander Allen really worked for, and you're far better off this way."

Hersnik's face was blank, and Jimjoy wondered if he had pushed too far.

"Orders to New Kansaw it is. Permanently, as far as the Service is concerned."

"I'll wait right here, after I've released the holds on your system, while you do the authorizations, Commander."

"Suit yourself, Major. Suit yourself. Not that you haven't already. This orbit's yours."

Jimjoy nodded. He just hoped one orbit would be enough.

... XXXVI ...

"Are you certain, Commander?"

"Of course not, sir. If I could prove it, it would have been handled in the ordinary manner."

The Admiral sighed. "I think we'll refrain from going into that right now." He rested his elbows on the wide expanse of polished wood beside the ornate console, leaning forward to pin the dark-haired Commander with piercing green eyes. "Let me summarize your surmises, and they are surmises, for all the circumstantial evidence you have presented.

"First, Major Wright managed to appear at Intelligence Headquarters without known use of Imperial Service transport or without being intercepted by any of your agents or by any friendly agents. Second, he admitted recognizing two attempts on his life by the late Commander Allen. Third, the health and service records of Commander Allen now in the data banks and the hard copies in Headquarters do not match the hard copies of the records found in the Commander's personal effects. Fourth, Commander Allen should not have had access to all of his own personal records—"

At the open-jawed expression of the Commander, the Admiral smiled and interjected, "My summary is not confined to just those facts you have chosen to present, Commander."

The Intelligence Service Commander closed his mouth without uttering another word.

"Fifth, Commander Allen was killed with the weapon found in his own holster inside a secure military installation by a Commodore who does not exist, but who knew background information known only to the senior watch officer, and not available to Major Wright under normal circumstances. Sixth, Major Wright detected and avoided two other assassination attempts you engineered indirectly and did not report to High Command. For whatever reasons, he chose not to even report all these incidents to you. Seventh, Major Wright still chose to return and to make a full, accurate, and detailed report, albeit with certain 'precautions,' and to request further orders, as far from Intelligence Headquarters as possible. Finally, he sent me a copy of the materials he presumably set aside to ensure his own protection."

The Admiral smiled at the Commander, but the smile had all the warmth of a wolf confronting a wounded stag. "Now, Commander, would you care to draw any additional conclusions from my summary?"

"No, sir. I would be interested in your conclusions."

The Admiral nodded. "I can understand that. First, despite your deviousness, your incredible stupidity, and your colossal egotism, your instincts happen to be correct. Major Wright represents a considerable threat to the Service. Second, your choice of an assignment for the man is also probably correct. And third, that is exactly what Wright wanted."

The Commander swallowed.

The Admiral waited.

"I don't think I follow your logic to the end, sir."

"Major Wright is a threat because he will never see the Empire's need for subtle action. Every direct action reflects poorly and stirs up greater resentment against the Empire. He will also destroy incompetence, one way or another, and most incompetents in the Service have strong political connections. They must be kept isolated and placated, but we do not have the political capital to destroy them."

The Commander squirmed slightly in the hard seat, but continued to listen.

"Major Wright also inspires great loyalty in the able people who recognize his talents. They would emulate him, multiplying the destructive impact the man can create.

"Last, he has no hesitations. He is a deeply ethical man, in his own way, with the same lack of restraint as a psychopath. With him, to think is to act, and no structure, authoritarian or democratic, can react fast enough to counter him."

The Commander cleared his throat softly, as if requesting permission to speak.

"Yes, Commander?"

"You make him sound almost like a hero. But you insist he is a danger, and you say that my actions were correct."

"Correct on all three counts. He is a hero type. He is a danger, and if he cannot be eliminated, he must be kept on isolated and dangerous duty at all costs."

"What if he deserts—" The Commander broke off the question as he saw the Admiral grin. "I see . . . I think. If he deserts, he destroys his credibility within the Service. And if he takes straight butchery assignments, he'll either have to reject them, for which he can be court-martialed or cashiered, or lose his ethics in accepting them. Is that it?"

"More or less, Commander. Although we will attempt, with more subtlety, to render the longer-term issues moot." The Admiral frowned. "That leaves the question of how to deal with Commander Allen. My thought is to leave the murder as unsolved, but to imply that he was indeed a double agent, and that a certain Major solved the Empire's problem. Since that Major will not be around to counter the rumors, that approach will bear double duty."

"Why are you telling me?"

"Because you will make the necessary arrangements, Commander. Need I say more?"

The Commander repressed a groan. "No, sir."

The Admiral stood, with a brief shake of his head, the backlighting glinting through his silvered blond hair. "That will be all, Commander."

... XXXVII ...

Still frowning after his quick look through the station screens at the scout ship in the docking port, Jimjoy sealed his suit and stepped forward.

The *Captain Carpenter* had seen better days. Much better days, but he couldn't say that he was surprised. Obviously, Hersnik wanted to get word to New Kansaw before his favorite Special Operative arrived. From the looks of the *Carpenter*, the good Commander might not have to worry about Jimjoy's arrival at all.

Jimjoy shrugged within his suit and tapped the access panel.

"*Carpenter*, Tech Berlan."

"Major Wright here. Temporary assignment for transport."

"Lock's waiting, Major. The Captain should be back in a few minutes with the clearance."

Jimjoy pursed his lips, then frowned again. Clearances were not picked up, but routed through the station comm system. Shaking his head, he studied the ship's lock as he stepped through the station portal and into the *Carpenter*.

Would what he was looking for be that obvious? He doubted it, but the clues were there.

"Cluttered" was the best word for the ship's lock. Although all the gear was secured, much of the additional

213

equipment was stowed in place with brackets added without much regard for the ship's original design, leaving only enough comfortable space for a single suited individual to walk through into the ship itself.

Jimjoy studied the lock, but all the equipment appeared standard, and the lock control panel, though battered, showed no signs of recent tampering.

The man who had identified himself as Berlan waited inside the courier.

"Major Wright?"

"The same." Jimjoy fumbled with his flat dispatch case, carried in addition to his kit and his flight equipment. The flight equipment bag also included several smaller packages with rather more specialized equipment. Commander Hersnik would not have been pleased with the contents, but then again, Commander Hersnik would not be carrying out the mission. The need to bring equipment meant that he was carrying more gear than usual, and the lack of personal mobility bothered him.

At last he managed to fumble out his I.D. and orders for the technician.

Berlan was red-haired, rail-thin, and stood perhaps five centimeters taller than Jimjoy. His short-cropped hair was shot with silver, and a thin white scar ran from the right corner of his mouth to his earlobe.

"Yes, sir. Senior Lieutenant Ramsour should be back shortly. You get the top bunk in the forward space—that's the spot of honor, since you're ranking on board.

"Hope you don't mind acting as the backup, but otherwise we don't go."

"No problem, chief. Let me stow my gear. Then I'd appreciate it if you'd show me around."

Berlan looked as though he might frown, but he did not. His lips pursed. Then he nodded. "Yes, sir."

Jimjoy eyed the clean but battered control area as he passed the open portal. In the Captain's cabin, scarcely more than a long closet, he found a single large and empty locker and placed his bags and case inside.

Berlan stood waiting.

"Drives?" Jimjoy asked as he knelt by the flush hatch that should lead to the space below that contained the grav-field polarizer, the screen generators, and the discontinuity generator, not that anyone ever called it other than the jumpbox.

"Standard. Beta class." Berlan made no movement to unseal the hatch.

Jimjoy touched the access plates, waiting for the iris plates to open fully. Then he touched the locks to ensure the hatch didn't reseal on him. He still wore his shipsuit, including the hood, with only the face membrane not in place. Drive spaces had been known to lose pressure during inspections, especially when the inspector was not popular.

"Coming, Berlan?"

"If you want, sir."

"Wouldn't hurt, especially since your equipment may have been modified since installation. Ships this old tend to have some unique modifications."

As he slid into the maintenance area, two meters square, from which in passage repairs were theoretically possible, the Major took a deep breath.

Ozone, as expected. A hint of old oil, also expected, and a rubbery sort of smell, the kind that always showed up after new or rebuilt equipment had been installed.

He waited until the tech's feet touched the plastplates, looking at the area to his right. The polarizer was untouched, clean, but with a fine misting above the exposed plastics and metal. The mist seemed to hover several centimeters above the polarizer.

"Not much to see, sir."

"Enough, Berlan. Enough."

Jimjoy looked straight at the jumpbox. The involuted blackness of the discontinuity generator twisted at his eyes, but he attempted to look around it, and at the thin power lines that ran to it. Superconductors were fine, but even a small gash could pose enough problems to turn the scout into disassociated subatomic forces. The silver finish on the lines he could see was unmarred. Besides, there were no recent marks around the field boundaries on the plastplates of the deck.

That left the screens.

"Had some screen problems last time out?"

"Why . . . ah . . . yes, sir. Nothing major, Major. But we kept going into the orange with debris."

Jimjoy forced himself to nod, as if he really didn't understand. "They fix it, or just replace part of the generators?"

"There. Pulled out the power links, replaced them."

Jimjoy followed the tech's gesture, noted the obviously newer, or at least less battered, section. He also noted, but did not call attention to the dullness of the thin power line running to the rear section of the screen generators.

"If that's all, sir . . .?"

"That's all, Berlan."

Clink.

"Flame . . ." muttered the Major as a stylus spilled from his belt pouch onto the deck and skittered to the base of the unpowered screen generator. "Lucky it went that way."

Berlan swallowed. "Need some help, sir?"

"No. Get it myself."

"I'll give you room, sir."

Jimjoy knelt and crawled under the apron of the generator, reaching for the stylus and checking the power connections. He did not nod as he saw what he expected, but, instead, reached for the stylus and eased it away from the equipment. His hand flicked a switch into an alternate position, a switch he doubted most of the crew knew even existed.

Then he eased himself backward and stood, carefully tucking the stylus back into his belt pouch.

"Everything all right, sir?" Berlan peered down from the hatch.

"Fine. Coming right up."

Jimjoy climbed the ladder slowly, though he would have

needed only two or three of the inset rungs to lever himself back into the scout's main corridor.

There were two possibilities, and he didn't like either. Lieutenant Ramsour's presence might tell him which was correct.

"The other tech?" he asked as he resealed the hatch.

"That's R'Naio. Should be back with the Captain. Wanted some real comestibles, not just synthetics."

Jimjoy grinned. "Can certainly understand that." He edged toward the control section. "Wouldn't hurt to check out the board, especially if I'm backup."

"Yes, sir. But the Captain's quite good."

"Understand, but sometimes the best can't do everything."

"Suppose that's true, sir, but it will be a short trip."

Jimjoy smiled and edged around the technician into the copilot's couch.

The control section smelled . . . used . . . and the section of the controls before the Special Operative was slightly dusty. He held back a sigh as he ran his fingers across the board, trying to refresh his skills, noting the slight differences in control positions and calibrations. The screen configuration was standard, with the power disconnects apparently operational solely between screens and drives.

The rationale was simple enough. Scouts by necessity often operated at high gee loads. Scout pilots were often inexperienced. The default system configurations allowed power diversion between screens and drives, but not between the grav-field generator and either drives or screens.

Jimjoy would have bet on two other factors, one being that the *Carpenter* ran hot. All scouts did.

With a wry grin, he eased himself out of the copilot's shell.

"You must be Major Wright," a new voice remarked.

The speaker was thin, dark-haired, hard-voiced, and female.

Jimjoy nearly nodded, instead answered. "The same. You're Captain Ramsour?"

"A very junior senior Lieutenant Ramsour, Major. And also rather new to the *Carpenter*."

"First command?"

"Second. Had the courier *Tsetung* for a bit over a standard year. Rotated into the *Carpenter* when her skipper made Major and was selected for staff college."

Jimjoy merely nodded politely.

"Major?"

"Yes?"

"What the flame did you do?"

"Enough that New Kansaw is the best assignment I'll ever get again."

Lieutenant Ramsour shook her head. "You know the board?"

"Yes. Not as current as you."

"Happy to have you here." Ramsour scarcely sounded happy, but more like resigned to an unpleasant duty. "Your gear strapped in?"

"In the empty locker. Sufficient?"

"What it's for. We're waiting for a R'Naio and a few local comestibles, since none of us care much for synthetics."

"Outbound from New Kansaw?"

"After we pick up Lieutenant L'tellen . . . fresh from post-Academy training."

Jimjoy frowned.

"Her father's deputy base Commander there."

"Wondered about that." Jimjoy looked toward the board.

The pilot followed his glance. "R'Naio should be here momentarily. She had an electrocart at the lock. You can start pre-break checks, if you want. I'd like a last look below."

"Go ahead. I'll wait. A few minutes won't matter that much." He wanted to watch her inspection of the drives.

The Lieutenant did not acknowledge his statement, but was already kneeling to reopen the hatch.

Berlan stood on the other side of the hatch, ostensibly checking the bulkhead panel containing the lock circuits and controls. As the Lieutenant dropped through the full iris of the hatch, he looked up to meet the Major's eyes, then looked away.

"Berlan!"

"Yes, Captain?"

"Did you run a full-surge through the screens?"

"No, Captain. Can't until we're clear of the station. We're at a standard lock port, not at a Service lock."

"Sorry . . . forgot about that."

Jimjoy nodded imperceptibly. She asked the right questions, although he wondered why the *Carpenter* had not been able to get a full-Service lock.

He caught Berlan's eye. "No facilities for couriers?"

"Not for a Ramsour, Major."

Jimjoy nearly choked, turned the feeling into a cough. "The Commander Ramsour? Her father?"

"Uncle." The tech's voice lowered. "She won the Armitage . . . understand they couldn't deny her pilot training . . . finished in top ten percent . . . with everyone out to bust her."

"Berlan . . . are you spreading gossip again?"

The Lieutenant looked up at the two men before flipping herself up and into the passage with a single fluid movement that Jimjoy envied.

Berlan flushed.

"Don't listen to him, Major. He thinks the whole universe is out to get me because Steven Ramsour was my uncle. But his paranoia counters my unfounded optimism." She resealed the hatch and straightened, brushing back short black hair with her left hand. The hair was too short to need brushing, but even that nervous gesture was graceful.

Jimjoy glanced at the standard embossed wings and name on her gray shipsuit—LT RAE RAMSOUR, ISC.

"Yes . . . the name is Ramsour. That's me."

Jimjoy merely nodded. The more he heard, the less he liked it."

"Have you ever heard of a Commander by the name of Hersnik, Lieutenant?"

"Hersnik? I don't believe so."

Jimjoy was convinced she had recognized the name, especially when she did not ask for his reasons for asking the question.

"*Carpenter*? Berlan, release the double-damned lock and give me a hand with your flaming fresh food." The gravelly voice issuing from the lock control panel could only be that of the missing R'Naio.

Berlan reached for the control.

The Lieutenant nodded sharply toward the control board. "Let's get you on your way, Major."

Jimjoy turned, took a step, and dropped back into the copilot's shell, this time cinching the straps in place.

"Skitter pilot, too?"

"Sometimes." He realized that the Lieutenant, while not experienced, was sharp. Too bad that she was being allowed to climb too fast, although that was also predictable. Intelligence, arrogance, grace, looks, and disguised femininity . . . and a case to prove for the entire Service—Hersnik had a lot to work with, and Jimjoy had probably handed him the solution to two problems on a platter.

He thumbed the checklist prompt.

"Power one . . ."

". . . standby," she answered.

"Power two . . ."

The checklist was quick enough, and the *Carpenter* showed in the green.

"Alphane beta, this is Desperado. Standing by for pushaway. Orbit break, corridor three. Clearance delta."

"Desperado, beta. Cleared for break. Estimate pushaway in three stans. Clearance is green. Report when clear of station."

"Beta, Desperado. Stet. Will report when clear."

"Lock links are clear, Captain." Berlan's voice was raspy through the board speakers.

Sssssssss.

Only a faint scraping sound marked the separation of ship and station.

"Don't," cautioned Jimjoy as the Lieutenant looked from the DMI to the course line display.

"Don't what, Major?" Her voice was low, sharp.

"Don't report clearance until we're actually powered."

"Sloppy procedure."

"Survival procedure."

"Care to explain, *Major*?" Rae Ramsour's face stiffened.

"No. You can trust me or not. Couldn't explain, but don't survive as Special Operative without trusting your instincts. Hersnik is out to get you and me. I set you up. Not intentionally, but I owe you. Now . . . trust me or not. Up to you."

Her mouth had dropped slightly, but only slightly, at his mention of being a Special Operative.

"Special Operative?"

"Why else would I be going to New Kansaw on a courier?"

She shook her head. "You handle the comm, then. Since you seem to think it will make a difference."

"Might not. Can't hurt, though."

Jimjoy could feel Berlan looking toward them, but the technician said nothing. Neither did R'Naio, wherever she was.

He waited as Ramsour's long fingers played across the board, watching as the DMI showed greater and greater separation from beta orbit control, waiting as the ship's acceleration built.

"Alphane beta, this is Desperado. Reporting orbit break this time. Outbound corridor three. Estimated time to jump point four plus five."

"Desperado, beta control. Understand four plus five to jump. Interrogative delay."

Jimjoy could tell that Ramsour wanted to ask the same question, but had not.

"Beta, Desperado. Require additional en route testing of equipment. Power shunts were not available Alphane station. Proceeding as cleared this time."

"Stet, Desperado. Your clearance is green."

Jimjoy continued to watch the panel, particularly the energy tracks on the EDI, to see if beta control would launch a message torp. But the EDI showed only the station and a single incoming ship, cruiser-sized, on corridor two.

"Paranoid as Berlan, aren't you?"

"More, probably," answered Jimjoy. "Would you mind another paranoid suggestion?"

"Suggestion? Or a strong recommendation?" Her voice bore a tinge of exasperation.

"Whatever you want to call it."

"I'm waiting, Major."

"Boost your angle . . . enough that we'll end up at about plus two by jump point . . ."

"Be happy to, but won't that actually delay our jump time, not to mention the distortion?"

"It would . . . if we wait until projected jump time."

Ramsour half turned toward the Special Operative. "Major, I do not appreciate half-explained, 'I know best,' patronizing schemes. While I appreciate fully your interest in maintaining both our hides, I personally operate a great deal more effectively when I fully understand what is intended. And I might actually be able to help."

Jimjoy repressed a smile.

"All right. First, what's the normal-matter-density distribution pattern relative to a system's ecliptic? Second, what's the purpose of a jump corridor? Third, why do the normal power cross-channels not allow diversion from the polarizer?"

"So we don't get turned into particles of various sizes?"

"Try again, and would you mind boosting our angle, say—"

"Since I don't yet understand your machinations, Major, please feel free to make the correction you would find appropriate."

Jimjoy could see the woman set her jaw. She also had the legendary Ramsour impatience, it appeared.

"If you wouldn't mind." He turned his attention to the board, blotting out her coolness, and began making the adjustments.

He could still feel her eyes on him, and on the board, as her fingers jabbed at her own calculations.

"Rather a subtle course pattern, Major."

"No sense in making it obvious. It should look like carelessness, at least for a while."

"All right, Major Wright. I'll go back to basics. First, matter density *normally* decreases with the distance from the mean plane to the ecliptic. A defined jump corridor is merely a path of lower matter density leading to one of the closer points outside a system where the matter density is low enough to permit a safe jump. Third, the grav polarizer is not cross-connected to the power shunts because a courier has an acceleration capability sufficient to damage an unfielded ship and its crew."

Jimjoy nodded. "Why do we have to stay in the ecliptic?"

"Because . . . oh . . . it's basically the lowest-power, least-error approach. But how much time will you gain? And how far into the reserves . . . ?"

"Not at all." Jimjoy grinned. "I took the liberty of restoring full cross-connections to the *Carpenter*. Figure we'll be clear enough to jump in about another one point five to two standard hours. In another ten, fifteen stans, start boosting accel. Drop to zero just before jump, and shift field and drives to screens."

"Are you planning the same sort of reentry?"

"Why not? If you screw up a jump and end up too far above the jump corridor, what else can you do?"

The Captain of the *Carpenter* shook her head slowly. "Should work." She paused. "But why don't more people figure it out?"

"It's in the more obscure tactics books, but what's the most expensive part of operating a ship?"

"Energy costs." She paused, then asked, "But how does that square?"

"It doesn't." He couldn't help grinning further. "Question isn't just energy. Matter of accuracy. Too far above the ecliptic, and the standard jump calculations don't work. They include a constant for matter density. The level of variation increases exponentially with distance from the mean galactic plane . . .''

"That's a fiction."

"Mean galactic plane . . . you're right again, but it's useful in approximations of this sort." Jimjoy paused to modify his early changes to the ship's vertical course angle. "Some of the commercial freighters use the tactic all the time, especially on runs where they know the density variations. They change over time, unlike the corridors, which exist because of internal system dynamics. But the changes are slow. Problem is that military ships go everywhere, and besides, we're not at war. So why complicate the business of navigation, not to mention boosting energy costs?"

This time Rae Ramsour was the one to nod. "And every hot pilot would be trying to cut time, and flame the energy costs."

"You've got it. Also, the debris level is uneven, and over time that can play hades with screens."

"So for economic and maintenance reasons . . ."

"And to simplify procedures for young pilots, not to mention increasing the defense capability of Imperial systems."

"How? What's to prevent attackers from copying your tactics?"

"Habit . . . and lack of information."

She laughed, brittlely. "It takes energy to determine local matter variations, and since no one but the Empire has the energy . . . but what about the Fuards, or the Halstanis, or the Arm traders?"

"If they have, they aren't telling, and neither would I."

Jimjoy continued to watch the board indicators as he talked, in particular those showing the cruiser inbound to Alphane on corridor two. But the cruiser bored in toward the Imperial planet and its orbit control stations on a steady course and angle.

"Major, you are dangerous. No wonder they want you off Alphane."

"So are you, Lieutenant. And consorting with me won't help." He tried to keep his tone light, even as he tapped an inquiry into the board.

"Desperado, Alphane beta. Interrogative time to jump. Interrogative time to jump."

"Rather interested, aren't they?" noted Jimjoy.

"Beta control, Desperado. Estimate three plus to jump. Three plus to jump."

"You lie effectively, Major."

"Just doing my best to preserve the Empire's assets."

Rae Ramsour shook her head again.

Jimjoy took a look at the spacial density readout and smiled wryly. If the thinning continued at the current level, jump was less than a standard hour away.

. . . XXXVIII . . .

"Less than ten stans to jump."

"I have this feeling," murmured the Captain of the *Carpenter*.

Jimjoy looked at the senior Lieutenant. "Recommend sealed shipsuits for jump, Captain."

Ramsour frowned. "What else haven't you told me?"

"Call it mere instinct. But if our shields have a flaw, the loving Emperor forbid, we won't be in any position to—"

"—make repairs. Or react." The courier's Captain straightened. "Berlan, R'Naio. Seal shipsuits for jump."

"Sealing suits, Captain."

Jimjoy sealed his own suit with the plastic shield, triggering the internal comm system. "Comm test."

"Clear, Major. Berlan?"

"Hear you both, Captain."

"R'Naio?"

"Clear enough."

"Would you like to set the jump, Major?"

"If you don't mind, Captain."

"Be my guest."

"All hands, strap in for maneuvers."

"Strapping in."

"Strapping in."

Jimjoy touched the controls, shifting power from the grav polarizer to the drives. A momentary lightness was replaced by the acceleration of the stepped-up drives.

"Major . . ."

"We'll be fine." Jimjoy's voice was calm, but crisp, as he concentrated on positioning the ship for the jump. He doubted that anyone would be waiting at the fringes of the New Kansaw system, but if they were, they would scarcely be prepared for the jump-exit velocity he had in mind.

"And I thought the Captain was a hadeshead . . ." The gravelly mutter was not meant to be heard, but the internal shipsuit pickups were voice-actuated and sensitive.

Jimjoy grinned. He might yet improve Rae Ramsour's situation, if only by comparison. Even if his presence as a noticeably senior officer had put her in an impossible position.

"Two stans until jump." Jimjoy could see the Lieutenant trying not to squirm in her shell.

With less than thirty seconds before jump Jimjoy diverted all power from the drives to the ship's screens, then watched the screen indicators, bleeding some of the power back to the jump generator.

"Ten, nine, eight, seven, six . . ."

At the word "six," Jimjoy dropped all power into standby, letting the ship's cutouts take over. Weightlessness brought his stomach into his throat. As he swallowed it back into place, the wave of blackness that defined a jump flashed over him.

The blackness subsided, though the weightlessness did not, as the *Carpenter* popped back into normspace.

As he studied the controls, Jimjoy was scarcely surprised. Internal pressure was dropping to zero, and the shields were inoperative.

"Remain suited. Internal pressure loss." He began to unstrap. "Captain, appreciate it if you left power *off* both drives and screens until I see if I can locate the cause of the problem."

"You don't seem surprised, Major."

"Would have been surprised if there hadn't been a problem."

Jimjoy unstrapped and made his way to the access hatch, where Berlan had already begun to open the iris. The tech said nothing as the Special Operative slipped down into the space below.

As Jimjoy suspected, one of the superconductor lines was black. That was the easy problem.

Berlan watched as Jimjoy eased the spent line from first one socket, then the other. Installing one of the spares was done almost as quickly.

"Captain, power up on the screens."

"Powering up."

The line shimmered dusty silver.

"Screens are in the green, Major."

"Course line?"

"Estimate two plus to New Kansaw orbit control. We're at about one and a half plus on the high side."

"What's the reserve on oxygen?"

"Two full pressurizations."

The Special Operative removed the temperature probe from the equipment locker and began to sweep the lower deck, concentrating on the inside hull plates.

One of the plates behind the screen generator was noticeably colder.

"Dropping the screen generator off-line, Captain."

"Can you make it quick, Major?"

"Debris?"

"Not for another fifteen stans at our inbound."

"Stet."

Jimjoy used the manual shunt to drop the generator off-line. Then he squeezed around the bulk of the generator. A neat hole had been drilled, probably with a laser cutter, at an angle to the plate, virtually invisible unless looked for. The secondary ship's screens probably had held a plug in place on the other side. When the screens failed, the internal pressure had knocked the plug out and depressurized the ship.

The sealant tube in the small equipment locker did the work.

Jimjoy repowered the screens.

"Ready to repressurize, Captain."

"Repressurizing, Major."

"Stand by for atmospheric tests, Berlan."

"Internal monitoring ready, Major."

Jimjoy climbed out from lower deck hatch, leaving the iris open. Then he strapped back into the copilot's seat.

"Wonder you Special Operatives can even function, you're so paranoid," noted the Lieutenant. her voice was dry.

"Some days we have trouble."

"Internal atmosphere tests normal, Captain. But it's still cold. Suggest you wait another five stans before you unseal."

"Thanks, Berlan."

Jimjoy studied the control board, looking for a discrepancy, any discrepancy. Surprisingly, he found none, and that bothered him.

"What next, Major?"

"We dock at New Kansaw orbit control, and you wait for Lieutenant L'tellen. I report planetside, and Berlan checks out all the hull plates and runs current tests on all the superconductor lines. You become more paranoid, and R'Naio poisons everyone with fresh food, assuming that any of those comestibles survived the instant vacuum packing they received."

"No more fresh food," muttered the other tech.

"I take it that we don't report inbound until we have to."

"Why give more notice than we have to?"

Lieutenant Ramsour shook her head. She said nothing, but readjusted the grav polarizer.

Jimjoy checked the screen indicators. All read in the green.

"If they're watching the system EDI, we should have an inquiry reaching us in about one standard hour."

"That the comm break point?"

"Roughly."

"Wonderful."

Jimjoy shrugged and leaned back in the shell. He eased

open his face shield, closed his eyes, and let himself drift into sleep.

The comm inquiry woke him.

". . . Interrogative inbound. Interrogative inbound. This is New Kansaw control. Please be advised that this is a quarantined system. This is a quarantined system . . ."

"Now they tell us."

Jimjoy struggled erect, squinted, and checked the time. He had slept for nearly one and a half hours. More tired than he had realized.

"You awake, Major?"

"Mostly."

"You heard the message?"

"The part about the quarantine? Yes. Was there more?"

"Asked for I.D. on pain of death, destruction, and dismemberment, or the equivalent."

"Mind if I reply?"

"Not at all. You have a certain way with words."

Jimjoy coughed, tried to clear his throat.

"New Kansaw control. New Kansaw control. This is Desperado one. Desperado one, clearance delta. Departed Alphane for crew change New Kansaw. Authorization follows. Authorization follows."

Jimjoy called up the authorization codes from the navbank, then continued.

"New Kansaw control, Desperado one, authorization follows. Delta slash one five omega slash six three delta. I say again. Delta five omega slash six three delta."

He touched the screen controls, toggled the Imperial I.D flash. While such flashes could be duplicated, any sector Commander who fired on a ship that had flashed such an I.D. would have a hard time explaining it away. Still . . .

"You have a torp on board?"

"Two, Major," answered Berlan.

"Program it with the information that New Kansaw control has declared a system quarantine, and that we have informed

New Kansaw control of our mission and are proceeding in-system.''

"What good will that do?" asked the *Carpenter*'s Captain.

"By itself, not a great deal. But after we've informed New Kansaw of our helpfulness in spreading the word . . ."

"Devious . . ." muttered Berlan.

"Why are you so determined to get to New Kansaw?" asked the Lieutenant.

"That's where I'm ordered, Captain. Failure to obey orders is a cardinal failure for a Special Operative."

Jimjoy cleared his throat again, then triggered the comm system.

"New Kansaw control, this is Desperado one. We are relaying your quarantine message to Alphane control via torp. Relaying your quarantine via torp. Proceeding inbound to assist in quarantine. Proceeding inbound to assist in quarantine."

He paused, then asked, "That torp about ready?"

"Input complete, Major. Permission to launch, Captain?"

"Launch when ready," replied the Lieutenant.

"Launching torp for Alphane."

Jimjoy tracked the thin trace of the small high-speed torp until it jumped from EDI display. He suspected that New Kansaw control also tracked the torp.

Then he forced himself to lean back in the shell, and wait. And wait.

The hiss of the old air circulation system and a faint whine from the open comm net were the loudest sounds in the courier.

"Desperado one, this is New Kansaw control. Desperado one, this is New Kansaw control. You are cleared inbound to alpha control. Cleared inbound to alpha control. Do not deviate from course line. Do not deviate from course line. We estimate your arrival in point seven five standard hours. Please confirm."

"Slight improvement, Major."

"New Kansaw control," answered the Special Operative, "this is Desperado one. Will maintain direct course line to alpha control. Will maintain direct course line to alpha control. Estimate arrival in approximately point nine standard hours. Point nine standard hours.''

"Still trying to give yourself a margin, Major?''

"Not much. They never consider standoff time, and I really don't want to give anyone an excuse. For either one of us, Lieutenant Ramsour.''

"Thank you for reminding me, Major Wright.'' The woman's tone was cooler than frozen ice.

Jimjoy suppressed a frown. He obviously hadn't thought that one through, but what could he say now?

"Sorry,'' he whispered, hoping the techs would not pick up on the apology.

"Quite all right, Major. Quite within the rights of a Special Operative.''

He did not shrug, but felt like it. Some days, even when he won, it felt like losing.

. . . XXXIX . . .

Jimjoy hefted the two ship bags and slipped the dispatch case under his arm. Once again he felt awkward with the amount of equipment he was carrying, but after the trip on the *Carpenter*, he couldn't exactly say he regretted it.

He looked up.

Berlan was standing by the cabin archway. The *Carpenter* only had curtains, not doors or portals as on larger ships.

"Major . . .?"

"Yes, Berlan?"

"We appreciate it." The tech's voice was pitched uncharacteristically low. "You have to understand . . ."

"Think I do, Berlan. Think I do."

He understood, all right, but wasn't sure what to do. Rae Ramsour was a person, not a mission.

"She'll understand in time."

Jimjoy nodded, took a deep breath, and made his way forward.

Lieutenant Ramsour was perched sideways on the edge of the control couch, looking neither at the controls nor at the Major, who stood there.

"Leaving, Major?" She did not look up.

"Not quite yet."

"Thought you'd burn your way through Hades to get to your mission."

"Only because I don't have the choices you do, Lieutenant."
She finally looked up. "What choices?"

He set down the bags and eased himself onto the edge of
the copilot's shell.

"Running out of time, Lieutenant. Learned a lot as a
Special Op. Learned enough to know that, one way or another, this is probably my last mission. If I can pull it off,"
he lied, "it's off to a desk. If I don't," he continued truthfully, "don't have to worry about desks, or choices.

"I know a lot about destruction and how to avoid it. But I
made a lot of mistakes about people. Fact is . . . still making
them. People matter." He laughed harshly. "Right? Special
Op killer telling you that people matter? Sentimental killer
and all that flame?" He shrugged. "Not much else to say.
Sorry I was hard on you. Hope I helped."

Slowly, he stood, picking up the bags.

"Anyway . . . good luck to you, Captain. And to your
crew." He straightened. "Permission to leave the ship,
Captain?"

"Permission granted, Major." There were dark circles under her eyes. "And thank you . . . I think."

Though she did not smile, there was no bitterness in her
tone, Jimjoy reflected, and that would have to be enough.

For some reason, he wondered, as he turned to activate the
lock, if Thelina would have approved of his attempt to clear
the air.

"Good luck, Major." Berlan, the first on the *Carpenter* to
see him aboard, was also the last to see him off.

"Same to you, Berlan. You've got a good Captain."

He did not listen for any response, but stepped through the
lock to New Kansaw orbit control and the pair of armed
technicians who waited to escort him planetside.

. . . XL . . .

"The main resistance headquarters has to lie in the Missou Hills." The Commander jabbed a pointer, awkwardly, at the wall projection. "We've cleared out all the other possibilities here on the central plains. The reeducation teams are having some success, and they would certainly have more . . ."

"If the rebels weren't so successful?" Jimjoy stood at attention, a rather relaxed attention that verged on insolence as the Operations officer summarized what he knew about the rebel positions. "How much does their success depend on your inability to find their base of operations? Do we even know if they require a fixed base?"

"Look, Major, this isn't a typical guerrilla action. We aren't talking small farmers up in arms about the Imperial onslaught. Most of the planet was held by large landowners. What we have here is a bunch of professional rebels, the same group the landowners were fighting to begin with."

Jimjoy tried not to betray the sinking feeling in his guts. "They didn't like the ecological transformations, I take it."

"Obviously. Why else would they sabotage the landowners? Remember, the Council asked for Imperial assistance when they failed to meet their repayment schedule for the planetary engineering. We didn't get called in until the minority landholders withheld their taxes and declared the High Plains independent.''

Jimjoy wanted to shake his head, but did not. Instead he asked another question. ''So the majority landholders claimed that the rebels and the minority landholders were somehow destroying the crops?''

''Worse than that. They were targeting the planetary diversion projects and the holdings of the landholders who supported them . . . anyone who supported the Empire.''

''I see.''

''That's why they have to have a fixed base. Because their operations aren't antipersonnel.''

Jimjoy knew better than to dispute the Commander's facts or logic, neither of which was totally accurate. ''What about a quarantine?''

''That's what we've been trying for the last three standard months,'' said the officer in crimson and red, ''but they don't have any conventional ties or transportation, at least nothing that we can track, even by satellite sensors. They aren't a large group, never mount more than a limited number of operations, but they have cost us more than fifty million creds' worth of equipment and three squads. We've lost one Commando team and one Special Operative. They were the only ones who inflicted more damage than they received.''

''Terrain too rough for conventional support?''

'' 'Rough' isn't the word for it. All you can do is land on the objective and hope the ground doesn't collapse under you. Take the badlands of Noram, add the winds of Coltara, the aridity of Sahara, and the ashes of Persephone, and you have some idea of the terrain.''

''Why so much difference between the hills and the High Plains?''

''The Plains sit practically on the bedrock. The hills were upthrusts where the aquifers broke out. Mess of fractured rock, silt. That's why they're collapsing now. No water supporting them.''

Jimjoy again refrained from comment on the Commander's

inadequate grasp of geology. "That why the area was never terraformed?"

"That and the fact that the alkalinity was phenomenal. It was too high to bother with, and too unstable. The Engineers just diverted the subsurface water tables and let it go."

"So there was a lot of vegetation there?"

"That's what they say. Supposedly, it climbed all over the cliffs, even down into the ravines. It's almost all dust and ashes now." The Commander cleared his throat and set the pointer down on the dull gray finish of the projector's console. He glanced over Jimjoy's shoulder toward the portal.

Since Jimjoy had not heard the telltale whisper of a portal opening, he knew that the other officer was hoping someone else would come in. He repressed a grin. The Operations theorists were never happy when they had to brief a Special Operative directly. It put them too close to the cold-blooded side of the mayhem. They all preferred to think of combat as either an art or unavoidable.

"I take it you want them neutralized?"

"Ummm . . . of course. Wasn't that why you were sent?"

"Yes. I was dispatched to find the quickest and most effective solution to your problem—regardless of the cost to the rebels or to the ego of Imperial forces. But no one would have dared to state that openly." Jimjoy paused before twisting the knife further. "They prefer not to ask too many questions about my solutions."

The Commander looked down at the drab and gray plastone floor, then back over Jimjoy's shoulder at the portal, and finally at the Major in his tan singlesuit without emblems or trappings—only the crossed bars of his rank on his collars.

The singlesuit was immaculate, as was Jimjoy. But neither looked traditionally military, since Jimjoy did not affect instantaneous obedience and the singlesuit possessed no knife-sharp creases, braid, or rows of decorations.

Jimjoy knew the only military aspects of his person were his eyes. Even Admirals had wavered before them. Not that he was anything other than superbly conditioned and trained.

He just wasn't military at heart, and probably shouldn't have been in the Service at all.

But he had survived for more than a decade in a field where the casualties ran eighty percent in every four-year tour.

He waited, his silence exerting a pressure on the Commander to speak.

"How long will it take?"

"Depends on what I have to do. One way or another, be finished in three months. Might be three weeks."

"Three months?"

The Major sighed. "You want a miracle. I'm here to do it. The difficult we do on schedule. The impossible takes longer. This is impossible. You can't take anything mechanized into the terrain except flitters. You don't know who the enemy is or where they are. You haven't been able to solve the problem in six months with five thousand Imperial Marines. You've lost Commandos and Special Operatives, and you want me to fix it overnight?"

He threw a skeptical glance at the Commander, who responded by stiffening and squaring his shoulders.

"Spare me a lecture about how each day costs money and troops," the Special Operative continued, his words stopping the protest from the senior officer. "Understand that. But you'll have even more delays and costs if I go off half blasted and get zapped. Now, if you'll excuse me . . . Is the rest of the material in the console?"

The Commander nodded, his face tight.

"Fine. After that I'll probably be wandering around to get a feel for the situation. Then I'll let you know what I'll need."

"What you will need?"

"Don't carry supplies with me, Commander," commented the operative as he drew the stool up to the console.

The Commander stood there, staring blankly at the Major's back, until he realized that he had effectively been dismissed by a junior officer. Finally, he turned and walked woodenly from the room.

As the portal whispered shut, Jimjoy glanced backward. "All alike. If it's not laid out in their order files, it doesn't exist. If it wasn't taught at the Academy or spelled out in Service policy, it's not possible."

He continued his scan of the background material, strictly a factual description of New Kansaw and the grain belt plains.

New Kansaw—T-type planet, variation less than point zero five from norm. Atmospheric oxygen content sixteen point five percent, and gravity point nine three of T-norm. Mean surface temperature within acceptable parameters . . . He skimmed through the facts.

The odds were that the statistics would tell him less than nothing, another fact that the Operations types never quite understood. He shook his head as he concentrated on the more detailed information about the higher plains where the Empire had expected the colonists to concentrate on grains and synde bean production.

The one number that might have some significance, he reflected, was the number of cloudy summer days. Why he could not recall, but somewhere, sometime, he had read about the need for an inordinate amount of unobstructed sunlight for successful synde bean cultivation.

Clouds usually meant rain, and rain meant moisture. Some grains did not do well later in their growing seasons with too much precipitation.

He keyed in the inquiry, more to see if the unit were connected to a full-research data bank.

Beep.

"Subject inquiry requires "Red Delta Clearance.' "

The Special Operative gave the screen a wry grin and closed down the console. Stretching as he stood, he stepped away from the console and began to pace around the bare-walled conference room, his feet hitting on the gray plastone tiles with a flat sound.

He found it hard to give his full attention to New Kansaw.
The Accord situation, especially the friendly detachment of
the Ecolitans, still bothered him. Even Thelina had been
professional. Only Temmilan had shown any interest, and
that had been for the express purpose of compromising him.

He had made his report, hadn't even been asked any
follow-up questions, which would not have been precluded
by his hurry-up departure. Hersnik just wanted him dead, one
way or another, without any blame on Hersnik or the Service
itself.

On the one hand, the Service was concerned about Accord.
On the other, the Admiralty really didn't want any new
information or insights, just an excuse to act against the
planet.

Running a stubby-fingered hand through his short black
hair, Jimjoy pursed his lips. He could worry about Accord,
about Thelina, *after* he had muddled through the New Kansaw
mess. *If* he muddled through.

He grinned—what else could he do?—and headed for the
portal.

As he stepped out into the humming of the main corridor,
he could not avoid the senior technician, fully armed, who
came up to him.

"Major Wright? Technical Specialist Herrol, sir. At your
service, sir."

Jimjoy said nothing, let his eyes survey the lean-looking,
dark-haired young man with the flat brown eyes. He did not
nod, but it was obvious that Technical Specialist Herrol would
be both bodyguard and expediter, if not assassin, at the
appropriate time, should one Major Wright show any lack of
suicidal enthusiasm in pursuing his assignment.

"You know where I'm quartered, Herrol?"

"No, sir."

"Neither do I. Let's find out. Where do I start?"

"You might try Admin, sir."

"Be happy to. Where is it?"

"Through tunnel three blue, sir."

Jimjoy gestured. "Lead the way."

Herrol's face was expressionless as he turned. "This way, sir."

Jimjoy followed. Herrol's mission was more than obvious. What was not obvious was how Herrol had been assigned that mission so quickly, and why. Herrol would be difficult to deal with, particularly if he knew nothing except his duty.

Jimjoy shook his head as he stretched his stride to keep pace with the technical specialist.

. . . XLI . . .

"Special Operative Wright," announced the black-haired man as he leaned over the console. "You have a bird for me."

"Wright?" asked the technician.

"That's right," responded Jimjoy evenly. "For a recon run at 1400. Code delta three."

"Oh . . . Major Wright. Yes, sir. That will be Gauntlet one, on the beta line. Sign-off and tech clearance are at the line console central." The woman looked away, as if she had completed an unpleasant task.

"Beta line?" asked the Major. "Could you point the way?"

"Sir. Take the corridor outside until it branches. Take the left fork. That serves the beta flitter line. The maintenance section is the second or third portal on the right after the fork, depending on whether you count the emergency exit as a portal."

The words rattled from her mouth with the ease and lack of enthusiasm created by frequent repetition.

"Thank you, technician." He turned and headed for the portal through which he had just entered, but not without glancing back to catch the fingers flicking over the console before her, as if to send a message.

He looked back again, just before the portal closed, but the technician had not looked up from her console.

Once through the portal, he surveyed the corridor, empty except for two technicians wheeling an equipment cart toward one of the flight lines and a junior pilot who trudged unseeing toward Jimjoy, the vacant look of too many hours at the controls overshadowing any other expression on the young woman's face.

"Afternoon, Major," the Lieutenant said mechanically, as she drew abreast of him.

"Afternoon, Lieutenant," the Special Operative replied politely as he turned toward the flight lines, swinging the small pack in his left hand.

Jimjoy had no illusions about eluding the persistent Technical Specialist Herrol, who would doubtless appear within moments, if he were not already waiting at the flitter. Jimjoy had not told him about the flight, but Herrol would know, and would be waiting or on his way.

At the proper fork in the corridor the Major in the camouflage flight suit stopped, as if to ponder which direction to take. He wondered what would happen if he wandered down the alpha line side.

Nothing—except he would eventually be directed back to the specified flitter on the beta line, a flitter doubtless snooped and/or gimmicked to the hilt.

Shrugging, he resumed his progress down the three-meter-wide corridor of quickspray plastic and unshielded glow tubes. At the third portal he stopped, then stepped through the opening and into the maintenance line area.

"Major Wright," he announced. "Gauntlet one ready for me?"

The technician beside the console jumped, but the black woman at the board merely looked up slowly.

"Yes, sir," replied the seated tech. She gestured toward the empty seat in front of a second console. "Plug in your particulars, and she's yours. Second one back once you're on the line."

Jimjoy wondered about the guilty-looking jump by the thin technician, but said nothing as he studied the small squarish room. Three consoles, two vacant, filled the center of the space. The walls to his left and right were nothing more than arrayed equipment lockers, but whether there were plastform partitions behind the lockers he could not see. Directly behind the consoles was another portal, presumably leading outside to the line where the base flitters squatted between missions.

The Special Operative glanced back to the chief technician, who had leaned forward in her swivel, but otherwise made no move to stand up. The other technician, who still wore a faintly guilty look, at least to Jimjoy's relatively experienced eye, had backed away, as if waiting for the Major to take a seat before bolting the maintenance line area.

"Appreciate your consideration, technician." He spaced the words evenly, fixing the chief technician with a steady glance that was not quite an order.

"Not at all, sir." But she stood up as he continued to study her, and her brown eyes finally flickered and dropped toward the plastone flooring.

"I do appreciate your working this flight in," he said more softly as he slid into the armless swivel in front of the console and began to enter his own identification, the mission code, the expected times of departure and return.

The screen cleared and brought up the maintenance records for his inspection. Jimjoy frowned as he studied them. Given the time since the flitter's last overhaul, there should have been more equipment failures, a longer history of technical and mechanical problems, and more comments by pilots.

The lack of documentation meant either lax maintenance, a light flying schedule, or something prearranged about the flitter.

As the thin technician finally made her hasty exit, Jimjoy caught the relieved look on her face as she edged out through the portal.

The chief technician had not reseated herself, but slowly paced around the area as Jimjoy studied the records.

Finally he stood. "Authenticated." He looked toward the remaining tech. "Second one back?" He picked up the small pack again.

"That's right, Major."

"Thank you." He nodded and stepped through the portal.

Outside, although the high clouds blocked any direct sunlight, the humid air seeped through his flight suit like heavy steam. Heat radiated upward from the plastarmac, and the olive-drab flitter squatted like an oversized insect waiting for its prey.

Jimjoy concentrated on the flitter as he approached, noting with amusement the carefully polished fuselage. The only way to conceal work on a flitter was to clean it thoroughly, which, he reflected with a twist to his lips, revealed that some work had been done.

The best way to conceal alterations would have been to assign him a bird straight out of the maintenance cycle, but that hadn't been done. No maintenance officer or senior tech would have allowed it. Which left an even more ominous implication.

He climbed up the handholds and triggered the pilot's side-door release. The puff of air that swept past him was warmer than the steamy atmosphere on the flitter line, but not much. After setting his equipment bag and all it contained on the seat, he descended to begin the preflight, wondering how long it would be before the ubiquitous Herrol arrived on the scene.

Rather than begin in the approved order, Jimjoy started by checking the turbines. Though the intakes showed signs of heavy abrasion, the turbine blades and casings were clean and spotless. Jimjoy filed the information for future reference as he continued his checks.

Nothing ostensible showed in the power system, but in several instances sections seemed far cleaner than normal or necessary. As he checked the connections on the tail thruster/stabilizer, he heard the hissing of the portal from the maintenance line. Jimjoy continued his preflight.

"Afternoon, Major," offered Herrol.

"Afternoon, Herrol. Ready for a recon run along the hills?"

"Been ready for a while, sir."

"Put your gear in the bird. Almost done with the preflight."

"Mind if I watch?"

"Suit yourself. Not very exciting."

Jimjoy continued the methodical checking, nodding occasionally as he went.

The skid linchpins were new. The cargo bay doors both worked, and showed signs of having recently been repaired.

At that, the Major did shake his head. He couldn't remember the last time he'd flown a beta-class flitter with fully operable crew doors. Most of the pilots ignored the door status, although a pilot could theoretically refuse to fly if the doors weren't fully operational. The only time anyone had bothered about that technicality was when the mission was a medevac or transporting brass or high-ranking civilian Impies.

"Everything looks good, Herrol. Let's strap in."

"You're done?"

"Finished a lot before you got here."

"Yes, sir." Herrol's flat voice was the single indication of possible displeasure with Jimjoy's failure to inform him about the flight.

Jimjoy ignored the tone. He had deliberately provided Herrol with no notice. The lack of advance information had slowed his assigned shadow only briefly, as had been the case all along. Jimjoy had ignored the "technical specialist" as much as possible, but invariably Herrol popped up, always unfailingly polite, usually apologizing for his tardiness, but never overtly alluding to Jimjoy's attempts to keep him scrambling.

Before Jimjoy slid into the pilot's seat and snapped the safety harness in place, he tucked the equipment bag and its contents into the minilocker under his seat.

Herrol's eyes darted to the bag quizzically, but he said nothing, and Jimjoy volunteered no explanation. The Major hoped he would not need the contents, but suspected that he would later, if not immediately.

The Special Operative began running through the checklist, answering himself as he did.

"Harnesses . . . cinched . . .

"Aux power . . . connected . . .

"Generator shunts . . . in place . . ."

Herrol watched intently but continued to maintain his silence as Jimjoy readied the flitter for light-off and flight.

"Starboard turbine . . . ignition . . .

"Port turbine . . . ignition . . .

"EGTs . . . in the green and steady . . ."

His fingers flicked across the board with the precision that had come from long practice. After clearing his throat, he keyed the transmitter.

"PriOps, this is Gauntlet one. Ready for lift and departure."

"Gauntlet one. Understand ready for lift-off ."

"Affirmative. Recon plan filed. Estimate duration one plus five."

"Stet, one. Cleared to strip yellow. Cleared to strip yellow "

"Gauntlet one lifting for strip yellow."

Thwop . . . thwop, thwop, thwop . . .

The regular beat of the rotors increased as Jimjoy added power, and the flitter lifted from the plastarmac and began to air-taxi westward toward the designated takeoff strip. The one farthest from the main flight-line structures, Jimjoy noted humorlessly.

"PriOps, Gauntlet one. On station, strip yellow. Ready for lift-off and departure."

"Gauntlet one, cleared for lift-off. Interrogative status."

"PriOps, this is Gauntlet one. Lifting this time. Status is green. Fuel five plus. Departing red west."

"Cleared for departure red west."

Thwop, thwop, thwop . . . thwop, thwop, thwop . . .

The flitter shivered as the beat of the rotors stepped up, and as Jimjoy lowered the nose fractionally. As the aircraft gained speed, he eased the nose back and established a steady rate of climb.

From the corner of his eye, Jimjoy noted how Herrol's right hand stayed close to the emergency capsule ejection lever.

All the power indicators and engine readouts remained in the green.

"PriOps, this is Gauntlet one. Level at five hundred, course two nine zero."

"Stet, one. Understand level at five hundred, course two nine zero."

"That's affirmative. Out."

Beneath, the even green of the synde bean fields stretched for kays in every direction visible for the canopy. Had he looked back, Jimjoy would have seen the Impie base as an island of grayed plastic amid the seemingly endless fields.

New Missou itself was a good hundred kays south of the base, and its low structures were invisible at an altitude of less than around three thousand meters.

What else besides agricultural vistas could you expect on an agricultural planet modified to supply the Imperial fleet?

Scarcely the place for a Special Operative, but here he was, with his deadly shadow seated beside him.

The EGT flickered as Jimjoy eased the nose back momentarily to begin the rotor retraction sequence. As soon as the blades were folded back, he dropped the nose again and began to twist on additional power with both port and starboard thrusters, letting the airspeed build, rather than stopping at a normal cruise.

He was gambling that whatever surprises had been planned for him were based on timing, not on fuel consumption or speed, and he needed to be as close to the badlands as possible as soon as possible.

"Really burning up to get there, aren't you, Major?"

"The sooner the better," replied Jimjoy, half surprised at

Herrol's observation. "Plenty of fuel. No reason not to use it."

"You're the pilot. Let me know if you want me to point out any of the key landmarks."

"Stet," replied Jimjoy evenly.

The EGTs remained steady, as did the fuel flows and the airspeed.

"Gauntlet one, this is PriOps. Plot indicates position ahead of flight plan. Interrogative position. Interrogative position."

The pilot smiled tightly. Didn't anyone realize they were tipping their hand? Or did it mean they didn't care?

He scanned the navigation readouts, compared them with the visual representation screen and the view outside.

"PriOps, this is Gauntlet one. Position is delta one five at omega three. Delta one five at omega three."

"One, PriOps. Understand position is delta one five at omega three."

"That is affirmative."

Not exactly, thought Jimjoy to himself. He had reported a position slightly behind the flitter's current position. He would have liked to fudge more, but Herrol's presence in the cockpit made any wild misstatement of location out of the question, at least until Herrol's position became clearer.

"Gauntlet one, say again position. Say again position."

"Stet, PriOps. Current position is delta one seven at omega four. Delta one seven at omega four."

Herrol was leaning forward, as if to take a greater interest in the series of transmissions. The technical specialist's eyes ranged over the position plots, as if to compare what he had heard with the flitter's position on the small screen.

"PriOps, this is Gauntlet one. Interrogative difficulty with base track?"

"One, that's negative. Negative this time."

The pilot refrained from smiling. One small momentary victory for the underdog, and one which might give him a little edge.

He inched up the power again, easing the nose down a shade. Ahead, he could see the hazy lines that marked the edge of the badlands area, assuming the charts were correct. He edged the flitter more toward the starboard, estimating the most nearly direct course toward the ruined lands.

Herrol did not seem to notice the marginal change, but his apparent lack of understanding meant nothing. In Herrol's position, Jimjoy would have betrayed nothing.

The EGTs flickered, and Jimjoy held himself from reacting, mentally calculating the distance remaining between the flitter and the badlands. If he could maintain speed and altitude just a bit longer . . .

He could feel the sweat beading up under his helmet, the dampness oozing out of his pores. Always, for him, the waiting was the most difficult.

His eyes flicked across the board, across the range of readouts, but the EGTs were steady, as were the fuel flows. He tightened his lips as he saw the fuel flow needles flicker in turn.

"Gauntlet one, this is PriOps. Interrogative status."

"PriOps, one here. Status green."

"Understand green. Interrogative position."

"That is affirmative," answered Jimjoy, ignoring the second question. From the left-hand seat of the flitter, Jimjoy frowned as his eyes shifted sideways for a quick glimpse at Technical Specialist Herrol's profile.

Herrol looked tense behind the casual pose.

Jimjoy kept himself from nodding. Before long, he would have to act.

"That the badlands perimeter up there?"

"That's it, all right," answered the man in the copilot's seat. "Have anything in mind?"

"Nothing special. Not yet. Wanted to get a good picture before I make a final decision." The pilot studied the board. All indicators were normal, even the EGTs and the thruster power levels.

Herrol fidgeted in the copilot's seat, shifting his weight, his left hand straying toward the capsule ejection handle.

"Gauntlet one, PriOps. Interrogative present course. Interrogative position."

"PriOps, present course three four eight. Three four eight. Status is green. Status is green."

"One, understand course is three four eight, status green. Interrogative position."

"That is affirmative. Affirmative."

Herrol's right hand hovered near the now unsealed thigh pocket of his flight suit.

Jimjoy took a deep and slow breath before snapping full power off both the port and the starboard thrusters and pitching the flitter's nose forward.

As Herrol's right hand lurched from his thigh pocket, the edge of Jimjoy's right hand snapped across Herrol's wrist.

Crack!

The small stunner struck the canopy.

Crunnnch.

The second backhand blow crushed the specialist's throat.

Wheeeeeeeeeeee . . .

"Emergency! Emergency! Ground impact in thirty seconds! Ground impact in thirty seconds!" blared out the flitter's emergency warning system.

Methodically continuing the emergency deployment of the flitter's rotor system, Jimjoy brought the nose back up to bleed off airspeed and reduce the rate of descent.

"Mayday! Mayday! This is Gauntlet one. Position is—" The pilot deliberately cut off his transmitter. He did not look at the dead man held in the copilot's seat by the emergency harness as he concentrated on his emergency descent.

The flitter was nearly over the transition area between the badlands and the cultivated High Plains as Jimjoy completed the turn to bring the flitter's nose into the wind. To his right he caught a glimpse of gray dust and cratered hills, a few marked with sticklike silver trunks of trees seasons, if not decades, dead.

He let the nose rise into a flare, then brought in full pitch on the blades as the flitter mushed into the golden and waist-high grasses that bordered the synde bean fields.

Shuddering as the blades slowed, the flitter sank into the soft ground.

Uuunnnnnnnnn . . .

The blades ground nearly to a stop as Jimjoy applied the rotor brake.

Thunk.

The final stop was more abrupt than any flight instructor would have approved, and the flitter shivered one last time.

As he unstrapped, his eyes scanned the control indicators a final time, checking the EGT and thruster temperatures, both of which were still well into the red. His fingers flicked across three switches in rapid succession, ensuring that the fuel transfer to the stub tanks would continue so long as there were power reserves remaining.

Flinging the harness from him and wriggling out of his seat, he unfastened the harness that held Herrol's body in place. Then he wrenched the dead technical specialist from the copilot's seat and levered him into the pilot's seat, strapping the body into place.

That misdirection completed, he manually opened the copilot's door and scrambled out, carrying his equipment bag with him.

He half tumbled, half jumped into the grass below.

Squishh.

His boots sank nearly ankle-deep into the damp mud from which the grass grew. He shook his head as he pulled his feet from the mud. Swamp grass between the cultivated fields and the badlands—that he had not exactly expected.

He flipped the pack into place as he moved toward the starboard stub fuel tank and began to loosen the filler neck.

Whheeeeee . . .

The sound was faint, distant, but increasing. Another flitter was heading toward the one Jimjoy had grounded.

"Don't leave much to chance, do they?" muttered the Special Operative as he wrenched off the tank's filler neck cap. Next he molded the adhesive around the small flare, and wedged both into the neck, giving the dial a twitch counter-clockwise.

Without looking backward, he began to lope northward through the grass, ignoring the squelching sounds and the tugging of the mud at his boots.

Whhheeeeeeee!

After covering the first fifty meters, he glanced back over his shoulder at the downed flitter, and beyond it at the black dot in the southern sky. He had another two or three minutes before the flare went, and perhaps five minutes before the pursuing flitter came close enough to see him.

By now he was within ten meters of the sterile ground that marked the edge of the rising and desolate slopes that lifted into the badlands. Changing his course to parallel the boundary, he kept up the long and even strides now more northwest and north.

Crummmp!

He dove headfirst into the still-damp ground. The grass, thigh-high, was deep enough to cover him, especially since he was more than half a kay from the fiercely burning wreck that had been a combat flitter.

WWHHIIEEEeeeeeee . . . whup . . . whup . . . whup, whup, whup . . .

From the sound alone he could tell that the pursuing Service flitter had deployed rotors and was hovering near the burning wreck.

Scuttling along with his back below the tops of the grasses, he continued his progress away from the wreck and the hovering flitter.

WHHUMMPP!

The shock wave drove him to his hands and knees, and he lowered himself all the way to the ground.

Whheeeeee . . . whup, whup . . . eeeeee . . . WHHHUMMP!

Jimjoy eased himself around and darted another look backward.

In a perverse sense, he was gratified to have his suspicions confirmed. The first explosion had been the metallic explosives he felt someone had planted on the flitter, although he had not been able to confirm that during his preflight.

He brushed the mud and grass off his uniform as well as he could and took a moment longer to study the devastation behind him. Where his flitter had been was nothing but dispersing smoke and a flattened expanse of grass and shredded synde bean plants. What remained of the chase flitter was a burning pyre, surrounded by smoldering plant life.

Someone hadn't known much about metallic explosives. Either that or they hadn't wanted to take any chances. A good fifty kilos of metalex had blown when the heat from the fire had reached the critical point.

The ensuing explosion had turned his flitter into a mass of shrapnel, which, in turn, had claimed the pursuing bird.

Jimjoy surveyed the scene, and seeing no immediate signs of life, reshouldered the small pack and began trudging along the edge of the field, ready to turn toward the highlands when the terrain offered some cover. He tried not to shiver as he stepped up his pace almost into a trot. No surprise that someone had wanted him dead. The surprise was how many. Herrol, with his background, had to have known the uses of metalex and would never have climbed into a flitter sabotaged with fifty kilos of it. Herrol had been watching the engine instruments.

So Herrol had either gimmicked the thrusters or had been told they were faulty. The technician had been duped as well. Which meant he would have died in any case.

But Jimjoy had killed a man who essentially had done nothing except make him nervous—that and pull a stunner in the cockpit.

The Imperial Operative kept walking, listening for the sound of another flitter, keeping close to the grass and hoping that he didn't have to worry about a satellite track. He felt cold, despite the heat and humidity.

More than one person had orders to eliminate him, that was certain. And without much regard for bystanders, innocent or otherwise.

As he reached the top of a low rise, he glanced back again. More than two kays separated him from the destruction he had left behind.

He started down the other side, studying the terrain ahead. From his earlier analysis, he estimated his jumping-off point was still another three kays ahead. He lengthened his stride, trying to ignore the tightness in his gut, his ears alert for the sound of the next wave of flitters that would be coming.

... XLII ...

As Jimjoy studied the rugged and chopped hills from his hiding place near the ridge line, he thought.

Had his analyses been correct?

He shrugged.

The rebellion on New Kansaw had been in the making for years, mainly the work of a small group of idealists—zealots, most probably. The scattered nature of the resistance, despite the overall population's sullenness, clearly pointed toward a single small group with well-prepared and preplanned bases.

His eyes drifted over the empty riverbed at the bottom of the rock-jumbled valley. Roughly one hundred kays to the east was the diversion dam which had siphoned all the water from the Republic River into the eastern side of the Missou Plains, turning what had been arid steppes into irrigated synde bean fields.

The western half of the Plains, beyond the point where he had crashed the flitter, was served by a similar dam across the old watercourse of the Democrat River. Like a wedge, the badlands separated the northern parts of the Plains.

While the diversions had changed the dry but fertile soils of the steppes into lush fields, the mere surface water rearrangements had not caused the powder-dry dust and spiked silver tree stumps of the badlands—all that remained of the junglelike growth shown on the early holos.

The Imperial Engineers had gone beyond mere dams. After charting the flows of the major aquifers, they had used their lasers and impermeable plastics to build underground dams far more extensive and critical than the two massive surface diversion projects.

The former highland jungle, according to background reports, had consumed nearly fifty percent of the area's available water. Since the steppe soils would not sustain the silverthorns and the rampart bushes, the jungle mainstays, once the surface and subsurface waters had been diverted, the silverthorns began to die out immediately.

The highlands had been the remnant of a more extensive upland forest network which had already been drying out as New Kansaw's climate edged toward another ice age.

The Imperial Engineers had not waited for the ice age. Defoliants and laser-induced fires had followed the diversion projects. Now all that remained were thorn thickets, spiked silver trunks, and hectare after hectare of drifting silver ash and dust.

In a few spots, the original dark blue dust thorns of the steppes were sprouting from beneath the silver devastation, seeking a new home away from the too damp synde bean fields.

Jimjoy shook his head again.

He couldn't say he disputed the rebels, but the whole situation was bizarre. The original colonists had opposed the water reengineering, but only because they had claimed it would not work. The Engineers had obviously made it work, and the synde bean plantations were producing protein and oil for the Imperial fleets—though certainly not in the quantities once projected by the Imperial Engineers.

The violence of the rebellion had caught New Augusta totally off guard, although the few captured rebels had claimed that the increase in the Imperial production tax from forty percent to sixty percent had ignited the unrest.

A puff of dust caught the Special Operative's eye as he continued to scan the dry riverbed and the overlooking ledges. He relaxed as he watched the small four-legged creature scuttle from dry rock to dry rock.

While he did not expect anyone or anything to appear in the open, for him to move until nightfall would be dangerous. Evening would be best. Later at night was almost as dangerous as full daylight, but not quite, since positive identification would be difficult for a satellite sensor.

His strategy had been based on two simple assumptions—water and location. He could only hope he had been right. In the meantime, he retreated back into the sheltered and overhung semi-cave and curled into a less dusty corner, stifling a sneeze.

A short nap would help, if he could sleep.

Either the heat or the silence woke him, and he rolled into a ready position, the stunner appearing in his hand even before he was fully aware he was reacting.

Both the heat, rolling in shimmering waves down the valley, and the silence were oppressive. He tried to swallow, but it took several attempts before his parched throat worked properly. He edged forward into the observation position, watching, listening. The silence was near absolute, with only the barest hint of a rustle of ashes.

Finally convinced that no one was nearby, he slipped back under the overhanging rock and retrieved his water bottle, taking a healthy but not excessive swallow. Capping it carefully, he replaced it on his equipment belt.

Then he pulled out the old-fashioned magnetic compass, useless for directions now but sufficient for his purposes, and studied the needle. Though the thin sliver of metal fluctuated, the range remained within the same bounds, reflecting the underlying low-grade iron ore. The heat buildups and the iron concentrations would provide the rebels with a near ideal barrier to any deep satellite scans. In that respect, Jimjoy wondered why no one in the Imperial services had not reached the same conclusion.

Or had they?

He listened for the distant whine of turbines, but all he could hear in the heat of the late afternoon was the soft sound of the wind beginning to sift silver-and-gray ashes from one pile to another, breaking the oppressive silence ever so slightly.

He surveyed the dry riverbed, particularly to his left, where it wound in a northwesterly fashion back toward the Imperial-controlled synde bean fields.

He shrugged and shouldered the small pack.

Not much sense in waiting, not when there was nothing he could do where he was except lead the Impies to the rebels, and that would be deadly for everyone, mostly for one Jimjoy Wright.

He did not sigh, but took a deep breath and began to move eastward toward the presumed rebel base, trying to parallel the now empty underground aqueduct that had predated the last massive restructurings of the Imperial Engineers.

With each step, the feathery cinders and dust rose around his boots. Some fragments flew higher, worming their way into every opening in his flight suit and boots. Ahead lay more ashes and cinders, more dead silverthorns jutting out like sticks—just like the ashes and desolation behind. The sunlight itself seemed weighted with ashes and death.

In the dryness, the ashes rose and fell, rose and fell, as if searching for moisture. Jimjoy's neck itched, as did his forehead, his back, and everywhere there was the slightest bit of perspiration. Ignoring all but the worst of the itches, he forced one foot in front of the other.

After a time, he stopped, easing himself down under another dust-covered rock outcropping in an attempt to reduce the chances of any satellite detection that might reach through the overhead clouds, the clouds from which no rain ever fell on the badlands.

Jimjoy shook his head, wondering if he would ever understand the intricacies of ecology, if Ecolitan Andruz would have been able to explain why it was so dead and dry where he sat and so wet it was nearly swamp ten kays westward—when the opposite had been true just a few years earlier.

With a half groan, he pulled the pack into place and resumed his hike through the ashes. Common sense indicated he should hike at night when it was cooler. Common sense was partly wrong.

Hiking late at night would have been a dead giveaway to a satellite infraheat scan, even through the clouds. Jimjoy needed to be undercover before the temperature dropped too much. At the same time, he needed to get into the rebel base, assuming it did exist where he thought it might, before the Impies were convinced he was still alive.

He put one foot back in front of the other, letting the ashes rise and fall, rise and fall.

When he stopped again, the light was dim, a dusk that was not quite true twilight. He itched all over, and the contents of his canteen were limited.

Keeping behind a still-hot boulder, he pulled out the combination nightscope and binoculars, carefully unfolding the gossamer plastic to check what appeared to be an unnatural rock overhang across the dry riverbed.

One look was enough, and he slid further behind the boulder and began to study the area section by section. The geology was less than natural, although from overhead, or from any distance, nothing would have shown, not even the concealed portal big enough to accommodate a small ACV. The lines of the portal showed that it was built for case-hardened endurasteel, nothing that a full battle laser or a set of metalex charges couldn't have sliced through in a matter of minutes.

While Jimjoy had the minutes, he lacked the charges or the laser.

The rebels could only be using passive snoops to monitor the area outside the entrance, since their base had not been discovered, and since Imperial technology would have tracked down any stray radiation. Especially in such an isolated and theoretically unpopulated area.

He eased the scope back into its small case, carefully folding the light plastic. Then he sat down behind the boulder out of sight of either a satellite heat trace or a direct optical scan from the rebel base, and opened a sustain ration.

The ration tasted like rust. Although Imperial technology had the ability to produce tasty field rations, the Service did not supply them. Not since a long-dead Inspector General had noted that the good-tasting rations were subject to a nearly eighty percent pilfcrage rate.

Jimjoy did not bother cursing the long-dead Inspector General, but choked down the rest of the sustain, forcing himself to chew in turn the even less tasteful but still nutritious outer wrapper as a last measure. A slow series of sips from the canteen completed his repast.

After checking his pack and the small stock of supplies and equipment, he stood and began to move eastward again. He was not looking forward to the next phase of the mission. But he needed to go underground, litcrally, before his former compatriots arrived in force, which they would.

The Special Operative sighed silently and continued his progress along the edge of the dust-and-ash-filled watercourse. The gloom deepened into dark, and the heat began to die as a breeze picked up. The silence remained near absolute, still enough for Jimjoy to hear his own breath rasping in the evening air. Overhead clouds blocked the light from either the nebula or Pecos, the single small moon.

He had covered almost a full kay before he reached what he was seeking. What had been an access tunnel for the early settlers had been reduced to a roofless ruin partly filled with a pile of rough-cut blocks.

Still cautious, Jimjoy approached the hillside ruin slowly, staying as far from the open dust and ashes as he dared, keeping on harder rock where possible and using the available boulders and dead thickets as cover. The loose ashes inside his camouflage suit seemed to be everywhere, and he itched continually.

Less than ten meters from the ruin, he halted behind the

last small heap of rock and slowly retrieved the starscope from his pack.

He studied the old maintenance building, originally ten meters square, but could see no sign of the onetime trail that must have wound through the jungle growth that had preceded the ubiquitous ashes.

He swallowed, trying to moisten his throat, and to ignore the bitter taste of ashes.

The warm night air, the taste of ash and dust, the lack of any living scents, the drifting heaps of ashes, and the gray light, gray stone, and sticklike trunks of the silverthorns all resembled a vision of Hades.

Jimjoy returned the refolded starscope to his pack, then took another sip from his nearly empty water bottle, still listening for either rebels or Imperial pursuit. Hearing neither, he shouldered his pack and stepped toward the maintenance ruin.

The doorway was vacant, without even a trace of the original door. The roofing material had been consumed by the old firestorm or removed at some earlier point. The back wall, where a large pile of stones had apparently fallen down, showed the greatest destruction.

The Special Operative glanced from one wall to the next. Only the stones from the back wall, the wall on the side of the building partly sunk into the hillside, had fallen. The other walls, except near the roofline, were intact.

Fallen stones? He grinned.

Next he studied the jumbled stones, looking for the telltale signs of traps, but could detect nothing. He sighed, and began the tedious job of removing the pile, stone by stone.

Although it had been a long day, he forced himself not to hurry, to move each stone, each bit of rubble, carefully, and to study the remaining pile before proceeding.

After he had removed the top layer, he could see the frame around the access hatch. Jimjoy nodded as he continued the methodical removal of stones blocking the hatchway.

As he stripped away the last of the old building stones, he

wiped his forehead. Despite the drier evening air, he was sweating from the effort, breathing more heavily than he would have liked, and plastered with fine ashes around his neck and forehead.

The hatch cover, or doorway, was of a dark and heavy wood that, despite its plastic covering, had turned black from the heat of the jungle fires. The plastic had run and bubbled in places. Jimjoy first tapped the wood, then pushed against the blackest section. The hatchway held firm.

He ignored the nagging thought that he was not as young or as well conditioned as he once had been, and turned to the small tool kit in his pack.

Taking one deep breath, then another, he sat down and tried to relax. A few minutes more now wouldn't matter, and once he had opened the hatchway, he well might need every bit of energy.

The hatch itself was held by a simple lock and two heavy industrial hinges. With a deep breath, Jimjoy stood up and removed the short pointed rod with the shining tip from the tool kit. He began to look for a rock of appropriate size.

Thud. Thud . . . thud . . .

Clunk. Clunk.

Whhssttt!

After removing the shattered lock, he sprayed the hinges and waited. While thumps and scattered impact noises always occurred in underground retreats, squeaking hinges meant something else entirely to anyone who might be listening.

He forced himself to wait longer than he wanted, though he worried about the growing possibility of satellite detection. In the meantime, he replaced all the tools in his pack, except the stunner, which he slipped into the left thigh pocket of his flight suit, the flash, which he held, and a small coil of cord, stronger than most ropes, which he put in his right thigh pocket. Then he reshouldered the pack.

At last he eased open the hatchway, looking to see whether there were pickups attached to the hinges or the doorframe. There were none, only a rough circular tunnel which ended in less than two meters. At the end of the tunnel was a shaft. Both tunnel and shaft were unlighted.

Stepping inside, Jimjoy eased the heavy wooden hatch door shut behind him but did not switch on the flash, instead listening for the sound of steps, breathing, reactions, or anything that might indicate his presence had been noted.

Nothing.

After a time that seemed much longer than it could have been, he flicked on the light and edged forward to the rim of the shaft. The light caught a shimmer of metal and glass as he studied the shaft area. He turned the beam on it. A lamp, bulb still intact, rested in a simple bracket, with a thin cable leading from it downward into the darkness.

A series of looped metal ladder rungs, each step set directly in the laser-melted shaft wall, led downward into the blackness beyond the reach of the flash.

Jimjoy studied the rungs, putting weight on the topmost with his boots. There was no give at all. He tried the set beneath. Also no give.

Clipping the flash to his belt, he switched it off and began the descent, testing each rung.

A dozen steps down, after anchoring himself with boots and one arm, he switched on the flash and studied the rungs beneath him. No break in the ladder and no sign of the bottom.

He continued his careful and nearly silent descent, testing each rung and periodically using the flash. After half a dozen uses of the light, his arms were stiffening.

Masking a sigh, he used the belt clip to anchor himself to a rung and let his arms dangle, shrugging his shoulders and trying to relax tired and tight muscles. By all rights, he should have been sleeping.

Each movement echoed slightly, but the sound died quickly.

Again he resumed the downward progress.

Later, after another half-dozen more checks with the flash, his probing leg found nothing.

Another check with the light, and he discovered a near

circular opening in the shaft wall. The next ladder rung had been offset to his right. With a deep breath, Jimjoy eased himself down and into the cross tunnel, where he listened, sniffing the air as well.

The atmosphere was dry, with a faint odor. His nose itched. At that, his back reasserted the need to be scratched.

The Special Operative began scratching, as well as rubbing his nose. The ashes and cinders from the badlands had dispersed to the least accessible portions of his flight suit and anatomy.

Even as he scratched, he continued to listen. The surface underfoot was flat, not curved as would be the case with a water tunnel. The tunnel had been built for maintenance or access purposes, presumably to the deep shaft which in turn accessed the old aqueduct beneath.

The maintenance tunnel where he stood, assuming that the ladder had not gradually twisted ninety degrees, headed west, back toward the location of the original maintenance station, the one that the rebels used.

Jimjoy sat down and pulled off his boots. He was tired, and in no shape to take on anyone. No one had used the tunnel recently, and he needed some rest before he tackled the three-kay walk back.

Asleep almost as soon as he had pulled the pack under his head, he dismissed the thought that he might be reacting to an oxygen deficit.

Waking with a start, he grabbed for the flash.

He did not switch it on, listening instead for whatever had awakened him, looking for the faintest glimmer of light. But the tunnel before him and the shaft behind him both remained silent. He could feel the slightest of breezes, flowing down from the shaft and into the tunnel toward the maintenance station.

As he sat up slowly in the darkness, he realized that he had a few bodily needs.

After convincing himself that there was no one nearby, he switched on the flash. The walls of the maintenance tunnel formed a half circle. The top of the arc stood about three meters from the floor. The widest section of the tunnel was about a meter above the floor, roughly four meters wide. The floor was melted rock, as if the Engineers had laser-drilled a circular tunnel, but let some of the molten material fill up the bottom to form a roadway for personnel and equipment.

Jimjoy pulled on his boots, then used the deep shaft to relieve himself. He doubted that there would be anyone below to object. Next he finished the very last of the water, scarcely more than a few drops, and checked the time. Four standard hours was all he had slept.

As he ran his fingers over his chin and felt the stubble, he grinned, imagining the sight he must present. He shrugged and set out, keeping the flash beam low.

Like the access shaft, the maintenance tunnel was lifeless. No insects skittered through it. There were no dragons in the dark. It smelled of long-departed moisture and ashes.

Like death, reflected Jimjoy.

Close to an hour later, he became aware of a faint glow ahead. Switching off the flash totally, he lightened his steps and continued forward, straining his ears.

The tunnel ended abruptly, blocked by a rough plastic partition. The glow was caused by the light which seeped around the edges.

Easing up to the partition, Jimjoy listened.

Outside of the faint hum from what might be a ventilation system, and an even higher-pitched and fainter sound that came from either old-fashioned lighting or electronics, he could hear nothing.

He used the flash to study the partition wall. With only minimal bracing and a thin layer of plastic overcoat, the partition had been constructed as a heat-and-light barrier, rather than as anything else.

With the knife from his belt pouch, Jimjoy carved out a small triangular niche in the wall, about half a meter off the floor, to scan the area on the other side.

His caution was wasted, since the space beyond the partition was nothing more than a storeroom, generally empty, with a scattering of opened and unopened cartons. Another wall, far more solid-looking, with a metal hatch, marked the end of the tunnel ten meters farther eastward.

Jimjoy used the knife to extend his viewing niche into three sides of a rectangle, creating a small "doorway" into the storeroom. After squeezing inside, he folded the thin plastic back into position, pressing the edges together. The cuts would not be that apparent to a casual observer.

Glancing at the hatchway to the main section of the station, he checked the contents of the boxes, discovering several sets of unused Imperial field uniforms, two cases of combat sustain rations, camouflage netting, and two unopened boxes of office supplies.

He shrugged. Everything so far had been merely preliminary. Now he had to tackle the main rebel base, preferably without too much chaos, in order to obtain his own passport off New Kansaw.

. . . XLIII . . .

Jimjoy took another look around the makeshift storeroom before approaching the hatch. Rather than a circular hatchway, the opening in the wall was more like an old-fashioned endurasteel pressure door set on massive hinges. The wall in which it was set was solid stone, fused to a smooth finish with no indication of joinings or mortar.

Keeping close to the wall, Jimjoy eased toward the steel door, repressing a smile as he neared it and saw the sliver of light cast on the floor.

Not terribly security-conscious, the rebels, he observed. Still, he stopped to listen again, right at the doorway, not that he learned anything from the silence on the other side. The air remained dry and musty, reminding him that both his nose and his back itched. He rubbed his nose and ignored his back.

Then he slipped the stunner from his thigh pocket and gently edged the door a few millimeters. No reaction. He peered through into what seemed to be an air lock of sorts. Shaking his head, he stepped into the small room. Of course, the original Imperial Engineers would have provided both protection and access if the aqueduct had ever backed up. The storeroom had been added later.

The next door was a bona fide watertight hatch with a

wheel to open it, closed, with no indication of what lay on the other side.

Jimjoy didn't bother to shrug. Holding the stunner in one hand, he spun the wheel until the dogs were released. Then he cracked the door and listened once more. The heavy metal would shield him from anything likely to be inside the station.

Other than a hum of lighting and a hiss from the ventilation system, the Special Operative heard nothing. This time he waited even longer. The rebels were probably not professionals, not at the waiting game.

At last he swung the hatch wider, peered around the bottom edge of the door, and saw an overturned table, a reddish smear across it. The sour smell of death oozed toward him.

The corners of his mouth turned down, and he bolted through the hatchway and across the room. The unitized and portable computer system with the map display still flashing indicated that the space had served as some sort of strategy or planning center.

He avoided the pool of blood and the single dead man who wore a faded purple uniform and stopped by the half-open doorway, ears cocked for any possible sounds.

This time he heard voices—male and female.

Before he could make out more than a sense of strain in the one woman's voice, the sound of closer footsteps echoed toward him. All he could do was stay close behind the doorway and wait, stunner ready.

"Pick up the most incriminating stuff, Dieler."

"What?"

"You know—maps with Imperial positions, anything with body counts, slots with data, anything to make Commander Moran happy. Nothing with blood on it."

Jimjoy smiled mirthlessly. Moran wanted bloodless extermination, like all Imperial tacticians. Like all too many modern tacticians, he thought.

"Right."

Two men stepped inside the rebel strategy center, not even looking backward.

Jimjoy let the first man pass and broke the neck of the second before the tech knew what hit him.

"Uhnnn—"

"Tech—"

Thrummmm!

Hoping that the high-pitched hum of the stunner had been less obvious than a shout would have been, Jimjoy listened intently as he dragged the figures, one dead, the other unconscious, behind the overturned table. He debated switching into one of the Marine's uniforms, but decided he didn't have the time before someone else showed up.

Moran had been smarter, much smarter, than Jimjoy had given him credit for. Jimjoy also wondered how Moran had kept track of him, what Herrol had planted on him. They had lost track of him once he had gone underground, but following his trail had clearly been enough. More than enough to lead them to the rebels and to assault the base.

He edged the door further open, but could hear only the voices coming from the hallway to the right.

Slipping out into the corridor, he darted toward the sounds. The first ancient doorway on the left was hanging on one hinge, and two bodies were sprawled inside, one sliced nearly in half.

Jimjoy swallowed hard and kept moving. Why the use of such fatal weapons? In close quarters, stunners were more effective, and less likely to destroy your own troops in the event of a mistake. Not to mention more humane.

Human soldiers, of course, always condemned inhumane weapons—except when necessary, which was usually.

Jimjoy slowed as he neared the almost closed door from where the voices came. He tried to listen for steps behind him or nearby as well.

"How many?" The tone was persistent, but assured.

Smack!

"How many were here?"

Smack!

Jimjoy stepped through the door, took in the two Marines and their Captain.

Thrum! Thrum! Thrum!

Only the Captain had had the time to look surprised.

The room was filled with the stink of sweat and fear, and Jimjoy wrinkled his nose in distaste. He closed the door behind him, quietly.

The woman tied to the chair did look surprised, her eyes widening as she took in the Imperial-issue flight suit . . . and the unsavory character wearing it. The other conscious figure was a man, gagged and bound to the other chair.

Jimjoy pulled the knife from his belt and stooped—once, twice, three times. When he straightened the third time, the woman's face was even whiter.

"Sorry . . . what they did was totally unnecessary. Appreciate it if you didn't scream. I intend to cut you loose."

She said nothing, but did not stop shivering. Her curly, shoulder-length brown hair rippled with the shivers.

He kept the knife low, away from her body, as he sliced the cords from her hands and feet. Then he did the same for the man, glancing back toward the door as he did so, listening for further sounds.

"How many are there? Impies, I mean." His voice was low.

"I . . . don't know," answered the woman. The man was still struggling with his gag. "We saw a lot, more than twenty, I guess, when they stormed through the portal."

"All wearing uniforms like these?" He gestured at the dead Marines as he moved back toward the heavy door, which he eased open a few centimeters.

"I think so." She rubbed her wrists to regain some circulation.

The man still had not spoken, although he had finally removed the gag.

Jimjoy nodded and smiled.

The woman shivered, and the man paled.

"Sorry. Have a few loose ends to tie up." He eased the

door closed and walked back to the three bodies. He reached down and removed two stunners from the Marine corpses, checking the settings. Lethal.

He reset the stunners to the widest beam focus and to a heavy stun pattern—enough to drop the strongest Marine cold—and handed one to the woman and the other to the man. The man handed the stunner back.

"It's only on stun," noted Jimjoy.

"Kordel does not use weapons."

He realized that she had a strange pronunciation pattern when she spoke, almost a cross between Old Anglish and Panglais. "Then you use them both if anyone looks in."

"Looks in?"

"If you see a face that isn't mine, shoot. The next crew that shows up will probably kill on sight. Or you'll wish they had."

"Like you?"

Jimjoy ignored the edge in the woman's voice.

"They've already tried to kill me about four times."

"And that justifies murder on your part?" Kordel's voice was soft, although the man looked trim and physically fit.

"No time for philosophy, Kordel. Could debate ends and means forever. Violence did save your lives, at least temporarily. And, excuse me . . . I'm going to attempt to ensure that our salvation is more permanent."

He edged out the door and worked his way farther along the corridor toward the two doors ahead. He chose the one which was ajar.

There were two Marines inside—one woman, one man. The woman Marine had a knife in her hand, wiping the blood off on the torn tunic of the dead woman on the cot.

The male Marine was pulling his trousers back on.

Jimjoy eased the stunner power level up to lethal.

Thrum! Thrum!

Even before the bodies dropped, he was inside the door, moving toward the dead Marines, forcing his stomach to stay calm, trying to keep his eyes away from the body on the cot, trying to ignore the retching feeling in his guts.

"You've killed before, Wright," he whispered as he checked the male Marine's stunner. "You've killed thousands."

But it hadn't been personal, and he hadn't gloried in it. He hadn't, had he? Pushing the questions away and leaving his nearly exhausted stunner, he took the stunners from both Marines, ignoring the laser rifle against the wall. He looked to see if both stunners were set on lethal. They were.

Listening for a moment at the door, he heard steps.

"Silzir, get on with it. They've had their fun. Make a last sweep and collect whatever we've got. Lieutenant wants the place cleared."

Jimjoy stepped behind the door and waited.

Thrum! Thrum!

The senior Marine tech died before he saw Jimjoy. The other's mouth opened.

Thrum!

The Special Operative laid the two technicians beside the other bodies. Four Impies and one female rebel. Back at the doorway, he could hear no other sounds close by. The former pumping control station sounded as it must have once before, with only the sounds of ventilation and lighting, scattered voices muffled by partitions and closed doors. The air seemed to thicken around him, and he put his head down and took a deep breath.

At his end of the corridor, the only room he had not checked was the one behind the closed door directly across from him. With a quick study of the still-empty corridor and a shrug, he slipped across the few meters between the doors, pausing outside the closed room.

He could hear two voices, both low-pitched, punctuated with silence.

He eased the door opened, saw two sets of eyes widen at his strangeness.

Wwwhhhsttt!
Thrum! Thrum!

Whhsstt!

Jimjoy was already diving away from the path of the laser cutter that left a clean slice diagonally across the door—a door left quickly behind him as he dove sideways.

Thrum!

Abruptly, the room was silent except for Jimjoy's heavy breathing, the only breathing in the room.

The Special Operative's eyes flashed across the gouged plastone flooring that bore the imprints of long-removed equipment. The laser rifle lay an arm's length from the man who had trained it on him—belatedly.

Jimjoy would have shaken his head, but he was still breathing too heavily as he moved back toward the slashed doorway, wondering how he had ever managed to avoid the laser, especially since he had *heard* the lethal weapon before he had fired, even before he had started to dive out of the way.

His eyes lifted to the silent figure in the straight-backed chair.

This time, he could not keep the contents of his stomach in place, could not avoid seeing in full the use to which the laser had been put by the dead Marine, before depositing the remnants of his last sustain bar on the gouged and already brownish tiles.

The last blast from the laser, the one that had cut the white-haired rebel in two, had not been sufficient to destroy the evidence of selective dismemberment. What had saved Jimjoy had been the Marine's need to refocus the laser. Even so, the dead Imperial Marine information specialist had nearly been quick enough to get Jimjoy.

Information specialist—his stomach turned again. While he had recognized the obscure rating patch, he had not realized that the duties were quite so hands-on brutal. His missions had been clean by comparison.

Jimjoy slumped back against the wall, forcing himself to take a series of measured breaths along with a short set of muscular readiness/relaxation exercises to put himself back together. His already dubious beliefs and his stomach were taking some severe punishment, and he hoped that he had a few moments before any more Marines showed up.

After wiping his dripping forehead with his arm, smelling his own stink—part animal, part filth, and part fear—he tried to center his attention on the next job at hand, which had to be getting out in one piece with the two remaining rebels.

"Hope—" He cut off the mumbled words. He had no time left for soliloquies, maybe not even for action.

With a last deep breath, he edged up to the scored and sliced doorway. The footsteps he heard were getting fainter, as if a two-man patrol were heading to the end of the other corridor at right angles to where he stood. He went through the doorway as quickly as he could and down the corridor, trying to maintain the high-speed glide step that was supposed to be virtually silent. He could hear his own steps as a faint scuffle.

Passing the room where he had left the woman and Kordel without a pause or checking at the closed door, he stopped short of the cross corridor and listened again.

". . . check . . . Silzir . . . ready to toss . . ."

He nodded as he could hear the pair headed back his way. Dropping low, he hugged the edge of the wall just behind the counter and kept listening.

". . . Commander . . . pull out . . . bring . . . out . . ."

". . . casualties heavier . . ."

"Not bad, not for just three squads and the battle cutter . . ."

"Lucky, if you ask me."

"No luck. We get wiped, and the Commander rams a tachead in. So sorry."

While the conversation was getting more and more interesting, Jimjoy was running out of time. He dropped around the corner and fired.

Thrum! Thrum!

This time he dragged both bodies with him back to the closed door, which he opened from the side. He waited for the rebels to see the bodies.

"That you?"

"Dumb question," he muttered, ducking and peering around the door at knee height. "All right, put down the stunners and drag these two in."

"Why?"

"Do it."

Whether reacting to the sensibility in his voice or to the cold matter-of-factness, each rebel dragged a body inside. Jimjoy eased the door shut and began stripping off his bedraggled flight suit. He glanced over at the woman, whose eyes widened and who looked at the stunner she had laid down.

"Forget it. If you want to get out of here, you'd better follow my example and find a uniform that halfway fits."

His eyes held hers for an instant, and he could see her face pale momentarily.

"Yes. It's that bad. Now move."

"And how bad is that, whatever your name is?" asked the man named Kordel.

"Bad as you wish to believe, maybe worse. Three to five minutes, the remaining Marines will discover the trail of bodies. Quick HE charges, maybe a tachead, to take care of everything, including any of their own left behind. No more pump station, no more us."

"There is a way out . . ."

"No. Came in that way. Couldn't get far enough. Compression wave." Jimjoy found that his conversation suffered while trying to keep his voice low and changing into the Marine uniform simultaneously. He had chosen a senior tech's uniform, leaving the dead Captain untouched. Too many would know the Captain.

"Who are you?" the woman asked as she pulled the Marine trousers over her legs.

Jimjoy had not seen her shed her own trousers, but then his concentration had been on the closed door and his own problems in changing.

"A former Imperial on the run. Did what worked. Not exactly what they wanted."

"So honorable yet." Kordel's voice was flat. He had begun to button the tunic, looser on him than Jimjoy would have liked, but they were running out of both time and luck.

"Hardly. Didn't happen to like unnecessary killing or killings for no real purpose. That and a few other things."

"You're about halfway honest, then." The brown-haired woman had a refreshing voice, and Jimjoy wished he could have spent more time listening. He folded back the Marine blouse in a standard tuck and reclaimed the beret.

The woman shivered as she saw him in the uniform.

"You look like you belong in it."

"I did . . . once. Ready?"

"For what?"

"To walk out to the outboard cargo flitter—the last one on the right-hand side. Keep the stunners holstered. If I yell 'Run,' follow me. Otherwise we march." He shrugged. "No great battle plan, but it's our only choice."

"At least we'll be shot on our feet."

Jimjoy thought of the woman in the next room and the tortured and dead rebel leader across the corridor and nodded slowly.

"The others?"

"What's your name?" Jimjoy asked as he put his hand on the door lever, ignoring her question.

"Luren. And yours?"

"Wright. Jimjoy. Major. Ex. Special Operative."

He thought he could feel the chill settle behind him, but he touched the lever and eased the door open, stepping into the still-empty corridor.

"March," he said quietly. "Try to stay halfway in step with me, not like a parade, but as if your steps mean business."

He could hear another set of steps when they neared the corner of the corridor. He gauged the sounds, his hand withdrawing the latest stunner he had appropriated. One set of footsteps.

"Tech—"

Thrum!

Almost without breaking stride, Jimjoy scooped up the falling figure and slid him around the corner and out of sight.

The main portal lay straight ahead, with no sentries in sight on the inside. Those controlling the portal would be outside, weapons trained on the portal.

With no one in sight, Jimjoy kept his steps quick and crisp, letting the old drill patterns take over while he sorted over the alternatives. He could tell from the orders he had overheard and from the desultory mop-up efforts, combined with the tail-end brutality, that the last step would be the total destruction of the former aqueduct control center, along with total destruction of its contents.

No doubt Moran would claim the rebels had left a self-destruct system.

The missing insignia on several Marine uniforms also told another story—one confirmed by the Marines' action after taking the rebel base. One way or another, Moran had raided the disciplinary battalion for his strike force.

Jimjoy straightened as he stepped toward the open inner portal.

"Keep it moving!" he snapped. "Captain wants us out."

Kordel stumbled.

"Gorski! Pick up your feet!" Jimjoy had noted the name on the uniform earlier.

Luren looked more military than Kordel did as the two marched out through the outer portal, each side of which stood jammed three-quarters open. The air reeked of ashes and blistered metal.

A single sentry stood ten meters away, laser rifle dangling negligently.

"How many more?"

"Captain's finishing up with the woman."

"How's he finishing up?"

"Told us to leave. Kept Dieler there." Jimjoy shrugged, keeping moving toward the troop carrier on the right. "Move it!" Jimjoy snapped again as he turned away and gestured toward the two rebels wearing the Imperial uniforms. "You might give some of them another call. Don't know how long the Commander's going to wait.''

''He'll wait . . .'' But the sentry looked back toward the portal.

All four troop carriers had the loading ramps down. None had guards outside, for which Jimjoy was glad. But then, the rebel base had supposedly been mopped up hours earlier.

His boots touched the bottom of the ramp, and he turned back toward the pair behind him, as much to shield his face from the copilot as to check on Luren and Kordel.

With a jerk, he turned back and covered the ramp in three quick strides.

Ummh.

The cargo-master fell to the stiffened hand without understanding what he hit him.

Thrum! Thrum! Thrum!

Ugh.

Thud.

Jimjoy shook himself, half coughing at the ozone from the stunner. Five more bodies sprawled around, from the pilot and copilot dangling in their harness to the single crew chief and the two Marines. More carnage, but he still hadn't seen any alternative. He had to keep moving faster than the reactions of the Impies.

''Get in here!''

Luren's face turned even paler as she surveyed the mess. Kordel turned greenish and swallowed—once, twice.

''Isn't there any other way?'' asked the woman as she stood inside the cargo space, one hand on the back of a troop seat.

''Not if you want to live. And I won't even guarantee that yet.''

Jimjoy began stripping the pilot from his harness.

''Anyone else shows up . . . let them inside and stun them.''

''Inside?''

''Inside. Don't need bodies falling out. Besides, we've got

enough lift here.'' Jimjoy eased the dead pilot from his seat and into the cargo space. He unlatched the copilot's harness and repeated the process. Then he turned to the pair of rebels. ''Strap in.''

''Why?'' Again it was Luren, her brown eyes hard upon him.

Kordel stood waiting, still swallowing to control his stomach, his face alternating between unthinking blankness and thinking nausea.

''Because we're getting out of here.''

''Where?''

''Accord.'' Jimjoy sighed. Luren wasn't going anywhere unless he explained. He had no time to act, let alone explain, and he was having to do both. ''Look. Unless all three of us get off New Kansaw, we're dead. The only place to get off-planet is at the Imperial Base. So I intend to borrow a shuttle and lift for orbit station.''

Luren shook her head. ''That's insane!''

''Right,'' agreed Jimjoy. ''Absolutely. Do you want to cooperate? Or do you want to get out, get tortured, raped, or worse? Like the ones I was too late to save. Do what I say or get the hades out. Your choice.''

Kordel shuddered, but said nothing.

Luren locked eyes with Jimjoy, then dropped her gaze and reached for the crew-seat straps.

''No. Up here. Take the helmet, and don't touch anything.'' He pointed to the copilot's seat.

The Special Operative checked the ramp mechanism to ensure that all the safeties were unlocked, then donned the pilot's helmet and seated himself at the controls.

''. . . three . . . do you read . . . do you read?''

''Cutlass two, can you see three?''

''That's a negative . . . you want me to send someone over?''

Jimjoy sighed. He had no idea what the pilot of Cutlass three had sounded like. But he needed to say something. He mumbled instead.

"Three here . . . here . . . breaker problem . . . up in four . . ."

"Gilberto . . . you always—"

"Clear it, two. Interrogative up time, three. Interrogative up time."

"Stet. Up in four. Up in four."

Jimjoy rushed through the first part of the checklist, gesturing at Luren to complete strapping in, hoping that Kordel could at least get himself strapped down. He used the unapproved checklist used by Special Operatives to get a bird airborne in minimum time. With the carrier ready for instant light-off, he unplugged the helmet jacks and slipped from the pilot's seat, heading toward the back of the combat carrier, looking for the emergency flare kit.

There was no flare kit, but there was a squarish case.

After twisting the seals off, he set to work, making the changes in one of the grenades, and clipping a small device to the side of the top one, and setting a timer loosely on top.

As he carried the heavy case back through the cargo space, he glanced first at Kordel, then at Luren. She was looking back at the man, who stared blankly at the open ramp.

Jimjoy set the case on the thruster console, then slipped back into the pilot's seat, plugged in the helmet jacks, and let his fingers dance across the board, listening to the audio. He levered the case onto his lap, checking to ensure that there was room for him to use the stick.

"Two. Gilberto back yet?"

"He's strapping in now, I think."

Jimjoy finished his preparations, sighed, and touched the studs.

"Three up. Commencing power up. Commencing power up."

"Negative on power up, three. That is negative."

"'Request power up. Losing aux system. Losing aux system." Jimjoy intended to power up in any case, but talking about it might get him permission and would gain time.

"That's negative until strike team is fully returned. Negative this time."

Jimjoy brought the thrusters on line at eighty percent and started the ramp retraction sequence, not that anyone but the sentry could see the action. That had been one reason for choosing the outboard cargo flitter.

"Gilberto! Shut down, or Nedos will have your hide."

"Stet. Will be shutting down. Need to break a shunt here." Jimjoy brought all systems on line and released the rotor brakes.

Thwop . . . thwop . . . thwop, thwop, thwop . . .

"Gilberto, shut down! Merro, get your gunner trained on three."

Jimjoy poured turns to the rotors and began to lift, spraying ashes and dust over the three remaining carriers as the flitter rose into the late morning. The whine and roar through the open cockpit hatch window was almost deafening as he began to edge the flitter up and over toward Cutlass one, the command carrier.

From the corner of his eye he could see a handful of figures streaming out from the shattered lock of the rebel base, but he ignored them as he locked the thruster lever in place with his knee and one-handedly levered the heavy grenade case toward the window, sucking in his stomach and barely keeping the carrier from pitching straight down into his target.

The grenades were meant to be launched from a laser rifle with an adapter, but the fused timer should create about the same result. He hoped.

"Merro. Once three clears, gun the flamer down. Must be Ferrill. Can't be Gilberto."

"Ready to commence firing."

"Negative! Negative! He'll drop on us."

Yanking the tab on the small detonator, he plastered it on the top grenade and levered the container out. Once both hands were free, he dropped the nose, fed full power into the thrusters and rotors, and began a sprint from the area.

"Fire, Merro. Fire!"

Crump! Crump!

WHHUMMP!

The troop carrier bucked twice with the shock wave, then settled down. Jimjoy did not look back at the greasy smoke that poured upward from the chaos behind him. He also ignored the smaller explosions that occurred when the fuel supplies of the three grounded flitters ignited.

Now all he had to do was get landing clearance and steal a shuttle.

Since the base always had a standby shuttle, finding the shuttle wouldn't be the problem. Stealing it well might be. But then, what was another impossible problem?

He glanced sideways at Luren, who refused to look at him, although she periodically glanced back at Kordel, who refused to look at either one of them.

Jimjoy didn't blame either one. Their chances were terrible and getting worse. But, as he had told her, there were no longer any alternatives. None. Moran would gladly destroy half the planet to get either Jimjoy or the remaining rebels, and Hersnik would be cheering him on.

"Now, Wright," he muttered under his breath, "isn't that taking too much credit?"

He did not answer his own question. Instead, he checked the readouts—less than sixty kays left before he reached the clearance call-in point. Less than sixty kays before the next confrontation. He shrugged his shoulders and tried to relax the tension.

He continued to scan the controls until he was certain that the carrier was functioning as designed. Then he set the autopilot, hoping that the cargo bird wouldn't fly into the ground. He watched the radalt for another few minutes before he eased from behind the controls and stepped into the troop space and began the distasteful job of stripping the copilot's flight suit. The pilot was too small, and since both uniforms were standard flight suits, no one would notice. But everyone would question it if a senior Marine tech landed the bird.

Kordel continued to stare straight down, with an occasional glance at the bulkhead before him, as if the rebel were still trying to gather himself together, or to escape from the nightmare in which he found himself.

Luren turned to watch, noting that Jimjoy did not change boots, and that his own matched both the pilot's and the copilot's.

"Yes, I'm a pilot, among other things."

He doubted she heard his words, although she shook her head sadly, the helmet bobbing as she did, the curly hair floating out from underneath momentarily.

Once he was wearing the flight suit, he used his own I.D. patch, the one thing he had kept besides his knife through three uniform changes. He doubted that the entire New Kansaw Base had been told that one Major Wright was persona non grata. Besides, Majors were scrutinized less intently than Captains and Lieutenants.

He scrambled back into the cockpit, noting that the flitter was less than two hundred meters above the plain. He made the corrections even before strapping back into place.

Then he shrugged his shoulders, trying to release the tension.

... XLIV ...

Jimjoy shifted the frequency from tactical control to field, listening for traffic at the Imperial Base before announcing his presence.

". . . PriOps, Gauntlet four. Departing alpha seven. Fuel status is three plus. Time of return one plus five."

"Four, cleared for departure."

Listening, he waited, then keyed his own transmitter with the ease of habit.

"PriOps, this is Cutlass three. Cutlass three, returning TacOp. Request delta three."

"Delta three clear. Interrogative threshold. Interrogative threshold."

"Estimate threshold in one zero standard. One zero."

"Cleared for delta three in one zero. Interrogative hunting status. Interrogative hunting status."

"Status is mixed green."

"Mixed green? What . . . ? Three, please clarify. Please clarify."

"Objective accomplished. Objective accomplished. Cutlass one, two, and four are strikes."

Jimjoy continued to scan the controls, mentally planning his approach to the Imperial Base and the shuttle it held. With a deep breath, he glanced sideways, then backward, to take in his two passengers—the one glancing speculatively at him, the other looking blankly at the gray metal decking.

"Interrogative assistance this time, three."

"Strike force will require outlift. Will require outlift."

"Interrogative intentions, three. Interrogative passengers."

"Negative on passengers, PriOps. Negative on passengers. Inbound for commlink. Then will resupply and join outlift."

"Understand resupply."

"After commlink, PriOps."

"Stet, three. Do you wish transfer to beta line after delta three?"

"That is affirmative."

He wiped his forehead with the back of his sleeve before shaking down the deeply tinted visor that disguised the three-day growth of dark beard.

He had thought about asking if a shuttle were scheduled for departure, but deferred. He needed the standby shuttle—after taking a few steps.

A tap on his shoulder, just as he began to line up for his final approach, brought him back to his immediate problems.

"What do you want us to do?" asked Luren.

"Drag all the bodies out of sight."

"Drag the bodies out of sight? Just like that?"

"Just like that." Jimjoy paused, then added, "When we land, just follow me and keep quiet. We'll all be heading for the main commcenter."

"Just like that?" repeated Luren.

"That's—"

"Cutlass three, interrogative time to threshold."

Jimjoy checked the EDR, then answered. "PriOps, this is three. Estimate threshold in four standard. Four standard."

"Three, please acknowledge Imperial I.D. I say again. Acknowledge Imperial I.D."

The suspicious Imperial mind, reflected Jimjoy. Only one of four flitters returns, and they want some reassurance that it's still theirs.

"Stet. Acknowledging."

He reached under the control board and triggered the cargo flitter's hidden transponder switch. The switch was in the first place he looked, although he knew all four potential locations.

"Stet, three. Signal green. Cleared to delta three."

"Understand cleared to delta three. Will report threshold."

"Stet, three."

Jimjoy's eyes flicked beyond the expanse of synde bean fields immediately before him and noted the gray of the Imperial Base structures and landing strips, and the black field tower. The fusion power plant was well beneath the base of the tower—standard Imperial design, and within a few meters of the standby shuttle, which was exactly where it should be.

"Why the commcenter?" asked Luren again, catching his attention by touching his shoulder.

"To get close enough to the standby shuttle. If you want to help, round up three or four stunners with full charges. Let me have two and keep two . . . and see if you can find an official holster for one of them."

She wrinkled her nose in reaction to either the proximity to the unwashed Special Operative or his latest request. "Can't you find a *peaceful* way to solve anything?"

"Wasn't trained that way. Besides, you rebels weren't exactly peaceful, either."

"Not after—"

"Excuse me." Jimjoy returned full attention to the controls. "PriOps. Cutlass three at threshold, descending to two five zero."

"Three, cleared to two five zero. Do you have visual on flitter at your two thirty?"

Jimjoy looked. The flitter was on a low-level departure.

"Stet. Have visual. Low level." The pilot added power as he completed the rotor deployment.

"PriOps, three descending to one zero zero. On final approach."

"Three, you're cleared to delta three. Interrogative crew service."

"That's negative until transfer to beta line. Request beta seven."

"Negative on beta seven. Beta four, five, and eight are open."

"Request beta eight."

"Holding beta eight for you, Cutlass three. Interrogative time on ground before transfer."

"Estimate one five standard."

Easing the nose upward, Jimjoy began dropping airspeed and adding power, gauging his descent to come to a full stop well clear of the tower, planning a sedate air taxi into the commslot.

The EGT on the right-hand thruster edged into the amber as he added power to bring the heavy craft into a hover. Cross-bleeding power left both thrusters in the green, but barely, as he edged the flitter toward the touchdown spot.

"PriOps, three on the deck. Shutting down."

"Stet, three."

Completing the shutdown seemed to take forever, but the clock only showed three minutes by the time Jimjoy was unstrapping.

"Have those stunners? And a holster?"

Luren pressed both into his hands, a sad look in her brown eyes. "I'm sorry I said anything. Thank you for trying."

"Don't thank me until I get you out of here safe. Let's go. You're witnesses to the nuclear arms the rebels had stored in their base.

"But—"

"I know. I know. But that's one of the few things that will get me where I need to be if anyone raises the wrong questions. And there's little enough left for anyone to dispute it by comm now." He set the stunners on the flat section of the controls, unstrapped, and attached the holster to his equipment belt.

Luren shook her head again.

Each time she seemed ready to accept him, he said or did something that set the woman off again.

For what seemed the hundredth time over the last few hours, he wondered why he was dragging the two along. Did he need some salve for his conscience? Or was he subconsciously thinking of a bargaining tool with Accord? He brushed the thoughts aside as he holstered one stunner and concealed the other, slightly smaller one in a thigh pocket.

He wished he had some of his own gear left. He'd had little enough by the time he'd left Accord, and bit by bit the rest had been used up. But all he needed was speed, force, and the luck of hades.

"Come on." He had triggered the ramp letdown already, and waited for the extension to stop.

"What do you—"

"Just follow me and look grim. Shouldn't be that hard for you."

He stepped down the ramp in smart steps, with a touch of haste, as if he were in a hurry but trying not to be too obvious about it.

"Major . . ."

The man who met him directly inside the portal to the flight tower was a tall Captain, taller than Jimjoy by half a head. The Marine Captain wore badges for combat proficiency and field command, and he was scrutinizing Jimjoy as if he had crawled from the nearest sewer.

Jimjoy did not shake his head. The Captain would be the next casualty.

"Captain. Urgent message uplink from Major Nedos."

"I'll be happy to take care of the details, Major. Since you are doubtless needed back in the . . . field." His voice conveyed a touch of disdain as he continued to survey the three scroungy-looking figures from the security of his height and impeccably creased uniform.

"I think not, Captain. But I would appreciate it if you would lead the way and verify both entry and transmission."

Their eyes met again, but the Captain, even from his superior height, looked away.

"This way."

Jimjoy knew the way, but saw no need for an uproar yet. He followed the Marine, letting Luren and Kordel trail him. The three received curious glances but no challenges as they took the old-fashioned stairs up two levels toward the commcenter.

The inner workings of the center were closed to all except restricted personnel, but several rooms with transmission consoles, directly outside the center and separated from the operations area, were available. They were seldom used, since station personnel could use their own consoles for the same purposes.

As the Marine gestured through the open portal, Jimjoy hesitated, stepping aside to let Luren and Kordel pass him.

"Go ahead, Captain. I'll need you as well." As the Captain reluctantly entered the small room, scarcely larger than a clerical cubicle, Jimjoy's hands brushed the portal controls. He turned.

Thrumm!

The Captain's face did not even register surprise. Jimjoy dragged his figure out of view behind the console.

"Not again!"

"Quiet."

Jimjoy pointed to the single console in the small room.

"Luren, sit here. Type out anything your heart desires on the screen. But type, and don't touch any of these three studs. Stand next to her, Kordel, as if you're reviewing it."

"Why?" asked Luren.

"For the benefit of anyone who may use the scanner. I'll be back in a few minutes. Just stay put. Use the stunner on anyone besides me who comes through the portal."

"Trust you?"

"Why not? Got anyone better?"

Jimjoy reversed himself and stepped back out into the corridor that led to the main commcenter. A young technician manned the access desk before the main portals.

"Major . . . were you looking for someone?"

"I was supposed to meet a Captain Tiarry here. Have you seen him?"

The technician glanced at her screen.

Thrum!

As he dragged the body out of sight, Jimjoy wished he had reset the stunner. He scanned the control board and shook his head. Totally tied with an interlocked security code. Any attempt to meddle would probably alert the entire base.

He turned his attention to the portal itself. It seemed relatively standard, despite the heavy casements.

He checked the stunner, refocused the weapon to the narrowest and most intense setting. Then he retrieved the second stunner from his thigh pouch. He stepped up to the portal, calculating the circuit placements.

Thrum!

Nothing happened. He moved the weapon slightly.

Thrumm!

The portal edges quivered.

Thrumm!

The doors spasmed, opening perhaps a quarter of the way before starting to close again.

Rippppyyyttt.

The Special Operative almost didn't clear the portal edges as he slipped into the commcenter, dropping the used and fused stunner and switching the replacement into his left hand.

Three people, the duty officer and two technicians, looked up with mild surprise.

"So sorry . . ."

Thrumm! Thrum! Thrum!

He grabbed the duty officer's stunner and jammed it into his holster, replacing the other weapon in his thigh pouch as he stepped up to the master console.

He entered the series of codes and instructions he was not supposed to know, the ones left over from the time of the Directorate, the ones used to ensure that no one captured an Imperial Base—and survived.

"Masada one, on line," scripted the console.

"Romans at the walls," he tapped in return.

"Time until sunrise?" inquired the ancient safeguard.

"Thirty-five standard minutes." Jimjoy hoped the time was sufficient, but if they didn't make it within the time limit, they wouldn't make it at all. Not after his trail of carnage.

"After sunrise?" the console asked in the uncharacteristic antique script.

"Neither legions nor the chosen people."

The console blanked, returning to its standard format. According to the program design, not even shutting the power off would stop the next steps. Only disabling the fusion power generator buried below the tower could do that.

The internal pressure on Jimjoy reminded him of another pressing need. He glanced around, trying to reorient himself to the more mundane necessities of life.

Trying to lift a shuttle on a high gee curve with a full bladder was likely to be uncomfortable, if not fatal. He sighed as he located the fresher and sprinted for it, shaking his head.

To be slowed by the merely physiological. He hoped that the minute or so spent relieving himself would not prove critical. His failure to account for nature would have amused Thelina and the Ecolitans, he suspected.

The fresher was plain, empty, and welcome. He also took several deep gulps of water from the tap, not caring if he dripped on the borrowed flight suit. Not that he would have cared even if it had been his.

Feeling less physically pressured, he left the fresher and moved back through the commcenter, with thirty-two minutes still remaining before the Masada trap triggered. Exiting through the portal was far easier, although he was ready to use the stunner, if necessary.

It was not. No one had discovered the missing tech, and he walked back to the transmission room where he had left Luren and Kordel.

"Finished? Good. Let's go."

"What have you been doing?"

". . . why . . ."

"Let's go," he repeated, setting the portal controls to lock behind them.

They were down the first flight of steps, fifteen meters from the access door Jimjoy wanted, when another officer confronted them, stunner in hand.

"You—where's Captain Tiarry?"

"Captain who?" asked Jimjoy.

"You know who."

"Tall Marine Captain who went with us to the commcenter? He's still there. Very upset."

"Now . . ."

"You would be, too, if you'd just found out that the rebels had wiped out most of Commander Moran's strike force and had managed to come up with half a dozen tacheads before he closed down their base."

"Tacheads?"

"Just class three," amended Jimjoy, edging closer while turning toward Luren. "You have that shot there?"

As he turned back toward the Lieutenant, something white in his hand, both hands flashed.

Ugghhh.

Clank. The unused stunner clattered on the landing, a crack across the muzzle tube.

Jimjoy dragged yet another body out of the way through the portal leading to the access tube to the standby shuttle.

"Someone should have caught us by now."

"They have, several times . . . but no one really believes they'll be attacked in their own base."

He locked the portal, hoping that any searchers wouldn't think about two strange Marines and a pilot in conjunction with the emergency shuttle, at least for a few minutes.

And he needed those minutes, he realized as he reached the lock portal separating them from the shuttle. With a sigh, he pulled out the sole remnant of his equipment, the small tool kit.

"No more explosives?" asked Luren softly. "No more stunning miracles? No more defenseless individuals murdered?"

"Kindly—shut—up," he mumbled, relieved that the panel controls and associated lock circuits were relatively straight-forward.

Still, the perspiration was streaming down his forehead before the five minutes it took him to persuade the locked panel to open had passed.

Clank. His fingers were shaking so much from the strain that he dropped the probe as he tried to retract it. Jimjoy shrugged, eased himself off sore knees, and picked up the instrument.

"Now what? Do we go back gently, killer, and plead for mercy?"

"Oh . . that." Jimjoy smiled and touched the access plate. This time it lighted, and the portal opened. 'No, you strap in. You get the copilot's seat. And, Kordel, you strap in where you can. We're running out of time. So you're on your own. Try to do it right."

Once they stood in the shuttle lock, Jimjoy dogged the manual seals into place. They might get blasted, but not assaulted by a following force.

"Onward."

Neither Kordel nor Luren said a word, but followed him along the narrow passage to the control cabin.

"Kordel . . . strap in there . . . you, Luren . . . there."

Jimjoy seated himself and strapped in, studying the controls, looking at the blank panel before him that would display an instant view from the scanners once he powered up the shuttle.

First came the pre-power checklist.

"Converters . . . shields . . . shunts . . ."

Next came the power.

The blank panel filled with a panorama of the New Kansaw

Base, with the flat stretch of plastarmac lined up right before the shuttle all set for an emergency lift-off.

He tapped the primary comm circuits.

"PriOps, Gauntlet one, approaching TacOps. Approaching TacOps. Will report ASAP . . ."

"Scampig Papa, at threshold . . ."

"Cleared to beta four, Papa."

Jimjoy bit at his lower lip. Gauntlet one would be reporting on the chaos he had left before much longer. He forced himself to remain methodical in attacking the remainder of the checklist, but he didn't resist a sigh when the board was fully green.

The right thruster began to scream. Then the left.

"Charon two, interrogative your intentions. Interrogative intentions."

Jimjoy was surprised PriOps would even ask.

"Missou PriOps, Charon two. Lifting for orbit control. Code Argent Black. Code Argent Black."

He brought both thrusters on line and tapped the panel stud to initiate retraction of the umbilical corridor to the tower, waiting for the light to signify a complete break.

"Charon two. Interrogative Argent Black."

Jimjoy added power to the thrusters, and the heavy shuttle began the roll out along the emergency strip.

"PriOps, Charon two. Clearance is beta theta seven. Logged with Missou commcenter."

"PriOps, this is TacControl. Request authentication from Charon two."

Jimjoy twisted the thrusters to full power.

"Charon two, this is PriOps. Interrogative authentication. Interrogative authentication."

The control readouts showed the thruster strain, but the thrusters remained on the border between green and amber as the ground speed built. The end of the emergency strip was appearing closer and closer.

"Charon two. Interrogative authentication . . . return to base."

"Missou PriOps, this is Charon two. Authentication logged in commcenter. Authentication logged in commcenter. Authentication follows. Jupiter slash five omega slash beta delta three four. I say again. Jupiter slash five omega slash beta delta three four. Lifting this time."

"What are you doing?" demanded Luren in a stage whisper from the copilot's couch.

Jimjoy ignored her as he eased the still-wallowing shuttle into the air, straight and level until he had enough speed to begin the turn necessary for orbit control positioning.

"Stalling . . . don't shoot while they're talking . . ."

"That gives you an advantage. You do."

Jimjoy dismissed the bitterness, watching with relief as the barely airborne shuttle cleared the base perimeter fencing, and as the airspeed finally began to climb when he retracted the wheels.

"Charon two. Say again destination and mission. Say again destination and mission."

"Missou PriOps, this is Charon two. Lifting this time for New Kansaw orbit control. Mission codes filed commcenter, as per ImpReg five four two."

Not that there was an Imperial Regulation 542, but that would confuse the issue for a moment or three.

Finally, the shuttle reached ramspeed, without a Marine combat flitter nearby yet. Jimjoy torched both rams, watching the airspeed build as the high-speed engines took over from the thrusters. Then he began to work with the course corrector, trying to merge his trajectory with the orbit control approach lane, easing the shuttle back toward the standard departure profile.

In another few moments, nothing from the base would be able to reach them. Then he could begin to worry about orbit control.

He darted a glance over his shoulder at the still-slack-faced Kordel, impassive as ever, and at the brown-haired woman, who continued to shake her head sadly.

"Have you thought about what you have done?"

"No. No time to think. Be dead by now."

Actually, he did think, but not about morality, which was what she had in mind.

"Charon two. Return base OpImmed. OpImmed."

"Missou PriOps, that is negative. Negative this time. Entering boost phase. Unable to comply."

Let them stew over that. The base had no long-range lasers, and no combat flitters close enough to reach them, even with tactical missiles. With the shuttle in boost, nothing on the planetary surface could reach them.

Another minor problem solved, with a mere dozen or so remaining before they could reach Accord. If they could reach Accord.

He shrugged and adjusted the steering rams. One step at a time.

. . . XLV . . .

History has shown that there are two kinds of warfare practiced. The first is the use of military forces and tactics to obtain territory, power, or position. The principal assumption underlying such 'power-seeking' warfare is that the participants will refrain from actions threatening their survival.

The second, and rarer, general classification is that of total warfare, where the goal is the total extermination of at least one of the participants. At times, total warfare may be limited to the destruction of a form of government of one participant or to the total destruction of a specific culture or racial type, but the goal is still the total destruction of *something*.

Governments and generals who fail to understand what kind of war they are pursuing (or opposing) seldom choose the proper strategies or tactics.

Patterns of Politics
Exton Land
Halston, 3123 N.E.

. . . XLVI . . .

Jimjoy didn't particularly care for what was about to happen to the Impie Base he had left behind and below the shuttle. But there hadn't been any real alternative. What it amounted to was that he valued his own continued existence over that of several thousand other individuals, many of whom were totally innocent.

"Charon two, this is Missou PriOps. Interrogative passenger status. Interrogative passenger status."

"Missou PriOps," returned Jimjoy, simultaneously adding boost, "status is green. Status is green. Entering lift phase two."

Why was the base still operational? Before long, if it hadn't already, the base security force was bound to discover the trail of bodies.

To his right, in the copilot's position, Luren sat quietly, but her eyes continued to check the screens and the controls, as if she had some idea what the readouts showed. Behind her, in the comm seat, was Kordel, his narrow face expressionless as ever.

He only wished that either one could help in operating the shuttle. He was tired, and it had been years since he had spent more than a few hours with a shuttle.

"Charon two, this is Missou PriOps. Authentication invalid. I say again. Authentication negative. Return to base."

"Missou PriOps, two here. Please say again your last. Say again your last." Jimjoy continued the stall.

SSSSSSSSSSSSSSSSSSSSSSSSSsssssssssssssss . . .

The scream of white noise across the audio was accompanied by a white flare that momentarily blanked the visual screen for the instant before the compensators reacted.

"What was that?"

"The end of Missou Base," answered Jimjoy evenly.

"The what?" asked Luren.

"End of Missou Base. Finis. Gone."

"You—you—you—?" finally stuttered Luren.

"How else could I keep them from alerting shuttle control? You think that Commander Moran and the Admiral would just let us fly off into the sun? After they'd sent five operatives after me? After your resistance cost them more than three hundred troops?"

"My god! Now what will they do?"

"What else can they do? They've already murdered every rebel they know about. Besides, that explosion won't have the resistance's name on it. It probably has my signature all over it."

"Are you sure? Wouldn't it be easier to blame the resistance?"

Jimjoy shrugged uneasily. "Could be . . . but they'd do that anyway if that's what they wanted."

"*What* are you?"

"Wish I knew . . . wish I knew . . . once I was a Special Operative . . ."

He kept scanning the controls, noting that the screen had dropped the glare filters.

"Where can we possibly go now, Mr. Planet-killer?"

"To Accord. Where else?"

"Accord?"

"Tell you later." Jimjoy began to make a series of minor power corrections. As he finished, with a sigh, he switched frequencies and keyed the transmitter. "Beta shuttle control, this is Charon two, beginning final boost. Beginning final boost. Interrogative status Missou PriOps. Interrogative status Missou PriOps."

"Two, shuttle control. Understand commencing boost. Say again your last. Say again your last."

"Beta, two here. Last transmission from PriOps garbled. Sensors indicate anomaly vicinity Missou Base. Missou PriOps does not respond."

"Two. Understand Missou PriOps does not respond."

"That is affirmative. No response Missou Base. No response on any frequency. Full boost this time." He shut down the struggling rams and touched the booster controls.

The surge of acceleration shoved Jimjoy back into the pilot's seat. Luren's breath whuffed from her. Kordel grunted.

"No response—two, can you return Missou Base?"

"That is negative. Beyond envelope this time."

"Stet. Interrogative your assessment of Missou Base."

"Comm status of Missou Base is omega. Comm status omega. Unable to determine other functions."

"Stet, two. Shuttle control unable to raise Missou Base. Report outer approach. Report outer approach."

"Stet, shuttle control. Will report outer approach." Jimjoy had to grunt out the transmission under the two-gee pressure.

"Why . . . are . . . you . . . telling . . . them?" gasped Luren.

"Why not? Want them to think we're on perfect orbit as long as possible. Less suspicion this way."

"Less suspicion?" Luren's laugh came out as a cough.

Jimjoy ignored her skepticism as he corrected the boost arc course, then ended up having to readjust what turned out to have been an overcorrection. The arc indicator lights finally all lined up green on the board, but the Special Operative repressed what might have been a sigh of relief as he caught sight of the projected closure rate.

Remembering his training, he did not shake his head but

began cutting the boost rate, rather than having to pile on high decel later.

"What . . . next . . . ?"

The pilot ignored the mumbled comment from Luren as he continued to make the necessary course and power adjustments. He wished he could have trusted the automatic computer controls, but once he allowed the linkage with shuttle control, he lost all control of the shuttle. Plus, the automatics were rough, and no shuttle pilot ever used them except in emergencies.

To add to that, he wasn't exactly planning a normal rendezvous.

Abruptly, he cut the boost to minimum gee and began reversing the shuttle's position.

"What are you doing now?" demanded Luren.

"Whatever's necessary." Next he began feeding in the parameters for the deceleration curve. Another few minutes would have to pass before he had to begin that operation. While he waited, he studied the control readouts. Finally, he called up the farscreens, trying to see if the shuttle were close enough to scan the orbit complex.

"Insufficient data," the screen announced.

"Oh, hades," he muttered. "Not again." He checked the times, then unstrapped and headed for the suit locker.

"Now what?"

"Time to get suited up. You won't have a chance later."

"Why do we need suits? Aren't we just going to lock in?"

"Not unless you want to be sent back planetside. So if you don't want to breathe vacuum, it would be most helpful if you got into one of these."

"Would you mind explaining?"

"Simple. We won't last more than a minute if we walk through a lock. We can't exactly lock in and ask them to give us a ship, if you please, to let us get away from them for Accord."

"I knew it. More violence . . . more bodies."

"You should have thought about that a long time ago—

when you got involved with the rebels." Jimjoy stopped talking as he finished struggling into the suit and began checking the connections and seals. He glared at Kordel, who cowered in the comm seat. When he turned to Luren, she was unstrapped and twisting her long brown hair into a knot at the back of her neck.

Kordel might prove useful on Accord, but for what Jimjoy had no idea. Jimjoy jabbed at the racks. "Here are the suits. Get into one now. You've got about two to three minutes."

"Do you want us to put on the helmets now?" asked Luren. She stepped toward the locker and caromed toward the overhead in the low gravity.

"No." Jimjoy caught her by the knee to slow her inadvertent flight. "Try one, and make sure you can get into it. But leave it on the rack. *Securely*. Don't need them bouncing around when we brake."

Kordel finally unstrapped himself and began to fumble with a suit.

Jimjoy finished his checkout of the single command suit and turned to see who needed assistance. Luren seemed to have mastered the process and stood quietly easing into the equipment, checking the connections as she did. She did not protest when Jimjoy adjusted several fasteners.

He turned his attention to Kordel, who held two identical suit sections and had a bewildered look on his face. Jimjoy sighed, took one section from Kordel's hand, and began to methodically stuff the man into the suit.

Cling!

"Hades!" he muttered as he let go of Kordel's shoulder clip so quickly that the other swayed toward the bulkhead in the low gee restraint. Jimjoy swooped back before the controls and delayed the decel for another minute. Pursing his lips at the thought of having to recompute all the inputs, he bounded back to Kordel and resumed completing the simple suit-up that the resistance man seemed to find insurmountable. Then he turned to Luren and ran over her suit.

"You're fine. Strap in. You, too, Kordel." Kordel did not

move. "Now." He picked up Kordel, who opened his mouth in protest, and jammed him into the comm seat, slamming the harnesses in place around the seeming incompetent.

Once back before the board, he began to recompute the decel vectors, realizing that he had gotten upset for almost no reason. He had never intended to bring the shuttle to an absolute stop in any case. Approximations would be sufficient . . . so long as the shuttle's relative velocity was relatively low when they exited.

He made the changes, rough as they were, and shifted his attention to the farscreens.

"Shuttle control, Charon two. Commencing back-brake. Commencing back-brake."

"Two, control. Interrogative status. Interrogative status."

"Shuttle control. This is two. Returning on manual pilot. Returning on manual pilot. Closure control delta. Closure control delta."

"Understand closure control delta. Do not attempt to lock. Do not attempt to lock."

"Stet. Will stand off. Standing off within scooter hop."

"Stet, two. Scooters standing by."

"Back-brake this time."

Jimjoy touched the fingertip controls as the gee force surged to four plus gees, then subsided to a constant three gees.

"Shuttle control. Two here. Interrogative courier for urgent pouch dispatch. Interrogative courier."

"Two. You're lucky about something. Both *Pike* and *Darmetier* on station."

"Stet."

Jimjoy knew there had to be some ships on station, but a courier would be best, with a small crew, high speed, and low profile. Armaments would be worse than useless. A scout would have been his next choice.

By now the farscreens were showing the general outlines of the shuttle control complex. He could make out several outlying ships, including one that bore the signature of a full battle cruiser. He did not shake his head, not under three gees. A full battle cruiser he did not need.

"Two, this is shuttle control. Suggest you increase delta vee. Closure rate above approach line. Suggest you increase delta vee."

"Stet. Increasing delta vee."

Jimjoy boosted the decel to four gees, this time waiting for shuttle control to acknowledge his actions.

"Two. You're under the curve."

"Stet. Monitoring this time."

He began backing down the deceleration according to his calculations, until the gee force was only slightly greater than one gee. He continued calculating the course line, trying to reset the decel schedule in a way that would not break the curve until the last minute, one that would not alert an already suspicious orbit controller.

Finally he found the combination he needed and entered it into the system. Fuel-wasteful, but the shuttle wouldn't be needing that fuel after he was finished with it in any case.

He concentrated on the farscreens. Both couriers' images were there, fuzzy compared with the solidity of the cruiser. The couriers were roughly equidistant from the shuttle's projected course line. He called up the EDI. One courier was distinctly colder than the other. That was his target.

Again his fingers returned to the maneuvering plot. He tapped in another small correction. The shuttle shivered as the attitude thrusters applied the necessary force.

Jimjoy keyed the transmitter.

"Shuttle . . . here . . . sssttt . . . on path . . . again . . . borthrop . . . again . . ." The skipped words should have given the impression of a malfunctioning transmitter.

"Two, this is shuttle control. Say again your latest. Say again your latest."

". . . control . . . on top . . . maneuver . . . sstteent . . . path . . . again . . . again . . ." Jimjoy repeated his stuttered effort.

"Two, shuttle control. Your transmitter is omega. Interrogative status. Interrogative status."

Dumb question. How could he answer if his transmitter were omega?

In his efforts to set up the approach, he had forgotten to check on the two passengers/resistance refugees. He glanced sideways at Luren, whom he found looking back at him. A quick look over his shoulder caught Kordel shivering and seeing nothing.

"Two, this is shuttle control. Can you read me? Can you read me?"

". . . trol . . . trans . . . broke . . . again . . . pact . . . brothrop . . . con . . ."

Jimjoy could tell from the corner of his eye that Luren was trying to figure out why he was using a pseudo broken-transmitter routine.

The readouts showed that the beta shuttle complex was less than twenty kays away as the shuttle hurled toward its final rendezvous. The pilot/Special Operative rechecked the calculations.

"Charon two, this is shuttle control. If you read me, key your transmitter. If you read me, key your transmitter."

Jimjoy nodded. Someone was getting smart.

". . . control . . . broke . . . gain . . . say . . . roga . . . en . . ." he replied as he watched the orbit control complex grow in the screens. Less than ten kays, and the shuttle was still under the approach max lines. But not for long.

He unstrapped and flung himself from the controls.

"Helmets on. Now."

He didn't even stop to let Kordel try, lifting the man from the couch and twisting the helmet on for him. Luren had hers on fast enough for him to check the seals by the time he had finished with Kordel. His own followed.

In less than two minutes the steering thrusters would ignite, adding some velocity to the shuttle, and the single message torp would also fire, both directly toward the orbit station. The shuttle would be piling toward the cargo holding section of the orbit control, the widest section of the station and the best target.

Palming the inner lock controls, he gnawed at his lower lip as he waited for the lock to iris open. Luren needed but a nudge before he shoved Kordel in after her and jammed himself in after them both.

While waiting for the inner lock to close and for the evacuation to begin, Jimjoy linked the safety lines around the other two. Then he checked his belt harness to ensure that both needler and stunner were firmly secured, and that the emergency tool kit was also in place.

When the outer door opened, he pushed the other two clear to give himself enough room to extract the broomstick—what passed as an emergency scooter on most Imperial shuttles. Nothing more than a metal tube with limited solid fuel jets and with a padded shock damper on the front.

The shuttle began to reaccelerate fractionally within seconds of his clearing the lock, even before he managed to draw Kordel and Luren to him. Both were gesturing wildly, obviously concerned that they could not talk to him.

He frowned within his helmet as he remembered that he had not told them that their suit communicators were inoperable. He'd taken care of that earlier, since he had not wanted the Impie comm techs to pick up any stray radiation or other indication of their presence.

Jimjoy checked the drift toward the nearest dark silvery hull. It would take most of the stick's power just to kill their relative velocity, assuming he could make contact.

By now the message torp should have fired. It packed more than enough power to dent the station, assuming that all screens were not at full power.

The dark hull of the courier loomed to the right. Jimjoy touched the broomstick controls, hoping his last-minute directional shift wouldn't break the safety line.

Thud.

The dull sound vibrated, rather than rang, through his suit as the damper end of the broomstick impacted the courier hull. The thin and fragile-seeming tube bent, but the damper grips held. Forcing himself to move methodically, hand over hand, down the tube from the spidery seat, the Special Operative at last reached the hull. He began to look for the bonding pattern that would identify a recessed loop link. After what seemed nearly a standard hour, and probably took but instants, he found the first loop.

To that he attached the two safety leads that led to Luren and Kordel. To the second, located even more quickly, he attached his own line.

As he moved toward the emergency entrance that all couriers had, leaving the two hanging behind him on their lines, he hoped that neither one would panic. But they couldn't move rapidly enough for the next phase of the operation.

The courier might have all four crew members on board, or none, or some number in between. The lack of radiation he had noted earlier argued for less than a full crew.

The simplest way to take the ship would be to force both inner and outer locks and require the crew to breath vacuum. That solution might create more problems than it solved, since there was no guarantee that the courier would have adequate reserves to reatmosphere itself, or that he could guarantee that the ship would remain airtight. In addition, he did not know whether the ship was undergoing maintenance, with the more sophisticated electronics exposed.

He sighed. Nothing to do but bluff it out, if necessary.

He reached the emergency entrance, not much more than a tube big enough to accommodate one suited spacer, and used the command suit's keylock to open the exterior door. Folding himself inside, he closed the outer lock and waited for the atmospheric pressure to build. Within seconds, the light blinked amber, then green, and he touched the lever.

The inner door squealed as it opened, loud enough to alert anyone, awake or asleep, within the small ship and a sure sign that the courier's crew was lax in its inspections. The scout was under minimum gee field, indicating someone was aboard.

He was clear of the hatch and had closed it behind him, quickly making sure that the seals were in place, before he heard the woman's voice.

"Turn around . . . slowly . . ."

He did, unfastening the helmet clasps but leaving the helmet in place, just cracking the faceplate.

She wore uniform gray shorts and tunic, both obviously thrown on in haste. Still, she had reached the lock before he had cleared it, which meant that she had reacted to the broomstick's impact on the hull. She held a needler firmly aimed at his midsection.

"Care to explain, stranger?"

"Wright. Major Jimjoy Wright." He inclined his head. "My shuttle malfunctioned. Have two passengers in emergency suits tethered outside. Didn't want to explain in advance."

'We'll see. Walk straight ahead, and don't make any sudden moves. Or I'll use the needler."

"Wouldn't dream of it. But can we hurry. One was hysterical even before I put him in the suit."

"Him?"

"It happens." He turned and took a step forward, as she had indicated.

From behind him, she laughed. "One point in your favor. No man would invent a hysterical male."

Jimjoy listened. There were no other sounds. Since the woman wanted him to move forward toward the controls, it meant no one else was aboard. He could feel his own stunner at his belt, but did not look down as he carefully stepped along the short passage, ensuring that he did not encourage the other officer to pot him on the spot.

After he entered the control area, he stopped.

"If you are who you say you are, you should understand the board. Call your control point and report you and your passengers are safe."

"Fine. Where are we safe?"

"This is Dauntless two."

She wasn't even giving him the courier's name, but he leaned forward slowly, his hand brushing the equipment belt and taking the stunner with it.

"Clumsy in gauntlets," he observed conversationally, letting his armored fingers click on the flat board's surface. He touched the activation stud before she could accuse him of stalling and waited until the automatic check sequence completed itself.

". . . shuttle malfunction has impacted gamma three. Beta complex in full-suit isolation. No casualties except for possible victims on shuttle."

"Two for you," observed the woman. "Maybe one minus for drek piloting. Go ahead. Report."

His timing would have to be perfect. He touched the activation stud long enough for the tone to sound, but did not actually key it.

Cling.

"Shuttle control, this is Charon two—"

Thrum!

Clang!

He had dropped, twisted, and triggered the stunner in a single fluid motion.

She had fired the needler, but not quickly enough, and the needle had ricocheted off the overhead. The needler bounced from her suddenly limp hand as she folded into a heap, mouth open in surprise. She was still breathing.

Jimjoy did not remember resetting the stunner, but he was just as glad the shot had not been fatal. He slipped the needler up and put it in his belt where he had kept the stunner. He held the stunner ready as he swept by the unconscious officer, checking each of the closet-sized cabins and the single small room that served as recreation, mess, and meeting room all in one.

His initial assumption had been correct. No one else was on board.

He refastened his helmet as he headed for the main lock, hoping the rest of the courier's crew was not returning.

Unless they were already en route, he doubted that they would be heading out until the mess in orbit control was straightened out.

With the main lock empty, he stepped inside, closed the inner door, and jabbed the bleed valve to vent the atmosphere. The outer door irised at his touch, and he scrambled out, scanning the emptiness around the courier. Nothing.

Kordel and Luren were still linked to the courier, but Luren had reeled herself into the hull and had begun to draw Kordel to her. She turned her head, alerted by the glint of his armor. Then she pointed to the still figure at the end of the safety line, and shook her head vigorously and negatively.

Jimjoy nodded in return to signify his understanding. Kordel was probably suffering from shock, space fugue, or who knew what. But it couldn't be helped. Not now.

He took over the job of reeling in the inert figure, slowly, until the man floated near his shoulder. Then he unclipped both rebels' lines from the ship and linked them to his belt. His own was attached to the courier's lock.

He could sense Luren's impatience with his slow and methodical progress—both in reeling in Kordel and in making his way back to the lock. But since weightlessness scarcely equated to masslessness, he did not speed up his efforts.

Once he had shepherded them both inside the lock, he almost breathed a sigh of relief. Instead, he used the manual lock seals to ensure that no one else would be able to surprise him.

Kordel sagged into a heap in the light grav of the courier. Aside from quickly removing the man's helmet, Jimjoy made no other effort to help him. As Luren removed her helmet, he snapped, "Crew quarters to the left. Get Kordel strapped into one of the lower bunks. Then come up here." He pointed. "Control room. Understand?"

"Yes, great and wondrous protector. I do understand."

"Wha—" Then he grinned. "You win that one."

"Everything's to be won . . ." She did not look at him as she began to struggle out of her suit.

He turned and made for the controls. He hadn't needed to hurry. The Imperial officer was still unconscious. Her short red hair framed her face like a halo. He checked her pulse. Regular and strong, and her breathing indicated she would be out for some time.

He unfastened the heavy gauntlets and clipped them to his belt, then extracted two equipment loops from the armor's regular supply pouch. The loops bound the woman's hands and feet tightly. For the moment, he left her laid out in the passage.

Luren had removed her own suit and knelt only a few meters away, easing the limp Kordel out of his suit. Jimjoy stepped around them both as he walked back to the emergency lock, where he checked the manual seals to ensure no unnoticed visitors would repeat his own entry.

Since the manual seals prevent easy exit, as well as easy entry, their use in space was generally forbidden by Imperial regulations.

Jimjoy rubbed his neck, then began to strip off his own armor, racking each piece into one of the recessed lockers by the main ship lock after he removed it.

He looked at Luren, who was still preoccupied with Kordel.

"Once you have him safely strapped in, would you please stow your suits into one of the empty lockers?"

She nodded, but did not look up.

Jimjoy again stepped around and over the pair, awkwardly, as he headed toward the control room. Before entering, he scooped up the slender officer and strapped her unstirring form onto the narrow couch behind the copilot's station. He thought about a blindfold, but decided it was irrelevant. She had seen his face, and besides, stealing a courier without murdering someone else was the least of his sins to date.

As he straightened, he watched Luren stuff an all-purpose space suit into the locker, close the cover, and sigh. She took another deep breath and headed toward him, looking over at the strapped-down woman.

"Now what?"

"She's only unconscious."

"Now you're just collecting them?"

"Got any better ideas?"

She shook her head tiredly, standing there as if waiting for him to move. He did, slipping into the pilot's couch. He scanned the board, then began to touch the controls necessary to bring the courier out of stand-down into full operational status.

He touched the audio, realized he was holding his breath as he did so. He forced himself to exhale, and to take a deep breath.

"Red four, beta secondary. Negative on transshipment this time. Negative on fatalities."

"Beta secondary, this is Medallion Strike. Interrogative instructions this time . . ."

Jimjoy listened even as his fingers began to key the courier for orbit break, hoping that the telltale emissions from the courier's systems would be overlooked as merely an emergency precaution.

He glanced up at Luren, who had been watching him from the archway between the passageway and the control section. "Strap in."

She started forward.

"Is Kordel strapped in? Look like he'll be all right?"

"Do you care, really?"

He ignored the bitterness. "Care as much as I can afford to. Any more, and I wouldn't be around to do any caring. Might give some thought to that."

"He's asleep. Whether he'll be all right or stay in that trance state, I couldn't tell you."

"Your straps secure?" he questioned, as the last of the pre-break telltales flashed green.

"Just about."

He nodded and touched the screen controls.

"Power . . . green . . .

". . . locks . . . secure . . ."

Forcing himself to remain deliberate, he went through the

entire checklist, until the console screen blinked and scripted the go-ahead.

"Ship is ready for break. Insert course cube."

Jimjoy did not have a course tape for Accord, nor would he have used one had he owned it. Instead he tapped in the instructions.

"Negative cube. Unprogrammed destination."

"Insert course and acceleration requirements."

He nodded at Luren. "You ready?"

She nodded.

Jimjoy tapped in the course line—a straight shot to the nearest point in the system that would allow a jump. At maximum acceleration. As he touched the last digit and keyed the override, he automatically straightened in the acceleration couch.

The nearly instant pressure gradually pushed him back into the cushions that felt less and less yielding.

"Hades . . ." The remainder of Luren's exclamation was lost as she worked just to breathe.

"Beta control . . . beta secondary . . . this is Medallion Strike. Interrogative on outbounds. Interrogative on departures."

Jimjoy cursed silently. Medallion Strike had to be the battle cruiser, and whoever the watch officer was, he was sharper than Jimjoy would have preferred.

"Beta control." Jimjoy forced the words out distinctly, in an effort to confuse the issue. "Dauntless two, departing as precleared. Mission omega orange four. Mission omega orange four. Sector radian blue. Sector radian blue."

"Dauntless two, this is Medallion Strike. Interrogative omega authorization. Interrogative omega authorization."

The Special Operative would have awarded the watch officer a medal, had he been on the other side. With all the dullards in the Impie fleet, he had to have blasted past one of the few bright stars.

"Medallion Strike, two here. Authorization filed with beta control. Authorization filed with beta control."

Jimjoy checked the acceleration and the separation from

the cruiser. He needed more time. The courier, despite its headlong acceleration and increasing velocity, was still well within range of the cruiser's long-range torps.

"Dauntless two, this is Medallion Strike. Interrogative omega authorization. Interrogative authorization. Medallion Strike stands Radian Crown. I say again Radian Crown."

Worse luck. Not only was the cruiser alert, but the ship was carrying the Imperial sector command.

"Medallion Strike, Dauntless two. Request authorization for interrogatory. Omega mission tee plus cleared."

Jimjoy grinned as he keyed off the transmission.

Even with instantaneous recall, it would take a few instants more for them to react to his perfectly legitimate, if fool-hardy, inquiry. Had he been captaining an actual omega rush mission, he would have been well within his rights to ask for disclosure authorization. The sector Commander might have seen that he never again saw an assignment closer to Terra than the Far Rim, but he could have requested it.

Jimjoy rechecked the separation. Then he began rekeying the jump parameters. Next he checked the perceived spacial density, on the off chance that the courier might be able to try an early jump.

The density was higher than average for his solar separa-tion. Within the confines of the acceleration shell, he frowned, waiting for the authorization he knew the cruiser would have back at him.

"Dauntless two. Medallion Strike vice Radian Crown. Au-thorization follows. Authorization follows. Delta victor slash five four theta. Delta victor slash five four theta. Request immediate your omega authorization. Immediate your omega authorization."

The Special Operative slowly sucked in air, thinking as he did. Finally he keyed the transmitter.

"Medallion Strike vice Radian Crown, this is Dauntless two. Omega authorization filed with beta control. Filed beta control. Omega authorization as filed follows." Jimjoy swal-lowed as he began to repeat the code, based on what he remembered from a far earlier authorization and updated from his more recent experiences.

"Gamma slash seven four slash four seven omega theta. I say again. Gamma slash seven four slash four seven omega theta."

Inputting the authentications would take only seconds, but it might take up to several minutes before the recheck was complete. Jimjoy hoped so, yet there was little he could do but coax the maximum sustained speed from the courier's drive and hope that the bogus authentication he had given had retained some semblance of accuracy.

He scanned the board before him, ignoring the anxious woman pressed into the copilot's shell. From his own instruments, Jimjoy could see that the cruiser had still not broken orbit. Nor were there any EDI traces for any of the smaller ships near the orbit control station. But the audio was suspiciously quiet.

With a second thought, he boosted the gain on the rear detectors, risking a burnout in seeking such sensitivity.

"Hades!"

He transferred all power from habitability and services into the drive, struggling to maintain consciousness against the immediate eight-plus gees that pressed him deeper into the couch, so deep that he thought he could feel every wrinkle in the couch liner scoring him like a knife.

HHHHSTTTTT!!!

The board went blank with the overload, but the immense pressure across his chest reassuringly continued.

Hssssssttt!

Jimjoy could only see the narrowest section of the board before him and barely feel the fingertip controls. But he waited until the blackness threatened to engulf him before he disengaged the bypass.

"Uhhhhhh . . ."

He realized that the groaning sound belonged to him and closed his mouth.

The screens swam back into sight from the swirling blackness, and he wondered why it was so difficult to move.

"Hades . . ." He fumbled for the fingertip controls, realizing that the bypass disengagement had only returned the acceleration to the preprogrammed three-gee level. The gravity dropped to a fractional gee level. He hoped enough power remained for jump and reentry.

He swallowed, that simple act made more difficult by the dryness of his throat and the soreness of his entire body. The bruises he would have . . .

1734. He had been out for only a few minutes. His fingers slowly began to check the ship's systems and reserves. Power was down to less than forty percent—adequate if he didn't have to evade anyone on the other end. None of the rear screens functioned, but the system checkouts indicated that the problem was in the sensors and receptors. He nodded minimally, remembering that he had never lowered the gain.

Moving his head slowly to the side, he looked at the still-limp figure in the copilot's shell.

Luren was breathing.

He strained to look behind him, but he could not see without unstrapping. He hoped the courier pilot was doing as well as Luren.

After completing the damage control scan, he waited for the results to script out.

Jimjoy saw the figures and permitted himself the luxury of a tight smile.

Dauntless two, *His Imperial Majesty's Ship Darmetier,* was functional, if overstressed, and on course to the nearest jump point in the New Kansaw system.

He checked the EDI readouts, since the rear screens were inoperative, and nodded at the EDI traces. Rather than send the battle cruiser after the torps, the Commander, or the bright watch officer, had dispatched the other courier, either to attempt to track or, more likely, to report the piracy of the *Darmetier* to Headquarters.

Definitely no turning back, reflected Jimjoy. The remaining question was whether he could persuade Accord, or the Institute, not to turn him over to the Empire.

The stakes were getting high enough that the Empire just might offer enough for one renegade to make it worthwhile for even the most discontented colonial government.

On the other hand, while the Impies might suspect the catastrophes had been caused by one Jimjoy Wright, there was little hard proof, especially since New Kansaw Base no longer existed—no fingerprints, no records.

Jimjoy pushed away those thoughts and returned his attention to the controls. One thing at a time.

Jump was approaching, and with the power drains he had placed on the courier, he needed a good jump. A very good jump.

Luren groaned, but Jimjoy did not look over at her. In less than fifteen standard minutes, he would have plenty of time, since jumps were not traceable, except with far more sophisticated equipment than possessed by the distant *Pike*.

He sighed and began to make the necessary entries and calculations.

. . . XLVII . . .

Cling . . . cling . . . cling.

At the first chime of the red-framed screen at the corner of the heavy wooden desk, the Admiral did not even look away from his own work on the main screen. With the second, he frowned. With the third, he put his own calculations on hold and reached for the emergency screen.

"Admiral, sir," stammered the Headquarters commlink watch officer. "Sorry to bother you, but Radian Crown has reported a major uprising on New Kansaw . . ."

The Admiral pursed his lips but said nothing, nodding his head for the woman to continue.

"Do you want the detailed status report or the executive summary, sir?"

"Both," replied the senior officer. "Both, if you will. Feed them right through."

"Yes, Admiral. Immediately, sir."

"That will be all, Captain Harfoos."

"Yes, sir."

The red-framed screen blanked momentarily, then displayed a title—*Executive Summary—New Kansaw Anomaly.*

Cling.

The Admiral tapped the controls on his own screen, shunting his work into storage and calling up the reports from the emergency communications system. The *Executive Summary* appeared on the screen before him, and the smaller emergency screen again blanked, and stayed blank.

The Admiral began to read, unconsciously rubbing his forehead as he finished the first page of the summary.

New Kansaw—either the rebels had proved too difficult for the talents of that Major Wright . . . or, even worse, he and Commander Hersnik had vastly underestimated Wright, and Wright had thrown in with the rebels.

The Admiral frowned as he began the second page of the summary. At the end of the three pages, he called up the body of the report.

By the time he had finished the complete report, he had the beginnings of a headache. He immediately routed a copy of the summary to Hersnik, mostly to give the Commander enough information to make the Admiral's next step a bit easier.

Rubbing his forehead again, he tilted his head sideways, then accessed the report again, searching for one section.

He nodded thoughtfully as he reread the part about the destruction of New Kansaw Main Base. That fit, and it had to be Wright, although he doubted that the Service would ever be able to prove the man had actually invoked the Masada safeguards. Because the issue was clearly under seal, he would not have to go public. But action was necessary, beyond a doubt.

How Wright had discovered the Masada safeguards was another question that would also never be known.

The Admiral sighed as he checked another section for the second time, then reread the conclusion, which lingered on the screen a moment before the Admiral relinquished it to permanent storage.

He shook his head slowly at the language.

"With the limited energy reserves on the *Darmetier* and the lack of atmospheric landing capabilities, the Service anticipates recovery of the vessel in the near future."

. . . XLVIII . . .

Jimjoy's forehead was still damp from the fresher, as was his hair. But at least he was clean, and shaved, for the first time in days.

The flight suit he wore had belonged to one of the crew members who had presumably been in New Kansaw orbit control at the time Jimjoy had appropriated the *Darmetier*. The suit's original owner was slightly shorter than Jimjoy, but a shade bulkier, and the difference in fit was not noticeable except that the flight suit's legs only reached down past the tops of his boots.

He glanced over at the control board, then at the woman in the copilot's seat, whose curly brown hair was already dry. Jimjoy had suggested that she use the facilities first once they had emerged from the jump, during the time when he was setting up the inbound course.

"You actually look presentable, Major."

"Jimjoy. Service wouldn't have me back except for an execution."

"Don't you deserve it?"

"Hades . . . but . . . probably so, at least technically."

"Technically? How about ethically?"

Jimjoy eased himself back into the control couch. "Ethically? Not sure about that." He did not say more, but the question sounded more like something a certain Ecolitan Andruz might have asked. Still might ask, if he ever got back to Accord. And he really didn't have an answer that would satisfy Luren or Thelina. Especially Thelina.

He sighed, and checked the board. He still had to get back to Accord. The brief recharge from the cleanliness and warmth imparted by the fresher was already beginning to fade, and he could feel the weight of the days of fatigue building behind his personal controls.

For another few hours, perhaps, he would be able to override it. Postpone payment for a time, but only for a time. His eyes were bloodshot and felt like they had been sandblasted. His legs felt like he wore twenty-kilo boots.

Still, once he got to Accord and locked in—

He frowned, wanting to pound his forehead.

"Hades!" He'd forgotten the simplest thing, the last hurdle. And the most troublesome.

"Now what—?" asked the rebel in the copilot's seat tiredly. "Another battle? Another set of impartial killings?"

Jimjoy ignored her. His problem was simple. Simple and impossible. So simple he had totally ignored the obvious.

His fingers touched the controls, and he studied the display screen before him. Just under three standard hours until he was within the defense perimeter of Accord. Just under four hours of power left in the *Darmetier*.

The problem was that Accord orbit control was Imperial territory.

Stupid of him . . . subconsciously believing that once he got to Accord his problems would be over. And the *Darmetier* was a spacecraft only, with no atmospheric capability.

He sighed.

"What's the problem?" Luren asked tiredly.

"How to get through Accord orbit control. It's an Imperial station."

"Walk through. No one could have traveled any faster than we have. How would they know?"

"Not exactly the problem. This is an Imperial ship. I have

no Imperial I.D. except my own, and that isn't usable. You and Kordel have none. Even if we could fake our way through and onto a down shuttle, it wouldn't take much to trace our steps. Then the Accord locals would have to return us.''

''I wish you'd thought of this earlier, Mr. Kill-them-all-and-think-later. Is there any place else we can go?''

''With four hours of power left?''

Still, Jimjoy called up the navigational display and studied the representation of the system.

Suddenly he grinned. Maybe . . . just maybe . . . he could work it out.

''What's so funny?'' snapped Luren. Her red-rimmed eyes peered out from the dark circles in her face.

''Nothing.''

''Nothing! You don't tell us anything. You have a drugged Imperial Lieutenant tied up, and Kordel's virtually catatonic, and you're laughing.''

''You're also alive,'' snapped the pilot.

Luren sighed and closed her mouth.

Jimjoy thought of another possible problem with his tentative solution, and his hands and fingers moved more quickly. He would have to plot a nearly powerless approach to avoid a telltale EDI track. Finally he had the figures on the screen.

''Strap in.''

''Again?''

''Just for a minute or two. We're headed somewhere safer,'' he said, not adding the words, ''I hope.''

As the acceleration pressed him into the shell, he continued to watch as the course change took effect. Then he cut the power down to the absolute minimum for habitability. Any Imperial detectors might have detected the burst of energy, but not the directional change toward the fourth planet's second moon, the one with the Ecolitan research station.

The next problem would be deceleration behind the planet to mask the radiation from the Accord orbit control detectors. And that would make the approach tricky, as well as hard on both of them, since he could not afford to make gradual changes. A gradual powered approach would hand the Impies a road map.

His initial power surges could have been a ship outjumping or merely passing through, unlikely as it might seem . . . but only so long as there were no energy tracks traced in-system.

He leaned back in the couch and watched the screens.

"Now what?"

"We wait."

"Until when?"

"Until we get there . . ."

Luren gave him a disgusted look. "Do you mind if I check Kordel?"

"Not at all. At least an hour before anything else happens."

As Luren fumbled with the straps, he wondered how he would explain it all to the Ecolitans, or to Thelina, assuming he ever managed to see her again. He was assuming there were no Imperial ships in the vicinity of Permana, the fourth planet. If there were, they were all dead. He shrugged and leaned back in the couch.

". . . I said, he's fine . . ."

". . . un . . . what?" Jimjoy jerked himself awake, realizing he had not remembered dozing off. He lurched to check the time—less than an hour had passed.

"Are you all right?"

"Fine," he mumbled. "Under the circumstances." He rubbed his neck to ease the stiffness and to lessen the pounding in his temples.

Then his hands reached for the navigational display controls. He began to replot the *Darmetier*'s position. Surprisingly, the courier was within the envelope he had earlier plotted.

The next step was to program the ship's tight-beam burst sender. With the correct focus and reduced power, he should be able to contact the Ecolitan Base without alerting anyone else.

He checked the ship's position again. Still too early for comm contact.

"Would you stop tapping your fingers, Major?"

"Not Major, just Jimjoy."

"Fine, Mr. Just-Jimjoy. Would you stop tapping your fingers? It's bad enough sitting here watching you fidget, without listening as well."

"Sorry."

"No, you're not, but thanks, anyway."

Jimjoy studied the nav screen again.

"You're tapping your fingers again . . ."

He sighed.

"What are you waiting for?"

"For us to get close enough to get rescued."

"Rescued? I thought we had plenty of power."

"Not that much, not now. And we need to be rescued in order to escape the Impies."

Luren looked away. Jimjoy did not volunteer more, instead checked both the screens and his calculations again.

The broadband audio frequencies remained in a hissing near silence.

Finally, Jimjoy cleared his throat, checked the power outputs, and triggered the tight-beam sender. "Nader Base, Nader Base . . . blue Mayday . . . blue . . . Sendak . . . failure . . . estimate . . . arrival . . . estimate . . ."

"Mayday? Is it that serious?"

"Only if we don't get rescued."

"Aren't you ever truthful?"

"I am this time. We need to be rescued."

Luren shook her head again, refusing to meet his eyes.

Jimjoy watched as her eyes rested on the display screens, watched as she tried to make sense of the information remaining on the screen.

"Unidentified ship, unidentified ship, this is Nader Base, Nader Base. Request your status and estimated arrival. Request your status and estimated arrival." The woman's voice was no-nonsense, but the phrasing was decidedly non-Imperial.

Jimjoy ignored the transmission. Instead, he continued to monitor the courier's instruments, particularly the EDI.

"Why aren't you answering?"

"Because they expect me to. Because any Impie on a fishing expedition would respond immediately, and because any ship with the power level I just used wouldn't be able to hear the Nader transmission."

Jimjoy checked the closure rate and the angle between Permana and Accord. He had another five minutes before he could pour on the remaining power to kill their inbound vector.

"Unidentified ship, this is Nader Base. Request your status and estimated arrival time. Status and estimated arrival time."

Again Jimjoy ignored the transmission, continuing to monitor the *Darmetier*'s screens and to watch Luren squirm uneasily in the copilot's seat.

After a time, he touched the comm controls.

"Nader Base . . . blue . . . blue Mayday . . . arm . . . Sendak . . . arrival in one . . . say again . . . one . . ."

"You don't let anyone know the whole truth, do you?"

Jimjoy looked over at the young woman, about to answer. Then he closed his mouth.

"You don't lie, either, exactly. You never let anyone know everything if you can help it."

"You may be right." He did not look at her, but at the navigational plot, which showed the *Darmetier* had finally coasted in behind the bulk of Permana. "Strap in again."

Luren said nothing, but he could hear the rustle of the harness and the shifting of weight.

"You ready?"

"I'm fine, Major."

Jimjoy did not argue about the title, but touched the stud to start the preprogrammed decel. The pressure pushed him into his seat, and the blackness narrowed his vision to a tunnel that kept trying to close in on him. He fought it until the pressure eased.

Cling.

He shook his head to concentrate, and was rewarded with an increasing throbbing in his temples as he studied the board, noting the post-jump entrance of another ship in the Accord system. He began to calculate its inbound path against the standard parameters.

The throbbing eased fractionally as he realized the inbound ship was Accordan and on course for Accord proper.

"Unidentified ship. Unidentified ship. This is Nader Base. This is Nader Base. Standing by for your arrival. Do you need medical assistance? Do you need medical assistance?"

Jimjoy nodded in response to the inquiry, but made no move to respond.

He continued to check the plot screen, trying to calculate whether he needed to step up the decel before the ship cleared the section of transit blocking a direct screen from Accord. Finally he stabbed the override and was jolted back further into the shell.

". . . uuufffff . . ." Luren protested.

He eased up on the extra decel and checked the parameters for near orbit around the moon. Given the six-hundred-kay diameter of Thalos, the orbit would have to be close indeed.

As he touched the controls again, the *Darmetier* shivered, once . . . twice . . .

"Unidentified ship, unidentified ship—"

"Nader Base, Nader . . . tier . . . medical . . . say again . . . med . . . stance . . . arrival ten . . ."

"This is Nader Base. Nader Base. Say again. Say again."

Jimjoy ignored the request. The base had already picked up the burst of power from the *Darmetier*, which would pinpoint the ship's location.

He was gambling that the Ecolitans would notify the Institute by their own courier, but not the Imperial orbit control station off Accord. From what he had seen on his guided tours of Accord, the Ecolitans, even plain local citizens, tried to avoid letting the Empire know anything.

With a mirthless smile, he monitored the last stages of his near powerless approach to the airless moon that orbited

Permana, the fourth planet of the Accord system, and home to an Ecolitan mining-and-research operation.

"Ohhhh . . ." The gasp came from Luren as he called up the front visual. Thalos filled nearly a quarter of the main screen.

As she took in the view, Jimjoy scanned the board. The courier's EDI detection system was picking up energy sources—both in space and on the satellite itself. Those from the satellite were barely detectable, something he might have expected, given the Ecolitans' consciousness of energy usage.

He frowned as he studied the two point sources in space, in orbit around Thalos, each roughly one-third of an orbit from the other, indicating the possibility of a third identical source.

Needleboats! With their only use that of space-to-space combat, the majority of Imperial needleboats were in storage. Those on his screens appeared marginally different. Why would the Accordans be using needleboats? And where had they obtained them?

Pushing those questions away, he focused on the delicate last stages of his manual approach, trying to use the last of his power to establish a generally stable orbit and hoping that the Ecolitans would ask questions first.

The sweat beaded up on his forehead. He wiped it clean with his shoulder, not taking his eyes off the screens and the readouts before him.

"Gentle . . . now . . . power . . ." The words slipped from his lips as he tried to fuse with the board, fingers adjusting, correcting, using the minimal power available, as if each erg were the last the courier possessed. He had already dropped all the screens and cut off the internal grav field.

"There!" He sat back, bouncing in his straps in the null gee, then wiped his forehead and leaned forward to reestablish a minimal gee in the courier for as long as the energy lasted. He took a deep breath and relaxed. But only for an instant.

"All right. Let's suit up."

"Suit up?"

"Right. We'll put Kordel and the Lieutenant into the bubble sled." He looked at her. "Before very long, someone will be here, and we'll need to be ready. They certainly aren't about to let an Imperial ship close to their base, even if the *Darmetier* were able to land."

"*Darmetier?*"

"Name of the courier." He was in his suit, except for the helmet, before she was halfway suited. While she finished, he located the bubble sled in one of the lockers next to the lock.

Then he checked Kordel. The man lay on the bunk, still staring blankly at the overhead, still wearing the harness straps. From there Jimjoy went back to the control area, where the Imperial Lieutenant was beginning to toss, as if the stun charges were wearing off. The last thing the woman's nervous system needed was another stun or drugs. He sighed and tied a makeshift blindfold over her face. Her hands and feet were still bound.

She might be rather uncomfortable, but for some perverse reason, he didn't want to hurt anyone he didn't have to, no matter what Luren and Thelina thought. Besides, the woman hadn't done anything wrong, except be in the wrong place at the wrong time.

Turning back to the main corridor, he found Luren suited, except for her helmet. "Turn around."

As she did, he checked over the suit connections, and found everything in place.

Clang.

"Our rescuers have arrived."

"Are they our rescuers?"

"Hope so."

He moved to the lock controls, and touched the stud to open the outer door. Through the narrow vision port he watched as two green-suited figures edged in. Both wore holstered hand weapons of an unfamiliar design.

He closed the outer lock and waited for the pressure to equalize, then cracked the inner door.

Despite the protection of her suit, Luren shivered as the cold air poured into the corridor.

Jimjoy said nothing, waiting with his empty hands in full view of the Ecolitans as the pair stepped inside the courier.

The taller one opened his faceplate. "You don't look that disabled."

"Not in the conventional sense," answered Jimjoy. "But I can assure you that both you and I would suffer a great deal if we had been forced to make Accord orbit control."

At the word "suffer," the first Ecolitan shifted weight and put a suit gauntlet on the butt of the holstered hand weapon.

"Refugees, then? You know we'll have to turn you back to the Empire, particularly if you mutinied and took the courier."

"We didn't exactly mutiny, since we weren't the crew. And I think you'll be in deep trouble if you act without contacting the Institute. You might check with an Ecolitan I once knew there. Andruz . . . Thelina Andruz."

"Who are you?"

Jimjoy grinned raggedly, belatedly recalling that he had told the man in the green suit nothing. "Sorry about that. Been a long time without much rest. My name is Wright. Jimjoy Wright. Guess you'd have to call me either a defector or a traitor, depending on your viewpoint."

He gestured toward Luren. "Can't the inquisition wait? Her . . . husband is lashed in the crewroom with deep-space shock trauma, and there's a rather angry Imperial Lieutenant trussed up and about ready to wake up in the control area. Luren here hasn't had much more than a few hours' sleep in the past four days."

"You still haven't explained why we shouldn't summon the Imperial Service." The Ecolitan's voice was cold and tired.

His silent companion had said nothing.

"Oh, that . . . it's really rather simple. You could execute me yourself—"

"No . . ." The involuntary cry came from Luren, who immediately closed her mouth.

"—but you might have a rather difficult time explaining why an Imperial courier with a defecting Major from the Special Operative section of Imperial Intelligence showed up near Accord with a commandeered courier. Even if you turn all three of us over. And you might have an even harder time with the Institute if you got rid of me without at least consulting with them. And last, if you insist on getting rid of us, how are you any better than the Impies?"

Jimjoy shrugged, then added, "And by the way, Luren and Kordel are the last survivors of the Imperial massacre on New Kansaw. You might find what they have to say about Imperial tactics and kindliness interesting."

Cling.

Jimjoy recognized the sound.

"Hold on. The grav's going, and we'll be down to emergency lights and no ventilation."

"Going?" asked the Ecolitan.

"We didn't exactly have a lot of power to play with, friend. Less than I thought . . ."

As the courier lapsed into weightlessness, the onetime Imperial Intelligence officer squinted, tried to hold back the blackness as the corridor swirled around him. Tried to hold on, to argue for Luren and Kordel, for himself, and for Accord. And failed.

The blackness of deep space swallowed his awareness.

. . . XLIX . . .

"Sit down, Commander."

The Intelligence Service Commander looked at the Admiral. A hint of a faint and sad smile flickered around the corner of his lips. He inclined his head, as if to ask where.

"Over there," added the Admiral, jabbing a long finger at the single straight-backed chair.

The Commander sat, gingerly, as if the chair represented a trap into which he was being forced to place himself.

"Commander Allard V. Hersnik, under the regulations of the Service, I regretfully must inform you that this gathering represents the initial Board of Inquiry to investigate your handling and conduct of the events leading to the destruction of the Service Base at New Kansaw, with the loss of life of more than twelve thousand souls. Indirectly, your actions may have contributed to the extensive damage suffered by the New Kansaw orbit control facility, and to the loss of *His Imperial Majesty's Ship Darmetier*.

"All proceedings here will be recorded on tamperproof vitraspool, but will remain under seal, due to the extremely sensitive nature of the material to be discussed. The findings of this Board will constitute a recommendation to the Admiral of the Fleets for disposition of the case.

"Anything you say will be retained for review by the

Admiral. Likewise, while in any future review proceeding, should there be one, you may elaborate upon any testimony you provide today, you may not introduce new evidence unless you can prove it was not known to you today.''

The Admiral paused before continuing. ''Are these conditions understood?''

The Commander in the straight-backed chair swallowed. ''Yes, Admiral. Perfectly clear.''

''Then let us begin.'' The Admiral nodded at the Legal Services Commander to his left. ''Commander Legirot will serve as your counsel as well as satisfy the requirement that at least one member of the proceedings be of equivalent rank to the Service member under inquiry.''

The Vice Admiral to the Admiral's right straightened in his seat.

''Vice Admiral M'tabuwe will serve as the Presiding Officer, and I will act as Inquestor.''

Commander Hersnik's eyes ran from the dark skinned Vice Admiral, clearly just promoted and quite junior to the Inquestor, to the Legal Services Commander and back to the silver-blond Admiral with the light and penetrating voice.

''May we hear the nature of the charges?'' asked Commander Legirot, his deep bass voice drawing out each word.

''The charges are as follows:

''First, failing to recognize and report unauthorized actions in a subordinate officer under the inquiree's command—a violation of Code Section 4004(b).

''Second, by not reporting such actions, becoming an accessory after the fact in a criminal action, that action being the murder of a Service officer in the performance of his duty—a violation of Code Section 5020(a).

''Third, by returning said subordinate officer to a field assignment without proper debriefings, medical examinations, and loyalty evaluations, allowing an Imperial command to be hazarded and lost—a violation of Code Section 6001.

''Fourth, ordering the elimination of an Imperial officer under emergency provisions of the Anti-Espionage Act without receiving clearance from a Board of Inquiry or an appropriate Flag grade officer—a violation of Code Section 6003 and Code Section 2012(c).

"Fifth, failure to report gross violations of security at an Alpha class installation, amounting to dereliction of duty—a violation of Code Section 3007.

"And sixth, falsification of official records—a violation of Code Sections 6006(b) and 6006(c)."

The Commander in the uncomfortable chair smiled bleakly, looking at his counsel, who did not return the smile.

The Admiral turned to the Vice Admiral. "With your permission, Mr. Presiding Officer, the Inquestor would request leave to present the facts at hand."

"You may begin, Mr. Inquestor."

Commander Hersnik slowly began to envy those who had been at the New Kansaw Base. Most hadn't known what had happened to them.

. . . L . . .

Jimjoy stretched out on the narrow bunk, glancing at the locked door, not bothering to stand. The door had been locked when he had awakened two days earlier, after his collapse in the courier.

At regular intervals a tray of food was slipped inside. Irregularly, the trays were removed.

The former Special Operative smiled, almost a real smile, as he waited. While he could not be certain, he doubted that the Ecolitans would turn him over to the Imperial Intelligence Service. Not after two days. They might dispose of him themselves. That was not out of the question. But if that had been their intention, they could have done so without letting him regain consciousness . . . unless they wanted to debrief him. That certainly would have been the Imperial way.

His eyes roved over the room. Standard asteroid station quarters, except for the small adjoining room with the fresher and toilet facilities. The hard rock walls and the minute fluctuations in gravity told him he was still on Thalos, awaiting who knew what.

He stretched again. This time he swung off the narrow bunk and stood, debating whether to run through his exercises again, doing his best to stay in shape for whatever might come.

With a flicker, his eyes ran toward the locked door and back to the foot of the bunk. Had he been so determined, he could have left the makeshift cell at almost any time, but he still would have been on Thalos. On Thalos with some rather worried and scared Ecolitans, and no one was more aware than Jimjoy that he now needed all the support, or lack of opposition, possible.

Someone was at the other side of the door, but he waited, forcing himself not even to look in that direction, not until there was a noise from the old-fashioned door itself.

Click.

Turning, he watched as the door opened and a silver-haired woman stepped inside. He suppressed the smile he felt. "Good day, Ecolitan Andruz."

"Good day, Major. I see you're still presenting problems." Thelina's voice carried a mixture of resignation and amusement.

"Forget the 'Major.' "

"I take it you are not interested in remaining on active Imperial service." Her voice was still dry.

He looked at her, wondering how he ever could have thought the woman impersonal, not with the piercing green eyes and expressive voice. "I have no doubt that the Empire would be most anxious that I do so. Not exactly eager to pay that price."

"I can guess why."

Before she could continue, he interrupted. "Been patient and waited, but isn't there somewhere else we could talk?"

"You're still the restless type." She paused. "You act as if it were your choice to stay here."

"Some ways it was. Not much doubt that I could have gotten out of here without any trouble at all—or not much. Probably could have taken over a good section of the base." He shrugged. "But that would have gotten everyone upset and given the local commander the perfect excuse to dispose of me. They weren't exactly thrilled with my arrival anyway."

A short laugh, half chuckled, came from Thelina. "You think you know us that well?"

"Don't know you at all. Know something about people." He smiled slowly. "Now . . . about talking somewhere else?"

"I don't see why not. Besides, I'm not about to stand and talk while you sit."

Jimjoy refrained from noting that the narrow bed was still wide enough for two.

She turned and walked back through the door she had never closed, speaking to someone outside. "Major Wright and I will be going to the small conference room."

Jimjoy moved through the doorway cautiously, nodding quietly to the pair of impromptu guards standing with the strange hand weapons. Both young, the man and woman inspected him closely, as he did them.

Although they had the look of solid training, the edge of experience was missing.

Thelina watched the proceedings, then gestured. "Follow me."

Once they were a good twenty meters down the wide corridor that had been drilled from the solid rock, she asked quietly, "And do you still believe you could have escaped?"

Jimjoy nodded. "But I'm glad I didn't try."

"So am I."

Another few meters and they stepped into a small circular room with a stone table sculpted out of the original rock. Around the circular and polished surface of dark gray were six functional wooden chairs, hand-carved, with the type of design that Jimjoy had come to regard as Ecolitan.

"Take any one you please."

Jimjoy plopped into a chair on the far side, from where he could watch both Thelina and the doorway. She made no move to close the door.

He grinned as she sat down to the side, taking a chair from where at least her peripheral vision could take in the corridor while she retained some distance from him. She pulled a small tablet from her belt, edged in dark green, as well as a stylus.

"Official record?"

"As official as we need."

"That bad?" His voice was even.

"Depends on what you mean. You left us with a bit of a problem. Two refugees and an Imperial Lieutenant ready to kill, given half a chance. Then you pass out." She shook her head.

He started to retort, then held his tongue and asked another question. "Can you help Kordel? Is Luren all right?"

"That's an interesting order of questions, Major. Especially given your background." Thelina shifted her weight in the chair, jotted something on the pad, and then pushed a strand of silver hair back over her right ear. "Space trauma can be cured. It will take time, but the Institute doesn't see any real problem there.

"The woman still doesn't know what to make of you. She insists that you ran the courier at multiple gees manually and that you didn't sleep for nearly one hundred hours."

"I had a few catnaps."

"For a hundred hours?"

"Closer to eighty."

"But you ran that courier single-handedly and manually under three-to-five gee loads?"

"Not exactly. First, there was the cargo flitter, and that was atmospheric. Then there was the shuttle, and that was a standard manual emergency lift. And then there was the courier. The courier was about three-quarters of the time involved."

"I see. But you did them all manually, and finished up in high gee with the courier?"

Jimjoy nodded.

Thelina made more notes. "Why?"

"To escape." He was afraid she didn't understand, that she thought he'd done it all because he was paranoid or macho-psycho, or both. "Look. Imperial ships are idiot-proof. Can't drop the shields and screens except on manual control. Without diverting power from screens and shields, you can't build in enough acceleration and variation from predicted course patterns to escape torps and other couriers or scouts.''

Thelina continued to shake her head. "So you ran on manual for what . . . sixty hours?"

"No. Hardly. I told you. First I had to get from the rebel base to the Imperial Base. Then I had to divert their shuttle. Boosted nearly through the center of orbit control while we used suits to take the shuttle. Had to drag Kordel through open space without brace or brief. That's where he went catatonic.''

Jimjoy took a breath before continuing. "After that I used a few techniques I know to get into the *Darmetier* through the emergency lock. From there it was maybe ten hours through the jumps till breakout. After we started in-system here I took a few catnaps. I did a minimum-power approach until I was shielded from Accord orbit control, then did a real abrupt decel. EDI probably registered, and might have caused them to ask a question or two, but I doubt it would have been a traceable course line.''

"So she was right . . ." mused Thelina.

"Who? What? Was it traceable?"

"No, you were right. The Impies screamed about our covert activities, but didn't connect you to that EDI blast." Thelina looked into the distance that was not there in the small conference room.

"Who was right?"

"Oh, that woman. Luren. I've already talked to her. She's afraid of you and probably worships the ground she insists your feet never touch.''

"For what?" Jimjoy shifted his weight. For some reason, the chair wasn't totally comfortable. "Just did what had to be done.''

"I know. I know. That's why you're a problem." The

Ecolitan looked at Jimjoy, and her voice was even as she asked, "Is there anything else we should know?"

"Probably a lot. Don't know what you know. Someone never wanted me to leave New Kansaw. Empire is scared to death of Accord. Couldn't prove it, but it's there. Guess is that they can't understand you. As for me . . ." Jimjoy shrugged.

"What is that supposed to mean? That we ought to take you in, like every other lost ecological nut or misfit?"

Jimjoy flushed slowly, but said nothing as he considered what the silver-haired Ecolitan had said.

After a few moments, he commented slowly. "So you're judge and jury, all rolled into one."

"For all practical purposes . . . yes."

Jimjoy continued to think, struggling to put into words what he had felt all along.

Thelina looked at the gray stone wall over his left shoulder.

The pair of de facto guards edged closer and stationed themselves within easy range of the conference table. A single female Ecolitan strode past, apparently oblivious to the drama taking place.

"You know," said Jimjoy, "from your point of view, it really might be best to dispose of me. Especially if you intend to knuckle under to the Empire. You could plant me back in the courier, drive it right into Thalos, and report the tragedy to the Empire. They wouldn't believe it, of course. But they'd accept it, and they'd believe that you were at least as cold-blooded as they were, and they'd wonder what you'd gotten from me before disposing of me.

"And you could take Kordel and Luren. Intelligence would figure they were deep plants they couldn't identify. But the Imperial Lieutenant would have to go down in flames with me."

"Do you think we could do that?"

"You're all quite capable of that. You, especially." Jimjoy shrugged again. "Besides, there's not that much I can do for you. I could destroy the Empire's control over Accord, I think, but it wouldn't be pretty, and the price would be higher than a lot of your idealists would be willing to pay. Loads of innocent people would die, just about everywhere.''

He did not look at Thelina, much as he wanted to, but continued to talk to the gray stone walls. "Not much good at talking, but there's a solution to almost any problem. Most technically good solutions never get adopted because of political problems. But everyone calls the objections 'practical.' ''

"Political problems?'' asked Thelina, as if the question had been dragged from her.

"People refuse to set their priorities. If liberty is the most important principle, then all others should be secondary. If they are not, then, whatever you say, liberty isn't the most important. The others are just as important.''

Thelina's mouth dropped open. "You really believe that?''

Jimjoy shrugged his shoulders without directly looking at her. "Try to. Haven't always succeeded.''

"You're . . . you're . . . mad . . .''

"Could be. Never said I wasn't. But I try not to fool myself. Like you and your guards there.'' He gestured toward the pair in the corridor. "Reason why I could escape is simple. If I choose to escape, that becomes the most important item. No hesitations, no worrying. I don't like killing, and I won't if I don't have to. But if it's necessary, I will. Means you don't commit to things wholeheartedly unless they mean a lot. In anything important, you have to make your decisions first. Not as you go along, but first.''

"So you think that the end justifies the means? Like every dictator in history?'' She pushed back her chair and stood.

"You said that. Not me.'' Jimjoy stood and stretched, but was careful to circle away from Thelina, staying in full view of the guards. "If you don't decide how to balance the ends and means before you start, you don't have a prayer, not in anything important. You decide your ultimate goal first. Then you adopt a strategy that goes with your principles. Then you plan tactics. If it won't work, you either abandon the goal or decide that it's more important than one of the principles getting in the way.

"In an action profession, you make the hard decisions first, if you want to stay alive. Sometimes you make mistakes, and in the end you're dead. But that's what it takes. And that's why your guards can't hold me if I choose not to be held. They may kill me, but they won't hold me."

Thelina looked down at the table.

"No wonder they want you so badly . . ."

"Have they actually said so?"

"This morning's message-torp runs contained an All Points Bulletin. It had a holo and your description, and said you were the most dangerous fugitive ever."

"I doubt that. They just don't like the idea I might escape their tender mercies. Hurt their egos."

"Major . . . let's cut the rhetoric and self-deprecation. You are a borderline sociopath with more blood on your hands than men and women who still live in infamy. You are damned close to the ultimate weapon. I have to recommend whether we pick up or destroy that weapon. You might represent survival or total destruction of everything we hold dear. And my problem is that I'm not sure whether your survival guarantees our survival or our destruction."

"Both, probably. Any decision you make will probably turn Accord upside down." He tried to keep his voice even, but could not keep the bitterness from it as he continued. "So what's the verdict, judge? String me along until I'm not looking, or use me until the cost gets too high, and then zap me? Or trade me in for credit to buy time?"

"Why did you come to us?" Her voice was flat.

"Not sure. Suppose it was because the Empire is dead. The future's here, so far as I can see. Here, or with Halston or the Fuards. I'm not much for single-sex politics or for tinhorn dictators. That left you." And you, he almost added, but choked back the words.

"For that slender a . . . hope . . . you left that trail of destruction?"

"Hope is all you ever have, Thelina." He turned toward the wall. If they wanted to shoot, they might as well have the opportunity.

The silence drew out as he tried to pick out the veins in the barely smooth rock wall.

"Major . . ."

He turned slowly. "Jimjoy . . . if you please. Never was a very good Major."

Thelina pulled out the chair and eased into it. Her hands were on the table.

"Sit down . . . please."

He sat, quietly, but remained on the edge of the blond wood chair, his forearms resting lightly on the table.

"I am not the final arbiter. I make the recommendations. Usually they are taken." She wiped her forehead with a green square of cloth, which she replaced out of sight. "Let me ask you another question. What could you do for the Institute?"

"Besides the inside information on the Imperial Intelligence Service? Not anything planet-shaking. Could design and run a better training course for any agents you have. Know a bit about small spacecraft and their design, and could probably help you improve couriers or scouts for your special needs.

"Don't know anything about ecology, biology, and all your specialties. Know a lot about killing and destruction, and when to use it, and when not to."

"Are you firmly wedded to your present appearance?"

Jimjoy refused to let himself hope. "Sort of like the way I look, but some changes wouldn't bother me. Prefer to keep Jimjoy as a nickname, since I'd find it hard not to answer to it."

"That *might* be possible." She added some notes to the tablet. "How would you handle your disappearance? And what would you do about the *Darmetier*?"

Jimjoy wanted to relax, but waited, still on the edge of the chair. "Wouldn't try to explain anything. I'd crash it somewhere where it would be found. I'd blank the last month or so from the Lieutenant's mind, if you can, and have her turn up in plain sight somewhere. And if I had a convenient body or three, I'd fry them in the wreck.''

''Would you keep the ship if you could?''

''No.''

''What if we can't, as you put it, mindblank the Lieutenant?''

''Drop her on some outback on a colony planet. That assumes that you haven't let her know where she is. By the time she gets anywhere, everything will be confused enough that it wouldn't matter.''

''What about you?''

''All I have to offer is experience. You park me or elimi-nate me, and you lose it all.''

One corner of Thelina's mouth quirked upward. ''That was not what I meant. What would you do, given a free choice on Accord?''

''Not much doubt. Work for the Institute, however I could.''

''What if the Institute wouldn't take you?''

''Try to find my own school to teach something. Work electronics on the side, I suppose.''

Thelina stood. ''That's that. You should be hearing shortly.''

''Hearing what?''

''When you report to the Institute. What else could we do with you?''

Jimjoy's hands tightened around the edge of the table. He stood slowly, forcing his fingers to release their grip on the stone, transferring the anger and his grip to the back of the chair as he moved behind it.

Thelina looked at his face and took a sudden step backward.

His words came slowly. ''Do you always play with people like this?''

''You were a little . . . unusual . . .''

He forced himself to relax, going through the mental pat-terns to loosen muscles and thoughts, taking one deep breath, then another.

''I see,'' he said. ''I see. I think . . . could be interesting . . .''

''What? The Institute?''

"No . . . the wars . . ." He chuckled, but it was a forced chuckle, although he could feel the tension ebbing.

"What wars?"

Jimjoy took a long look at the silver-haired woman, but refrained from shaking his head. "All of them," he answered. "All of them."

THERE WILL BE WAR

Created by J. E. Pournelle
John F. Carr, Associate Editor

T H E   S A G A   C O N T I N U E S . . .

Buy them at your local bookstore or use this handy coupon:
Clip and mail this page with your order.

Publishers Book and Audio Mailing Service
P.O. Box 120159, Staten Island, NY 10312-0004

Please send me the book(s) I have checked above. I am enclosing $_____
(please add $1.25 for the first book, and $.25 for each additional book to
cover postage and handling. Send check or money order only—no CODs.)

Name _____

Address _____

City _____ State/Zip _____

Please allow six weeks for delivery. Prices subject to change without notice.